Halo
and the
Devil's Tail

A fictionalized account of genuine paranormal experiences

Lewis D. Ladd
&
Trish Lindsey Jaggers

LADD & JAGGERS

SMITHS GROVE, KENTUCKY

Lewis D. Ladd & Trish Lindsey Jaggers
Smiths Grove, KY
https://HaloandtheDevilsTail.com

Publisher's Note: This is a work of fiction. Names, characters, places, and incidents are a product of the authors' imagination. Locales and public names are sometimes used for atmospheric purposes. Any resemblance to actual people, living or dead, or to businesses, companies, events, institutions, or locales is completely coincidental.

Book Layout © 2019 BookDesignTemplates.com
Book Cover Fiverr.com

Halo and the Devil's Tail/Lewis D. Ladd & Trish Lindsey Jaggers -- 1st ed.
ISBN 978-0-578-56457-9

A long standing argument waged in the early twentieth century between Albert Einstein and the researchers in the mathematical science of quantum physics. The discoverer of time dilation once remarked to Neils Bohr, the discoverer of the fundamental atomic radius, "Your science is incomplete."

Einstein may have lent credence to a larger perspective when he also remarked, "Imagination is more important than knowledge."

The Twin Law

Any act or intent which impedes a separate thing from being all that it can be is evil.

Any act or intent which allows a separate thing to be all that it can be is good.

Contents

Prologue

An important foundation of 20th century science is Einstein's principle of Time Dilation. For example, the rapid orbital motion of GPS satellites requires their signals to be calibrated to adjust for the "positive-time" displacement occurring within the satellites. It is well established that spacecraft traveling near the speed of light could operate as one-way time machines. However, the classic idea of the time machine must first unravel a deep and mysterious question: Does the past truly disappear? The answer to the question may involve a mathematical issue known as "Probability Invariance." The perception of an orderly universe seeks to identify linear, constants, and limits—the so-called "Time Barrier" is an example. Moving forward and backward in time might be possible if random, mixing motion can be seen to contain Variant patterns and rates. Every day, ongoing outcomes could then be seen to permute or "link," literally, with prior, past events. The reality of "negative-time" displacement, as a mirrored principle to 'positive-time' dilation, would lead to scientific innovations and perhaps resolve many current mystical quandaries. The authors' shared psychic bond is one such example and the inspiration for this story. The author's (Ladd) mathematical and empirical research (Probability Variance Theory) and other (psy) artifacts mentioned in the novel can be witnessed on the novel's website.

******

Details concerning many of the paranormal episodes referenced in the "Halo" story can be accessed on our website. For example, the plot involves a vision of the New York City "9-11" disaster. The author wrote a short story of this account, "Sandcastles," in 1988. This can be viewed along with many other corroborative psychic artifacts. Research into the scientific theory and much more can be found there.

To reach us, visit our website:
http://www.haloandthedevilstail.com

Reader Paranormal Artifacts Bonus!

Areas in the novel marked with an asterisk indicate related paranormal artifact files are available for you to view/download.

These artifacts include original artwork, images, photographs, and other documents.

So when you see an asterisk * in the text, check out the "'Halo' Artifact Files" page on the HDT official website:

https://haloandthedevilstail.com

CHAPTER ONE

The Duel

Aaron and Helen stood within a spinning vortex; the only solidity was their grasp on one to the other. A spinning cloud of dim light, which might be experienced on a mountaintop in an early morning mist, seemed to have engulfed the now standing and dizzied couple.

Helen asked, "Aaron where are we? This has never happened before!"

Aaron responded, "Do you feel the total mind?"

Helen shouted, "No! I'm still just Helen. What's happening?"

As the two held each other close, the nearly terrified explorers saw that the cloud surrounding them was beginning to brighten and clear. They realized that they were high in the sky. Behind them, both could see a vast expanding city and a clear blue sky above. Before them, an unspeakable terror was at work. A vast wall of billowing flame and blast appeared to be retreating. The houses and buildings beneath the holocaust seemed to be returning from flame and destruction, jumping to their original pristine state.

The huge towering mushroom cloud shrank quite quickly to a smaller and smaller size. An entire metropolis was springing back into reality. A vast expanse of skyscrapers jumped from the ground up to claw at the beautifully clear winter sky.

It was as if the couple was chasing the Genie back into the bottle. The green expanse of Central Park appeared, and in the distance, One World Trade Center stood again. The blast shrunk down to the size of a building and then a house and finally seemed to emerge from the corner of a thoroughfare that made its way around the Manhattan Park.

At that instant, an intense pure white light burst out from a single point on the street. It was as if 10,000 Suns burned in that small spot. Aaron spoke out, "It's amazing. We can look right into it and there's no discomfort whatsoever!"

Helen grabbed tightly onto Aaron. "Do you hear it!? It's growling! It's as if it were something living!"

In just an instant, a white Chevrolet van sat at the point from where the light had emanated. The couple saw men in protective garments. One was closing the van's back door and began walking backwards towards two other men. All the men stood together briefly and the two men dressed in suits also began to walk backwards to a black vehicle.

Helen shrieked, "Oh, dear God! It's you, Aaron! It's you and some military General!"

Aaron steadied Helen in his arms. "Helen, you must have faith in (Y). We're being shown this for a reason. I think I understand!"

At that instant, the couple was sped along the streets and thoroughfares of New York City. Both marveled at the traffic and pedestrians as they went about their business, all completely oblivious to the fact that their lives were stuck in complete reverse.

(circa 2014 parallel [Y]time line)

In the year 2014, I was an associate professor of English and literature at a Mid-Western university . . .

"Helen, are you in a daze or something? You don't seem yourself today," a friend, Professor Alyssa Black, asked.

Smiling, Professor Helen Lovelace remarked, "I had the oddest dream last night and I can't decide what it meant. I guess I'm just preoccupied today." The intellectual, but decidedly feminine, teacher snatched up papers and books, her thick auburn locks swirling as she dashed out the copy room door. "I'll catch you after my 2:00 class!"

Running into class minutes late, Helen blushed as the roomful of students began to chuckle. A broad smile filled Helen's face, her brilliant green eyes sparkling. "I know we're studying European classics. But, let's skip Shakespeare's *Tempest* for a moment and come back to H. G. Wells' *The Time Machine*."

Zoe, Helen's assistant, began typing as the projector filled the class screen with the title work. A picture of the nineteenth-century author loomed large before the class.

Helen spoke assertively, "All right, someone read me his/her thesis statement regarding this work." Helen smiled as she saw an unexpected number of hands go up around the room. "Well, I guess we have a number of 'sci-fi' enthusiasts?"

Zoe was Helen's "Radar" in the class. She quickly responded, "It's Professor Aaron LaSalle, Helen!"

Helen's fine features strained as she turned to her adoring French grad student. "What did you say, Zoe?"

A few chuckles emerged from the class again. Helen turned to the class; her expression belied her deliberate aplomb. She pointed to a young man in the back of the class; his raised hand was the most enthusiastic. The white shirt and pocket protector almost materialized in Helen's imagination as the young man jumped to his feet.

"H. G. Wells was right, Professor Lovelace! There's a physics professor who has broken the time barrier. Several of us have his class. He's determined that negative time surrounds all events, even in our thoughts."

Helen turned to the huge screen in front of the class, her fingers combing through her still disheveled hair. In truth, she didn't want the class to detect her disconcerted expression. It was that name, LaSalle.

She knew the name, but Helen Lovelace was a published poet. The qualitatively graceful topics which consumed her palette of fine arts rarely entertained the crass notions of scientific types. The professor gazed at the towering picture of the noteworthy nineteenth-century writer and decided on a bit of humor to change the tone and commence the class work.

Helen spun around to her class, smiling broadly. "Well, that's quite interesting! I don't suppose he looks anything like this distinguished Englishman?"

The unexpected laughter was quite loud this time. The young college nerd stood smiling broadly. "Yes, Professor, he does! We all thought for a moment you had put the picture up deliberately!"

Helen's mind dizzied as her thoughts returned to the recurring dream. In the dream, she stood holding the right wrist of this autocratic gentleman. She kept repeating frantic questions. His silence and the intense stare from his soft brown eyes were haunting.

Helen grimaced, deciding to surge ahead with the class's work agenda. "We'll start with your thesis then, young man. I'm sure that you've prepared a poignant exposition."

Helen set the stack of books and papers on her office side table. Zoe smiled as she dropped the stack of class work beside the other piles. "Are you going to need any more help, Professor?"

Helen hugged the young student. "Oh, you dear, if it weren't for my grad students, I'd have to move into this office! No, Zoe. Bailey Smith will be here shortly. Have you met her? This is her first semester."

The sprite of a smile returned to Zoe. "I'm so anxious to meet her. But I have to run. Can I meet her tomorrow?"

Helen sat at her desk as she turned to see the student awaiting her answer. "Of course, Dear. You have a good afternoon!"

Helen began to type into her computer as she heard Bailey's voice.

"Helen, Alyssa Black said she was buying us a late lunch at the Red Dragon Restaurant."

Helen stopped typing and looked up at the clock on her wall. "I am starving!"

She turned to see the first-year grad student standing at the door. Helen jumped to her feet, grabbing her purse. "Okay, let's go!"

The three women laughed as Bailey swallowed a bite of the Chinese cuisine. "I've never had chicken stir fry like this. It's really good!"

Alyssa Black smiled. "My husband and I eat here often."

Helen took a sip of coffee. "Alyssa, you're a history professor. Do you know why the dollar bill says 'In God We Trust'?"

"That's an interesting question," Alyssa replied. "Bailey," she continued, eyeing Bailey, "you don't know this, but my husband is a physicist. Anyway, it's out of character, but he takes a lot of interest in history and social issues. He's always talking about American history."

The young student's grey eyes sparkled with the directness of the professor's remark. Bailey responded, "My father is really big on the history of the Masons. He says the dollar bill mentions God because the American Revolution was prophetic. I guess it's somehow mentioned in the Bible."

Alyssa took a sidelong glance at Helen." Why do you ask? I'm an expert in world history," Alyssa mused. "I'm not sure I have a pithy response."

(circa 2012 [Y]time line)

Helen's mind dizzied again; the momentary experience from the classroom lecture had returned. The normally crisp focus of the bright, green-eyed academic became a blur. Helen looked up from her steaming cup of coffee to see the seated presence of Professor Aaron LaSalle. The startled look on Helen's face was matched by her frantic glances around the table and around the room.

The dazed English professor was about to shout as an inexplicable calmness filled her mind. "You're the physics professor. We've known each other since . . . ?"

Aaron laughed his patented laugh. "Oh, you green-eyed demon! Let's see; it's been since 2009. That's right, almost three years!" Aaron's brown eyes squinted as he peered curiously at his luncheon companion. "You can't get out of the discussion that easily! All right, next month the Mayan prophecy will take place on the night of December 21st, 2012. My research in variant random sequences is taking me places. I think ancient societies, like the Mayans and the Hebrew prophets for that matter, knew about the loophole that exists in time."

Aaron took a drink of his hot tea. Gazing suspiciously at his dearest friend, he timidly asked, "Helen, are you all right? What are you thinking about?"

Helen blinked as she struggled to clear her head of the dizziness. She clamped her left arm with her right hand. "I guess I'm all right. I had the funniest thought, but now I can't remember what it was. Oh, I remember now! I wanted you to tell me what the inscription on the dollar bill says."

Aaron blinked as he tried not to appear concerned. "Well, it says, 'In God We Trust.' What else should it say?"

Helen smiled as her complexion and manner returned to normal. "Well, of course it does! All right, so tell me about this - what did you call it - a Reveal? Tell me how this works."

Aaron returned to his comfort zone. "The Hebrew prophecies have always been of interest to me."

Helen smiled as she studied Aaron's olive complexion and striking brown eyes. "Well, naturally."

Aaron continued, "I have uncovered a technique that I believe may have been used by Nostradamus and perhaps many of the prophets. It involves selecting Bible passages by random means and recording the passage, one at a time, for each day. I call it a Reveal.*" (See the "Halo" Artifact Files* page on the https://haloandthedevilstail.com website.)

Helen took a drink of coffee as she thought about Aaron's comments. "Do you think this will tell you whether the world is going to end next month?"

Aaron chuckled. "You and I have discussed my dreams. I know how New Age you are. You're the only one I can discuss this with. I'm worried that something terrible is going to happen on the 21st."

Helen wiped her mouth and grimaced. "You know a lot more about these ancient notions and modern science than a professor of poetry. When do you start this Reveal?"

Aaron smiled. "It's a simple procedure. I do it each night or the morning before the day in question. There are sacred steps that must be observed. In this case, I'll start on November 21st and stop the morning of December 21st, 2012."

Helen's expression was intense. "Aaron, can you tell me in simple terms what your research is really about?"

Aaron was hearing the exact words he had hoped to hear. "Helen, in quantum physics, something magical is observed. There is a remarkable duality. For example, light can be a particle or a wave. It really shouldn't be doing that. It's as unexpected as the asymptotic limit for all speed being something just as peculiar - again - the speed of light. I've done simple experiments with random systems, things like tumblers and card flips, and found phenomenon in the macro-world just as unexpected."

Helen smiled. "Okay. Remember, I'm an English professor."

Aaron continued, "Einstein's Relativity says that if you travel at just about the speed of light, you'll quit aging, your watch will slow, and you can travel into the future. It could be a day, a year, or 10,000 years. Here's the point. I've found that the simple act of mixing the contents of any random system actually produces negative time connections."

Helen grimaced, her green eyes sparkling, and asked, "You can actually see this in your card flips and those revolving ping pong ball tumblers of yours?"

"Yes!" Aaron replied. "There is this hyperspace motion that is linking past outcomes to the given real time event. It arcs backwards in time, like two mirrors facing one another. It reaches backwards to a distance of negative pi time. I call the graph the 'Halo.' It trails behind all interactive motions. There's another anomaly that extends the multiple set counts; it acts to counteract the orderliness of the phenomenon. I call it the 'Devil's Tail.'"

Helen winced as she drank deeply from the hot cup of coffee. "So there is some weird science that produces order and disorder?"

Aaron's gaze focused on his tea cup as he rocked it back and forth on the table. "I'm more impressed than you know. There must be some reason you're here. The math says reality is just one long corridor. There is no end or beginning to the path that each of us is on. But here's the point. At one end of the hall, we may still be experiencing birth, but I don't think there is an ending at the other end."

Helen smiled. "You're telling me that reincarnation is real!"

Aaron continued, "The prophecy about next month's Winter Solstice portends great evil. My scientific theories are based on what are called binomial relationships. Apparently, the Universe operates just like my tumblers. The outcomes pivot back and forth eternally between twin possibilities."

Helen's expression turned blank. "You're scaring me. I've always thought there was one God, maybe? But I've never considered that goodness might not prevail."

Aaron's soft brown eyes began to water. "Helen, I need you. There's something I haven't shared. I'm quite psychic. I experience lucid dreams of the future. They're often quite interpretive, but for the most part, they come to pass. It appears to run in my family. You're a writer. I wrote a short story in 1988 describing 9-11. Here it is."

Aaron pushed the eleven-page story to Helen. Her wide-eyed expression conveyed both surprise and genuine trepidation. She sat quite still, staring at the pages. Several moments passed.

Helen spoke slowly as her gaze made unblinking contact with Aaron's eyes. "The story is titled 'Sandcastles';* it's dedicated to the Woman and Victory. Why does that title seem to disturb me?"

Aaron chuckled quietly, his soft brown eyes never leaving the jade depth of Helen's stare. "You're the Woman. The date of these pages could be checked. That story shows the destruction of the World Trade Center on September 11th, 2001, the attack on the Pentagon and the three planes involved. It's written symbolically, but here's the point. I also saw you! Many years ago in the dreams, there was only one person who could help me prevent something even worse. It's you, Helen."

The stare never paused between the two. Helen's hand cupped her mouth as she almost whispered, "Somehow, I know this must be true, but why?"

Aaron blinked as he timidly looked away. "It's the binomial math, Helen. Everything comes in pairs. There is some expanded aspect of reality that religion and science are just beginning to touch on. The revelation is that mankind has reached the point where we must advance or possibly become extinct. The historians talk about the Dark Ages. The truth is we've never left them. For all the science and technology, we really know just enough to harm ourselves."

Helen picked up the story and began to read as she trailed the question, "What can I possibly do?" A good bit of time passed silently as Aaron waved off the waiter. Helen turned the last page and looked up at Aaron. Her expression was whimsical. "How did a physics and math wizard ever write such a story?"

Aaron smiled broadly as he looked into Helen's eyes. "Thank you. Very few people have ever read it. I didn't know if it was of any value."

"Aaron this is absolutely beautiful," Helen said softly. "You call this a children's story? It's truly a wondrous parable. The three feathers are the planes that were used as weapons. The Twin Towers are the child's sandcastles that were torn down. And the building that was not square but had one extra corner is the Pentagon. You saw '9-11' in 1988 and wrote it as a beautiful allegory!"

Aaron continued to pivot his empty tea cup as he gazed into it. "In the dream, I saw the skyscrapers fall as if they had turned to grains of sand. I saw the three planes flash to flame like feathers in a furnace. I saw a building which was not square but held one extra corner. The extra wall smashed by violence."

Helen's expression was blank, matching the moments that passed. "Did you see this using your Reveal technique?"

Aaron looked up and shook his head. "No, it appeared in my dreams. I've had such dreams my entire life. But there's something else you need to understand. I was not shown the date it would occur. Sometimes, I see incidental things. Once, I was driving with a friend, and I told him that, when we pulled into his driveway, there would be a bookcase in his yard--with the books all turned backwards. The dream came true when my best friend Mick and I arrived at his house to find a van delivering phone books. The side door was open, and it was filled bottom to top with the books neatly stacked, pages out."

Helen grimaced as she shook her head. "What did he say?"

Aaron smiled as he answered, "His response has always reminded me that such things are completely natural. He looked at me and quipped, 'I've gotta give you that one!'"

Jade eyes grew intense as Helen replied, "I had something very odd happen on the day of 9-11. A small and screaming wren flew into my car as I was about to leave for work that morning."

Aaron's eyes stared into the distance as he responded, "That's rather poetic. A mathematician named Christopher Wren proved in 1658 that the square of the circle is the cycloid shape that inscribes the circle."

Helen smiled impatiently. "Remember, I'm an English scholar."

Aaron smiled, wryly. "You'll understand in time. The connections that we see in the real world are not coincidences. There is a far deeper, far-reaching reality that the human race is quite colorblind to perceive."

Helen leaned forward as she spoke intently, "You said there was something far worse that may happen."

Aaron continued, "The Reveal can only be performed when a sign is given. The Mayan warning is such a sign. After the Solstice, I want to show you how to perform your own Reveal."

Helen grimaced as she repeated the question, "What do you think could be worse than 9- 11?"

Aaron gazed deeply into Helen's eyes. "The same set of dreams in 1988 showed me multiple atomic blasts, in perhaps more than one major city."

Helen's eyes widened as she threw her right hand over her mouth. Aaron reached across the table and took hold of her left wrist with his right hand. "Helen, 'keep calm and carry on.' I was shown a way that we might prevent it."

(Aaron's home [Y]time line)

The room was pitch-black. Aaron LaSalle kept his bedroom blackened out to prevent interruption of his dreams. Flat on his back, the thoughtful man's eyes riveted from left to right, right to left. A faint, gossamer light gave witness to the rapid eye movement of his shut eyelids. Aaron began to dream a strange dream.

A lamb was being chased by a lion and a bear through a strangely-shaped field that was not square, but had one extra corner. The lamb ran until it became exhausted and collapsed. As the lion and the bear surrounded the lamb, the lamb began to speak.

"Why must you kill me?" asked the lamb.

"Because that's our nature," said the bear. "You're a lamb and I'm a bear."

"Speak for yourself," said the lion. "I'm going to kill you because you're weak and deserve to die."

"Before you kill me, let me ask you both one question," said the lamb." Bear, you are a creature of the woods and the wilderness. You sleep for half a year in the bosom of the forest and you fish the endless brooks and streams of the mountains. Why then, must you kill a harmless creature that does no more than graze the pastures well beyond your domain?"

The bear shrugged his huge shoulders and said, "Yes, that is all true, but I am still a bear and you are still a lamb."

"Lion," said the lamb, "you say I am weak. Are not your lion cubs innocent, soft and weak, also? Would you kill them for being lion cubs?"

The lion pawed the ground and tossed his great hairy mane to and fro, and then he became very quiet and said, "Yes, that is true, but I am a lion and you are a lamb."

The lamb shook his head slowly back and forth and spoke very softly, "Bear, you have found an excuse to do something that is easy to do but not necessary. Lion, you have found a lie that allows you to blame others rather than yourself. I know now that you must kill me and I must let you, but I want you to know one last thing. It is more important to me that you understand the truth of what you have said than what you are about to do to me."

Then, the bear and the lion slew the lamb.

Aaron's eyelids began to flutter as he nearly left the deep sleep state. He thought for an instant, *What year is this? Those passages were from "Sandcastles." Is it 1988? No, it's December 14th, 2012.*

Aaron's eyelids tightened again as his eyes began to flicker, left to right and right to left. He was taken high in the air and could see the towering New York City skyline. Suddenly, the city burst brightly with the intensity of the sun. Blast and flame followed, consuming the ordered structures of man as a towering fiery red mushroom cloud filled the sky. Aaron's breathing became that of a panting animal as he tried desperately to break free of the dreams. He again asked himself, *Are these the dreams of 1988? Why, are they recurring?* Pulled again into the deep sleep, Aaron watched as the towering specter reversed itself and shrank into a pinpoint of light - the towering skyline returning before him.

The scene changed as Aaron flew along the New England coast. He found himself hovering before a Connecticut school house. The happy and delicate elementary children filled the scene as their smiling teachers welcomed them. Time itself seemed to blink. In rapid snapshots, Aaron watched as the minutes turned to tens of minutes. A man approached the school, now in session.

Aaron watched the flickering scene as the walking man turned hideous. A grotesque creature erupted from his shoulders. Where there was a head, a red regurgitated shape now formed. It was comprised of many eyes, and mandibles seemed to hover hungrily about them. Aaron's thoughts became frantic. *Where is this place? I must know this place! What time is this? What year is this?* Aaron shouted, "Dear Yahweh! Please, tell me how to stop this!"

Aaron snapped straight up in the bed as he heard the words, "The sandy hook, 9:30."

Aaron rushed out of bed to his computer and began to search Google, frantically, talking to the screen filling with links and images. "Let's see; it was Connecticut. What does a 'sandy hook' mean? All right, it was a school, small children. Yes, it was an elementary school. I'll look at all the elementary schools."

Aaron's eyes widened as he found Sandy Hook Elementary, Newtown, Connecticut. "It's 4:44 in the morning which means its 5:44 in Connecticut. I have time! I can send a message to their police. I must!"

Aaron's heart sank as he realized and spoke to the computer's monitor, "It's the date; once again. Satan has confounded me! I don't know what year it will happen!"

Aaron began to weep out loud, "How long must I live with this torment? Must mankind always know only the companionship of death?"

Aaron threw the keyboard against the computer monitor's edge as his nude form paced wretchedly into the kitchen. Muttering to himself, he lamented, "My only companion will be death and my hot tea."

Aaron stood combing his hair, nearly dressed and looking into his bathroom mirror. With a dignified expression, he stared into his own eyes. Suddenly, a shot of adrenaline coursed through his body.

"Oh, dear (Y), I could have left this house and not done the Reveal!"

Aaron laid out a clean hand towel and washed his hands. Drying them very carefully, he was even more careful not to touch anything directly. He pulled open the bedside drawer after covering the handle with the towel. Reaching in, he pulled out the dice, again covering them with the towel. The private prayer was repeated in Aaron's mind. It could not be recited out loud. He pulled the KJV Bible out with his hands and laid it onto the towel, next to the cleansed dice. Sitting at the den table, he set out the handwritten Reveal. The last entry was 12/13/12. Aaron performed the ritual and entered the date and verse.

It read 12/14/12 – Numbers 14:3 "Children made prey."

The adrenaline rushed through Aaron as he reassembled the computer and keyboard. "I must contact the Newtown sheriff. There must be a 911 website? All right, it was at 9:30 EST! It's 6:56, their time. There's plenty of time. This can happen! Wait! The warnings from 1988! I have to check with the Woman of the story. I was warned in 'Sandcastles!'"

The frantic professor banged at his phone as he muttered, "It can only be Helen that can prevent the ultimate destruction. Please, Helen! Why aren't you answering? Answer the damn phone! Please, dear Yahweh! What do I do?!"

The tears clouded Aaron's eyes as he muttered, "I can't let the children die - the lamb must be saved. I don't care about the city. These blood sacrifices Will Not occur!"

Aaron depressed the "send" key as the room began to spin. The professor of physics fell in slow motion, his left wrist grasped vice-like by his right hand as laws of gravity and some greater injunction were decreed upon the man.

(circa 1703 Switzerland [S]time line)

The seventeenth-century scholar worked tirelessly. The hand-carved craftsmanship of the French accouterments was an exquisite extension of his limbs. The ceaseless cadence of the hand-built pendulum clocks testified to a time when quietude was certain. The repository of a lifetime of travels and exploration were reflected in the books and artifacts surrounding the middle aged man. Francois L'Hospital was on the forefront of his science. The frailties of the new disciplines of the mathematical calculus and the kinematics of Newton were being established as building blocks of a new world. Philosophy and fact were thought to be inseparable.

Francois returned the quill pen to its well as he grasped his left wrist firmly with his right hand. The tingling and numbness seemed to fill his entire body. The immediate fear for his health was replaced with a dizzying rapture. In the time of a single breath, a flood of images overwhelmed his considerable mind. As if the revelation of birth had been duplicated several times over in just that instant, the classic Swiss personality saw a world telescoped beyond description. Francois arched backwards in the baroque chaise, a kaleidoscope of reality filling his mind. The tactile images were at once pain and pleasure. The impressions of the mind were suddenly experienced as graduations in the known and the unknown. The pain of the crawling infant hitting his head could be held in one's hand. The laughter of the school yard joke could be tasted. The mother's love became as a dexterous skill; the child's image of his own written words.

"Francois! What are you doing?" Shri'Ani cried out as she stood watching her husband twisting in his chair, trying to regain his composure.

The dignified Swiss man turned to see the statuesque form of the youthful Hindu woman who was his wife of 25 years. "I'm all right, Shri.'"

Francois held out his hand as he gazed into the jade eyes of the approaching rapturous beauty. Pulling his dearest companion close, he pressed his face into her bosom. The jade-colored sari held the scent of rose petals. Shri'Ani's thick locks of ebony hair entangled Francois's face. Francois breathed in the moments as the ticks of his clocks paced forward.

Looking up into the fine features of his Hindu companion, the staid disposition of his personality could be seen from a new perspective. He smiled as he tenderly said, "I love you so much."

Shri's fiery jade eyes sparkled as her supple lips turned to a broad smile. "You want to love Shri' now? Yes!"

In an instant, the reality of three lifetimes flashed through the mind of one solitary brain. The seventeenth-century scientist was in awe of the twentieth-century means of warfare. The skyscrapers falling like meaningless mounds of sand in a child's backyard box, jet aircraft, spacecraft, submarines and mushroom clouds: 300 years of creation and destruction were instantly compressed in one vision.

Francois looked deeply into Shri's eyes. The sparkling refraction of the green iris, the opulent arch of the childlike lashes seemed to reach across time itself. His gaze fell to see her face as a whole. The same fullness of lips, no one has that dimple in their chin. Jakob Bernoulli was always calculating the possibility of a snowflake ever being duplicated. The austere French natural scientist would never ingratiate him by agreeing. He knew, however, the mathematics must be true. No two faces are ever exactly the same, even spanning three hundred years! He thought to himself, *This is the Woman. It's all connected. Shri'Ani is Helen!*

Francois unseated himself and stood next to Shri'. Taking her in his arms, he kissed her as deeply and passionately as he had those twenty-five years earlier in the jungles of India. The teenage girl had followed him like a stray cat. The man in his 20s had taught her much of his language during the two years of exploration. Francois held her limp form at arm's length. Shri' slowly opened her eyes and muttered, "You love Shri' now? Yes!"

The dignified Frenchman laughed as he hugged her gently. "You don't know, do you, Shri'?"

Shri'Ani frowned as she responded, "I know I love you."

Francois smiled. "I promise to love you all afternoon, after the Academia of Science meeting. I promise, Shri'!"

Shri' frowned again. "You give that desk more love than you give Shri'. I'll get the tea. You will not forget the promise. I guarantee that you won't, Francois."

The nubile beauty flipped around and walked from the room. Francois watched her every step. He sat in wonder with the phenomenon that was life itself. His gaze drank in her exquisite pear shaped bottom, the lithe sensual form. Just as Shri' reached the doorway, she snapped around to catch Francois's gaze. She smiled wryly as she quipped, "I guarantee you won't forget to love me!"

Francois turned to his desk. Pulling a fresh sheet of paper and dipping the quill pen, he thought to himself, *I'm going to start by recording the Variance Theory equations. If the seventeenth century knows that consciousness is a natural physical property, then the substantive belief in God is a short step. Perhaps the warfare and sacrifice of the twentieth century can be avoided. If the world knows there truly is a God, then we'll stop killing each other. I'll need the Science Academy to publish the work. I'll have to get that arrogant Swiss man Jakob Bernoulli to endorse the work. I've still got time, before the meeting.*

The mind of three men wrote for many minutes. Suddenly, the dizziness and numbness returned to the body of Guillaeme Francois de L'Hospital. His left hand wrenched tightly to his right wrist as he lost consciousness.

(circa 2012 [S]time line)

Aaron LaSalle's eyes opened as the numbness and tingling filled his body. The death grip on his right wrist by his left hand seemed to have a mind of its own. He blinked repeatedly as the kaleidoscope of events across time and space filled his mind. He was the same man who had lived 300 years earlier. But it was as if he stood at the opposite end of a long hallway, watching himself approach from both directions.

He thought to himself, *This can only be described as a "total mind." I know I finished the manuscript and argued with Jakob Bernoulli. I made love all afternoon with Shri'Ani. Dear (Y), I miss her already! No, wait she's still here. But most importantly, I now know I only have twenty-one minutes before I forget almost everything. Yes, I remember my clock. It was twenty-one minutes and the rapture occurred again! I have to write fast! I have to record every memory.*

Aaron picked himself up and ran to his den. Seating himself, he grabbed a notepad and began to write as fast as he could:

"I don't dare use a computer. If any information from the past interacts with current time it may produce a paradox. Even something as small as a name from a previous century might cause a change in the future history books. I can't risk that. Wait! What am I saying? I just introduced twenty-first-century quantum physics into the seventeenth century! Just write what you know Francois, Yuri, Aaron. We'll figure out what we've done, after this twenty-one minute window closes. At least, I'll have this diary to help me know if anything has changed."

(circa 2014 Helen's College [S]time line)

"Helen, are you in a daze or something? You don't seem yourself today," Professor Alyssa Black asked.

Smiling, Professor Helen Lovelace remarked, "I had the oddest dream last night, and I can't decide what it meant. I guess I'm just preoccupied today."

Professor Black inquired gently, "Was it some kind of nightmare?"

Helen pursed her lips then took a deep breath as she replied, "I don't really know how to explain it, even to myself."

Alyssa Black retorted, "Try me! Now, I'm really curious."

Helen spoke disconcertingly, "Alyssa, it's as if I keep seeing ghosts. I keep dreaming of students in my classrooms who disappear when I call on them."

Alyssa looked curiously at her friend. "Well, go see Aaron LaSalle in the meta-physics department. He has theoretical work that he says may explain paranormal phenomenon."

Helen's expression became quite distressed. "I've met with LaSalle. There's something unsettling about him."

Alyssa shook her head, smiling. "You'll figure it out. I still say you should be tested. You may have real psychic abilities."

Helen snatched up papers and books, her thick auburn locks swirling as she dashed out the printing room door. "I'll catch you after my 2:00 class!"

Running into class minutes late, Helen blushed as the roomful of students began to chuckle. A broad smile filled Helen's face, her brilliant green eyes sparkling. "I know we're studying European classics. But let's skip Shakespeare's *Tempest* for a moment and come back to H. G. Wells' *The Time Machine*."

Bekah, Helen's Swedish grad student, began typing as the projector filled the class screen with the title work. A picture of the 19th Century author loomed before the class.

Helen addressed the students, "All right, someone read me his/her thesis statement regarding this work." Helen smiled as she saw an unexpected number of hands go up around the room. "Well, I guess we have a number of 'sci-fi' enthusiasts?"

Bekah was Helen's "Radar" in the class. She quickly responded, "It's Professor Aaron LaSalle, Helen!"

Helen's fine features strained as she turned to her adoring European grad student. "What did you say, Bekah?"

A few chuckles emerged from the class again. Helen turned to the class; her expression belied her deliberate aplomb. She pointed to a young man in the back of the class; his raised hand was the most enthusiastic. The white shirt and pocket protector almost materialized in Helen's imagination as the young man jumped to his feet.

"H. G. Wells was right, Professor Lovelace! There's a meta-physics professor who says he can break the time barrier. Several of us have his class. He's determined to go back to the 2012 Holocaust and save New York City."

Helen turned to the huge screen, in front of the class, her fingers combing through her still disheveled hair. In truth, she didn't want the class to detect her disconcerted expression.

Helen looked wide-eyed at Bekah, whispering, "He promised me! This cannot get around. Even in the meta-physics department, this cannot be common knowledge."

Bekah looked up from the keyboard and said softly, "I think it's okay. I'm good friends with Bailey Smith, his 'Girl Friday' grad student. He hasn't said that much, really. . ."

Helen Lovelace was a published poet. The qualitatively graceful topics which consumed her palette of fine arts rarely entertained the crass notions of scientific types. The professor gazed at the towering picture of the noteworthy nineteenth-century writer and decided on a bit of humor to change the tone and commence the class work.

Helen spun around to her class, smiling broadly. "Well, that's quite interesting! I don't suppose he looks anything like this distinguished Englishman?"

The unexpected laughter was quite loud this time. The young college nerd stood smiling broadly. "Yes, Professor, he does! We all thought for a moment you had put the picture up deliberately!"

An intense moment of Déjà vu filled the beleaguered English professor's mind. Helen thought to herself, *It's the recurring dream! The huge face of H. G. Wells does resemble Aaron LaSalle. In the dream, I stood holding the right wrist of this autocratic gentleman. It was this moment, in this classroom, but there were students I've never known! There was a young French girl. I think she was trying to tell me something, but what?*

Helen grimaced, deciding to surge ahead with the class work agenda. "We'll start with your thesis then, young man. I'm sure that you've prepared a poignant exposition."

(circa 2014 [S]time line)

Helen set the stack of books and papers on her office side table. Bekah smiled as she dropped the stack of class work beside the other piles. "Are you going to need any more help, Professor?"

Bekah's blue eyes glistened as Helen gave the blonde Swede a hug. "No, I'm fine, dear. If it weren't for my grad students, I'd have to move into this office."

Bekah spoke excitedly, "Oh, I almost forgot! Alyssa said Bailey Smith is stopping by."

Helen replied, "This is her first semester and I haven't met her yet."

The sprite of a smile returned to Bekah. "Bailey is fabulous. I just adore her!"

Helen sat at her desk and began to type into her computer as she heard Bailey's voice from down the hall.

"Hi, Bekah! Guess what? Alyssa Black said she was buying Helen and us a late lunch at the Red Dragon restaurant."

Helen stopped typing and looked up at the clock on her wall. "I am starving!"

She turned to see the first-year grad student standing at the door, hugging Bekah. Helen jumped to her feet, and walked over to the smiling physics student. "I've heard great things about you!"

Bekah grimaced. "I've got a class! I never get to go anywhere!"

Helen grabbed her purse and gave Bekah one last hug. "I'll see you in the morning then, dear. Okay, Bailey, let's go!"

Bailey, Alyssa and Helen walked into the restaurant as Alyssa spoke, "Oh good, there's Aaron. He's already got our table."

Helen gave Bailey a sidelong glance as the physics student responded with a broad smile. "Yea, Professor LaSalle's having lunch with us, too."

Bailey's soft grey eyes sparkled as she swallowed a bite of the Chinese cuisine. "I've never had chicken stir fry like this. It's really good!"

Alyssa Black smiled. "My husband and I eat here often."

Helen peered sternly into Aaron's eyes and took a sip of coffee. Without shifting her gaze, she said, "Alyssa, I have a question. Do you know why the dollar bill says 'On God We Depend'? "

Alyssa quipped, "That's an interesting question. Bailey, you know my husband, Robert. He and Aaron are the reason we all know each other."

Aaron interjected, "Bob's a world-class physicist. He's an expert in electricity and magnetism."

Alyssa continued, "Anyway, Robert takes a lot of interest in history and social issues. He's always talking about American history."

Bailey's grey eyes sparkled with the directness of the professor's conversation. "My father is really big in the history of the Masons. He says the dollar bill mentions (Y) because the American Revolution was prophetic. After all, it was prophesized in the Bible."

Alyssa took a sidelong glance at Helen as she spoke, "Why do you ask about the inscription?"

Helen's mind dizzied again; the momentary experience from the classroom lecture had returned. The normally crisp focus of the bright, green-eyed academic became a blur. The intense feeling of Déjà vu had returned. Helen looked up from her steaming cup of coffee and looked deeply into Aaron's eyes. The startled look on Helen's face was matched by frantic glances around the table and around the room.

The dazed English professor was about to shout as an inexplicable calmness filled her mind. "Aaron, you're the physics professor. We've known each other since . . ."

All four people laughed as Aaron said, "Oh, you green-eyed demon! Let's see; it's been since 2009. That's right, almost five years!"

Helen leaned across the table, her fiery jade eyes sparkling as she looked deeply into Aaron LaSalle's eyes. "Aaron, do you remember our conversation that early morning on December 21st, 2012?"

Aaron smiled wryly as he answered, "Of course, I do!"

Helen pursed her lips, furled her brow. "It's happening, Aaron! You were right. I was wrong. The 'total mind' you spoke of is happening. You said it would happen."

Aaron's gaze never left Helen's face as he softly queried, "Do you remember what I told you would be the sign that we could undo the Apocalypse?"

Helen's eyes began to water as she nearly shouted, "Yes, I saw it in the dreams. The dollar bill is wrong! It's supposed to say 'In God We Trust.'"

Aaron leaned forward and said, "Helen, I need to explain something to you." His brown eyes gazed intently into the jade depth of the perplexed woman's eyes. "I want to take you back 300 years. You must know what happened if we are to correct a divine error. The past does not disappear. There is, in fact, a greater reality; there is an *eternal now.*

"In the year 1703, there were two well-known mathematicians: Jakob Bernoulli and Guillaume Francois de L'Hospital. There was a conflict between them regarding the question of man and God. They actually engaged in a swordfight to resolve a pivotal mathematical issue."

Helen smiled wryly. "I can understand their frustration".

Aaron sighed and continued, "There exists a unique shape called the cycloid. The issues regarding this are known as the Brachistochrone problem. If understood, the shape suggests that time itself might be manipulated and that time is at the heart of all human awareness."

Helen replied blankly, "I see why they were fighting."

"If Francois won the duel," Aaron continued, "Jakob would present Francois' work to the Academy. Each was a masterful swordsman, but it appears that L'Hospital did in fact win, and I'm quite sure now that that result must be altered."

Helen's expression shifted, her pained confusion obvious. "I don't understand."

Aaron explained, "This is the reality we now exist in. Your academic society directly embraces the existence of God."

CHAPTER TWO

The Reveal

(Early morning, December 21st 2012 [S] time line)

Aaron sat motionless in his den, the writing table and its contents consuming his total concentration. Staring intently at the open Bible, he was aware of the hand-built pendulum clock ticking incessantly as if the inanimate object possessed a mind of its own.

A stern expression filled the scientist's face, his brown eyes wide. Aaron knew that the tsunami of world-changing events he had witnessed for the last seven days were about to truly devastate the world. He pushed the Bible and dice forward as he grasped the handwritten Reveal page and took hold of the pen. He began to write . . .

> *12/21/12 Ephesians 6:13 Take unto you the whole armour of God, that ye may withstand the evil day, having done all, stand.*

Aaron took the completed Reveal and hurried to his desk, punching up Helen's e-mail address.

> *Helen,*

> *I must see you at your office, on campus at 8:00; it's urgent. I know we haven't talked much since our lunch last month, but I must share the results of the Reveal. I must verify something with you, and I now am desperately afraid that there will be a terrible devastation today! I must meet with you so both our minds will be unified in this knowledge.*

Aaron

Helen sat at her side table in her college office. Taking a sip from her hot coffee, she peered through the steam at her clock on the wall. She muttered to herself, "Well, it's precisely 8:00 a.m. That door should open within 30 seconds. If there is one constant in the Universe, it's the timely compulsion of one Aaron LaSalle."

Helen set down the cup and smiled to herself as she admired her precious drinking vessel. She pivoted the dark green cup back and forth, studying the bright gold 4-leaf clover which adorned it. Her mind wandered to the dream several years earlier in which she saw herself drinking from such a cup. A wry smile crept across her face as she remembered spotting the exact cup the next day, or was it two days later, at the mall. She wondered to herself if such things genuinely spoke of a reality beyond the confines of human thought. Perhaps, the future truly could be foretold.

The office door opened to the wide-eyed presence of Aaron LaSalle. The breathless professor appeared to Helen as somewhat forlorn. She experienced a fleeting thought. For the briefest moment, the dignified English professor avoided his eyes. This reaction, too, was quite new to Helen's repertoire of Aaron LaSalle experiences. The quite youthful and genuinely beautiful academic suddenly felt quite vulnerable. Aaron shut the door and rushed to the L-return of Helen's desk, seating himself across from her. Helen's distraction turned to total focus as Aaron began to speak.

Aaron leaned forward into Helen's green-eyed gaze as he spoke nervously, "Helen, I know we don't really know each other that well. I mean, we've only met, what, three or four times in college surroundings?"

Helen smiled as she studied Aaron's soft brown eyes. She became quite comfortable as she responded. "We had that lunch at the Red Dragon Restaurant last month."

Aaron smiled as he felt comforted in the difficult topic he must broach. "Helen, there is going to be a catastrophic world event today." Aaron paused, awaiting the distraught reaction he had been anticipating.

Helen remained quite composed as she spoke quietly, "I think I know that something terrible is about to happen. I've prayed to (Y) that my dreams don't come to pass."

The meta-physics professor smiled broadly. "So you are psychic. Have you ever been tested?"

Helen shook her head. "No, I've never wanted to develop these abilities. I don't have the courage. I don't want to know when people are going to die in a car wreck or have some child's mother begging to know if her child will live. I don't know how you card-carrying psychics have the courage to deal with it."

Aaron pushed several papers in front of Helen, ordering them on the desk and pointing as he spoke, "Helen, this is the Reveal, my total-mind diary from 1703, and a dollar bill. Each of these contains earth-shaking information."

Helen's eyes widened as her expression became quite grim. "What kind of nightmares do you experience, you poor man? What is a total-mind? What are you talking about?"

Aaron handed Helen the dollar bill. "Read the inscription."

Helen grimaced as she took the bill. "You want me to read this?" Aaron nodded.

Helen shook her head as she began to recite, her eyes never looking at the bill and never leaving Aaron's gaze. "On God We Depend." Helen frowned. "Is it supposed to say something else?"

Aaron held up the Reveal, pointing at the 12/14/12 entry. "Read the entry."

Helen leaned forward and read:

"Numbers 14:3 "Children made prey."

Helen's nonplussed expression returned. "And, what, pray tell, does that mean?"

Aaron queried, "Have you ever heard of the Sandy Hook Elementary School massacre?"

Helen's look became distressed. "Dear (Y), what are you talking about?"

Aaron held up the third stack of handwritten sheets. "This diary is from a handwritten account of a man describing his wife in the year 1703 in Switzerland."

> *Francois gazed deeply into Shri'Ani's vivid jade green eyes, the childlike arch of the excessively long lashes remained immutably in his memory. His gaze moved to absorb the delicacy of her features. The distinct dimple in her chin seemed a divine improvement to the classic beauty mark. Its unique signature could not be duplicated by any artistic hand. A tiny, divinely prescribed snowflake seemed to adorn her chin as if God himself had sought to re-write the mathematics of the improbable.*

Helen averted her eyes from Aaron as she cautiously grasped her chin with her right hand. Several moments passed as both sat silently. Helen meekly returned her gaze to Aaron. "You said something terrible was about to occur."

Aaron picked up the Reveal and pointed to the entry made a few hours earlier. "Read the entry."

Helen leaned forward and read:

> "12/21/12 Ephesians 6:13 "Take unto you the whole armour of God, that ye may withstand the evil day, having done all, stand."

Helen blinked; a befuddled look filled her expression. "What does it mean?"

Aaron set the papers down and reached across the table, taking Helen's right wrist with his left hand. He gazed intently into the depths of Helen's wide, green orbs. "At 12:21 p.m. today, New York City is going to be annihilated in a nuclear blast."

Helen's eyes began to tear. "It's the dream! You were saying those words to me!" Tears fell down her cheeks as she wiped them helplessly with her left hand.

([Y] time line)

The office door opened to the wide-eyed presence of Aaron LaSalle. The breathless professor appeared to Helen as somewhat *dazed.* For the briefest moment, the dignified English professor avoided his eyes. This reaction, too, was quite new to Helen's repertoire of Aaron LaSalle experiences. The quite youthful and genuinely beautiful academic suddenly felt quite vulnerable. Aaron shut the door and rushed to the L-return of Helen's desk, seating himself across from her. Helen's distraction turned to total focus as Aaron began to speak.

Aaron leaned forward into Helen's green-eyed gaze as he spoke nervously, "Helen, I know we don't really know each other that well. I mean, we've only met, what, three or four times in college surroundings?"

Helen smiled as she studied Aaron's soft brown eyes. It occurred to her that she felt just a bit uncomfortable as she focused on his face. "We had that lunch at the Red Dragon Restaurant last month."

Aaron smiled as he felt comforted in the difficult topic he must broach. "Helen, there is going to be a catastrophic world event." Aaron paused, awaiting the distraught reaction he had been anticipating.

Helen remained quite composed as she spoke quietly, "I think I know that something terrible *could* happen. I've prayed to God that my dreams don't come to pass."

The physics professor smiled broadly. "So you do believe in psychic abilities. I need someone to discuss such things with. It's a bit of a leap for a scientist to discuss the paranormal with associates."

Helen nodded. "Yes, my dreams are much of the inspiration for my poetry. But I don't want to know when people are going to die in a car wreck or have some child's mother begging to know if her child will live. I suppose that's why people don't experience such things very often."

Aaron pushed several papers in front of Helen, ordering them on the desk and pointing as he spoke, "Helen, this is the Reveal, a diary of my total-mind dreams, and a dollar bill. Each of these contains earth-shaking information."

Helen's eyes widened as her expression became quite grim. "What kind of nightmares do you experience, you poor man. What is a total-mind? What are you talking about?"

Aaron handed Helen the dollar bill. "Read the inscription."

Helen grimaced as she took the bill. "You want me to read this?" Aaron nodded.

Helen shook her head as she began to recite, her eyes never looking at the bill and never leaving Aaron's gaze. "In God We Trust." Helen frowned. "Is it supposed to say something else?"

Aaron held up the Reveal, pointing at the 12/14/12 entry. "Read the entry."

Helen leaned forward and read:

"Numbers 14:3 "Children made prey."

Helen's nonplussed expression became wide-eyed. "That's the date of the Sandy Hook Elementary School massacre!" Helen's distressed tone continued, "Dear Lord, what are you talking about? Are you supposing that this Reveal technique of yours identified the children's deaths?"

Aaron held up the third stack of handwritten sheets. "This diary is from a handwritten account of a man describing his wife in the year 1703 in Switzerland." He began to read.

> *Francois gazed deeply into Shri'Ani's vivid jade green eyes, the childlike arch of the excessively long lashes remained immutably in his memory. His gaze moved to absorb the delicacy of her features. The distinct cleft in her chin seemed a divine improvement to the classic beauty mark. Its unique signature could not be duplicated by any artistic hand. A tiny, divinely prescribed snowflake seemed to adorn her chin as if God himself had sought to re-write the mathematics of the improbable.*

Helen averted her eyes from Aaron as she cautiously grasped her chin with her left hand. Several moments passed as both sat silently. Helen meekly returned her gaze to Aaron. "You said something terrible was going to occur. Do you mean today?"

Aaron picked up the Reveal and pointed to the entry made a few hours earlier. "Read the entry."

Helen leaned forward and read.

> "12/21/12 Ephesians 6:13 "Take unto you the whole armour of God, that ye may withstand the evil day, having done all, stand."

Helen blinked as a befuddled look filled her expression. "What does it mean?"

Aaron set the papers down. "The ancients possessed knowledge which now eludes our modern society. There is connectivity in all things. We don't simply disregard this; we deny it today."

Aaron reached across the table, taking Helen's right wrist with his left hand. He gazed intently into the depths of Helen's wide, green orbs. "New York City is going to be annihilated in a nuclear blast. It's not going to happen today, but it is going to happen. Helen, you and I have prescient dreams. I see things which come to pass, but I can't see the dates."

Helen's eyes began to tear. "It's the dream! You were saying those words to me!" Tears fell down her cheeks as she wiped them helplessly with her left hand. "It was this moment. Your right hand was free. My left hand was free."

Aaron smiled sheepishly as he glanced at his grasp on Helen's wrist. "I didn't realize I had even done that!" As he released his grip, Helen rose to her feet, hesitated for a moment, and walked over to Aaron still seated. Looking up, Aaron gazed into Helen's tear-filled jade eyes. He reached around Helen, holding her close, pressing his face into her bosom. The smell of rose petals filled his nostrils. A single tear fell from Aaron's right eye and was quickly absorbed by Helen's azure silk blouse.

Standing up and still holding Helen close in his arms, Aaron spoke, his gaze never leaving hers, "You don't know, do you?"

Helen spoke timidly. "I know something, but I'm not sure . . ."

Aaron reached into Helen's thick auburn locks, his hands framing her face as his fingers combed into her hair. Each closed their eyes as their parted lips drew close.

The sound of the door was as shattered glass. The resonating voice of Bekah was like a cold shower. "Hi! It's me . . . Oh! Did I interrupt something?"

([S]time line)

Bekah stood transfixed. The white-blonde, blue-eyed Swede held an expression as translucent and remarkable as her full and enviable head of hair. She stood stiffly as the moment in time dilated. The instant might leak across not only the morning, but dampen slowly across the day, the week, and perhaps further. Was she a grad student in a faraway country? Was this her adored English professor, embraced in a shocking, wet, and completely titillating lip-lock with the most unexpected, austere partner imaginable?

Time indeed had stopped. The four-year-old stood at the bedroom doorway of her family's Stockholm brownstone. She watched the same scene as her mother turned instantly, her face filled with a reassuring smile.

Helen pulled her face from Aaron's hands; her thick auburn locks resisted the command. Her wide-eyed expression was, at once, both blank and quite vulnerable. The sidelong glance to Bekah's eyes was deliberately brief. In a somewhat off-balanced cadence, Helen quickly deposited herself at her desk and began fingering her computer keyboard. A distinctly inaudible sound could be made out as Helen held her closed left fist to her mouth and cleared her throat.

In the same brief instant, Aaron had taken his cue in the silent scene and held his back towards Bekah as he appeared to scoop paperwork into his arms from across Helen's side table. She continued watching the comic scene as the distinguished meta-physics professor turned with an "eye-to-eye" stare towards Bekah. With choreographic precision, at just that moment, a dollar bill fluttered from the disheveled pile of papers in his cuddled arms. Bekah's blue eyes twinkled as she immediately covered her mouth with her right hand. She knew that she could not possibly hide the chaos of expression that her face must be announcing. The young girl held her breath as her sky-blue eyes were filled with the image of the bill, falling leaf-like to the floor, finally completing its journey.

Returning to Aaron's frozen image, Bekah held her breath and was quite pleased to find her hand holding back the laughter. She realized that the poor disheveled man had no idea that the bill had even fallen from his grasp.

Aaron mustered a timid smile. "Well, I'm glad we were able to discuss things, Professor Lovelace . . . I uh . . . I will speak to you around lunchtime. And yes, hello, Bekah! It's nice to see you. Oh, I have to hurry, now! I can't miss my 9:00 o'clock class."

Aaron shuffled to the door, grappling with his armful of papers as he leaned over and just managed to turn the door handle. The middle-aged professor appeared quite forlorn as he scuttled from the room.

Bekah turned to Helen as the silence continued. Her failed attempt to secure any mute response from the woman, absorbed with her typing, was understood. Glancing at the bill on the floor, Bekah's focus was brought to the gold four-leaf clover cup sitting quite solitary on the table.

She spoke up brightly as she retrieved the dollar bill from the floor and reached for Helen's special drinking mug on the desk's edge. "I'll get you some hot coffee." Bekah stepped to the cabinet and poured a fresh cup. Returning dutifully, she placed the mug in just the right spot next to the chorus of clicks and clacks from the busy keyboard.

Helen's gaze never left the screen as her lips meekly leaked a single word, "Thanks."

Bekah boldly pulled a chair from the side table up to Helen's desk. She sat silently next to her precious professor, quietly awaiting her first drink from the coffee cup. Finally, Helen gripped the cup, sat back, and drank deeply. The steam swirled across Helen's vivid green eyes as she silently turned her gaze to Bekah. Moments passed as the two vitally feminine women waited for the other to speak. Bekah's gaze was scarcely diverted as she laid the dollar bill in front of Helen. She studied every nuance in Helen's faintly perceivable reaction.

Helen's lips puckered before speaking, "Do you think it says the right thing?"

Bekah grimaced as her gaze fell to the bill. "What? What do mean?"

Helen smiled wryly as she continued, "You know today is the Winter Solstice, the day the Mayans waited 6,000 years for."

Bekah's confidence was gone. Her attempt to understand the preceding events had been preempted by someone very much wiser and by possibilities very much more important. She spoke nervously, "I have dreams that confuse me sometimes. As a child, I had bad nightmares of being burned alive. This 'end of the world' thing seems somehow familiar to me."

Helen spun her chair around and took Bekah's hand. "I'm sorry, Dear. I want you to stay close to me today. And I want you to call your parents early this morning and tell them you're here with me today. Promise me you will."

The expression on Bekah's face was palpable. "I will. I promise. Something *is* going to happen, isn't it?"

Helen's look turned blank. "Where's Zoe? Oh dear (Y)! Where's Zoe? She's always here to help us. Bekah! Where is she?"

The look on Bekah's face was both befuddled and frightened. "Helen, she's in New York City with her family. She's from New York, Helen, remember? She's due back tomorrow . . ."

Helen's purse fell to the floor as she latched onto the cell phone. She punched frantically, muttering to herself. "Answer Aaron, answer now." A look of relief filled her face as she held the phone to her ear. Bekah's blue eyes filled like a warm pool of azure water as she listened. Helen's voice trembled as she nearly shouted.

"Aaron, Zoe is in New York City! . . . Yes, with her family! I'm going to call them. They have time to get out!" Bekah's expression turned to terror as she listened to Helen's shouts. "No, don't you dare tell me that. Don't you dare!" Both women began to tear as if on cue. "I will warn them! They must get out of that city . . . Aaron, please don't say that. They have time. They have time. You said it happens at noon . . . I'm coming over there! I don't care. Dismiss class! I'm on my way . . ."

Bekah and Helen jumped to their feet and looked at one another desperately. "Bekah, do you understand what's going to happen?" Helen asked.

Bekah's expression turned to that of a frightened four-year-old child. "It's my dreams. I've had the nightmare since childhood. New York City will be destroyed by fire. Today."

([S]time line)

The office door slammed behind the two women as both ran pell-mell down the hallway. The meta-physics department was twelve minutes away in the science building. Helen intended to make the trip in four.

The halls were filled with students. Helen thought of the Yukon salmon swimming upstream against a river torrent. She pondered, *Why do events always turn against the intention?* It occurred to her that she had suddenly lost sight of Bekah. If a giant wet bear paw appeared and began to clear a path, the morning would be no stranger. The bedraggled professor wondered if perhaps the eccentric Aaron LaSalle might be right. Does the Universe truly possess a mind which toys with humanity? A human female hand, waving in the air, returned Helen's focus to the moment.

Bekah spoke loudly from behind her, "Helen! Aaron's standing in front of the office. He's waiting for us."

Helen swerved past the last student, narrowly ducking an unexpected swipe of a young man's backpack. She stopped adroitly in front of the meta-physics professor, her tone quite terse, "Aaron, we've got to talk!"

The two women entered the aging scientist's office. It occurred to Helen that the objects, shelves, and desk all had a tidy appearance. With a sidelong glance to Bekah, she muttered, "How can one with a mind so complex keep his office so neat?"

Bekah smiled as she whispered, "I think it's Bailey's work. I enjoy keeping your office picked up, Helen."

It occurred to Helen that the bear was still swiping at her. That time, she had swum right into the claws. A few feet away, Bailey Smith sat at Aaron's side table. She reached up, taking Bekah's hand as she guided her into the chair next to her. Helen looked at Bailey and felt her stomach tighten as she saw the distress in her eyes. It occurred to her that the adorable grad student was on the verge of tears.

Helen and Aaron sat down as Bailey spoke up. "Helen, neither you nor Aaron know this, but Bekah, Zoe, and I almost consider you and Aaron our adopted parents. The three of us are dedicated to taking care of our two favorite bachelors. I've had a bet with Zoe that you two either were married in your last lives or would be married in this one."

Helen forced a smile, listening to the kind words. She averted her eyes from Bailey's tender expression as she considered the frightful subject. "I guess you're telling me what we all know. We all love Zoe. Do you also know what Aaron told me this morning?"

Bailey's wet, grey eyes blinked as she wiped them with a Kleenex. She hesitated for a moment, looking directly at Aaron, before she spoke, "I actually have a psychic quotient almost as high as Aaron. I've had terrible dreams that suggest something horrific today. Aaron has the 'total mind' documentation. But there is something far more complicated going on, Helen. We've been working on this since Aaron began the Reveal."

Aaron leaned forward and began to speak, "The world knows that the mathematical work of the prophet Francois L'Hospital demonstrates that consciousness is a natural physical property. For 300 years, mankind has known that God exists. The nuance is troubling. There are, in fact, two Gods - a creator and a destroyer. Here's the problem. I am now convinced that this knowledge was not supposed to be known for the last three centuries."

The look on Helen's face was blank. She wondered, *Had the bear caught the poor salmon?* Perhaps she had swum directly into the fisherman's net. She looked up from the table, and drew a bead on Aaron LaSalle.

Helen's vivid green eyes grew stern as she poured all her energy into a response, "I am warning Zoe! I am getting on this phone. She has almost two hours before it happens, is that right? You said it happens at 12:21. Is that right?"

Aaron's eyes began to water as he appeared almost frozen in his seat. The image seemed to Helen like some National Geographic parody. The flapping, red-headed salmon wriggled desperately in the flesh-ripping claws of the Alaskan brown bear.

The words fell slowly from Aaron's lips. "Helen, it has to do with the Twin Law. If we intercede, we have stopped a divine destiny from being fulfilled."

Helen's eyes grew wide. The vulnerable expression had turned to fury. "What in the name of (S) are you talking about? Card-carrying psychics prevent disasters every day. By the divine reality of Hell itself, you're a 3rd degree psychic! The Supreme Court decrees your right to act on your (psy) credentials. If someone disobeys your considered intervention, they can go to jail. Every day, people are saved. (Y) only knows how many ships and planes have been saved by the (psy) International Law. Don't even hand me this! You tell me what's really going on!"

Helen grimaced as her peripheral vision captured the image of Bailey's tears falling down her cheeks. Helen glanced at Bekah; the same distraught reaction was being duplicated. Helen's expression became quite blank as the moments passed. Looking directly at Aaron, she awaited his response.

Aaron's soft brown eyes appeared to focus far beyond Helen's piercing gaze. "Helen, I've caused this . . . And I don't just mean the annihilation of New York City. I mean all of this. A parallel time line has been created by my actions. I was trying to explain to you that even the dollar bill doesn't say what it's supposed to say. We're not even supposed to be sitting here discussing this."

The incredulity of the moment drove deep into Helen Lovelace. "I always knew that I hated all psychics," she said. "I have always denied even my own déjà vu experiences. All right, I'll bite. Why can't I call Zoe?"

Bailey swiped her eyes again with the moist Kleenex. "Helen, Aaron and I have just pieced it together. There is a grand conflict from within the Authority. Yahweh and Satan are fighting over the control of mankind."

Helen grimaced. "What does it have to do with Aaron causing all of this?"

Aaron spoke up with renewed confidence. "People want to believe that the Universe is like a big pinball machine. The ball bounces around and the results are unknown. It's not true! It's not true in a couple of ways. Things really are predestined."

Helen interrupted, "I need a *simple* answer!"

Aaron pursed his lips before speaking, "Helen, the only spontaneity which truly exists is mankind's free will. Our moment-to-moment decisions are discreet from some patterned future, but it's like a relief valve in a pressure cooker. (Y) Knows the future. (S) Can't see it clearly. This is why the fallen angel works on our impulses to control destiny."

Helen retorted, "But how did *you* cause this?"

Aaron smiled as he continued, "Right now, Helen, there is a nearly identical time line with all of us sitting at this table. But in that time line, there are ships that *did* sink! The World Trade Center in New York has already been destroyed on 9/11/2001. And an elementary school full of beautiful children was massacred by a demonic man just one week ago."

The image of Aaron LaSalle appeared to recede telescopically in Helen's vision. She found herself trying to find the words to respond to the impossible concept just described. The words which she uttered seemed to be spoken by someone else.

"This," Helen said, "is the (S) time line and the other is the (Y)."

Aaron blinked. He appeared quite befuddled. "Yes, that's right. You do have the dreams, don't you?"

Helen's face remained quite blank as she sat motionless. She pondered a silly question. Somewhere, somehow, someone else laughed at the abject absurdity of the idea. She silently heard herself speak the question: *Is this how the poor salmon feel just before they're disemboweled? All they want to do is complete their destiny, their divine purpose; they just want to swim upstream and bring forth another generation. Why does that have to be replete with such brutality?*

Helen's disquiet continued as she calmly queried, "What did you do to cause this, Aaron?"

The soft, brown-eyed gaze of the aging meta-physics professor never varied as he meekly responded, "People say, 'God works in mysterious ways.' But the problem is Satan works in ALL ways. Evil never seems to rest. I intervened in the children's massacre on December 14th, 2012, one week ago in the (Y) time line."

Helen drew a deep breath as she spoke softly, "Yes, you did, didn't you? So what do we do now? Is there no way to save just one more child? Please say yes, Aaron, *please*!"

A deeply forlorn expression remained as Aaron replied, "I have to figure out how to get back to the event that caused this, Helen. I have to return to the past. It happened when my math-physics work was delivered by myself to myself in a 'total-mind' state 300 years ago."

Helen continued, "So why does that mean we can't tell Zoe?"

Aaron grimaced as Bailey spoke first, "If any more intervention comes as a result of Aaron, the fate of New York City cannot be reversed. You see, Helen," Baily continued, "this is a satanic trick. If Aaron breaks the Twin Law again, (Y) will not act to prevent the works of (S)."

A ringing phone brought all eyes to Bekah as she pulled the phone from her pocket. Her blue eyes grew wide as she frantically glanced around the table, covered her phone, and whispered. "Oh dear (Y), it's Zoe!"

"Zoe, I've been thinking about you." Bekah's blue eyes sparkled as she sat wide-eyed and quite still, the words falling lifelessly from her lips into her phone. The three other faces at the table were equally blank and intensely focused.

Zoe's tightly cropped black hair seemed to almost float as she shook her head. "Bekah, I needed to talk to you! There are strange things happening all over New York City. Last night my mom and my sister, Hanna, were out on the patio, and they saw the strangest lights in the sky. Every time I went out, they disappeared. There are all these weird stories on the internet, but Mom said the morning paper had President Obama as saying that today would be no different than any other day."

Bekah spoke briskly, "Zoe, is your dad home today?"

Zoe answered, "No, but my sister took off work and my mom's here. Hold on. Hanna's saying something."

Zoe's identical twin sister spoke assertively. Her china-doll, yet decidedly French, features grew distraught. "Get to it, Zoe. We need to know!"

Zoe spoke eagerly into the phone. "Can you get to Helen? We want to know if she could get to Bailey or maybe Professor LaSalle. I tried Bailey's phone, but she must have it shut off."

Bekah responded, "I'm sitting here with Helen right now . . . Do you want to talk to her?"

Zoe's voice crackled, "Yes, yes! I want to ask her something."

Bekah handed the phone to Helen.

Helen grimaced as she spoke out. "Zoe, hi, Dear. Is everything all right?"

"Helen," Zoe answered, "I guess I'm getting a little scared. There are a lot of people leaving the city. My dad is a fireman. Hanna and I tried to talk him into driving all of us out. He said, 'Only an atheist would abandon the fire station.' Helen, can you get to Professor LaSalle or Bailey and see what they think."

Helen spoke calmly, "Hold on a second, Zoe."

Helen covered the phone as she dropped it to her side. Glaring at Aaron, she spoke up brusquely, "Well, Aaron, do I tell her or not?!"

Aaron gasped as he responded, "Of course, this changes everything. She called us! Tell her to flee the city. There's still time!"

Helen held up the phone and spoke calmly, "Zoe, now listen carefully. Bailey and Aaron LaSalle are here with us. We want you to take Hanna and your mother and get in your car and drive as quickly as you can. Drive out of the city!"

Aaron quietly whispered to Helen, "Tell her to drive directly west from the area around Central Park."

Zoe's rich brown eyes grew wide as she retorted. "You're all there together! It's about this, isn't it?! The psychics are right. New York's going to get hit today."

Helen spoke up assertively. "Listen to me, Zoe. Listen! You're all right, now. You have about two hours. Take a route out of the city that will place as much distance between you and Central Park as possible."

The phone seemed to vibrate in Helen's hand as the shouts erupted from the phone. Zoe's mother and Hanna, shouted in unison, "Dear (Y)! Tell her we all live one block from Central Park!!"

Zoe turned her back from her family as she spoke, "Helen, I'm not leaving without my dad! I tried to call him a few minutes ago; we can walk there in just 10 minutes."

Helen interrupted urgently. "No! Zoe, please, listen. He's a dedicated civil servant. He won't leave!"

Zoe retorted. "I don't want to live without my father. We're walking to the station!"

Helen interrupted. "Zoe, Aaron LaSalle wants to talk to you!"

Aaron's expression went blank as Helen jammed the phone in his face. "Zoe, this is Aaron. Listen. I'm a 3rd degree (psy). I am credentialed. You must listen to my authority. You must take your family and leave the city, now!"

Helen grimaced, pursing her lips as she grabbed the phone back from Aaron. Helen's wet jade eyes seem to glisten. "Zoe! Can you hear me, Hon?"

The phone crackled in Helen's hand. The inanimate object

seemed to speak with a quiet voice of its own. "Yes, I'm here."

Helen pleaded gently, "Please, Zoe. Take your mom and Hanna and drive directly out of the city. Please ,Zoe, tell me you'll go right now!" The phone went mute in Helen's left hand.

The three women marched quickly through the crowded streets. Zoe held her Siberian husky in her arms tightly.

Hanna spoke up. "You can set Balto back down. The crowd's thinning again."

Zoe's mom spoke up. "That man is a devout Catholic, but I swear he has absolutely no belief in the paranormal!"

Zoe's mind returned to the day that her father, Captain Blankenship, took all of them to the bronze statue of Balto in Central Park. The young child stood transfixed looking at the date below the lifelike edifice, "The Winter of 1925." She was quite proud that she was able to read the engraving and the date. Zoe always remembered the tiny puppy her mommy handed her that day on her 6th birthday, March 14th.

She had always wondered why the details of the heroic trek through the frozen Alaskan wilderness had remained so strong in her mind. The Siberian husky and the sled team had performed an amazing feat. The diphtheria serum had arrived just in time to save so many children in Nome. It occurred to Zoe that the bronze statue of Balto in the Park had been the focus of much of her life. She always intended to be married on that spot. She wondered if her precious Balto might actually be one and the same.

The three pilgrims ran through the open door of the FDNY Engine 39 Fire Station. A fireman was at work on a truck.

Zoe approached as her cold breath lingered before her face. "I need to talk to Captain Blankenship!"

Behind the smiling face of the New York City fireman, Zoe

caught sight of a large clock. The time reflected by its pointing hands sent a shot of adrenaline through the cold, red faced girl.

The young man spoke, "He won't be back for at least an hour. He's finishing up a run!"

Zoe turned and looked into the shared expression of the other two forlorn faces. "It's a quarter-to- eleven. The psychics over the internet said it was going to happen at noon. I have to call back and find out what time Aaron thinks it will happen." Zoe's grievous expression spoke before her words. "Daddy's on a run. The fireman said he would be at least an hour!"

Hanna blurted out the desperate question. "How can we all get out? That's only about one hour from now!"

Zoe stood punching her cell phone. She pursed her lips as she repeated the action. "Oh dear (Y) please, this is no time to lose a signal!"

The women watched as Zoe held the phone to her ear and spoke, "Bekah, let me speak to Professor LaSalle!"

Aaron took the phone from Bekah and concentrated to hear the words.

"This is Aaron."

Zoe asked, "Professor, what time is this going to happen?!"

The faces of Bailey, Bekah and Helen might have been their death masks as their eyes pierced the man speaking into the phone.

Aaron spoke quite deliberately. "Zoe, I saw three ground blasts. They consumed the entire city. One is at the Towers, downtown, one is uptown, and one is in Central Park. I saw the time was 12:21 PM . . ."

Zoe spoke tersely. "I'll call you back."

Aaron slowly lowered the phone to the table as the barrage of shouts and questions began. Helen was the loudest. "Where are they?"

Aaron spoke timidly. "I don't know. She only asked when it was supposed to happen. Then she hung up again."

Helen cupped her face with both hands, leaning into her arms and the table. Speaking meekly through her palms, she said, "There must be a Hell and this is how one is admitted."

Aaron gave Helen a sidelong glance, watching as the tears fell silently down her cheeks. He wondered to himself if his thoughts were psychological or psychical. *Is my mind trying to escape the moment or am I really seeing this?*

(circa 1703 Switzerland [S]time line)

The tears of Shri'Ani fell like water from an open spigot as she pulled the arm of the precious child from the surreal mound of charred ash. It had been burned off cleanly, just below the elbow. The Hindu birth rings of Pyara wrapped colorfully around a piece of paper, gripping it tightly. Francois L'Hospital wondered how the finely written pen and ink document could escape being consumed by the fire, the fury of which had turned the entire body to crisp black dust.

(December 21, 2012 New York City [S]time line)

Zoe's mother spoke up. The vapor of her breath trailed her words. "Look at the sky! It's getting dark. Where did the sun go?"

Zoe stepped closer to her twin. The appearance of the scene might have been that of a beautiful, petite, magazine cover girl looking into a mirror.

Zoe nearly whispered, "Hanna, the professor said 12:21. Mom isn't going to want to go. We have to make her!"

Hanna grabbed her mother's shoulders with both hands. "Mom, daddy won't be back in time. We're going to the car!"

The maternal response was perhaps years out of place. "Girls, we all agreed! We're not leaving without your father!"

Zoe turned and insisted. "Listen, Mom. If we can get out and call Daddy while we're driving, he may come to us. He would damn us all to (S) if we stayed right here and committed suicide!"

Zoe felt the kiss on her forehead as her mother muttered. "You always were the logical one."

The trio bounded through the open doors as Zoe pulled the retractable leash from her pocket. "Come, Balto. Home, Balto, home!"

As the harried group headed up the first town house row, three rapid sounds could be heard in the distance: Pop, pop, pop!

Zoe's expression turned wide-eyed as she looked at her sister. "Did you hear that?!"

Hanna responded, "Do you think it was . . ."

Zoe interrupted, "Yes, I do!"

The group had turned down the avenue leading back to their house when the melee could be seen. The street was awash with throngs of people. The walking had slowed to the point of a crawl when the family car came into view.

Zoe muttered, "If we can get in, maybe they'll clear out of the way." It appeared to Zoe that there was a zealot with a sign blocking the road. "Look, that man in the turban with the sign is stopping traffic!" Zoe gave out a whistle. "Balto, foe! Balto, foe!"

The Siberian husky snapped to attention as Zoe double wrapped the leash around her right wrist. The ancient instincts of the faithful predator were formidable. Balto's gut wrenching growls and barks forced the mass of people to fall over themselves as the way was cleared. Zoe's mom reached into her purse and handed Hanna the keys.

Zoe shouted to them as they got into the car. "Start the car and follow me. Balto and I will clear the way!"

Some progress had been made when one (S)atanist, sign in hand, stood his ground. "You cannot escape the judgment of the Authority. The End is nigh!" The Shamar-clad man stood with his sign between him and Balto. Zoe read its proclamation, "(S) is the one true God."

Zoe's disgust had reached the breaking point as she screamed, "Attack, Balto! Attack!"

The lunge of the Siberian husky had been known to crash through plate glass windows. The retractable leash had been pulled to its breaking point when the tumbling zealot stopped rolling.

Zoe whistled. "Balto, home!" She held the back door open as Balto vaulted in.

Hanna stepped on the gas as a good distance was made between the scenes. The trio made it to the Lincoln Tunnel when the traffic stopped.

Zoe glanced at her watch. "We can't get out. We're going to Balto's statue. If we can reach it, Daddy can get there with a city truck. He'll get us out with the lights on. The people in this city know to get out of the way of the FDNY!"

Zoe's mom responded, "Captain Blankenship will come for us. If he knows we're stranded, the fires of Hell won't stop him."

Zoe nimbly thumbed her phone as the resonating motion within her palms banged back. She looked up, realizing that their car had lurched backwards into another vehicle. Her wide-eyed look was mirrored by the curious face of Balto staring back.

She called out to Hanna. "Do you know what you're doing?!"

The driver-seated doppelganger called out, "I'm turning this car around and getting us back to the park! This traffic isn't going through that tunnel any time soon."

Zoe questioned her mom, "Is Daddy answering his phone?"

Her mother replied, "No, I'm going to call the fire station dispatcher and have them radio him on the truck."

Zoe said, "Tell them to tell him we're at Balto's statue, and we're getting scared!"

Zoe's call finally connected. "Bekah! Is that you?"

Bekah held the phone to her ear as she replied, "Zoe, we're all scared to death! Where are you at?" The group's hopeful expressions turned grim as Bekah repeated Zoe's words. "You're driving back to Central Park? There's no way to get out of Manhattan?!"

Aaron's complexion turned white as he let out a gasp. "Oh dear (Y), what have I done?"

Helen reached across the table and took hold of Aaron's right wrist with her left hand. She quietly implored, "Aaron, it's 11:45 in New York! They won't make it out!"

Aaron yelled to Bekah, "Tell them to get to their father. He's FDNY! There's a chance he can get them out!"

Bekah nodded her head rapidly. "Yes, yes! Zoe's saying they've heard back from him. He's coming for them at a meeting spot in Central Park. They have a chance!"

Helen's grip tightened as she demanded, "Aaron, I want a simple answer. How is this happening? How do you know the details so perfectly?"

Aaron drew a deep breath as he leaned into Helen fierce gaze. "I told you, Helen, I caused it! I caused all of it!"

Helen released her grip as she spoke in a soft voice, "Please, tell me you can undo this."

Aaron said quietly, "Bailey and I are close to the answer."

Helen grimaced as she retorted, "I asked for a simple explanation."

Aaron looked about the table. The faces greeting him were a combination of bewildered and terrified. "Helen, you know that there is always a faction in the (Y) followers that say the 2nd Amendment should be repealed, right?"

The bewildered look on Helen's face deepened as she replied, "Even the atheists aren't that stupid! For generations, the statistical analysis has proven that the most effective way to prevent murder is with carefully implemented gun laws and registration."

Aaron continued, "That's right. The greatest volume of gang-related murders and faith executions happens in cities and countries where guns are banned. I have a question for you. If you could have done it, would you have shot Adolf Hitler? Would you have stopped the death of millions, including the Jewish Holocaust?"

Helen grimaced as she answered, "Hitler was a zealot for the Nazi Fundamentalist sect in the Great Religious War, but I think he was really just a psychotic (S)atanist."

Aaron quipped, "I asked you if you would have assassinated him if you could have?"

Helen leaned into the table and nearly shouted, "You know I loathe the thought of taking another person's life, but of course, I would have! Do you think (Y) would greet me in Heaven if I hadn't tried to save millions?"

Aaron smirked as he replied, "What about the Twin Law?"

Helen demurred. "Oh, for the love of Yeshua! There are all sorts of dispensation to the Twin Law and the Torah."

([Y]time line)

Aaron felt a tingling in his right wrist as he realized his words would not emerge from his lips. The image of Helen's incredulous image seemed to telescope before him. Aaron blinked as he scanned the room. His blank expression was greeted with Helen's solitary presence, drinking deeply from her gold clover cup.

"Aaron," she was saying, "you can't be serious! You believe people are safer with guns! I've seen you almost tear up when you discussed the 12/14/12 entry in the Reveal. If gun control hadn't been stopped by the damn NRA and the radical right, those children might still be alive!"

Aaron blinked as he heard the question fall from his lips. "Helen, tell me what the inscription on the dollar bill says?"

Helen replied, "Are you all right? What are you talking about?"

Aaron asked again, "No, please answer me, Helen.

She shook her head. "The dollar bill says 'In God We Trust,' what else?!"

([S]time line)

Aaron gripped his right wrist firmly with his left hand. Looking up, he saw the blank expressions of Bailey, Bekah, and Helen staring back at him.

He blinked and looked at Helen. "I saw the nukes destroying New York City. I was carried to Newtown, Connecticut, and was given a choice. I couldn't let the children die. At that moment, I wasn't rational. I now know that humanity is being influenced by a mind far greater than ours."

Helen shouted, "You're a 3rd-degree, card-carrying (psy), and you just realized that? Damn you! How are you going to fix this?"

***

The desperate trio and Balto jaunted to the bronze statue of the canine hero.

Zoe shouted, "Everybody listen, I hear Daddy!"

The deep, repeated blast of the FDNY ladder 16 fire truck was unmistakable. The resonant harmony of the shrill siren sent an irrefutable call to one and all. Zoe turned to see the image of the huge, charging red rhino headed straight through the green grass of the park. The milling crowds of both the innocent and the zealots dove out of its path.

The huge NYFD truck stopped a short distance from the Balto memorial statue. The shouts and smiles from Captain Blankenship's family were tumultuous. Balto barked loudly, beating the children and their mother to his beloved master. Zoe looked at the charred smudge across her mother's face as she pulled back from the deep kiss with her father.

Captain Blankenship was a commanding presence. He stood well over 6 feet and had a jaw line to match any well-used fire ax. Zoe noticed that he wore his complete reflective fire gear. The bomber jacket was drenched wet. She caught her father's stare as "pop, pop" sounded across the Park.

Speaking up loudly, Zoe implored, "Daddy, what's going on?"

Robert Blankenship unzipped his coat as he shook his head. "New York's coming apart. The damn (S)atanist zealots are setting the city ablaze. They've set fire to cars, blocking the tunnels and bridges. There's all kind of crazy chatter on the radio!"

Zoe continued as she grew close, focusing on her father's gaze, "Daddy, you have to get us out. The city's about to get hit!"

Robert's expression was forlorn as he pulled Zoe into his arms. "I love you with all my heart. I would normally give you a big argument. But only a fool would refuse to see; there's some kind of terrorist action about to occur."

Zoe stepped back from her father and began banging on her cell phone again. "I've been having a problem getting through. We have to get back to Helen and Professor LaSalle."

Captain Blankenship's eyebrows furled. "Isn't LaSalle one of those psychics at your college?"

Zoe's voice crackled as she held the phone to her ear and spoke out, "Helen, is that you? Yes, yes! Daddy made it! Give the phone to LaSalle." Zoe thrust the phone at Captain Blankenship. "Here, Daddy, it's Professor LaSalle. He can tell us what we need to do!"

Robert's expression turned almost sour as he spoke into the phone. "This is Captain Blankenship."

Aaron looked deeply into Helen's eyes as he began to speak to the New York City fireman. "Sir, you have a dire situation on your hands!"

Robert's expression remained stern as he answered, "I agree with that, Professor. A massive assault is at work on my city."

Aaron continued, "Captain, what I have to tell you is going to be difficult. I want you to work with me. Please say you will!"

Robert grimaced. "I will do my best, Sir!"

Helen's complexion grew white; her eyes strained as she listened to Aaron's words.

"Captain Blankenship," Aaron said, "there are multiple thermo-nuclear bombs placed strategically around New York City." Aaron hesitated; he listened carefully as he heard Robert's faint response.

"Oh Dear (Y), tell me this can't be real."

Aaron continued, "Sir, one of the bombs is in a van parked on the street there in Central Park."

Helen could hear the shouts coming back through the phone. "How in the name of the one true God do you know this? No one is that psychic!"

Aaron spoke calmly. "Sir, I told you this was going to be difficult."

Helen's attention was brought to Bailey. The young meta-physics student had begun to write something. Helen stared at the paper to see some sort of graph and equations. Bailey looked up, catching Helen's gaze. At that instant, Helen felt a deep numbness come over her left arm.

The scene began to telescope before Helen's focus. Aaron's words slowed to a stop as the image became that of a woodland trail. Turning toward Helen was a young soldier. A musket was held against the soldier's shoulder, and the scene was filled with other colonial troops. Staring intently into the soldier's grey eyes, Helen realized that this was Bailey. His hair was short. This person had a rugged vitality, which was similar, but still the same perfect and recognizable features. It occurred to Helen that the soldier appeared to be frightened.

Helen heard herself saying, "You must lead the men on this trail; do not take the left fork. It will lead to defeat."

(circa 2012 [S]time line)

Helen blinked. Her focus had returned to Aaron on the phone with Robert Blankenship.

"No, you can't. The way out is blocked. Captain, I know how impossible this sounds, but you must believe me. The only way out of this is for you and your family to stay right where you are!"

Robert looked at Zoe. Shaking his head, he handed the phone to her. "You need to talk to this man. You're the brains in this family. What the Hell is he talking about?"

Zoe took the phone and said, "Aaron, what do we do?" Zoe turned to Hanna; an odd thought crossed her mind as she peered into the mirror image of her sister. "You're telling me that there is a twin reality. This reality will be washed away and the city will not be destroyed. So we just stay right here and we aren't really about to be incinerated. Well, Professor! I see why Daddy is troubled with this approach!"

Robert shouted over Zoe's voice, "I see why Father Hannity

thinks all psychics are empowered by (S). You're all crazy as Hell!"

Zoe turned from her father's shouts. "Aaron can't we get into a cellar or something? We still have some time!"

Aaron warned, "Don't try it, Zoe! The bomb will excavate down hundreds of feet. If you do manage to survive, you won't be dug out. You'll lie for days, horribly burned, and eventually die of dehydration."

Zoe retorted, "But don't we have to try? It's an eternal sin to commit suicide."

Aaron pleaded, "Listen, Zoe. I know what I'm talking about. This is not suicide! If you stay where you are, there will be absolutely no sensation. You may hear a very slight crackling sound in your ears. It will last for the very smallest fraction of a second. You will then be greeted by your grandparents in Paradise. You will then be returned to this very instant, and you won't remember any of this. But listen! If you are injured or suffer during this transit, (S) will plague you after this. You can be affected in the parallel reality."

Zoe turned back to her father and placed her arm around his waist. She spoke up, so her father could hear her words. "Can you give us some kind of sign? I know you can! I've heard that a (psy) has that ability. I'm not worried now! But please give us a sign for Daddy."

Aaron responded, "I'm going to recite Psalm 23. Put the phone on speaker. All of us will pray until the moment comes. I don't quite know what I'm feeling, but there is a strong spiritual presence there. You are going to see something to help you through this."

Helen, Bailey, Bekah, and Aaron all held hands as Aaron began to pray into the phone: "The Lord is my shepherd; I shall not want. He maketh me to lie down in green pastures; he leadeth me beside the still waters . . ."

Captain Robert Blankenship held his family close. Hanna, Zoe, and their mom—his wife—stood close to him as Balto began to pull urgently against the leash.

Zoe called out, "Balto, stay! Stay, Balto! Stay!" The strong animal pulled relentlessly.

Robert called out, "Let him go, Sweetheart. He knows something we don't!"

Zoe reached out and snapped the leash loose at the collar. Balto bounded the short distance to the brass statue of his namesake and jumped up on it. Turning back to the family, tail wagging, Balto began to bark eagerly.

Zoe shouted out, "He's happy! It's like he's greeting us when we come home." Everyone smiled and agreed. "He's telling us he knows we're coming home!"

The family listened to Aaron's voice as he recited, "Yea, though I walk through the valley of the shadow of death, I will fear no evil; for thou art with me; thy rod and thy staff they comfort me."

Aaron blinked as the phone he was leaning into made a slight 'puff' sound. He spoke into it. "Zoe! Zoe can you hear me?"

Aaron, Helen, Bailey, and Bekah all turned in unison and looked at the analog clock on Aaron's wall. No sounds could be heard as each read silently. The time in New York City was12:21.

CHAPTER THREE

Dreams

(Helen's College, circa 2014, [Y]time line)

"Helen, are you in a daze or something? You don't seem yourself today," a friend, Professor Alyssa Black, queried.

Smiling, Professor Helen Lovelace remarked, "I had the oddest dream last night, and I can't decide what it meant. I guess I'm just preoccupied today."

Professor Black inquired gently, "Was it some kind of nightmare?"

Helen replied, "I don't really know how to explain it, even to myself."

Alyssa Black retorted, "Try me. Now, I'm really curious."

Helen spoke disconcertingly. "Alyssa, it's as if I keep seeing ghosts. I keep dreaming of students in my classrooms who disappear when I call on them."

Alyssa looked curiously at her friend. "Well, go see Aaron LaSalle, in the physics department. He has theoretical work that he says may explain paranormal phenomenon."

Helen's expression became quite distressed. "I've met with LaSalle. There's something unsettling about him."

Alyssa shook her head, smiling. "You'll figure it out. I still say you should be tested. You may have real psychic abilities."

Helen snatched up papers and books, her thick auburn locks swirling as she dashed out the printing room door. "I'll catch you after my 2:00 class!"

([S]time line)

Helen lay snuggled in her bed. The detail-oriented woman would methodically end her day with a cup of hot cocoa and her reading lamp. She let the galley proofs of her poetry relax from her hands as she pondered to herself, *How would a compilation of these poems be titled?* Her eyes drooped and then closed as a pleasant dream consumed her.

A blue sky rose above a lovely scene. The green grass reached to grasp at its azure coattails. The tall trees rustled gently in the wind, their leaves full and breathing. The sound of children playing could be heard. Helen scanned the scene, but search as she might, she could see no one. On the cusp of her awareness, a dog could be heard barking. It seemed to be headed in her direction. Helen smiled and could see herself embrace the happy and loving animal. It was a Siberian husky. She saw herself smile happily. She knew that she had always wanted a Siberian husky. The power and faithful adoration of this vital creature was the truest expression of spiritual reality. In that instant, the limitless tranquility of the summer day, and perhaps the vessel of rapture itself, shattered.

A tender voice, but somehow pleading, crackled in her ear: *Helen! Helen, it's me, Helen. How can you forget me? Helen, please, you can do it. The two of you must do it.* For only an instant . . . did the girl's face appear? Helen jerked straight up from her sleep.

([Y]time line)

She brushed her thick auburn locks as she looked wide-eyed, leaning into the mirror. She smiled, turning her head slowly left to right and right to left. She had always found it so curious that the only way to see one's eyes move in the mirror was to move one's head. She exhaled deeply and resolved herself to the inevitability of one Aaron LaSalle. She had met him once, or was it twice? Alyssa Black would know the best time to stop by the physics department.

Helen muttered to herself, "I don't want to announce myself. I don't know why. But that's how I'm going to enter into this conversation."

The door crept open into the physicist's office. Helen looked about at the widgets and artifacts. Her eye was drawn to a huge length of wood mounted on the wall. It occurred to her that this was the type of board that would be found making up a floor or a roof. She read the large hand-written letters on it, "Planck's constant." She found herself standing in front of Aaron LaSalle's desk. He was typing into the keyboard, furiously.

Helen chuckled to herself as she realized, *He doesn't even know I'm standing here*. She thought that it might be fun to see how long the impossible circumstance might continue, but she thought better of it.

"Excuse me." Helen smiled gleefully as the absorbed professor nearly jumped out of his chair.

Aaron looked up, wide-eyed. "Oh, I'm sorry! Hello. Oh, I know you, don't I?"

Helen fought back the strong impulse to giggle. She held out her right hand to shake his as she said, "Don't you remember me? We talked at some length about your research."

Aaron felt the deep and discarded masculine impulses well-up, with the image of the riveting, green-eyed woman staring back at him. Helen wiggled her extended arm as she smiled with more emphasis. Aaron's blank expression turned to a smile as he reached out and shook Helen's hand.

He spoke assertively. "Well, yes! I've actually been intending to come and see you."

Helen furled her brow as she replied curiously, "Really? I never heard from you after we had lunch that day with Alyssa."

Aaron stepped over to his side table and pulled out a chair. "Please sit down. I'll get you some coffee. You like it with just cream."

Helen sat down as she mused, *It's been over 2 years, and he remembers how I like my coffee.*

Aaron returned moments later and set two cups on the table, one coffee and one tea. He smiled. "Well, it's just wonderful to see you!"

Helen drank deeply from the cup, studying the aging professor's soft brown eyes. Setting the cup down, she queried, "What is that plank of wood doing on your wall?"

Aaron's smile widened. "Yes, that's Right! The German scientist's name is pronounced like a 'plank' of wood. The sardonic joke among physicists is that possibly the smallest thing in the Universe should have such a formidable name."

Helen grimaced as she took another drink of coffee. The steam swirled into her glistening jade eyes. It occurred to her that there must be something quite humorous in that, but she was, in fact, quite dumbfounded.

She leaned across the table, her jade eyes sparkling as she looked deeply into Aaron LaSalle's eyes. "Aaron, do you remember our conversation that early morning on December 21st, 2012?"

Aaron smiled wryly as he answered, "Of course, I do!"

Helen pursed her lips, her brow furled. "It's happening, Aaron! You were right. I was wrong. The 'total mind' you spoke of is happening. You said it would happen."

Aaron's gaze never left Helen's face as he softly queried, "Do you remember what I told you would be the sign that there could be an Apocalypse?"

Helen's eyes began to water as she nearly shouted, "Yes, I've been having odd dreams. I'm seeing people I've never met. But it's as if they're supposed to be here, like I should already know them. And there is something else. The dollar bill is wrong! It's supposed to say 'On God We Depend.'"

A thin smile crept across Aaron's face as he reached out for a pad of paper. He drew several arcs across the paper. Each arc touched the preceding at just the beginning and the end.

Aaron said, "If you think of a straight line as possibly a set of arcs, connected to form 'sort of a line,' that would be the Variant Universe. It's not linear. It's 'almost a straight line,' but it's not. We just think it's straight. In fact, these arcs can run up onto themselves like a stack of curved quarters. They'll stack nicely, but you suddenly realize there really isn't any beginning or end. The straight line you thought you started with was probably just an illusion."

Helen leaned into the desk. Her eyes seemed to twinkle as a smile crept across her face. It occurred to her that the ecstasy she had experienced in each of the troublesome dreams had just been put into words.

She spoke up, eagerly. "These dreams begin quite marvelously. In one, I held a dollar bill, and it was if it were something good. It almost was happy that it could be spent to buy good things and pay people for good work. Then, there was this other bill that was 'sneaky.' It knew that it was just an excuse to trick people into doing things that might not be so good. I really don't know how to explain it!"

Aaron pursed his lips. His expression grew intense. "Helen, what I have to tell you is going to be difficult. I need for you to work with me. Please say you will."

Helen thought to herself, *I don't seem to have any choice, but I'm not about to tell him that.* She spoke out, "I'll do my best."

Aaron continued, "Do you remember our conversation about natural psychic abilities and dreams?"

Helen nodded.

Aaron continued, "You aren't aware of this, but you have very powerful psychic abilities."

Helen felt a bit ajar. It was an odd statement. She thought to herself, *People aren't supposed to talk like that. How does he know something that intimate about me?*

She spoke up, "Well, I guess I really do know that must be true."

Aaron continued, "Do you remember our conversation about the technique I developed from my research? I use the King James Version of the Bible. I call it the Reveal."

Helen nodded.

Aaron continued, "I need for you to conduct a 30 day Reveal session, and then, I can explain to you what's really going on."

Helen's expression turned a bit intense. The same thought passed through her mind. *It's not 'correct' for someone to know more about you, than you know about yourself.*

Helen returned to staring at the odd physics professor through the steaming hot coffee. Her mind had returned to the dreams that had begun to plague her very existence. She deliberately studied Aaron's reaction as she set the cup down.

"I keep seeing a beautiful, petite student in my dreams," Helen began. "I've never met her. But she is desperate for me to help her."

Helen stopped right there and soaked in every nuance from Aaron's expression. Aaron blinked; his eyes avoided Helen's stare. She felt a powerful and thrilling sensation fill her mind. She thought to herself. *I knew it! He knows who it is! He knows!*

Helen's eyes began to tear up.

She heard herself blurt out the words, unable to restrain the excitement, "Can we save her? Can we bring her back?!"

Helen's gaze never left Aaron's face. As his eyes finally met hers, she could see the intensity in them. They had become wet. She knew he was on the verge of tears.

"Yes," he almost whispered, "and many, many more who won't have to die."

Helen sat quietly, considering the moment. She pushed for details. "I know all of this has to do with your research. Is there an easy way to explain what's going on?"

Aaron hesitated, pursing his lips before he spoke, "It's like the curved line segments. Reality somehow loops back on itself. There's some type of duality in all of nature—the math term is binomial. I've done experiments with random tumblers and observed results that match magical phenomenon. It's what's called quantum physics."

Helen softly said, "Well, I knew better than to ask. I'm a poet, and I juggle imagery, not tumblers. I'm not sure I'll ever think the way you do . . ."

Aaron laughed, abruptly. "You just proved yourself quite right and wrong."

A perplexed expression filled Helen's face. "I don't get it!"

Aaron responded, "You just illustrated 'entanglement'. You're here because you represent the mirrored counterpart to, well . . . Me."

Helen smiled meekly as Aaron continued, "I've discovered a way to enhance the naturally occurring psychic dreams that most people have. But it's limited. I'm not able to see certain aspects. I see events in the future, but I can't see the exact time the events will occur. I think you're here because you'll be able to."

Aaron continued, "I'm going to show you how to perform the biblical Reveal. It will lead us to the complete explanation."

Helen looked concerned. "Is this dangerous or somehow sacrilegious?"

Aaron guffawed. "Oh, yes—to both questions."

The stare between the two was quite intense as Aaron awaited a response.

Helen smirked as she retorted, "I don't consider myself officially religious, but I do consider myself deeply spiritual, and I believe there is one true God."

Aaron smiled broadly. "Sometimes, I'm so astute, I surprise myself."

Helen felt a bit uneasy with the overt confidence she was witnessing in the physics professor.

Aaron leaned forward, his gaze never leaving the lovely English professor's eyes. "You must not be timid with the things I'm going to show you. There are several revelations that you must come to understand. One of them is that there are two Gods. One, Yahweh, is the creator God. The other, Satan, is the destroyer. There are many details around all of this, but there is something you must know. Nothing is self-evident. Things in the Universe are convoluted. Childlike perceptions are Never complete. If there are no serious signs to perform the Reveal. It must Not be performed. Further, if it is not performed with absolute reverence and in the sacred manner that I will instruct you in, then the evil God will intervene. Now, show me how smart you are . . . Tell me how you have met the first requirement."

Helen sat meekly for several seconds. Her expression became intense. "The child and a Siberian husky need my help."

Aaron smiled broadly. "I know those two souls, and you are quite correct. It's why you're here."

Helen queried, "The world is shaking itself apart over religious and political ideology. You said that many might be saved. Is something truly terrible coming?"

Aaron averted his eyes from Helen's gaze. His voice was low as he answered, "Do you ever wonder where your mind goes when you sleep?"

"I guess I believe it goes to some spiritual realm," Helen replied, thoughtfully. "I've experienced dreams that come true. I've seen things in my dreams that I wouldn't have understood in the real world."

Aaron's expression was quite approving. "I knew (Y) would send me the Woman to prevent the vision."

Helen's face contorted. "What does that mean?"

Aaron pursed his lips, expressing consternation. He spoke cautiously, "I'm going to show you how to perform the Reveal in our next meeting. I can't explain too much more until then. I know you're tormented by the dream about the girl. So I want to leave you with a thought over the next 30 days. She, her family, and her faithful canine companion are alive in this world right now as we speak."

Helen's face contorted as she muttered, "So they're not ghosts?"

Aaron continued, "Again, you're right and you're wrong! A parallel world has been created. In the one, they've been annihilated along with all the inhabitants of a major city. In this time line, the event hasn't occurred. Yet."

Helen's vivid jade-colored eyes glared back at Aaron. "If you think that helps, you're quite mistaken!"

Aaron spoke assertively, "We've both been given a sign. It's all either of us needed to know at this point."

Helen nearly jumped from her seat as the door to Aaron's office opened abruptly. The young voice was immediately recognizable.

"Hi! It's me, Bailey. I can't believe it! Hi, Helen, I'm so glad you're here! You get to meet my Ibrahim."

Helen studied the slight look of bewilderment in Aaron's soft brown eyes. He stood to greet Bailey and her friend. It occurred to her that Aaron hadn't met Ibrahim.

Bailey began the introductions. "Aaron, Helen, this is Ibrahim Abdulaziz."

The blank expression on Aaron's face was replaced by a faint and somewhat forced smile. Helen wondered if this was the natural reaction from a surrogate paternal instinct or perhaps the ethnical background had some influence.

Aaron spoke up, "Well, I thought I had Bailey all to myself!"

Bailey grabbed the young man by the arm. "Ibrahim and I met at the Casino in Louisville."

Helen chuckled as she maneuvered a handshake. She spoke up gingerly, "It's very nice to meet you, Ibrahim. Are you here on a scholarship?"

"Yes, I am, but I must make good grades to keep the scholarship. We must maintain a 3.0-4.0 for SCAM."

"SCAM? So you are from Saudi Arabia then?" Helen asked. "What is your GPA right now?"

"Yes, I am. 3.2, Professor. But my literature class is very hard for me, and I'm worried about my grade," Ibrahim said.

"Who is your literature professor?" Helen asked.

Ibrahim pulled up the last empty chair in the office and sat down close to her and pulled a folder marked "ENG200" from his backpack.

As Helen and Ibrahim read over the papers, Aaron rose from his desk and motioned for Bailey to follow him just outside his office door.

He pursed his lips before speaking in a near whisper, "Well, I didn't think you spent much time at the Devil's workshop."

Bailey laughed as she said, "Aaron, you're going to scare my fellow foreign student. He doesn't know any of our code. He doesn't know that another name for our math-physics research is 'game theory.'"

Aaron spoke assertively, "Well, I hope he hasn't learned any of our secrets."

Bailey grimaced. "You know better than that."

Aaron grunted as Bailey turned and walked back into the office. Aaron slipped around her when she stopped behind Ibrahim where he and Helen were poring over his syllabus and assignment list. Aaron's chair gave a small squeak of protest as he, rather abruptly, sat down.

Helen's attention was brought to Aaron's expression which had turned decidedly intense. Ibrahim put all his papers back in his backpack and stood. Helen moved her chair closer to Aaron's desk as Bailey once again grasped Ibrahim's arm.

Bailey's smile was contagious as she turned her attention to Helen. "So what's the occasion? Have I missed anything?"

Helen smiled broadly as she answered, "Oh no, Aaron and I had some things to discuss since our luncheon."

Bailey maneuvered her grasp on Ibrahim's arm, turning him slowly as Helen spoke. Aaron found himself poised directly in front of Ibrahim as Bailey's eyes quickly met his. The deliberate sidelong glance posed an unavoidable request. Aaron extended his right hand as a thin smile crept across his face.

The young Arab smiled broadly. The thick middle-eastern accent added to the difficult moment. "I have heard so much about you, Professor LaSalle. I am so pleased to meet you!"

The nervous youth's right hand almost shook as he grasped the stoic man's hand. It occurred to Helen that the scene was fit for a Hollywood production. The image might have been the moment from *Lawrence of Arabia*, when Omar Sharif met Peter O'Toole. All that was missing was the hot sun and the desert sands. The oddity of the image was matched by an errant thought. It occurred to Helen that it wasn't the desert sands which contained the moment. It was, in fact, something more tragic. Perhaps, it was Omar Sharif in Helen's favorite movie. *Yes*, she thought, *this moment was a scene from <u>Dr. Zhivago</u>.*

Helen's expression turned to a wry smile. "So Ibrahim, you two met at a Casino, but you're a student here on scholarship?"

The strained handshake ceased as the young man turned to Helen's voice. "Oh yes, I have not yet decided on my major! But I am so happy that I have met Bailey to help me with such decisions!"

Bailey spoke up, "Ibrahim is brilliant; he can do anything he sets his mind to."

Helen observed the obvious target of Bailey's words. She watched the blank expression on Aaron's face turn slightly sour. Bailey continued as she released her grasp on Ibrahim and grabbed Aaron by the right arm.

The staged moment only lacked a cued kiss on Aaron's cheek as Bailey completed her script. "Aaron knows I couldn't have any interest in someone who's not brilliant."

Helen concentrated on not displaying too much enjoyment from Bailey's stellar performance. It occurred to Helen that *Dr. Zhivago* was the correct theme. The nubile young woman was developing some sort of rising action.

Aaron spoke up, "Bailey, are you coming back this afternoon for our lab?"

Bailey relaxed her grip on Aaron's arm as she spoke adroitly,

"Of course, I have the research in my file. All the data leads to the year 1703."

Helen's ceaseless fascination with the scene reached a climax as she intently studied Aaron's reaction. The nonchalant demeanor had become genuine, for the first time, since the play act had begun.

He spoke crisply, studying Bailey's eyes, "You found the corollary!"

Bailey's chest expanded slightly, her face beaming. "It was right in front of us, all along. L'Hospital had to obtain approval from Bernoulli. They couldn't publish on their own in those days!"

Helen blinked; her face went blank as Aaron's reaction turned genuinely intense. She watched as he turned from the group, placing his right hand to his chin, standing silently.

Bailey turned to Helen and smiled. "It was so nice to see you this morning. We've got to get to class."

The two students stood for a moment at the door. Bailey watched her mentor, reassuring herself that her parting words had not gone unheeded. Aaron's apoplectic state continued as the couple departed.

Helen seated herself at the table, waiting for a moment to see if Aaron would take the hint. Impatiently, she finally broke into Aaron's distraction. "Aaron, sit down for a moment!"

Aaron snapped his head back to Helen's voice. He pulled the chair from the side table and resumed his seat.

He spoke somewhat disjointedly, "Do you ever wonder what the point of youth is?"

Helen grimaced as her bewildered expression turned to a chuckle. "Where did that come from?"

Aaron's focus seemed to return slowly as his eyes reluctantly returned to Helen's gaze. "You and I have so much to explain to one another Helen. We knew each other before this life."

It occurred to Helen that she might as well be in some sort of movie. The distracted expression that had overcome Aaron now possessed her.

She leaned forward into Aaron's gaze. "Let's start with the reason I came here. What have I been dreaming about?"

Aaron's professorial tone returned. "I created two time lines. More correctly, I created three parallel reality sets."

Helen fought back the urge to grimace. She decided the best thing to do was to sit quite still. If she moved, it might somehow change the impossibility of what she was hearing.

Aaron continued, "The Reveal intensified the natural time-slip abilities of my mind. My variant rate data shows that all systems are echoing themselves in time. We're not just 'self-deceived' computers like the dark-age intelligentsia would have you believe. There is something much more wondrous going on, something much more miraculous. We are 'self-aware' - we are happy, sad, angry, and so forth, because there is a universal mechanism of both negative and positive time involved. We are mirroring ourselves with every thought."

The words which Helen spoke seemed to fall from her lips. It occurred to her that the voice speaking was reaching from across the table. The intense, yet soft brown eyes sat safely in their orbits, but the mysterious man was, in fact, speaking through her lips.

"Bailey's pregnant."

Aaron exhaled deeply as he muttered, "You have no idea how much this complicates everything. She and her family are Catholic; quite devout, I'm sure."

Helen's jade eyes blinked as Aaron's brown pigment seemed to pull from her sockets. It occurred to Helen that she felt slightly numb as the curious moment shifted.

She clasped her left wrist with her right hand. "I'm not sure how to say this, or even if I should. But I will. Aaron, I feel suddenly quite relieved. I've never said anything like this to anyone before. I feel like we just had sex!"

A wry smile formed on Aaron's lips as he calmly spoke, "That's good. It helps to prove what I already know."

Helen grimaced as she spoke abruptly, "Well, I'm glad it was good for you! I'm still waiting on some sort of explanation."

Aaron stood and moved to his desk chair. He grabbed a pen and a Post-it pad and scrawled feverishly. "It has to do with our shared 'total-mind', Helen. We've lived as man and wife for our entire lives."

Helen nearly shouted, "What the Hell are you talking about?"

Aaron snapped his head to Helen's voice and spoke softly, "Oh, I'm sorry! You really don't know, do you?"

Helen sat mutely, staring back at Aaron's gaze.

The physics professor spoke tersely, "It's too much to explain now. Here's the instruction for your Reveal. You must not deviate from this. And I mean not one bit. If you do, you will leave that child from your dreams, and millions of others, quite irrevocably dead."

Helen's riveting jade eyes began to water as her thick, ridiculously-long lashes dampened. She rose to her feet, towering over Aaron. It occurred to Aaron that he could not read her feelings. He watched as a single tear fell across her face, filling the wondrously shaped dimple on her chin. He stuttered as he fought back the words. He could hear himself speaking them silently. *I love you so much Shri'Ani.*

Helen held the Post-it and read for a moment. "All right, I'll do it, and then . . . we'll talk some more."

The English professor grabbed her purse and walked to Aaron's door. She hesitated for a moment and turned back to peer into Aaron's eyes.

She studied his expression for a moment, before speaking softly, "I'll see you in 31 days."

Aaron sat motionless as the door to his office closed. He drew a deep breath and exhaled. He knew that an impossible challenge lay ahead.

***

Helen stood in her night shirt as she dried her face. Leaning into the mirror, she peered into her jade eyes. She couldn't go to bed with any mascara hiding in her lashes. She plucked at a suspicious spot and decided that they were pristine.

Helen muttered to herself, "All right, I'll wash my hands one last time before I dry them with the clean hand towel."

Helen wriggled her fingers together, reassuring herself that they were completely dry. Holding the towel over her hands, she walked to her nightstand. She used the towel as a mitt to open the drawer and covered the waiting dice with the terry cloth. She rubbed them briskly, letting them fall from the towel onto her bedside table. The weary academic laid the towel open neatly onto the table and stood momentarily looking at the scene.

She muttered methodically, "Towel, dice, pencil, and pages of the diary."

Helen began to pray her private prayer as she returned to the nightstand and pulled the King James Version from the drawer. The heavy grain cover of the book felt crisp and tactile in her hands as she continued to pray.

She sat down as she muttered the words out loud, "Amen."

Reaching out, she began the process of rolling the single die and opening the tissue-thin pages to the guided verse. Helen drew a breath and sat quite stiff as she read:

> Ezekiel 43:11 "And if they be ashamed of all they have done, shew them the form of the house, and the fashion thereof, and the goings out thereof, and the comings in thereof, and all the forms thereof, and all the ordinances thereof, and all the laws thereof: and write it in their sight, that they may keep the whole thereof, and all the ordinances thereof, and do them."

Helen drank deeply from her gold clover cup. The hot cocoa was like family. She sat the cup down and picked up the diary page for one last review. She scanned through the nine forgoing entries and reread the current entry for the 10/4/14 date.

She smiled wondrously as she spoke out loud to herself, ""Show them the form of the house and the comings and goings thereof.' It really is like I'm being spoken to. 'Write it in their sight'. Thank you, Lord. And I thought I was having a lonely birthday."

Laying the diary back on the nightstand, Helen switched off the lamp and trailed off to sleep. In the dark room, a faint light gave witness to Helen's closed eyelids and the riveting motion of her eyes as they moved left to right, right to left. A vivid dream filled Helen's mind.

(circa 1703 [S]time line)

The Hindu language had been spoken very little before Pyara's arrival. The young Indian girl stood barefoot before Shri'Ani. The midday sun beamed down upon the two like the smiling God Brahma. The two women plucked at the carrots and cabbages from the garden.

Shri' smiled. "The gardens grow well here in Switzerland, but it is a short season. I never understood that seasons could change, before I came here with Francois. It's been since I was your age that I was back home. My mother and father made the long trip just once since I've been here these twenty five years."

Pyara spoke plainly, "My mother was killed by the Thuggees. My father was killed in the war against them. I am so pleased that the English brought me to live with you and master Francois."

Shri'Ani leaned forward over the girl and stole a kiss from her forehead. "You are our only daughter. We love you. You have brought us great joy, Pyara. Vishnu is known to work His mysteries."

The two soiled women raced into the Swiss homestead laughing and shouting as Shri'Ani grimaced. "Shhh . . . We can't disturb the great white scientist! I think he's in his lair of treasured books and the wooden desk."

Pyara laughed. "Let's sneak up on the foreign beast and see if we can learn his secrets!"

The four eyes peered from behind the slightly open door and gazed for several minutes at the seated man. Francois's quill pen danced across the paper. He sat transfixed, oblivious to the undetected scrutiny.

Shri'Ani spoke softly to her compeer, "If only my beloved husband truly knew how jealous I am of that exquisite wooden desk."

([Y]time line)

Bailey Smith grasped the door knob firmly. If it turned, professor LaSalle would be seated at his office desk, typing away at the computer. The routine of the two early birds was rarely disrupted by little more than the odd retrieval of coffee and tea. The knob turned silently as two eyes peered from behind the slightly opened door and gazed at the seated man. For a moment, the physics grad student paused to absorb the image. It occurred to her that she must remember to take a picture of the distinguished professor. The image of the distracted man, pen in hand and the computer somehow incidental, was made noteworthy by his remarkably ornate wooden desk.

Bailey walked quietly to her corner; she knew the simple spot held little character. The computer dominated its importance, but she was proud of her special place in the office/laboratory of her mentor. Bailey unlocked her desk and retrieved the document which had held her attention for over two years. The mystery described in these pages was special in ways that would push the limits of both science and man's awareness of thinking itself.

Flipping through the small bundle of papers, she smiled as the odd thought passed through her mind. *How could Aaron have written so much in just 21 minutes?* She muttered to herself, "It's as if he instinctively has an extra appendage of communication. Words normally transformed to speech were handily converted to written print." She wondered if the societal loss of cursive writing was truly a wise decision.

Punching up the file, Bailey flipped back and forth between the bullet points in her notes. She smirked, muttering to herself, "If anyone else had spoken of such things, they'd be locked up. I suppose Michelson and Morley would only have been believed by another physicist. If only they had known that static light speed was the simplest aspect of what the universe really has in store for the naked ape."

Bailey read the computer screen. L'Hopital met Johann Bernoulli in 1691 at his estate in Oucques, France. Bailey grimaced as she spoke out loud, "That's it! It's slightly different from Aaron's account."

Bailey's grey eyes grew wide as her thick brown locks jumped back from her face. The smell of hot coffee brought her straight up in her chair as she heard Aaron's voice.

"Well, today it's my turn to startle you," he said, smiling.

Bailey smiled as she reached for the hot cup and drank deeply.

Aaron continued, "So are you ready to show me, now? It was over a week ago that you said you had the corollary."

Bailey set the coffee down and turned her chair towards her professor. She spoke quietly as she shook her head slowly from left to right, right to left. "Aaron, why haven't you published your Variance Theory? You've worked on it for over a decade."

Aaron beamed, he knew Bailey like he knew the elementary equations of kinematics. "You have it, don't you?"

Bailey smiled back. "I know what's going on. Aaron, did it ever occur to you that I might doubt your sanity?"

A thin smile crept across Aaron's face. Bailey studied his soft brown eyes. She was eager for every nuance his answer to her question might take. Aaron pulled up the side chair, seated himself and took a drink from his hot tea.

An intense expression changed Aaron's face. "Well, it may seem strange that a general physics instructor might take such an interest in the paranormal, but I really had no choice."

Bailey's gaze never left Aaron. "I know you have déjà vu as I do. And I know we've discussed the suggestion from the experiments that events are somehow intertwined. But do you really believe it means that awareness is extending across time?"

Aaron interrupted, "Are you afraid to say it clearly?"

Bailey smirked. "You're right! I didn't use the "R" word, did I?"

Aaron took another drink from his tea and answered, "You don't know, do you?"

Bailey grimaced as she retorted, "Know what?"

The aging professor turned and gazed distractedly. "In

pendulum motion, the period of motion is not dependent on the mass. It's dependent on the length of the arm."

Bailey pursed her lips and furled her brow. "Aaron, I know I'm supposed to connect that to the issue. I mean, yes, that's what we physics nerds do. We just love the cryptic mysteries. Okay, I mean, yes, we love them! But I'm going to need some help with this one."

Aaron spoke up, "Type into Google and look up Matthew 17, verses 10 through 13."

Bailey's eyes grew wide as she read,

> [10] And his disciples asked him, saying, Why then say the scribes that Elias must first come?
>
> [11] And Jesus answered and said unto them, Elias truly shall first come, and restore all things.
>
> [12] But I say unto you, That Elias is come already, and they knew him not, but have done unto him whatsoever they listed. Likewise shall also the Son of man suffer of them.
>
> [13] Then the disciples understood that he spake unto them of John the Baptist.

"Oh my God," Bailey breathed, "if I ever showed that to my dad he would just die."

Aaron looked at Bailey and responded, "You're Catholic aren't you?"

Bailey nodded slowly. Her expression grew quite blank.

Aaron continued, "Well, in every lifetime there are extreme issues which define who we are. These issues test us, and the choices involved determine more about what we become than what we are. That's quite a contrast to the dogma of the cause and effect reversal our society operates on today, isn't it?"

Bailey grimaced slightly. "Okay, I got that one. You're saying that the victimhood excuse that predominates politics is wrong."

Aaron smiled. "You never cease to amaze me with how smart you are."

Both took a drink from their cups, almost on cue.

Bailey, at last, said, "Well, this is the part where whoever speaks first gets proven wrong."

She smiled broadly as she continued, "Am I going to tell you why your diary is right, or are you going to tell me why the world's view of reincarnation is wrong?"

Aaron grimaced as he continued, "Let's start with the world being wrong. If the physics demonstrate that the root of causality always involves a restatement of the properties, then why do people try to reduce things to the simplest proposition?"

Bailey's thick brown hair shuddered as she retorted, "Boy, I'm glad it's just us two geniuses here. If the world knew that two Frankenstein's existed, the straights would be at the door with the pitchforks and torches. *Okay*, people are childish and simplistic. Perhaps the choices we make extend beyond rote information, but does that mean that our identities have extended beyond this life?"

Aaron leaned into the desk and stared directly into Bailey's grey eyes. She blinked and appeared a bit startled. Aaron squinted; his penetrating brown eyes seemed to pierce into the young girl.

He spoke intently, "Open the diary to the section with L'Hospital and Pyara. Describe Shri'Ani's orphan daughter."

Bailey read, "'The young Hindu girl was lovely. Her handsome features were adorned with distinctive, grey eyes. Her thick hair was not as dark as most Indian girls'. It was dark brown. The intelligent and comely lass would sit and study me while I worked at my desk for hours on end.'"

Aaron watched as Bailey's eyes began to water. Her expression grew blank and pliant as her mind drifted from her own presence.

She muttered quietly as if she spoke from a distant and lonely place, "I was Pyara."

***

The Smith family's pew had remained exclusive for many, many years. Those years had passed in anxious anticipation of the long-awaited birth of their precious daughter, Bailey.

Bailey sat holding hands with her mother, who sat next to her father. The three souls were a vision of love and stability in the sanctuary of the church in a world never sanctified by such grace. Father Adams held service.

"It was a month ago," Father Adams began, "that the 13th anniversary of the 9-11 attack occurred. In memory of this great evil, I will read from 2 Peter 2:4, 'For if God did not spare the angels when they sinned, but sent them to Hell . . .' if he did not spare the ancient world when he brought the flood on its ungodly people, but protected Noah, a preacher of righteousness, and seven others; if he condemned the cities of Sodom and Gomorrah by burning them to ashes, he made an example of the ungodly; he rescued Lot, a righteous man - if this is so, then the Lord knows how to rescue the Godly from the trials and to hold the unrighteous for punishment on the day of judgment. This is especially true of those who follow the corrupt desire of the flesh and despise authority."

It seemed to Bailey that Father Adams was looking straight at her as he continued,

"From Isaiah 6:6, 'The wolf shall dwell with the lamb, the leopard shall lie down with the kid; and the calf and the young lion and the fatling together and a little child will lead them.'

"And from John 5:24, 'Verily I say unto you, he that heareth my word, and believeth on Him that sent me, hath everlasting life, and shall not come into condemnation, but is passed from death.'"

The throngs of people emptied from the church as the Smith family shook hands with many smiling friends. Saying their farewells, the family began their trip home. Bailey sat in the backseat as she had for nearly two decades. Her father looked in the mirror at his most precious daughter; the "tell-tale" look on Bailey's face was still present.

William Smith spoke up, "I'm so glad you made it today, Bailey. Your mother and I know you are a grown woman now with many distractions."

Bailey's grey eyes riveted to her father's eyes. She knew that he had just read her mind.

She spoke up bravely. "I know I told you that you would meet my friend today. He didn't show up did he?"

Sarah Smith answered, hopefully, "Oh darling, men are unpredictable - and I guess that's why we love them." She reached across and squeezed William's hand.

William smiled. "You'll find love, Darling."

Bailey grimaced as her gaze became downcast. "The thing is he does love me."

Sarah's expression turned sour as she turned around and looked at Bailey directly.

"What's going on, Bailey?" Sarah demanded.

Bailey knew that the foreign name she was about to speak could cause a car wreck.

"Ibrahim promised me that he would attend the Catholic Church with me, today."

The terrified looks on the faces of Bailey's parents were more than she could stand. It was a horrible moment that Bailey had not really considered, until recently. The penetrating voice of Father Adams began to echo in her head. *Hold the unrighteous for punishment on the Day of Judgment.*

Sarah nearly shouted, "Well darling, you've just had your first reality check in the intolerance of the non-Christian! Maybe the righteousness of the scripture and the evil of false prophets from 2 Peter will now be understood."

Bailey muttered meekly, "I asked him to convert to Catholicism, and he demanded that I convert to Muslim."

The intensity of the moment was broken with the near-hysterical laughter from the front seat.

William spoke up loudly, "Child, the sands of the Middle-east will melt in Hell before those acolytes of Satan will ever convert to the Judeo-Christian miracle."

William gazed into the rearview mirror to the vision of his true oracle of worship—and the young girl was a truly wretched sight. Bailey's vivid grey eyes were now quite indistinguishable. She appeared as if, in just the time of a single glance, she had pulled her head out of a muddy rain soaked puddle.

William implored, "What is it darling?"

Bailey struggled out the words, "Ibrahim will not allow me to remain a Catholic. He says I have to convert to Islam, or he won't marry me!"

Sarah burst into tears as she appeared to almost grow faint. "Oh, dear Lord, Bailey, you promised me. You made vows. You swore you would be a virgin on your wedding day!"

Bailey's voice rose, "Mom, Dad, I am a virgin! I, I . . . don't understand myself. I, I . . . mean, well, we drank too much and played around a little, but I didn't do anything wrong. I don't know how this could have happened!"

Bailey's Slip

(October 5, 2014—[Y]time line)

Professor Aaron LaSalle glanced at his watch as he leaned into the closed hallway door. The hands confirmed that the "early bird" was indeed busy. The door's attached whiteboard* was a symbol of the dedication Helen Lovelace held for her students. The aging professor looked at the morass of emoji scrawls and dates and decided they could be sacrificed. He reached into his pocket, retrieved a Kleenex, and began to erase.

Grasping the pen hanging by its cord, Aaron began to draw a large number '4' on the board. He wanted it thick, so he painted it in, creating an unmistakable image. Then, he drew two large eyes with long, pronounced eye lashes. The simple circles were filled with darkened pupils. It occurred to Aaron that he should have thought to bring along a green pen. One eye was inside the closed triangle of the '4', the other rested next to it above the horizontal intersecting line. Aaron studied the image and shook his head agreeably as he thought, *That's what I saw in the dream last night. She was looking through the "4."*

"What are you doing?" Aaron jumped as he heard the melodic female voice behind him.

Turning to see the broad smile of the subject of his graffiti, Aaron stuttered, "Well, I, I . . . never imagined that anyone else got up as early as I do."

Helen leaned around Aaron and peered at the odd artwork. She chuckled as she said, "Do you want to come in and have some coffee? Oh wait, that's right, you don't drink coffee. You drink tea."

Keys jingled as the two shuffled into the office and Helen set her armful of materials on the desk.

"Have a seat," she said. "I'm glad you're here. In fact, it's quite odd you're here. Maybe, it's not as odd as the foreplay on my door. But it's not as odd as the dream I had last night."

Aaron sat quite silently as Helen worked about her kitchenette, talking at length with some distraction. Setting the cups down, Helen sat down and gave Aaron a quick smile as she drank deeply from her Irish-green coffee cup, emblazoned with a gold 4-leaf clover.

Aaron took a drink of his tea and set the cup down. Smiling broadly, he said, "Did you do that deliberately!?"

Helen smirked as she retorted, "Do what?"

Aaron bemused, abruptly. "That cup! It has a 4-leaf clover on it."

Helen laughed loudly as she responded, "Oh, you scientific types!" She turned the cup around and looked at it as she laughed again. "You're right; it does have 4-leaf clovers on it." She set the cup down and leaned her face onto her left palm, with her elbow on the table. Her jade eyes sparkled as she continued, "All right, I don't know why I find all this so interesting! I can't wait to hear the explanation."

Aaron quipped, "You don't know, do you?"

Helen retorted, "Know what?"

Aaron chimed back, "Know what I'm doing here?"

Helen guffawed. "I know I've got a million things to do, but no, I don't know what you're doing here."

Genuine warmth filled Aaron as he looked deeply into the bright jade eyes and the smiling face seated before him. "I had a dream last night. I call this type of dream a DV. It means 'dream vision.' They are quite distinct. The things I see come to pass are things I don't know, but I come to find out are real."

Helen blinked, remaining motionless as she responded, "I finished the 10th entry for the Reveal last night. Yesterday was kind of a lonely day for me, but the verse I turned to was exhilarating. I had the most remarkable dream I think I've ever experienced. I guess that's what you mean by a DV."

A thin smile crept across Aaron's face. "In my dream, you were peering through the number '4.' It was an intense flash of an image. It was brief, but you were there and it meant something quite important to you. It was as if you were breaking through—or into—the number itself."

Helen leaned back and shook her head slightly as she spoke up, "You are truly amazing."

Aaron sat motionless as the moments passed. He finally spoke, "All right, yes, I don't know. Please tell me what it meant."

Helen drank deeply from her coffee. Its steam swirled across her green orbs. She set the cup down and continued, "My birthday is on October 4th. I pushed into the fourth decade of my life yesterday. You didn't look up my birthday or something, did you?"

Aaron guffawed as he answered, "You know how computer illiterate I am. I have to have Bailey's help just to find my car keys."

Helen smirked as she replied, "Well, we're certainly on the same page. I think Bailey may well be the point of the most remarkable experience of my life. Uh, well, I mean 'lives.'"

Aaron leaned forward eagerly as he asked, "You experienced your past life?"

Helen smiled thinly as she said softly, "You mean *our* past life, don't you?"

Aaron continued, "Did you see us together?"

Helen quipped, "Nothing was very different. You sat at the same desk. I really think it was the same desk. Where did you find it?"

Aaron answered, "I had a dream, and the next day in a flea market, there it was."

Helen grinned as she held up her unique coffee cup. "That's exactly how I came to buy this. I dreamed it just a day, maybe two, before I saw it and I had to buy it." She continued, "Okay, here's the real point. There was this beautiful Hindu girl. Oh, by the way, I was Hindu or maybe Buddhist. Anyway, you were a quite handsome Frenchman. You had a weird name! But I can't quite remember it. Anyhow, this young Indian girl was like my daughter, or something. But here's the real point. I looked at her very closely. She had dark brown—almost black—hair, grey eyes, and I already knew her."

A very reassuring expression came over Aaron. He said, "This means the issue is working itself out. The Authority has taken notice!"

Helen retorted, "What does *that* mean?"

The professor of physical science explained, "When you finish the Reveal, we'll talk more about what I call the Super-consciousness. Anyway, Helen, the Twin Towers were destroyed. The Titanic sank. The children at Sandy Hook died. But I have a diary I wrote after my experience that says all those things never happened. The World Wars weren't nation-state conflicts; they were religious wars. Even the American Revolution was different."

Helen queried, "Where is this different world?"

Aaron continued, "You might as well ask where you go when you dream. It has to do with information, Helen. In quantum physics, the particle and the wave are indistinguishable. It's called the de Broglie Principle."

Helen knew that she must keep the discussion on track. She interrupted, "Aaron, you told me before that you caused some sort of rip in time. Does this mean that you changed the past?"

Aaron nodded, agreeably. Helen continued, "Okay, so if you changed the past, why isn't anything any different now?"

Aaron smirked, disappointingly, as he spoke up, "Helen, was your dream of the 17th Century lovely and blissful?"

A joyous smile came across Helen's face as she responded, "Oh, yes. It was the most delightful birthday present I ever had. I now know how much I love you."

Aaron's soft brown eyes began to water, even as his expression went quite blank.

The aging professor demurred from Helen's gaze as he meekly responded, "You see, Helen, I have the diary because I am the same man in all time lines. There are actually three parallel realities. I messed up the whole universe, or at least maybe the solar system." Aaron's gaze returned to Helen as he smiled whimsically.

Helen continued, "All right, so the ghosts of the students that I keep dreaming of—and that wonderful Siberian husky—they're supposed to be here. But they died in New York on 2012 in the other time line."

The look in Aaron's eyes was that of a truly forlorn soul as he muttered, "I'm going to try to say this without losing it. It's my fault. I intervened in Divine Destiny. I was taken back to the 17th Century and left my work behind. My name then was Francois L'Hospital, a mathematician. The world wasn't ready for the information I delivered. It caused a rip in time that must be repaired."

Helen's expression grew stern as she asked, "What can I do? I'm just another lesser professor. Hell, I don't even know half the words you speak!"

Aaron grinned, broadly. "Helen, we're all just naked apes. Humanity knows just enough to blow itself up and keep the deities entertained."

Helen interrupted, "There you go again! All right, the first thing you need to explain to me is whether you're being metaphoric when you say these things about God!"

Aaron grimaced as he nodded his head in response. He spoke up quietly, "Helen, I just explained to you that matter and energy—waves and particles—are just information. That means that they're contained in some sort of processing mechanism. Don't you see we're just ideas in the mind of God?

Helen nearly shouted, "Then why is everything such a damn mess if there is this 'perfect mind' running everything!?"

Aaron retorted. "There isn't one perfect mind running everything! There are two perfectly disagreeable minds running everything! You don't know this, but you currently exist in what I call the (Y)time line. The creator God's name is Yahweh. The name begins with the 10th letter in the Hebrew alphabet, the smallest letter. The time line I created is the (S)time line. The destroyer god has limitless names, Satan, Beelzebub, Devil, Apollyon, the Angel of Light, or in your life with me as Shri'Ani you would know the name as Shiva."

Helen continued, "You said something about an Authority. What does that mean?"

Aaron's smile thinned as he answered, "You haven't gotten to that part in the Reveal. I really didn't expect to see you this morning. I can't explain any more right now."

The look on Helen's face was quite nonplussed as she quipped, "Well, one thing is for certain. That Happy Birthday card on the door definitely wasn't foreplay!"

Aaron rose to his feet, leaned over and kissed Helen on the forehead. "I better get going. Bailey's going to wonder where the 'early bird' is."

Helen watched as Aaron walked to the door and turned back to her as she spoke up, "Tell our daughter we love her."

Aaron smiled warmly. His gaze penetrated Helen's eyes as he responded, "Love is what will unravel the riddle."

Bailey stretched back in the hot water. The young grad student finally found the quiet time to luxuriate in her tub. Her eyelids fell slowly closed as she inhaled deeply. The scented candles and the flickering light might last for all eternity, if not for the realities—both without and within. The only imperfection was the ceaseless "drip, drip" of the tub's spout. Bailey ran her wrinkled foot over the spout. She smiled to herself as she considered the physics of hydrodynamics.

Her grey eyes grew wide as the nubile young woman muttered to herself, "All existence is fluid. The deeper the water, the greater the natural force. The weight of the ages are all constructed one drip at a time." Bailey jammed her big toe into the leaky orifice. A smile crept across the young scientist's face. "It's all a magic trick. One moment, it's a drippy stick; the next instant, it's a corked bottle."

She reached for the bottle of bath oil and poured a small sampling of the creamy white fluid on her belly. "There's the issue, the milky waters of life." Bailey's fingers traced spiraling circles around and around on her flat belly. The target of the bubbling, aromatic sojourn was her deeply pronounced umbilicus, the navel of life. She closed her eyes, punched the stereo's remote and listened to the soft music. The tones of the timeless band Hybrid played. She listened as the lyrics spoke to her, "wild, wild horses running free." She thought of the playful time with her impassioned Ibrahim. She considered that it must have been a mistake. The cool-down shower, in fact, resulted in a much hotter episode. But how could all the rinse water allow even one wriggling seed to make the trek to her core?

Bailey's mind drifted to the intense argument with her mother. Sarah was as furious as Baily had ever witnessed. Sarah had nearly snarled as she spoke, "You will not dishonor your father with an illegitimate child!"

Bailey retorted sarcastically, "Well, I guess he'll enjoy going to Sunday services with his daughter dressed in a burqa."

Sarah's expression turned sour. "The only thing worse than that is the thought of an abortion. You'll have to make the choice!"

Bailey's tender world suddenly crashed. Flickering images of her idyllic childhood came to mind. For some odd reason, the little girl's memory of her puppy's death came to mind. She spoke up, distractedly, "Mom, do you remember Fluffy?"

The stiff-backed stance of Sarah Smith gave way, and she stooped over as her hands covered her eyes. She began to weep intensely.

The candlelight danced across the image of Bailey's wet face. Her closed eyelids betrayed the rapid eye movement as they riveted from right to left and left to right. The lotion-laden fingertips of her right hand slapped helplessly at her left arm.

The nearly comatose state of the young girl was abruptly interrupted with the harsh words, "Pyara, how long are you going to linger in that tub!?"

Shri'Ani seemed impatient as she lifted her sage oil lamp before her dear adopted daughter.

Bailey sat straight up in the tub and shouted to herself, "What was that!? Am I losing my mind?"

(phone text [S]time line)

Helen,

It's Bailey Smith. I need to talk to you. Is there a time I can stop by your office?

****

Yes, Bailey...

Today, after the 3:00 classes . . .

Helen

The door to Helen's office crept open to the sounds of typing. Bailey peered around and meekly announced herself. "Hi, it's me Bailey."

Professor Helen Lovelace could type with her eyes closed, and more importantly, she could still carry on a conversation. Bailey stood transfixed as Helen's dexterous choreography remained unperturbed. The professor of fine arts looked up, smiling at the young student. "Hi, grab some coffee. It's fresh!"

Bailey set the cup of coffee down at Helen's side table and seated herself. She watched for some minutes as Helen continued the typing cadence. Turning to the smiling face of the grey-eyed girl, Helen spoke at last, "So, how can a befuddled English professor assist one of LaSalle's physics scholars?"

Bailey smiled broadly. Her thick, dark brown locks swirled as she began her characteristically animate conversation. "Helen, I've got something going on. I wouldn't normally discuss this with anyone, but I know that you and Aaron know things that I don't."

Helen smiled thinly as she took a drink of her now-cool coffee. Bailey studied the unique, gold 4-leaf clover decorated cup. Helen smiled as she asked, "Do you like my cup?" Bailey nodded, approvingly. Helen continued, "I dreamed of it before I saw it. I went shopping one day, and there it was. I can only assume that it has some purpose for being here."

Bailey grimaced slightly as she spoke, "It's a funny idea, isn't it? I mean the idea that anything has a purpose . . ., a cup . . ., or even people."

The gaze between the two was intense. Helen's green orbs seemed to smile as she spoke quietly, "Okay, I guess I already know some things. But why don't you go first."

Bailey's grey eyes seemed to squint as she pursed her lips. The words were nearly pushed from her mouth, "I'm pregnant, and Ibrahim won't marry me unless I convert to a Muslim."

Helen grimaced as she spoke out sympathetically, "Your parents aren't going for that, are they?"

Bailey answered, "And, I'm not either! The only thing is I consider it a mortal sin to have an abortion and, maybe worse, to bring an illegitimate soul into the world."

Helen grappled to help the young student. "I wish I had a solution. It's an impossible issue. One of my favorite phrases is 'On the horns of a dilemma.'"

Bailey continued, "I don't know how much you know about the other issue, but I now know that Aaron's obsession with his time line thing is real."

Helen perked up as she studied Bailey's expression intently. "What do you mean, dear?"

Bailey's focus on Helen's expression increased as she continued, "Helen, I've had unusual dreams my entire life. I've had some truly remarkable déjà vu experiences. But I experienced something, while dozing in my bathtub, which I've never experienced."

Helen smiled thinly as she queried, "I'm on pins and needles!"

Bailey's voice crackled as she seemed to almost shiver, "Helen, I was carried back to some ancient time. And you were there! I think you were my mother! In the instant that the dream image lasted, I was in a bathtub, and you were standing there with this old-time lamp. You told me to hurry up and get out of the tub!"

Helen spoke up, "Was that all?"

Bailey continued, "No. I knew your name, and I knew mine."

Helen smiled curiously as she spoke, "What was my name?"

Bailey answered, "Shri'Ani."

Helen's expression turned quite blank as she spoke, "It's really interesting that you have proven to me what I dreamed by what you dreamed, and I can now prove to you that what you dreamed is true by what I dreamed." Helen laughed uproariously as she continued, "Boy, if one of my students handed in a thesis with a run-on sentence like that, I'd fail them."

Bailey interrupted, "Science is the ultimate run-on sentence. There's a lingering question! Helen, do you know about Aaron's diary?"

Helen answered, "Yes, I know about it."

Bailey continued, "Well, here's the thing. The diary is what we've been poring over for two years. I don't exactly know what I'm looking for. But we've been trying to find historical things in the past that don't match up with his diary."

Helen asked, "Have you found what he's looking for?"

Bailey continued, "I think I have. But here's the thing. Aaron pointed out this girl in the 17th Century, and when I focused on the details of her life, I knew it was me in a previous life. Now, I don't understand why he didn't show me that the woman in the diary—the woman who was my mother—was, well . . ., you! You're the woman. And he has to know their names, but they aren't named in the diary."

Helen grimaced as she replied, "You have three choices. You can betray your faith; you can have an illegitimate baby, or you can have an abortion."

The gaze between the two women was troubling. It seemed to Bailey that the moment might have lasted for an hour. Or perhaps the curious sensation stemmed from some invisible 3rd party, listening intently for the words that might be spoken.

Bailey muttered quietly, "Do you suppose there is an ultimate diabolical purpose in things? I mean is everything just an accident, or is there some larger authorship in things?"

Helen smiled as she replied, "Well, I know about authorship. Aaron seems to be in conflict with the idea of trial and error. He appears to think there is some kind of higher mind involved in everything."

Bailey continued, "It's odd that I met Ibrahim at the casino. And then I found out he's a student in some of the same classes. Was it destined, or was there some architect in so many foreign students being in my world?"

Helen, still smiling, said, "There have always been strangers in strange lands."

Bailey continued, "Well, the academics tell us that Yahweh and Allah is the same God . . ."

Helen laughed uproariously as she interrupted, "Don't tell your father or Aaron LaSalle that. They'll have a Rabbi and a Priest ready to exorcise you." Helen looked deeply into Bailey's forlorn eyes. "Are you telling Shri'Ani that you've decided what to do?"

Bailey smiled lovingly at the professor as she responded, "Well, after all, you were my mother 300 years ago and you believed in many gods. Will you tell your daughter that the gods are all alike? Would it be permissible to convert?" Bailey's grey eyes grew wide as she peered into the depths of Helen's riveting jade orbs. "You do believe in both (S) and (Y), don't you? Will you tell your daughter that both gods are the same?"

Helen pursed her lips as she furled her brow. She spoke intently, "Bailey, the resolution to the great issue of good and evil rests with the Authority. Scientists and ecclesiastics study it ceaselessly. I mean, after all, we vote every four years on what the spiritual catechism should be."

Bailey grimaced, "I need for you to tell me what to do."

Helen responded sternly, "You go to that young man and you tell him that he will convert to (Y) or you will damn him to Hell. You tell him that he will convert to Catholicism!"

([Y]time line)

Aaron LaSalle scuttled through his office door. The "early bird" was surprised to find his fellow insomniac already sitting at her desk.

Aaron spoke up, "Well, I think we've beaten our record."

Bailey chuckled, "It's almost 6:00 AM. Yep! We've beaten our record."

Aaron set his satchel down on his side desk. He walked over to the kitchenette as he spoke, "You got me some fancy tea! I guess I'll try this Earl Grey."

Aaron walked over to Bailey as she continued uninterrupted at the computer. She spoke, "Are you ready for the big issues?"

Aaron sipped the hot tea while gazing down at his student through the steam. He watched as Bailey's thick locks twirled around in his direction. Looking up, she smiled broadly. Aaron pulled up a chair and sat down beside her desk.

Bailey flipped through the thick stack of hand-written pages. Her animated demeanor was in full gear. She turned in her chair and held the mass of papers up, in front of her teacher's face. "Aaron, how did you write so much in just 21 minutes? I mean, was it really 21 minutes? I've watched you writing, and it's really weird how you write so fast, but this is ridiculous. It's like 17 pages!"

A thin smile crept across Aaron's face as he sat silently. Bailey matched his stoic response. She knew after one or two seconds that the sparring match had begun. She spoke up first. "No. I'm serious. I probably should have asked this long ago. But now, I want to know! I mean, okay? I don't know cursive, and I've had to translate three languages, but really!"

Aaron took a deep drink from the Earl Grey. The steam from the cup created a wavy aberration in the image of Bailey's wide-eyed stare. Aaron pursed his lips before speaking quietly. "You really believe all this now, don't you?"

Bailey stammered, "Well, of course I believe it! Do you think I would have worked on this for two years if I thought this was just a fantasy?"

Aaron smiled genuinely as he replied, "Well, yes, I think you would have. It's much too interesting, isn't it? I mean, it redefines truth and fiction, doesn't it?"

Bailey muttered, quietly, "Well, yeah, it does. I mean it's like the most interesting thing I've ever seen. It makes quantum physics look like 'tinker toys.'"

The look on Aaron's face was quite genuine. "I know about the problem."

Bailey's attempt at confidence suddenly eroded. The child's face returned to an expression of limitless quandary. Aaron spoke again, gently, "Did Helen have any advice?"

Bailey's eyes began to water as she stuttered frantically, "I . . . I don't see any other option. I can't have an abortion. I guess I have to learn the Koran." Bailey's tone shifted as she pleaded, "Is there anything you don't know? You were a master swordsman, weren't you?"

Aaron held out his arms as his dearest friend nearly jumped into his lap. Bailey swiped at her face with her right hand as she fought back the tears. She muttered, her voice choking, "Okay, we have too much to figure out and not much time. An hour isn't much to try and understand 300 years and two time lines."

Aaron spoke up as Bailey climbed back into her desk chair, "It's not two time lines; it's actually three."

Bailey's bewildered expression matched her questioning tone, "How are there three?"

Aaron shuffled through the pages as he answered, "Look here, on page 13. This describes the (Y)time line, our time. This is you and me with our current memories. This reflects the current state of our minds. Your best friend is Bekah. Look, you see, I even mention her name. Now, look over here on page 15. I mention you and Bekah with another female student."

Bailey smiled curiously as she said, "I never noticed that! On page 13, you mentioned that I would help you with the research, but that was before December 14th, 2012. You mentioned Bekah and the other girl, but I never paid any attention to it because you never mentioned her name."

"Do you and Bekah have another best friend?" Aaron asked.

Bailey shook her head timidly as she muttered, "Well, no! I guess we don't." Bailey's frozen expression remained as her jaw dropped slowly. The timidity in her voice grew palpable as her left hand covered her face. "Oh, dear God, there *are* three time lines."

Aaron took another sip of tea as he studied the young girl's reactions. He spoke tenderly, "I suppose now, you truly understand that all of this involves more than some H.G. Wells fantasy."

"It really is macro-quantum mechanics, isn't it?" Bailey asked. Aaron nodded, approvingly. Bailey continued, "So your mathematics explains how memory really works."

Aaron smiled broadly as he replied, "Of course! The same loophole that I've identified in random motion is happening in the bowl of fatty lipid neural molecules inside our skulls. It's the mirrored counterpart to Einstein's Relativity."

Bailey's smile widened as she responded, "It's all about time, isn't it?"

Aaron continued, "Of course! And the weirdest part in the science is that the memories continue in and out of what we think of as death."

Bailey's tone became quite intense as she spoke, "What about the friend I've never known. Who is that girl!? No wait! I see something now! It's how you wrote so much, so fast." Bailey's grey eyes pierced deeply into Aaron's brown orbs as she spoke up insistently, "You know all three time lines! You have some sort of eidetic memory from the 'time-slip.'"

Aaron smiled broadly as he answered, "Well, I did for the 21 minutes when I returned to the floor at my home, on December

14th, 2012. But now most of it is like trying to remember what I had for lunch last Thursday."

Bailey's animated tone returned as she nearly shouted, "But why are there three time lines? If all of this is a real world manifestation of quantum entanglement, why are there three? I mean when I put on a glove, it's just the shape of my hand. The glove is just the hollow hand!"

Aaron grimaced as he spoke, "Smash your hand into soft clay. You have half of the hand. If you look at the cast of your hand, you'll wonder if you're looking at the left or right hand. DNA replicates itself perfectly. It's like filling the glove full of 'plaster of Paris'; you have the same right or left hand. But the universe is binomial. It requires the kaleidoscope of opposites, up, down, hot, cold, protons, electrons, good, bad, life, death . . ."

Bailey's expression became intense again. "Now, I'm really scared. It's like all I can think of is that friend I never met in this life, I mean time line . . . I think!"

Aaron chuckled as he spoke quietly, "Now, you know how she died, don't you?"

Bailey swung her stare back to Aaron's eyes. She nearly stuttered as the words fell from her lips. "She died on the darkest day. Now, I know why you call 12/21 that. It's the Solstice, the day of the year with the longest night."

Aaron nodded, approvingly. "And, you understand that the (S)time line must be returned to simply one (Y)time line."

Bailey looked meekly into Aaron's eyes. "She died in New York in the (S)time line, didn't she?" Aaron nodded, agreeably. Bailey continued, "You left certain names out of my copy of the diary, didn't you?" Aaron nodded. Bailey smirked as she asked, "I couldn't know too much too soon, could I?" Aaron nodded, approvingly. Bailey's expression grew quite focused. "I can almost see her name. It's like the bomb was somehow destined to get her. It's like her name says something about the bomb."

Aaron spoke up assertively, "Bailey, you've got other things to worry about right now. We know enough to fix what happened; let's discuss that."

Bailey's eyes became a torrent as she lurched upright from her chair. "Oh dear God, it's the physics of mass death. It's her name! It has to do with the term Ground Zero. Zoe . . . Oh, dear God, Zoe! Please, dear God, help us . . . all."

Aaron blinked as he watched Bailey grab her left wrist with her right hand. He sprang from his chair and took the comatose girl in his arms as she fell. Leaning her into his legs, he lowered her gently onto the floor.

He muttered to himself, frantically, "Please, dear Yahweh! Please, let it work this time . . . You can do it, my brave daughter. Get the message through. It has to work this time . . ."

(circa 1703 Switzerland [S]time line)

Pyara muttered to herself, in her Hindu dialect, "Dear Vishnu, what's happening?" The dizziness and the numbness in Bailey's left arm were overwhelming. She moaned deeply, releasing the death grip of her right hand. "This is our home in Switzerland . . ."

Lurching to her feet, the teenage girl flailed in the darkness at the doorway to Francois's library. Her young voice crackled, softly, "Yes, Aaron knew it all along. It was Satan himself that shifted all of time." The total mind of three lives settled into one innocent soul. Pyara thought to herself, "Kala, the God of time and its destroyer, Shiva, are at war with Vishnu!"

Bailey knew what she must do. Pyara steadied herself, staring down at her young legs as control of her body grudgingly returned. Shakily, she walked to the desk of Francois L'Hospital. Bailey sat down and gazed wondrously at the quill pen and ink. Reaching into the stack of paper, she smiled, thinking to herself, *The paper's much thicker now. What do I say that he'll believe? I know! If I start with the equations, he'll know I'm speaking the truth. There is no way that Pyara would know the mathematics, so he'll listen when he reads it.*

Bailey smiled as she muttered to herself, "Now, I know why I took all those French classes."

The young hand dashed across the 17th Century parchment as Bailey's warning continued, *"You Must Not win the duel that you will fight with Jakob Bernoulli. Please! Francois, your work must not be published at this time! I cannot explain, but when you read what I have written, you will know that your Hebrew God does not wish it. Please listen to your obedient daughter!"*

As Bailey finished her penmanship, she sat quite still as her mind wandered to the 'total mind' of multiple lives. Blissfully, she considered the charming life of love and dedication with her precious Shri'Ani and Francois. In the distracted moment, she did not notice the intense pinpoint of red light forming lowly on the floor in front of the desk.

A voice in perfect Hindi dialect queried, "What are you doing, child?"

Pyara leapt straight up from the finely-crafted French desk chair of Francois L'Hospital. "Who is it, in this room!?"

"Do you not know?"

The red light before her grew larger, its scarlet cast filling the room. A voice softer than a man's, but clearly not a woman's, continued, "Bailey, have you not given your soul to the Word of Allah? Have you not traded your faith for another?" The articulation in colloquial English was almost musical. "You may answer if you wish, Pyara." The voice again spoke in perfect Hindi dialect. "Do you not recognize the Lord of your fears? Do you not know the God of the eternal cycle of all the seasons, of all the time that ever has or ever will exist?"

Pyara's body began to shiver. The twin mind of a single soul began to spin as she realized that Aaron's worse fear had transpired. The child's soft grey eyes were wide as she frightfully uttered the question, "What do you want?"

"I am your Lord. I am the mind that holds your mind. I am the vessel which holds your form. I am He who owns your fealty. Will you obey my Word?" The voice was, at once, one voice and yet, at once, a cacophony of voices. It was hard to understand. Pyara heard it as a screeching siren. The young girl knew its power must be more in her mind than in her ears.

The child mustered every ounce of strength across both lifetimes to bleat the uncertain question, "What is your desire, Lord?"

"I am your Lord. Your written word is not my Will. Look upon your composition; the lamp flickers upon the paper and ink. Place it upon the lamp that it may be consumed by the light." The painful voice echoed within Pyara's head. Its trance-like resonance reached deeply into the young woman who stood shivering before the desk. Pyara stepped to the desk and lifted her printed words close to the lamp, struggling to place the paper over the lamp and its flickering fire within the globe of glass. She watched as the parse smoke exiting the opening at the top began to cover the paper and darken her words.

The moment protracted as each instant seemed to linger. The teenage girl struggled to maintain her complete identity. Her expanded consciousness had somehow been diminished. In her mind, Bailey saw the beleaguered face of Aaron LaSalle and heard his words.

Her young face grimaced in pain. "No, no, I've seen the death, the destruction! Millions of lives incinerated. This impossible reality must be overturned."

Pyara jerked the paper from the lamp and held it tightly to her chest. "No, no, I've seen the death! I will not destroy this message. Its purpose must be fulfilled!" Bailey heard herself shouting and gripped the paper tightly with all her might. The room was suddenly filled with a deep grumbling sound. The young girl felt that she might be overcome with the fear that seemed to redouble itself within her very fiber.

The crimson-colored aura before the desk seemed to approach the shivering girl. As it neared, the form seemed to compress into a shape, and a swirling tail appeared to follow, snakelike. The foreboding presence transformed into a grim and powerful face. Pyara blinked as she lurched back and turned from the terrifying embodiment.

A voice then spoke with such power that she imagined for a moment that the wall she was pressed against was shaking. "You cannot disobey my Word! You are among my flocks. You will not commit this blasphemy!"

The soul wrenched between worlds and time itself stood only shivering and silent. Bailey wondered for a moment if the future still existed. *Will I ever see that life again?*

Pyara muttered, "I must get to Francois and Shri'Ani. I must move now! I must run—now!"

The form before her seemed to surround her, and she heard the same voice, but now, somehow more deeply. "You are removed from this world! The light that creates your being is made void! The light that was in you since the beginning of the Universe will be made absent from your birth unto this moment!"

The shivering in the child ceased. The horrifying voice went silent. The last image in Pyara's grey eyes was an intense fiery red, which flashed for the briefest instant.

The beleaguered library of Francois L'Hospital seemed to glow in a dim, but rich, azure light. The collapsed form of Pyara lay before her patron's desk. The desk chair toppled. An intense blue light emanated from her body. It was as if the human being lying there was indeed some type of compressed sponge. The light leaving her body was her very existence. As it bled out, its blue intensity displaced the red shroud that covered her. The flesh and bone that was her being was now discarded. The teenage girl had been converted to cinder and ash.

A short time later, the room went dark. The rich woodwork and priceless books that covered the walls were now pasted with greasy soot. Looking down at the crisp black ash, the trace of a twisted human form could be perceived. One part of the human remained.

The right forearm grasped firmly by the left hand, lay inviolate. The bifurcation from the ash and the remnants of the limbs was distinct. It was as if, in the incineration of this being's life, her soul was still shouting out. On her hands, her sacred birth rings glistened, untarnished from the preceding oblivion. And in her right hand, the message to Francois was still tightly held.

Bailey's Revelation

(circa 2014 [Y]time line)

Aaron stood over Bailey's limp form. She now lay stretched out and reclined in the professor's high-back, padded desk chair. It was a bit of a struggle to hoist her flaccid body into the chair without disturbing her wrist-hold. The look of distress on his face increased with each glance at the second hand of his analog wall clock. Glancing down at the side table, he verified the items needed upon Bailey's return to consciousness. The stack of fresh lined paper and several pencils and pens sat at the ready.

Aaron furled his brow as he counted the minutes. He muttered to himself, "I'm sure it was less than two minutes. Yes, definitely much less than two minutes." Aaron blinked disconcertingly as he pried open Bailey's left eyelid. The riveting action of the rapid eye movement was uninterrupted. The professor of physics held some knowledge of medicine. He checked the young woman's pulse. The grip on Bailey's left wrist by her right hand remained firm. He considered her pulse to be within safe limits. Leaning over closely to her face, he listened to her breathing. The deep and steady inhalation suggested the girl was in a simple sleep-like state. He held his hand to her forehead and wondered if Bailey might be a bit warm.

Glancing at the clock again, he let out a small gasp. "Oh dear (Y), it's been almost four minutes. Maybe, I'll apply a wet cloth to her forehead." At the kitchenette, Aaron wrung out a wet dishcloth. Walking back to the limp form of his student, the aging professor stopped dead in his tracks. He blinked repeatedly as the image before his eyes shifted impossibly. He watched steadfast as the surreal scene before him appeared to shimmer like water through a clear bowl. Before his eyes, in an instant, the image of Bailey Smith's right hand grasping her left wrist was transformed. As if in a mirror, the girl's prostrate form now had her right wrist held, vice-like, by her left hand.

Aaron rushed to her side as her eyes opened and she drew a deep breath. Looking up at Aaron, Bailey exclaimed frantically, "Oh! Cher Brahma! Francois, Francois C'etait horrible!" The grip on the young woman's right wrist became a full and desperate embrace of Aaron, about his neck. Sitting up in the chair, Bailey looked about the room. "Did I do it? Is anything different? What does the dollar bill say?"

Aaron answered, "It still says 'In God We Trust,' but there's still no Zoe. Nothing has changed in my memory."

Bailey rose to her feet and felt her face with her right hand as she stammered, "Francois, I sat down at your desk . . . Uh, I mean Aaron. I left a note for Francois. I started out by writing down the Variance equations. I told Francois to lose the duel and Not publish the work!"

Aaron peered deeply into Bailey's frantic expression as she continued, "Aaron, some hideous creature came at me. It was some kind of supernatural force. Part of me wants to call it Shiva and part of me wants to call it Le Diable! Aaron, I think it destroyed me. Somehow. I held the warning in my hand. It wanted me to burn it in the lamp. I wouldn't do it!"

Bailey reached for the waiting cup of coffee and drank deeply. The breathless girl settled down as she continued, "I think it consumed me somehow. The last thing I saw was an intense red light and intense heat!"

Aaron held the wet cloth to Bailey's forehead as he combed the thick locks from her face. He spoke softly, "Calm down, Dear. Calm down. You're all right, now. Listen, I'm going to get you some more coffee. Pull up your chair and begin to write everything that's in your mind. Do you have a 'total mind' of everything? Do you feel lucid?"

Bailey's grey eyes sparkled vibrantly as she answered. "Oh Aaron, I've never experienced such rapture in all my life. I've never imagined such an incredible vitality! And Aaron, it's not just Pyara and Bailey. There was a third life. I lived an entire life during the Revolutionary War, and Aaron, I was a man!"

Aaron's expression became deeply befuddled as he calmly placed the pen in Bailey's hand. "Write, Dear. Write as fast as you can. Put me to shame. I know you can write even more than 17 pages."

Bailey peered into the clamorous noontime cafeteria. She was definitely hungry. But her real appetite wasn't culinary in nature. Her grey eyes widened as she caught sight of Ibrahim sitting discretely in a far corner. Her curiosity was satisfied for the moment. After the "stand-up" at St. Michael's, she had wondered if he would have the courage to meet her at their agreed rendezvous.

Bailey entered the line of hungry patrons, grabbed a plate, and began the waiting process. She shook her head and grimaced slightly as she considered the kaleidoscope of events which had consumed the morning hours. She mused to herself, *Life!? Here it is almost Halloween 2014 and for the first time I understand the Spanish tradition of Dia de Muertos.*

Smiling to herself, she considered the fresh perspective of the simple activity of "having lunch." Was it really about sustenance? The absorbed background chatter and smells of the room seemed, at once, new and yet quite hackneyed. Bailey considered the revelation, which had occurred just hours earlier. She wondered if the trauma should have been enough to dissuade her from such a pedestrian activity.

An errant thought entered Bailey's mind. Francois L'Hospital had used the term "extra-color." The 300-year-old conversation bled into the moment. "If you think you see all there is to see, you do not see its meaning."

The thick dark locks of Bailey's hair almost dipped into her tray as she reached for the chocolate pudding cake. She stood upright and gazed at the crowd. A thin smile crept across her face as she considered the class work with her beloved parents. Shri'Ani translated her French father's words. "Whatever you think you see, there is always something more." The beautiful face of Pyara's green-eyed Indian mother lingered in the girl's mind.

"Girl! You're hungry today!" The smiling dark face of Ginnie suddenly filled Bailey's eyes. The cafeteria worker had been a long standing fixture in the student's life. Ginnie continued, "That baked salmon is sooo delicious! You're gonna love it!"

A distracted mind leaped to the 21st Century. The broad smile and wide eyes returned to the intense young woman as she responded, "Oh, Ginnie, I'm always so glad to see you at lunch! It wouldn't be school without my Ginnie!"

A genuine glow filled the cashier's face as she spoke, "I remember the first time I saw you, Bailey Smith. You walked into that line, way down at that end, and I said to myself, 'That beautiful young girl is somebody important. All these college professors and big thinkers are going to learn something from her!'"

The animate expression of the dark-haired, grey-eyed girl returned. "Ginnie, if my hands weren't full, I'd kiss you."

Ginnie keyed her register. "I've got your code, Sweetie. And I will hold you to that promise." The grey and black eyes of the two women met for just a moment as the smiles departed.

Holding the tray with both hands, Bailey began to walk the distance to Ibrahim. In just the short time since her arrival, the cafeteria had filled with more and more people. Threading her way through the crowd, Bailey lurched to a stop as a chair suddenly blocked her path. A startled boy spoke up, "Oh, I'm sorry! I didn't see you."

Bailey grimaced as she peered at the contents of her tray. She thought to herself. *I guess my meal and I have something in common.* The image of spawning salmon, swimming furiously upstream, flashed through her mind.

At that instant, a loud voice became recognizable. "Bailey! Bailey, we're over here!" The beleaguered Bailey turned a sidelong glance to the waving hands of Bekah and another student, Samantha.

Bailey thought to herself, *I better walk over and tell them I can't sit with them. Otherwise, they'll come over and bug us.*

Bailey pursued an expedient path and corrected the course from her destination. A glance at Ibrahim was met with a curious expression. Bailey nodded and grappled with the tray. She managed a single finger in the air to convey a signal. As she waggled the appendage, she mouthed the words, "Just a minute!"

As Bailey approached the two striking blonds, it occurred to her that the one disadvantage of being genuinely pretty was having a best friend who was the Viking Princess of Stockholm. She chuckled to herself as she muttered, "And then, there's Samantha Stewart. She definitely is the incarnation of some Scottish nymph goddess. The two of them need my company just to keep the wolves at bay."

Bailey mused one of Aaron LaSalle's inane jokes: *What do you call two blonds in the library?* She remembered her exact aplomb as he recanted the answer, *You call them book ends!* The endearing smile from the thought was planted on Bailey's face as she arrived at the girls' table.

Standing quiet and erect before the vivacious twin beauty queens, Bailey spoke up, "I have a date to sit with Ibrahim today." Bailey looked down at Bekah as she spoke.

Bekah's rapturous blue eyes twinkled as she responded. "Well, he is a handsome dark devil, isn't he?"

Bailey grimaced as she continued, "Are you meeting me at the Red Dragon after classes today?"

Bekah nodded. Bailey cast a quick glance at both girls and the contents of her tray as the directive to her legs was intervened by an unexpected incoming signal from her auditory senses.

"Bailey, tell me you're going to proctor LaSalle's physics test today!" Samantha sat eagerly, awaiting Bailey's answer.

Bailey resettled her stance as she abjectly responded. Her forced courtesy was obvious as she smiled meekly. "Yes, Sammy, I am."

Samantha smiled broadly. The fine contours of the girl's Gallic origins became pronounced. It occurred to Bailey that the facial delicacy of both Bekah and Samantha was quite similar. *An errant thought passed through Pyara's mind. Francois stood at the blackboard of their library. He traced the geometry of the "golden ratio." She recalled that, at that point, she could speak French quite well. "Oui, papa! The beautiful proportion speaks to the observer in a transcendental voice."*

The question which followed, in Bailey's mind, seemed odd. It had never occurred to her. *How could the Scottish people, a country as high in latitude as Sweden, have such a propensity for brown eyes? Both Francois, and of course, Aaron have brown eyes. They are both distinctly European in origin, but his eyes are almost identical to Ibrahim's.*

Samantha seemed to almost vibrate as she implored Bailey, "Bailey, I've been cramming all night! I don't know if I'll be ready this afternoon. Bekah's pretty good at this, too, but tell me you'll give me some hints during the test. Please, Bailey?"

Bailey looked over her lunch tray to see the open physics text. A sidelong glance at Bekah was greeted with a nonplussed grimace.

Bekah chewed patiently, swallowed, and responded, "I'm not going to be hungry all day. She's not even eating."

Samantha queried, "How could anyone even figure this stuff out? Listen to this question: 'If a fish weighing 42.2 Newtons is rapidly swimming upstream and jumps straight up from the water, how fast does it have to leave the water if it reaches its maximum apogee in precisely one second?'"

The look of bewilderment on Samantha's face was genuinely endearing. Bekah chuckled quietly as she studied Bailey's expression. The young Swede was enthralled with anticipation.

Bailey's normally animated demeanor returned. She glanced at her tray, wondering if the salmon was having the last laugh. She spoke up. "Samantha, it's a trick question! The mass of the fish has nothing to do with its thrust. The height is only dependent on the instantaneous velocity at the moment the fish leaves the water. The thrust from its tail will cease when it leaves the water!"

Samantha looked bewildered as she glanced at Bekah. Bekah grimaced, shrugging her shoulders as she answered, "Don't ask me! I don't have a clue!"

Bailey continued, "You'll find the correct answer by using {velocity equals the gravitational acceleration times the time}."

Bailey turned and began walking away. Calling back over her

shoulder, she spoke loudly, "Speaking of flying fish, mine's getting cold. Yes, I'll try to help you on the test."

Walking briskly, the beleaguered girl set her sights on her destination. She tracked Ibrahim's facial expression as she approached. It seemed to Bailey that the young man might be described as cowering in the corner seat. The complex mind of more than one life must now address a question far more involved than the physics of motion quandary.

Bailey set the tray down, making no eye contact with Ibrahim. She then sat down, quite abruptly. The only sound to be heard at the table was the jostling of silverware and a deep breath as the young woman prepared for the first bite of her lunch. Ibrahim continued to chew slowly, all the while studying his aloof dining companion. With each drink of cold tea, Bailey would peer over the glass, returning the stoic gaze. The couple's obstinate and mute demeanor lingered as Bailey continued eating.

Bailey's thoughts slowed, and for several moments, she considered the regret of her life without the total awareness of the previous incarnations. She recalled Aaron's comment, *"I know who I have also been, but it's like trying to remember what I ate for lunch last Thursday."* Bailey wondered if the lingering trauma of spontaneous human combustion would also pass as equally unremarkable. The clinical mind of the young scientist finally determined that the scales of indecision had tilted in Ibrahim's favor.

"Well, I guess we could play this child's game until I finish eating, and I then walk away, just as silently." The pert expression on Bailey's face spoke volumes.

Ibrahim's stare remained inviolate. He paced his response with the precision of a virtuoso, speaking softly, "I wanted to come to your church and meet your family. I truly did. I am lonely in your country, and you have given me my only companionship."

The mind of the colonial soldier, Riley O'Reilly, spoke out to Bailey's intimate friend, "That's a touching sentiment. Given the predicament we find ourselves in, I would like to accept it as genuine."

Ibrahim shifted his head slightly as he suppressed the urge to blink. He posited his question delicately, "You do believe me, don't you?"

A thin smile crept across Bailey's face as "Riley" continued, "I believe you love me. But I also believe that you just defined love a bit too succinctly."

Ibrahim adjusted himself in his seat as he took the first drink from his cup of coffee. His soft brown eyes widened as he set the cup down and leaned across the table, returning Bailey's gaze. A warm smile came across his face. "Yes, I do love you."

Bailey smiled warmly and answered, "I love you, too."

A moment passed as "Riley" held Bailey's expression fixed. He knew that the child's game conveyed much more meaning than the academic realized. The opulent grey and brown embrace of the couple's stare held a deeper promise. Ibrahim's paced tone shifted as his gaze turned from Bailey. Returning the coffee to his face, he peered into the dark steamy fluid and blinked.

Bailey studied the Middle-Eastern features of the handsome young man. "Helen says you look like Omar Sharif."

Ibrahim looked up and blinked hard. "Who is this Omar?"

Bailey perked up as she answered, "He is a famous Hollywood actor. He's Egyptian in origin."

Ibrahim grimaced as he answered, "The faithful of the Shia Islam know the blasphemes of the Hadith of the Sunni tribes."

A bewildered expression filled Bailey's face as Pyara muttered out loud, *"Whatever you think you see, there is always something more."*

Ibrahim's brown eyes strained as he queried, "What is that, you say?"

Bailey smirked as she answered, "I've always found it so remarkable that people become so irate over the religious convictions of others."

Ibrahim retorted, "You would find it less mysterious if the others you speak of had killed your brother or your children."

Bailey inhaled deeply as she reminded herself of the "horns of the dilemma" upon which she was impaled. She spoke quietly, "How do you think I could have become pregnant?"

Ibrahim spoke up, eagerly. "It is the Will of Allah! He wishes for me to bring sons to this world."

The mind of three people stared back at the foreign young man. Bailey considered the great knowledge she possessed and the transcendent wisdom which had been thrust upon her. Riley knew that such cerebral acumen meant little when combating the mind of a zealot or a child.

([S]time line)

Bailey queried, "Do you know about the work of Francois L'Hospital?"

Ibrahim guffawed. "I hate the Masons more than I hate the Sunnis!"

Bailey grimaced as Riley spoke out of her mouth, *"What do you think of the American Revolution?"*

Ibrahim almost snorted. "The Revolution against the British was good. The British suppressed my people for hundreds of years. When Sharia Law is allowed to coexist with your constitution, America will be a great country!"

Bailey drank deeply from her glass of tea. Her sidelong glance at Bekah and Samantha was met with hectic waves and beaming smiles. The forlorn faces of three lives meekly smiled back. The thought of the New York City apocalypse and the fate of Zoe saddened her. Bailey muttered to herself, *"Yes, time travel is quite real. I guess Helen and Aaron are right; the dollar bill is wrong. It's supposed to say 'In God We Trust.'"*

([Y]time line)

The mind of three people stared back at the foreign young man. Bailey considered the great knowledge she possessed and the transcendent wisdom, which had been thrust upon her. Riley knew that such cerebral acumen meant little when combating the mind of a zealot or a child.

Bailey queried. "Do you know about Aaron LaSalle's work?"

Ibrahim guffawed, loudly. "I hate all science that tries to replace religion!"

Bailey grimaced as Riley spoke out. *"What do you think of the American Revolution?"*

Ibrahim almost snorted, "The Revolution against the British was good. The British suppressed my people for hundreds of years. When Sharia Law is allowed to coexist with your constitution, America will be a great Country!"

Bailey drank deeply from her glass of tea. Her sidelong glance at Bekah and Samantha was met with hectic waves and beaming smiles. The forlorn faces of three lives meekly smiled back.

Bailey muttered to herself, *"Yes, time travel is quite real. I wonder if that should be Zoe sitting there with Bekah. I can see her and feel my love for her, but it's harder to see the second (Y)time line where New York City isn't going to be destroyed. I guess Helen and Aaron are right; the dollar bill can't be changed. It must never say 'On God We Depend.'*

Bailey looked at Ibrahim thoughtfully and asked, "Have you ever owned a pet?"

Ibrahim's expression remained stoic as he answered, "I had a dog for a while when I was very young. It was taken when the village didn't have enough food to feed them. The Imam decreed that pets weren't allowed."

Bailey looked at her empty plate. She fought back the sadness as she spoke, "Did you love your puppy?"

Ibrahim nodded silently, affirming the question. Bailey continued, assertively, "Do you think your puppy loved you?"

The expression which leaped into Ibrahim was disturbing. Bailey blinked defensively. The young man became reactive, and exclaimed, "What kind of nonsense do you hit me with? I think little of the beasts. Allah has love only for the faithful servant!"

Bailey waved her hands in a fanning motion as she spoke encouragingly, "Calm down, Ibrahim, calm down! Here's the point I'm making. All life is sacred. Love is not exclusive to a point of view, a society, or even absent in animals."

Ibrahim spoke intently, "You sound like a Rabbi. In Genesis, chapter 2, all the animals were named by Adam and the law was given."

Bailey sat in wonder with Ibrahim's impressive response. She continued, "Well yeah, that's what I'm talking about! God made the point that all life is sacred."

Ibrahim shook his head, disapprovingly, as he retorted, "You do not know the Hadith 38. The Wilayah tells us that Allah loves those who are the closer servants to Allah."

Bailey's eyes widened as her brow line furled. She grimaced slightly before speaking. "Do you understand the concept of circular reasoning?" A look of bewilderment came over Ibrahim.

Bailey leaned into the table and looked intently into Ibrahim's gaze. "You have demanded that I convert to your religion for us to be married. I've been reading the Koran. I have a question. What do you think of chapter 9, verse 5?

Ibrahim's expression demurred. "You are a smart woman. I knew that you had a soft heart. Now, I know that you are much stronger."

Bailey smiled curiously. "So you know the verse?" Ibrahim nodded, affirmatively. Bailey continued, "Don't you think the phrase 'kill the idolaters wherever you find them' is a little convenient if you just don't happen to like somebody?"

Ibrahim remained stoic as the moments passed silently. Bailey continued, "All right, I could go on about the subjugation of women, death to homosexuals, and a rather flagrant contempt for other religions, but here's the point. I want you to tell me how any God could be so callous?"

Ibrahim responded, quietly, "The world must be purged of idolaters. It is called the Caliphate. The world will become as one with the Islamic prophet."

Bailey grimaced as she continued, "There is an interesting correlation to the New Testament Book of Revelation. The 66th Book, The Apocalypse of John, describes a world at war between good and evil. Which side do you believe you stand on?"

Ibrahim interrupted, "Your 1st Book of Genesis describes the destruction of Sodomites. God will only preserve the righteous."

Bailey smiled broadly as she spoke up. "That's right! And there is something you must consider. Tell me what this Caliphate believes to be the new Sodom and Gomorrah?"

Ibrahim smirked as he answered. "Only the sheep don't know the answer to that question."

Bailey spoke up. "That may be the case, but I am no sheep. I will tell you why the Islamic terrorists will fail. I will tell you why the prophecy will fail. I will tell you why Yahweh will save New York City."

Ibrahim's expression remained cold. The voice from the young woman grew stern as the spirit of three lives spoke her words, "In Genesis 18, verses 16 thru 33, Abraham argued with God. No, he pleaded with God.

'If there be but 50 good men, would you sweep away the righteous with the wicked? And the Lord said, for fifty I will spare them. And Abraham, again spoke. Lord, what if there be but forty, will you not spare them? And God answered, for the sake of forty, I will not do it. Abraham humbled himself with his question. Lord, what if there be but thirty? He answered; I will not do it for thirty. Again, the question came. Would you not do it for twenty good men? I will not do it for twenty. Abraham implored God's forgiveness. Lord what if there be but ten? And He answered. For the sake of ten I will not destroy it."

Bailey sat silently, peering into Ibrahim's intense stare. No words were needed. Bailey spoke quietly, "I was going to convert to your faith. I know many good and true Muslims who follow the poetry of the Koran's verse. The good and the evil can be found in all religions. I pass no judgment on your faith. I only pass judgment on intolerance. I follow a belief in which goodness allows separate things to exist. And evil works too capriciously to destroy something that's different, even if other options exist. This morning, I experienced the wrath of Hell for my betrayal of my faith. I cannot pass judgment on you, but I will bring the flesh I'm bringing into this world unto the faith of a God of love. I will not marry you, Ibrahim."

Bailey stood up and looked timidly at the young man seated before her. Ibrahim's stare appeared to have no focus as the soul and wisdom of many lives turned and walked away.

(October 26, 2014 [S]time line)

Helen shuffled the stack of typed papers as she spoke. "Boy, today was crazy. I had to pick up a test. The student was cheating!"

The papers and other items rested on Aaron's side table. Helen looked up at Aaron LaSalle sitting a few feet away at his desk.

Aaron spoke up, "Bailey's last class should be over about now, and she'll be along." The professor of natural science glanced over his left shoulder to see the gaze of the vivid jade eyes of his fellow academic.

A wry smile crept across Helen's face as she spoke, "Do you want me to make us all some coffee?" Aaron raised his eyebrows as he nodded, approvingly.

Helen stood up and walked over to Aaron's kitchenette as she said, "I have had such vivid dreams since I began the Reveal!* It's very odd. I sleep much more heavily, and I don't know how to explain it. But I feel like there's . . . Well, I don't know how to explain it. It's like I'm a child and I know mom and dad are in the other room."

Aaron looked up from the computer. His look was met by Helen's smiling face, her dark green eyes returning his stare.

Aaron stepped over to the table and took a drink from the hot tea as Helen said, "Here're the sheets. Oh, I typed out the hand-written diary. I wasn't sure you could read my writing."

Aaron sorted through the sheets. He stopped suddenly and looked up, peering at Helen with a questioning stare. A rather nervous look filled the English professor's face as she whispered. "I know. There are 31 entries. I forgot to number the entries . . ."

Aaron read the last entry:

"October twenty fifth, two thousand and fourteen II Corinthians

4:18. 'While we look not at the things which are seen, but at the things which are not seen: for the things which are seen are temporal; but the things which are not seen are eternal.'"

Aaron smiled warmly as he spoke, "The technique invites guidance and instruction. This last entry shows me that your Reveal has been guided."

Helen smiled broadly as she replied, "It's really interesting isn't it? It's talking about the issue isn't it? I mean look at the words—things that are seen are of time; things that are not seen are eternal!"

Aaron's soft brown eyes seemed to twinkle as he spoke, "My random studies have repeatedly shown connectivity across time. The step-by-step invariant rate is subject to variance when compared to the geometric expansion."

Helen grimaced as she replied, "I understand that you were French, but you really need to stick with English right now."

Aaron retorted, "I have an important phrase that I use a lot. 'Whatever you think you see, there is always something more.' I call it the principle of the 'extra-color.'"

Helen asked, "So it's okay?"

Aaron responded, "Did you do everything else scrupulously?" Helen nodded her head in agreement. Aaron smiled as he continued. "Well, I won't try to explain this right now, but this means that a woman must do the Reveal 31 times. I was told in the DV of 1988 that I was not to perform it more than 30."

Helen spoke up. "Well, there's something else. The entry for 10/21/14 called for the exact same entry as 10/8/14! How could it do that?"

Aaron flipped to the entry and read:

"Genesis 28:15 And, behold, I am with thee, and will keep thee in all places whither thou goest, and will bring thee to this land:

for I will not leave thee, until I have that which I have spoken to thee of."

Helen spoke up. "You know, it really is uncanny. The verses speak of a return to location, like the double entry in the diary."

Aaron grimaced. "Well, it corrected itself, didn't it? There are 30 entries!"

A distressed look filled the sharp features of the jade-eyed beauty. Helen shook her auburn locks back and forth, disagreeably, as she spoke up. "Well, that's not quite right either. For the 10/17/2014 entry, I was led to Genesis 28 :17. Just as I recorded the entry, the die fell to the floor! I don't really know how I did it, so I recorded the 'second time' entry."

Aaron guffawed. "So there really are 31 distinct entries!"

Helen's expression was timid as her hair bounced vertically in agreement. Aaron read the twin entries:

"Genesis 28:17 And he was afraid, and said, How dreadful is this place! This is none other but the house of God, and this is the gate of Heaven. (Jacob's 'ladder' dream) And the second entry Colossians 3:12-13 (12)Put on therefore as the elect of God, holy and beloved, bowels of mercies, kindness, humbleness of mind, meekness, longsuffering; and (13)Forbearing one another, and forgiving one another, if any man have a quarrel against any: even as Christ forgave you, so also you, also do ye. Humbleness, love, forgiveness."

Helen and Aaron both looked up, a bit startled, as the door to Aaron's office opened.

"Hi! It's me . . . Well, I might as well say, it's us." The smiling face and animate personage of one Bailey Smith smiled from the doorway.

Aaron reached over and picked up the thick, hand-written pages as he spoke up. "Grab some coffee, Bailey. You're right on time!

Helen and I just went over her Reveal. I have several thousand questions for you. I want to discuss the Authority with both of you. It's the most significant aspect of the (S)time line we're in."

Bailey set her backpack and materials beside the empty chair at the side table. "Give me your cups," she said. "I'll freshen your drinks. After all, a servant is the most loved."

Aaron and Helen's eyes met in perfect cadence. The synchronous curiosity required no audible words.

Bailey set the steaming cups on their napkins and sat down with a beaming smile. "Boy, I'm glad this day is over! My last class had a calculus test. It was interrupted when a student almost got his test picked up. The boy was messing with his cell phone."

A curious sidelong glance returned to both professors as Aaron spoke up. "There really are no coincidences."

Bailey caught the shared expression and queried, "What have I missed?"

Helen responded, "You made two rather poignant comments. Of course, that's why we're here isn't it?"

Aaron smiled wryly as he chimed in, "It's interesting how some people relate to one another more readily than others. I've always been curious about the colloquial comment, 'I don't like him or her.'"

Bailey completed the "Round Robin." "Well, if there were ever three people that had a reason to like one another, it would be us. Mom and Dad aren't any happier with my new decision than they were with the old one. Dad said, 'A child without his last name will be neither a son nor a grandson.'"

The forlorn look in Bailey's eyes reminded Helen of her recent dreams. It was as if she could hear the doleful howl of Balto through Bailey's eyes.

Helen smiled broadly, peering deeply into Bailey's damp, grey eyes as she spoke, "Well, I know we all have fragmented memories from 300 years ago. But for whatever reason, I can ask this like your mother. What do you really think about the pregnancy?"

Bailey's expression remained stoic as she answered calmly, "I think it was (S). I think that little wriggler was given wings, or maybe a jack hammer. I mean, let's face it; there is some sort of serious agenda afoot. And New York City getting nuked two years ago was just part of it. I mean, what's next!?"

Aaron peered at the two women through the steam of his tea. Setting the cup down, he asked, "Bailey, when you came in, you referenced the love for a servant being the greatest thing. I guess my ethnicity is showing, but I know something about that issue."

Bailey smiled wryly as she responded, "That's funny. I didn't even realize it. I was giving a signal, wasn't I? Maybe, it's Pyara or Riley working through me. It would have to be Riley. Pyara only knows Shiva. Riley knows the bible, forwards and backwards. Why wouldn't he? It's funny to think that I was a Catholic priest in the Revolutionary War."

The look on Helen's face turned to astonishment as she blurted out, "What!?"

Aaron's attention to Bailey never ceased. "I want to know about the conversation with Ibrahim."

Bailey responded, "He and I had a rather intense religious conversation. I mean, the ecclesiastics at the United Nations should be so pithy, yet loquacious." Bailey diverted her eyes to Aaron, with a quick smile as she continued, "One of the things I wanted to ask about today was the proficiency of the 'total mind.' Like right now, I look at you and I know you're 300 years old, but all I see is Aaron. But when I had this somewhat frightening conversation with Ibrahim, I was Riley O' Reilly. And man, you don't want to frick with me! I mean, I should have been a warrior/priest in the

2nd Great Religious War!"

Aaron queried, "So he quoted the verse in the Koran about the servant being the most loved by Allah?" Bailey nodded her head, agreeably. Aaron asked, "And how did you answer?"

Bailey responded. "Well, I referenced Genesis 2:20. I used this to illustrate that all living things are sacred and that companionship is more important than servitude. The 21st verse is the parable where (Y) took Adam's rib to make Eve. He didn't have a clue!"

Aaron smiled broadly as he spoke, "The true God admires our service, one to the other, not idolatry or servitude in any form."

Bailey nodded her head agreeably as she spoke, "I didn't even try to explain. I finished the point by asking if he understood circular reasoning. I mean, what kind of God wants nothing but sycophants!?"

Helen leaned forward as she asked tenderly, "So what have you decided?"

Bailey's eyes demurred as she answered, "I will have to suffer the shame of illegitimacy. I will bring the child into this vicious world, already handicapped by an imbalanced family. Every child instinctively hungers for a mother and a father." Bailey picked up the napkin from under her coffee and wiped the tear from her right cheek as she continued, "It's so odd. I have four of the finest parents any soul could ever want, and my child will only have me. I guess (S) will win after all. I guess that's why 'It' incinerated me."

Aaron spoke assertively, "Don't be vague, Bailey. Say it clearly."

Bailey grimaced as she responded, "Yeah, you're right. (S) likes to mess with people who seem to have everything going for them, but we have to allow it."

Aaron nodded, approvingly.

Bailey spoke meekly, "It happened because I told my parents I was going to betray my Catholic faith and convert to Muslim."

Aaron's stare never left Bailey's riveting grey eyes. He continued to nod as he spoke. "Spontaneous human combustion has nothing to do with flammable oxidation. It results from macro quantum physics and can therefore be caused by a conscious divine entity."

Bailey's thick dark brown locks swirled characteristically as she mused, "All right, we tried for two years to figure out what happened to change the time line. We've all been devastated by the meeting, at this table, when we heard Zoe's voice for the last time. But we also know there is an alternate (Y)time line. So how do we get back to the right reality? How do we undo your mistake, Aaron?" Bailey shifted in her seat as she became emphatic. "No, what I'm trying to say is this: If everything is interconnected, will the return to the original (Y)time line mean I won't have this baby? Does the punishment I suffered as Pyara, trying to fix it, mean that I've only made the problem worse?"

Aaron fanned his hands in a calming fashion as he spoke quietly, "Bailey, the real question is, 'How did you slip without even doing a Reveal?' I knew there was some possibility that your read of my diary might trigger it because I already knew you were Pyara. But here is the question. Was it (Y) or (S) that triggered your slip?"

Bailey's expression turned blank as she answered, "I see what you're saying. I've assumed that Satan sent you to your previous life to create his dominion when you intervened and prevented the Newtown sacrifice. So when you interrupted the Authority, (S) sent you back to deliver the information that there is a Super-Consciousness. But if (S) sent me back to the 17th Century, why would he run the risk that I might succeed in returning the (Y)time line."

Aaron sat quietly with a wry smile on his face.

Bailey nearly jumped in her seat. "It was Yahweh that sent me back!"

Helen grimaced as she interrupted their conversation, "Oh, you beautiful physics nerds. I wish I had a clue what you're talking about."

Aaron retorted, "Not physics . . . It's meta-physics. Look, the reason that Bailey slipped is because of her world view. Her acumen of scientific knowledge and spiritual level allowed (Y) to intercede. He attempted it because Bailey's freewill was being tested. She might get back there and either leave the message or burn it up. It passed the rules of the Authority, and that meant that (Y) could intervene!"

Helen responded, "You spoke of the Authority before Bailey got here. I've heard the concept; I had religious courses, of course. Frankly, I didn't even know the term meant anything. But here's the point. My 8th entry in my Reveal diary spoke of the Authority."

Aaron grabbed Helen's diary as Bailey jumped from her seat and ran to Aaron's side.

Bailey mouthed the entry as Aaron read out loud:

"October second, two thousand fourteen, Saint Luke 20:2 'And spake unto him, saying, tell us, by what authority doest thou these things? or, who is he that gave thee this authority?'"

Helen looked aghast as she watched Aaron and Bailey begin hugging and exclaiming uproariously. She meekly queried, "What . . . What is it?"

Aaron resettled himself and turned to Helen. "It's you, Helen! You're the key!"

Bailey leaned across the table as she spoke up, "Helen, I now understand my broad-mindedness. I was Hindu, Catholic, a girl, a man, and now a woman and a Catholic scientist. Aaron is like a divine fixture. He was a scientist, a soldier, a man, a man, and now he's a scientist and a man. If that's not like boring enough, he was Jewish—every time! And he's still fighting for things like a soldier. He's so stable; he shouldn't even have been reincarnated. His karma is like divine!"

Helen's meek expression turned sour as she spoke, "Oh, I get it now! I'm the gentile. I'm the pagan liberal who has to make the choice for the good God . . ."

The wildly-joyous expression returned to both faces as Helen sat dumbfounded. Aaron leaned forward and spoke encouragingly, "Well, sort of, but it's more complicated than that. If you weren't somebody who had done, or tried to do, something really wonderful, something that required your total sacrifice, you wouldn't be here!"

Helen again, spoke timidly, "Is that supposed to make me feel better?"

Bailey spoke up, "Yes. All this means that you will have a 'time-slip.' You had to have had one more extra life, like Aaron and I. But you haven't had a slip. So none of us have any awareness of it."

Aaron chimed in, "Do you see the infinite poetry in it? We were all together, three lifetimes ago, separate in our second lives, and we've been brought back together to set the world right. Helen, we even get to see our grandchild this time!"

A befuddled look filled Helen's face as she said, "I don't think I'm up to it. You two don't get it. Aaron scares me to death. I try not to even think about him. Look, I've never been intimidated by anyone in my life. Now, there're two of you Titans. What the Hell can I do?"

Bailey laughed uproariously. "Oh, Helen! I guarantee you. You were something to be dealt with. Have you looked in the mirror lately? You aren't simply ravishing; those piercing eyes of yours could kill!"

Helen spoke meekly, "So I can expect one of these raptures, like you two experienced?" Heads nodded as she continued, "Will I be sent back by (S) or (Y)?"

Bailey and Aaron spoke up, synchronously, "(Y), of course!"

Aaron continued, "I need to give you a quick meta-physics lesson. It will prepare your spirit for the rapturous encounter. When you experience the 'total mind,' your world view cannot be in conflict with the genuine nature of reality."

The look on Helen's face appeared as a child being urged to take her first step. She spoke up cautiously, "Is this going to turn me into a Republican!?"

CHAPTER SIX

Supra-Natural

(October 26, 2014 [S] time-line)

Helen's expression appeared befuddled. "All right, I believe in a transcendental reality, like any other good Buddhist, but here's my question: I now know I was Hindu, and if that isn't strange enough, I was also married to the ecclesiastic Francois L'Hospital! If that's why this is happening, how does it involve me? I mean, L'Hospital is a cornerstone of the Masonic Religion."

Bailey and Aaron turned one to the other and smiled wryly. Bailey answered, "Helen, the curriculum for a bachelor's degree only requires (Psy) 101. But there are no bachelor's degrees in meta-physics. A student must have a bachelor's degree in physics to apply for a graduate degree in meta-physics. And you must pass tests proving that you have psychical abilities."

Helen's jade eyes sparkled. "I guess I didn't know all that, but I've taken the (psy) tests. I score very high, particularly in the empathic senses." The professor of Literature and English pursed her lips as her curious expression returned. She continued, "So there are no undergraduate degrees in paranormal studies?"

Both Aaron and Bailey slow-shook their heads, left to right and right to left, in concert.

A comedic smile filled Helen's face as she quipped, "Why didn't I know that? I'm not sure that's generally understood!"

Aaron responded, "You are aware that the (psy) department is sanctioned by the Supreme Court, right?"

Helen nodded. "Sure, I know that. And I know that some

graduates hold police powers, like my ex-husband here." Helen smiled broadly as she smirked in Aaron's direction, "Just kidding, Aaron!"

Helen continued, "I'm a tenured professor. Why am I ignorant of something as remedial as the curriculum requirements for one of the university departments?"

Aaron spoke up, "It's not supposed to be generally known. Did you know there's a program for 'remote viewing'? We study the files of freshmen. The department contacts eligible students, but we do so through clandestine, indirect methods. They don't even know it's been contrived."

A thin smile formed on Bailey's lips as she piped in, "Bekah has the dreams. I was sent to determine if she should be contacted."

A look of exasperation filled Helen's face. "Are you serious? I had no idea! So you people really are just mysterious Druids. You exist outside the real world, don't you?"

Aaron replied, "Bekah was my daughter in my second life, during the 2nd Great Religious War. She's suffering trauma from an episode in her youth as a German child. She hasn't come to terms with it. We can't accept her in the department."

Helen nearly shouted, "Well! Are you going to help her?"

Aaron grimaced. "That's not how the Twin Law works. We have to be very subtle in these matters. It has to do with Berlin when it was bombed and on fire. I can't speak of it."

Helen exclaimed, "Who were you, then? Don't you still love her?"

Bailey gave Aaron a side-long glance as he responded first, "Helen you're demonstrating why you were never contacted."

The jade fire in Helen's eyes grew hot as she jumped up in her chair. "Well, if I'm too sensitive, then, why do you need me now?"

Aaron grimaced as he waved his hands in a calming fashion. "Helen, I've dreamed of Bekah since the time-slip. Yes, it's painful. I was with her during the city's destruction in 1944. But she now has a sister."

A curious expression filled Helen's face as she turned to the smiling face of Bailey. Helen guffawed as she said, "Look, I said it earlier! I can't do this! You two Jedi's will have to do this on your own."

Aaron spoke quietly, "Helen, there are no coincidences. Don't you get it? Even this distraction has a point. The city's mass death by fire, two years ago, has been brought even closer. You are the only one that has been given a sign that the Authority may intervene."

Helen's eyes softened as she spoke quietly, "Is there no other way?" Bailey and Aaron again slow-shook their heads left to right and right to left—again, in concert. Helen rose up and looked in the eyes of her two dearest friends. She spoke softly, "What do I need to know?"

Aaron sat quietly for a moment, staring at the table. He glanced up at Bailey and asked, "Would you get us some fresh coffee and tea dear?"

Bailey perked up and collected the cups.

Aaron adjusted his chair and looked directly at Helen. "Okay, I have less information to explain and much more attitude to share. Are you familiar with Shakespeare's Hamlet?"

The English professor's thick auburn locks bounced eagerly in affirmation.

Aaron continued, "Well, one of my favorite quotes from Hamlet is 'Brevity is the essence of wit.'"

Helen's rich green eyes sparkled as she chimed in, "I always liked Samuel Clemens' 'Truth is stranger than fiction.'"

Aaron smiled broadly as he responded, "Yes, you get the idea. There are pivotal ideas that either we grab onto and make use of in our thinking or we ignore them. I'm going to begin by telling you the old New England crab fisherman's tale." Aaron smiled as Helen's attention remained fixed. "There was a young Jack on a blue crab fishing boat. The old ship's mate told the lad that there was one important rule. 'Lad you must never place just one crab in the bucket.' The youth wondered about the rule, but agreed. Now, the crab bucket is a large metal pail about the size of a 5-gallon bucket. You can put a lot of hand-sized crabs in it."

Helen smiled broadly as she drank deeply from her coffee cup and settled in for the story.

Aaron continued, "Now, as time went on, the lad worked hard and carried thousands of crabs in the large buckets. From time to time, the boy would ask about the rule. 'Why must I not put just one crab in the bucket?' The wise old seaman would only smile and ignore the question. One day, the lad was about to pour the bucket of crabs into the hold when the old ship's mate told him to stop and set the bucket down. 'Lad, what do you see in the bucket?' The young sailor answered, 'A bucket full of crabs.' The old mate asked. 'Is it full of crabs?' The lad answered. 'It is full to the brim!' The old mate asked. 'Can a single crab escape from the bucket?' The lad laughed loudly. 'No, I've never seen a single crab escape from the bucket!'"

Aaron continued, "The old seaman reached out and took one crab from the bucket. Then, he told the lad to empty the bucket of crabs into the hold and set the bucket on the deck. The old mate then placed the solitary crab into the empty bucket. 'Now, watch the bucket lad.' The young jack sailor watched as the crab reached up with its pincer towards the bucket's brim. It did not reach. The lad watched as the crab clamored on its eight legs to reach the brim. It did not reach. The sailor stared in amazement as the teetering, frenzied creature just managed to balance itself on its side and pinch the very top edge of the bucket with the very tip of its scissor-like appendage. The young man watched as the crab pulled itself up, teetered tightrope-like on the brim, and fell out of the bucket onto the deck."

Aaron sat back in his chair and, taking a deep drink from his tea, peered into Helen's sparkling green eyes.

Helen smiled wryly as she said, "Well, it might be a physics lesson. Gravity was involved."

Aaron chuckled as he answered. "You can do better than that."

Helen grimaced. "Okay, let's see. What is the moral?" The teacher of literature sat for a moment with a ponderous stare. She spoke up, meekly, "You know, it really must be obvious, but I'm not sure how to say it best. One moral would be, to work hard and you'll succeed."

Aaron grimaced as he repeated himself, "You can do better than that."

Helen grimaced indignantly, "Now, I know how my freshmen feel."

Aaron smiled broadly as he replied, "That's a good answer! But here's the point. When the crab is confined with others, it will never escape. The other crabs will always 'pull the solitary crab down.'"

Helen appeared somewhat dejected. "I get it. The survival instinct is a balancing act."

Aaron guffawed. "No! The example doesn't speak about balance, equivalence, fairness or even pragmatism. It speaks of all aspects of life. It refers to any consideration. 'Too many cooks can spoil the soup.' 'The committee that designs a horse ends up with a jack-ass.' 'Cast your pearls before swine, lest they turn to rend you.' And it even speaks of selfish abandon."

Helen giggled as she retorted, "But what about cooperation and love?"

Aaron sat quite stoically, his soft brown eyes peering back at Helen indignantly. "What about it?"

Helen grimaced as she answered meekly, "Well, that's how things go forward, isn't it?"

Aaron retorted, "Why didn't the old ship's mate tell the sailor jack the answer to the riddle to start with?"

Helen pondered for a moment before she answered. "I guess it wouldn't have meant as much."

Aaron rebuked, "Do you just say those words, or do you really understand their meaning?"

Helen's gaze remained as she sat pondering.

Aaron continued, "Earlier, I spoke of the 'extra-color.' 'Whatever you think you see, there is always more.' The old sailor was reaching into the boy's soul and giving him much more than information. The foolishness of the priesthood of academia, of all forms of politics, is a bias for information. It is a trite thing. There is a spectrum of truth—information, knowledge, wisdom. There are larger realities. Sensation is split into pain, bliss—awareness splits into emotion, logic, the cardinal emotions being love and hate. The ascent to wisdom teeters on the bifurcation of the fabric of reality itself—good and evil."

The table and its party sat silently for some moments. Bailey leaned forward, retrieved her cup of coffee and took a drink.

She asked, "Helen, was the crab that escaped the bucket a socialist? Did the young sailor learn something about human nature?"

Helen laughed. "I really do get the point. We start out like the boy on the fishing boat. But do we ever grow up?"

Aaron smiled approvingly as he spoke, "Winston Churchill

said, 'If someone under 30 isn't a liberal, I worry about their heart. If someone over 30 isn't a conservative, I worry about their brain.' Now, you know why you were given the sign. Everything is connected. Sometimes the mind is the object of its own self-interest. Sometimes it must remain selfless. I now know that for the last 300 years, the creator God didn't want itself known. We are all just cells in a far larger organism. Each mind is its own universe. But there is a Super-Consciousness. And that mind is bifurcated into twin hemispheres of good and evil. The information would not have prevented the world wars or stopped the crabs from cannibalizing themselves."

Helen's intense stare reached beyond Aaron's gaze. "Humanity is capable of anything. But our childish preconceptions prevent so much."

Aaron retorted, "You're getting there. But explore these words. 'Any act, or intent, which impedes a separate thing from being all that it can be, is evil. Any act, or intent, that allows a separate thing to be all that it can be, is good.'"

Helen smiled as she peered into Aaron's soft brown eyes. "All right, so people will always show their worse nature, particularly when stressed. And that says a lot about political and social realities, but what does it tell me about productive cooperation?"

Aaron shook his head gently as he said, "You're demonstrating how diligently the mind works to maintain its own preconceptions."

Helen smirked as she retorted, "Well, all perspectives must be considered a working theory or even a holistic concept."

Aaron rebuked, "You have enough information right now to experience a revelation in your world view."

A befuddled look crept across the English professor's face. "Well, I guess I do think more qualitatively. Okay. I'll shift more blood to the left side of my brain."

Helen sat silently, awaiting Aaron's response.

"It really is about the crabs," he finally said. "The orthodoxy of socialism is built upon the fallacy of Central Planning. It's a compelling notion which motivates a great many naive souls. The acolytes of Identity politics, the mind control of politically correct speech, denial of a higher Being—ultimately, the sycophants of their own moral superiority always hand themselves over to a tyrant. As hard as they try to deny it, the collectivists demonstrate that atheism is simply another religion."

Helen chuckled as she muttered, "You really are an alien aren't you?"

Helen gave Bailey a sidelong glance. Her gaze was greeted with a broad smile.

Aaron continued, "Helen, the Big Bang occurred about 14-1/2 billion years ago. The first generation stars contained only hydrogen. Billions of supernovae explosions threw heavy elements into the Universe. Around 10 billion years ago, solar systems began to accrete. The lighter elements formed new stars and the heavy elements formed planets."

Helen drank deeply from her coffee cup as she said, "Keep going, I'm all ears."

Aaron continued, "Around 4-1/2 billion years ago, the earth was a rusty, muddy ball. The atmosphere was mostly carbon dioxide and nitrogen. Here's the point. It stayed like that for around one billion years. Then, the first step in the evolving process occurred, spontaneously. Early cyanobacteria algae formed, and over eons, precipitated fossilized limestone mats called stromatolites. These can be seen from orbit in the waters, mostly around Australia. Now, here's the wonder. The photosynthesis produced by this primitive plant life filled the atmosphere and the oceans with oxygen. The earth became a blue world, one that could support complex life."

Aaron smirked as he continued, "I know it's pretty boring, but I'm getting to the interesting part. The only life that existed 3-1/2 billion years ago was this first plant-like cyanobacteria. There was no survival of the fittest, no mutation, and no natural selection. Period! The DNA in each cell in our bodies could be stretched out from your feet to the top of your head. It's only a hundred or so atoms in cross section, so it can be spindled down to fit in each microscopic cell. It contains so much information you could fill many encyclopedias. Now, here's the magic! The DNA in the nucleoid of the cyanobacteria can be stretched out to reach from your feet to about your waist."

Helen interrupted. "You mean most of the information that makes me "me" is necessary just to make one bacterial cell?"

Aaron implored, "Do you really understand what I'm saying? There was no natural selection involved. There were no simpler cells. The incredible amount of information necessary to create the algae cells that turned the earth into a living planet occurred spontaneously. Now, amino acids can be made in a high school chemistry lab. They've even been found in meteorites. But that's as different from the DNA molecule as a few scattered alphabet letters are from Shakespeare's Hamlet."

The English professor smiled as she quipped, "I know there's an eight-legged point to this, isn't there?"

Aaron smiled broadly as he continued, "You see how smart you are? Yes, they'll scuttle back into the conversation any second now. Around 3-1/2 billion years ago, the earth's atmosphere began to contain oxygen. This Pre-Cambrian period gave way to complex life on earth around 500 million years ago."

Helen mused, "So life is just a string of data and we really don't have a clue where it came from?"

Aaron smiled wryly as he continued, "Exactly! The earliest crustacean life—like lobsters, crabs—they fed on varieties of early pre-skeletal creatures. Did you know that spiders aren't insects, they're the early crustaceans that came out of the oceans and chased the six legged creatures that evolved in the early tidal pools?"

Helen interjected, "So the crabs ate the fish and learned to eat insects."

Aaron nodded his head in agreement. "Here's the thing about evolution. Even if we assume the survival of the fittest idea finally came into the issue. There aren't enough 'in-betweens.'"

Helen quipped, "Like kids that aren't quite teenagers?"

Aaron nodded his head in agreement. "There's a term. An atavism is a lingering prehistoric, biological trait. Your abdominal appendix is an atavism. The useless arms on the T-Rex is an atavism. There aren't even remotely enough of them in the biology. All the species are too perfect. Consider the hummingbird. It's hardly even a bird. It's so successful at filling the niche of the bumble bee it's become one. How did every single biological system in its body change so radically for it to survive to reproduce? In genetics, this is called the 'rapid change' quandary."

Helen reflected for a moment and spoke up quietly, "I was just thinking about something that always stuck in my mind. In the Nazca lines, there is this huge hummingbird. Did those ancient peoples draw it for a reason? I mean, did they know something we've forgotten?"

Aaron continued. "Modern science, like any individual person, has an agenda. Truth sits in the back of the bus. Creatures survive by consuming unlike creatures. They thrive by finding a niche and barely coexisting with like creatures."

Aaron held up one of the documents on the table as he

continued, "In my math-physics manuscript, I've identified binomial variations. Everything is comprised of like and unlike, up, down, high, low, even, odd, life, and death. The Universe evolves, but not in the simplistic fashion our Dark Age science preaches. There's a loophole in randomization. It's a natural principle* of counter-entropy. This information network reaches across time and space. It's the mirror counterpart to Einstein's time dilation. Our minds exist outside the 3-pound mass of lipid fatty cells which is our brain. We are not just self-deceived computers. Our magical sense of self-awareness is the result of a natural property of time-slip."

Helen' jade eyes sparkled as she asked, "The Universe is filled with earth-type planets isn't it? Do you suppose well-meaning aliens are talking to those who want to listen by using the crop circles? I read a book called 'Circular Reasoning.' The flattened patterns in the crops are actually braided and the stalk nodes are burst from the inside by some unknown energy. The math and patterns are far too complex to be done by a few people with boards and strings in the middle of the night."

Aaron replied, "The Kepler satellite has shown that at least 100 million earth type planets exist in our Galaxy alone, inside the habitable zones of their stars. They're said to orbit in the 'Goldilocks' Zone.'"

Helen furled her brow as she anxiously asked, "You don't suppose there are smart crabs that can figure out how to get here, do you?"

"That's a good question," Aaron replied. "There are three ideas around the proposition of extraterrestrial life, the Jungle hypothesis, the Zoo hypothesis and the Fermi paradox. The Jungle hypothesis supposes that we're just ants and the aliens are so advanced that we can't even perceive their activities. The Zoo hypothesis says that we're primitive but not entirely different. So the aliens would probably take some interest but keep us isolated. Enrico Fermi was a physicist around the time the nuclear bombs were developed. He asked a question. He asked, 'Where are the others?' No scientist doubts that the Universe is filled with life. Nuclear power can be used to propel a space ship to near light speed. NASA has designs. Ships could be built to travel to the stars. And the astronauts would return far in the future, but they would only be a few years older. That fact makes it impractical, but the question must be asked, *Where are the aliens*? Out of millions of worlds, some species should have visited!"

Helen smirked. "I hope they're not space lobsters. I'm pretty selfish. I'd rather have them on the plate instead of me."

Aaron responded. "The great lesson from science and religion is that life is a very selfish proposition. It is fortunate that it stumbles in the direction of selflessness. But we need to be cautious and understand that the distance between predator and prey is as close as our nearest neighbor. Each and every thing is, at once, separate and connected. 'The human mind is the most complicated thing in the Universe,' sounds like it should be right, but it's not. Science might say that the Zoo hypothesis must be correct. But a mind attuned to the spiritual phenomenon would recognize the Jungle hypothesis. There is always more than we see—the extra color."

Helen drank deeply from her cup of coffee. Setting the near-empty cup down, she held it with both hands and seemed to stare into its remaining contents for some moments. She remained stoic as she spoke softly, "So all people, places, and things need to be viewed as potentially both positive and/or negative. 'Hope for the best, prepare for the worst.'"

Helen raised her eyes from her revealing comment to the

ambivalent stare of both Aaron and Bailey.

Bailey smiled wryly as she added, "That's right and any perspective that does not first consider that axiom is making a mistake."

Helen's eyes grew wide as she pursed her lips before speaking. "I guess the difference between those that do and those that don't are pretty much the difference between the liberal and the conservative." Helen's words were met with an approving nod from both her friends.

Aaron held Helen's stare for some moments before he spoke, "What did you learn from the ideas regarding life on other worlds?"

Helen raised her eyebrows curtly as she remarked, "There's something quite revealing in what you just told me. The Zoo Hypothesis sounds like planet Earth may be blocked from proof of alien visitation."

Aaron responded, "When the SETI array (Search for Extra Terrestrial Intelligence) was first switched on, a signal was heard from deep space. It was a complex radio signal. It's called the 'Wow' signal. Nothing like it has ever been received since."

Helen chuckled as she asked, "They knew we were listening and blocked us from any more signals?"

Aaron smiled wryly and nodded his head.

Helen continued, "Well, here's something perhaps even stranger. Suppose the 'Jungle Hypothesis' is right. Suppose these super advanced life forms—which are so different we hardly notice them—suppose that this is the ongoing 'mind' of all life. Suppose that there is an entirely distinct reality in which no mind, no memory, ever disappears. It's the Super-Consciousness you spoke of. It's not physical at all—at least, not all the time."

Aaron turned to Bailey. Helen's expression turned blank as she watched the two smiling whimsically, one to the other. Aaron commented to Bailey, "I've never seen anyone put that together, by themselves, so quickly."

Bailey exclaimed, "Well, that's why we love Shri'Ani. She's a Hindu princess! No one knows more about the spiritual realm than my mom."

"'We are all much more what we're born to be," Aaron added, "than what we learn to be. Our attitudes and interests are directly linked to the reality of Karma."

Helen nodded her head, approvingly, as Aaron continued, "All right. The last thing we need to do is explore the final connecting issue. I think everybody is on the same page. Bailey, I want you to read through your diary and tell us about your incarnation as Riley O'Reilly. This is the final key in explaining how the 'temporal refraction' occurred. The introduction of the 4-year vote for the 'Ecclesiastical Dictum' into the Judicial Branch of government has transformed the last 300 years of history. It's the reason we're sitting here in the (S) time line."

(circa 1762 Boston (S) time line)

"Another ale, Sire?" The vivid grey eyes of the young barkeep sparkled as he inquired of the familiar and notable patron, Samuel Adams.

"Aye, bring another, lad." Adams wrote intently, his eyes never looking up from the parchment even when he spoke. The pen and ink were kept on hand for the Bostonian gentleman.

Riley returned to the table and carefully wiped it clear of clam shells, peanuts, and moisture.

"I see you are writing another epic, Sire." The smile on the face of the young indentured servant was broad and sincere as he set the draught judiciously on the table. He took care to place it both in reach and a cautious distance from the intent patron's work.

Adams scrawled a flamboyant signature upon the narrative and, with a sidelong glance, peered upwards, approvingly, towards the servant.

"Tell me, lad, how many years have ye attended my party at this table?"

The beam upon the bright face broadened. "Well, Sire, let me ponder. It is now the year 1762. I left for the New World . . ., hmm, my mother and I departed Dublin in Spring of 1760. I was graced by my master to the service of the Green Dragon Tavern in January of 1761. I think my accounting would ascribe nearly two years to be the answer, Sire!"

Samuel Adams leaned back in the heavy New England oak four-legger. With a sincere smile, granting approval to the teenaged servant, he furthered his inquiry, "Are ye bestowed with the skills of the read and the write?"

An intent expression came over Riley's face. "Quite so, Sire! I am skilled both in the King's English and the Hindu colloquial script."

Adams smiled gingerly. "I've heard this about ye, young man. Your intelligence is known to those of merit here in the Boston commune."

Riley's voice belied a nervous departure, "Sire, I am most honored."

Adams spun the parchment round and pushed it towards the barkeep. "Can ye read the correspondence? Who is this written for?"

Riley peered closely and answered, "Yes, Sire. I see that it is intended for the honorable Sire John Hancock." The young man's face was blank and exposed his astonishment.

"Do you notice the style of my signature? What do ye think of the queer symbol I place beside it?" Adams studied Riley's face intently while he drank deeply, peering over the fresh mug of dark ale.

Riley spoke confidently, "Well, yes, Sire. I see that you adorn your signature with the 'hooked X.'" Riley heard himself saying the words before he had time to think of what he had just exposed. Nervously, the 16-year-old stood quite still, trying not to betray his composure.

A wry smile seeped from the crevices of the Bostonian gentleman's face. He spoke quietly, leaning imperceptibly into his words, "I'm now even more curious. How do ye know about the 'hooked X'? I fear we have much to discuss, lad."

Adams' studied every contour of the distinct features of the grey-eyed youth, awaiting his response. "Well, Sire, I read and study with Dr. Joseph Warren. I have great interest in the Masonic wisdom." Riley stood quietly, hoping for an approving response.

Adams' intensity never left his comportment. "What might ye think of the use of the 'X' with my name?"

Riley flung his bar towel over his left shoulder; his characteristic energetic nature slowed as he responded, "Sire, I fear I may speak out of my station."

Adams smiled. "Ye are with a friend. Speak, lad."

Riley spoke cautiously, "Well, one thought comes to mind. The 10th Book of the Hebrew testament is Samuel, the second Book. It is your name." Riley peered deeply into the dark-eyed gaze of the 40-year-old gentleman.

A rich smile filled Adams' face for the first time. "That is the most inspired answer I have ever received to that question. It is a correct answer. The 'X' is also the 10th letter of the Latin language. And there is much more meaning"

Riley stood smiling and quite relaxed; he felt that a most

important event in his life had surely just occurred. Adams continued his query, "Tell me, lad. I've heard your English father was killed in the Indian conflicts with the Thuggees."

Riley demurred as he spoke plaintively, "This is true, Sire. I never knew him. I'm known by my last name. My Hindu name does not fit with my station."

Adams spoke respectfully. "Ye will be as free as our new nation, lad."

(circa 1774)

The two colonial gentlemen sat quietly at the Green Dragon Tavern's table, a place which might have been considered their private locality.

Riley O'Reilly spoke up gingerly, "Samuel, I feel the old tavern has become the seat of much controversy."

Adams drank deeply as he queried. "Do ye think the English Governor has the list of the 'Sons of Liberty'?"

Riley shook his head vigorously. "Nay, there would be not a man to betray us."

Adams continued, "There is a man attending a meeting soon who may play an important role in forthcoming events. He is a strong patriot and hails from Virginia."

Riley queried, "Is he privy to the Order?"

Adams gave a quick side-long glance to Riley. "Aye, his name is George Washington; he is high in the Masonic wisdom."

(circa Winter 1777 Valley Forge, Pennsylvania)

George Washington stood in the small house reading the heart-wrenching news. The supplies, so desperately needed by the 12,000-man Continental army, would not be arriving.

Washington looked into the intense grey eyes of the courier as he spoke, "Is Colonel Danforth and Commander Lafayette aware of this message?"

The shivering, red-faced soldier stood at attention as he responded, "Yes, General. They are shortly behind me. I was sent ahead. They are with the small train of provisions."

Washington queried, "I see you are with the Massachusetts militia."

The near-frozen soldier stuttered, "Yes, General. I'm from Boston."

Washington smiled wryly as he spoke, "We've met, haven't we?"

Riley O'Reilly smiled gingerly as he answered, "We met with Sire Adams, just two years hence."

Riley's gaze dropped to Washington's coat. His focus fell upon the unmistakable presence of a bullet hole.

Washington's continued study of the young man recaptured his stare. A wry smile filled the beleaguered face of the Continental Army's Commander in Chief. Washington turned from the courier and proceeded to his chair beside the fireplace.

The beleaguered commander sat down and spoke softly, "Come over and warm yourself."

Riley stooped before the hearth. He closed his eyes as the radiating heat purged the cold from his very soul. The two remained silent for some time.

Finally, Washington inquired, "You are very close to Joseph Warren, isn't that right?"

Riley turned, smiling broadly as he answered. "Yes, Sire. He and his books have been my College. All I know, I owe to him."

Washington continued, "It will require action by God Almighty for our war against the British to succeed."

Riley responded, "God is with us, Sire."

"In the Battle of the Monongahela, in 1755," Washington continued, "the fighting was intense. I found that my coat and hat were filled with bullet holes. I was unscathed. Earlier this day, I walked into a cold field to watch the sunset. I turned to find the Indian Chief—we fought those many years ago—standing in my presence. He told me that the Great Spirit came to him in a vision, that day in the battle. He said that I must fulfill a great destiny, that I could not be killed."

Riley sat dumbfounded as he listened to the surreal story told by his revered General. "I found many bullet holes in my coat, my hat and my horse was shot dead. Recently, my garments have been pierced once again, but by some divine providence, I again remain unscathed."

The day was bright; a clear sky provided the canopy for the raging battle. The Continental troops poured into the clearing as the ranks of Red Coats fell before the rag-tag troops. The battle seemed to turn in favor of the militia troops under Riley O'Reilly's command. As the wave of soldiers advanced, the forward march converged on a forked trail in the approaching woods. Riley's suspicions were aroused.

He wondered,. *These fleeing Englishmen, they're heading into the left fork of this trail.* At that moment he heard a tender voice.

As if in a dream, he heard a woman's words, "You must lead the men on this trail. Do *not* take the left fork. It will lead to defeat!"

At that instant, another voice was heard. "O'Reilly! Which way do we proceed?"

Riley turned to see General Washington on horseback. The young field commander responded, "General, we must follow the right fork and fall back to reinforce the battle field!"

(circa May 1787 Philadelphia, Pennsylvania)

"O'Reilly, this is James Madison. I have spoken to him of your research."

The smiling face of the revered author of the American Constitution stood before the humble Indian-Irish citizen of the new American nation. Samuel Adams guided the party to their table.

Madison asked, "Do you believe this mathematical work of Francois L'Hospital is correct?"

Riley answered eagerly, "If we charter the Judicial Branch with the task of citing the Will of God, we can ensure that secular freedom will continue with obedience to Holy principles. A populace vote on ecclesiastical dictum can be held every four years on religious tenants."

Madison responded. "I suppose that would satisfy those at odds with the strictly secular notions of the Order, while providing a voice to the prevailing religion."

Riley's expression spoke volumes as he nodded.

Madison continued, "There are ancient symbols in the Masonic lexicon. Our revolution has been ordained. I propose that our currency should bear the phrase 'On God We Depend.'"

Titanic

(circa June 2015 [Y] time line)

A blue sky rose above a lovely scene. The green grass reached endlessly to grasp its azure coattails. The tall trees rustled gently in the wind, their leaves full and breathing. Helen's momentary diversion paused as the peripheral scene came into focus. The deck table held stacks of papers, phone, pads, and more work than the beleaguered professor wanted to embrace. Fanning briskly, she successfully intercepted an eight-legged invader. She took up her morning coffee and drank deeply.

She muttered to herself, "The thing I've worked the hardest for was just this moment, my country home, the solitude of my patio, and a beautiful Saturday morning."

Helen's gaze fell to her phone as she wondered *I think Bekah said she'd call later this morning.* The quiet moments continued as the green-eyed, dark-haired woman nestled in her comfy deck recliner. From above the prosaic scene, the fine contours of the woman's features appeared immutable, a sculpture of infinite detail in flesh. A glint from the morning light of the sun gave witness to the eternal snowflake, divinely carved into her chin. Her eyes swept the scene from left to right and right to left.

Then, her eyes snapped wide as the distant sound of a dog barking startled her. Her expression grew intense as she pondered the moment. *Was it Balto? Is Bekah coming over? No, it's Zoe. No, not Zoe, it can't be Zoe.*

The tender expression of the ageless feminine soul turned to grief as she blurted out loud, "Oh, that damned Aaron, Yuri, Francois - and he says Beelzebub has limitless names!"

Helen sat upright and reached for her iPad. She muttered to herself as she searched feverishly through the mails. "When did this start? When did I get drafted? Maybe it's all fantasy."

The newly-energized woman punched the pad with the dexterity of a virtuoso as she exclaimed, "'The Red Rose on the Moon.' He always names everything. Yes, it was dated 8/6/14. The first American decapitated by ISIS was August 20th, 2014."

Helen read the mail:

Two nights ago, I experienced one of the lucid dreams. In this, I was looking at the moon, and in this dream, the panorama was completely real and almost overwhelming. In the vision, the sun was casting a red illumination which danced across the surface. As I watched, this sunset light formed odd crystalline or geometric features on the surface. These were large designs that were centered across a large portion of the entire sphere. Suddenly, the design twisted into a beautiful shape, which I can only describe as resembling a rose. The main aspect in the shape is that it was 5-sided . . .

As I have described to you before, I was suddenly lifted right out my sleep, and my eyes were immediately set on my digital clock. The large red numerals read "222." The Moon is the astral symbol of the Muslim spirit. The Sun can be equated to an astral symbol of the Judaeo-Christian. Why? The 3 Rules of Consciousness prescribes that each contained personage or entity represents a "bubble" of reality which is manifest across All time:space. The Sun produces light and exists eternally in daylight. The moon reflects light and exists eternally in darkness. This binomial relationship represents a contained randomizing system, the First Rule. The Second Rule says that the interaction of the twin elements must result in one or the other obtaining dominance in each event or cycle. The Third Rule says that the observer of these events participates in the outcome of each discreet cycle. The event and the observer are linked.

Red is not a good sign. The five-sided shape is not a good sign. Recall "Sandcastles." This worries me . . .

* *The absolute reality of the "dream vision" and the sharp, crystalline blood-red shards, erupting on the moon, are a warning of impending conflict and death.*

Aaron

At that instant, the harried English professor found herself jumping from the lounge chair as she chased several loose papers across her backyard. The wind had invaded the moment. As Helen reached down for the most precious of her papers, that being the journal sheets containing her heart-felt poetry, she noticed an oddly shaped branch. Its forked and twisted presence made itself known by nearly poking her eye. Helen thrashed at the branch, pulling back to keep the dried, prickly scrap of wood from her face. Aggravated, her focus broken, she muttered to herself, "Never a moment's rest! Just when I've collected my thoughts, I find myself collecting all the fettering of the physical world."

Helen stood frozen, the focus and gaze of the classic artist admiring and pondering the scene before her had returned. She walked all around the "forked" branch, sizing up its peculiar twisted shape; the detail and exactness was uncanny.

"This can't be right," she said out loud. "Oh, I've been spending too much time around that mad scientist."

Helen reached over, ready to grasp the branch. She stood frozen in her tracks as she blurted out. "No, I'm not going to touch you. I looked at you already. I didn't want to 'see' you then, and I don't want to look at you now! You are not there. You can't be there.

You are not the 10th letter of the Hebrew alphabet, and you can't be sitting on the ground in my backyard. You are a river in the sands of Ramadi, Iraq. You are *not* here!"

Helen grimaced, reached into her pocket and retrieved her phone. Holding out the 21st Century device, she tapped the screen, focused the view, and snapped a picture. "Well, this is going to make Aaron quite satisfied. I can hear him now: 'I told you, you will be given a sign. You will be given a . . . sign."

The phone fell to the ground as Helen's right hand grabbed her left wrist. The thick locks of reddish auburn hair fell forward as she tried to steady herself. A cold intense tingling filled her left arm. The last thing Helen could see as she lost focus was the (y)-shaped branch, again nearly poking her in the eye. The lovely morning had gone completely awry as the beautiful lady lay sprawled indignantly across her lawn.

(circa 1914 RMS Titanic [S]time line)

"So Molly, tell us about that night. I've heard about the maiden voyage to New York. I simply must be told. What was the Captain's facial expression when you told him to get the ship out of the ice field?" The German accent was pronounced as the poised, middle-aged lady drank her tea, her pinky extended.

The struggling young entertainer was pleased that her new acquaintance and potential benefactor was taking a sincere interest in the little known episode. Margaret Brown was known in (psy) circles, but she was weary of the academic realm and wanted to see the world and experience fame and fortune. It had been two years since their original voyage to New York on April 15th, 1912. Soon, she would actually be on the stage in burlesque.

Molly's tea cup fell from her hand as she grasped her left arm. The young, vivacious woman's green eyes went wide as she let out a gasp.

Gertrudt exclaimed, "What is it dear? Are you all right?"

Molly steadied herself against the table, "I'm not sure. I feel really dizzy." The young psychic focused on her jade bracelet,* encircling her grasping right hand. "I'm better, I think. You're Gertrudt, and this ship, this ship . . ."

Molly's voice went silent as Gertrudt Cohen spoke up, "This ship is the ship you saved, or at least that's what I believe. Many don't pay any attention to such things. But I have my intuitions as well. You are a 3rd-degree, card-carrying psychic, and you, my dear, saved this ship and all its passengers."

Molly fumbled and reached into her purse, extracting her compact mirror. Gazing at her face in the mirror, she spoke quietly to herself. "I'm Molly Brown, and I'm on the RMS Titanic in the year 1914, two years after it sank!"

Gertrudt's look was puzzled, "What did you say, dear?"

Molly continued to dig frenziedly in her purse. Pulling out an American dollar bill, she pulled it taught and read the inscription silently, *On God We Depend.*

Taking a deep breath, the wide-eyed young woman muttered, "I'm in the (S) time line. Oh, my (Y)! Aaron and Bailey are right. It's all true."

Looking up at her dining companions, Molly's aghast expression remained as she realized that she and Gertrudt were much younger than they should be.

"Gertrudt, I'm 23 years old, and you're about the same age!"

Molly's remark was met with concerned looks. Gertrudt spoke up assertively, "W.B., should I send for the ship's surgeon?"

The Irish poet peered over his spectacles and inquired gently,

"Molly, we adore your perpetual jests, but I think you must depart to a serious tone. Are you well, dear?"

Molly's piercing, jade-colored eyes grew wide as a bemused expression filled her face. She spoke gently, considering how she must appear. "Oh, yes, Mr. Yeats. I'm fine. Really, I am!"

The distinguished Irish poet smiled wryly as he spoke, "Well, I'll take you at your word, if you return to my casual address."

Gertrudt grimaced as she repeated her question. "All right, now, I want you to tell W.B. what you said to Captain Smith the night of April 15th, 1912. Oh, W.B! I awoke at 2:00 in the morning, and Molly was gone from our cabin. When she returned, she told me what she had done, and at first, I didn't believe her. Tell us, Molly. I want W.B. to hear the story!"

Molly blinked as she considered the few minutes that had passed. She thought to herself, *I have a total of 21 minutes, and then I'll return to 2015. I have to talk to Yeats. I'll never have a chance like this again. I actually have a chance to speak to the greatest English poet of the 20th Century. Oh, dear (Y), I'll have to satisfy Gertrudt quickly.*

Molly leaned into the table and retorted, "Gertrudt, everybody knows that W.B. is skeptical of the dark arts. He has just spent months studying the Holy writings of the Irish Book of Kells." Molly studied the distinguished poet's expression to determine if her wiles were encouraging. She was pleased to see his wry smile as she spoke, "W.B., I had an intense dream. I saw the Titanic hitting an iceberg." Molly paused as her companions responded in grins and bewilderment.

W.B. spoke up, "The irony of the largest ship in the world sinking on its maiden voyage would indeed speak of the Dark Arts!"

Molly continued, "Well, I marched right up to the bridge of this ship, I pulled out my (psy) credentials, and I demanded that the ship must be taken out of the ice fields!"

Gertrudt interjected, "International Law requires that a 3rd-degree credentialed psychic must be obeyed if it could prevent a catastrophe."

W.B. shook his head in agreement. He queried, "I bet the Captain was amazed?"

Molly continued, "Oh, by the stars! He demanded to know how I knew the ship's latitude. I have to tell you, honestly. I am proud to be an activist for suffrage and women's issues. I could feel it in his mind. He called me a 'bulldyker.' Of course, I read it in his thoughts, so I forgave him."

The well-bred poet demurred. He shook his head and spoke sympathetically. "Molly, I am glad that you are such a courageous spirit. You are blessed by (Y). I could not bear the responsibility of such talents."

Molly smiled gleefully; she knew her moment was at hand. She spoke encouragingly, "Now, W.B, please tell me what you found in the Book of Kells. Which of the four Gospels gave you the deepest inspiration?"

Yeats looked deeply into the piercing jade eyes of young Molly Brown as he spoke. "Well, Molly, I should enjoy telling you about the ancient mysticism. For once, I actually believe I'll have a chance to entertain you."

(circa June 2015 [Y] time line)

From above, the sprawled female form appeared, at once, lifeless and irresistible. The omniscient mind considered the curiosity of the scene. The early morning sun illuminated the images in stark contrasts. The well-manicured, bright green grass expanded far beyond the smallness of the central image. Just above the prostrate form, the Yellow Birch and White Oak shivered in the sporadic breeze. A discarded branch levitated upwards and returned to the arboreal choreography of the divine stage.

Shimmering, like water held in a clear bowl, the moment stuttered. As if a mirror had been held to the lithe body, the right hand released its death grip on the left wrist. Now, the left hand furiously clasped the right limb. Helen's green eyes opened wide to the image of the forked stick nearly poking her face. She rose to a sitting position as she swept back her thick reddish-brown hair. She breathed in the damp morning air. The instinctive urge to cough was fought back as she realized the dry, salty ocean breeze no longer filled her lungs. She considered the infinite wonder of the preceding revelation. The rapturous vitality of three lives filled the inscrutable space of just five cups of neural tissue.

Helen scanned the scene for her phone. Looking down, she saw that both the proof of the 21st Century and a small prize of her cherished hobby lie in the crux of the (y) shaped stick. Molly reached out and delicately plucked the four-leaf clover from the grass. Helen snatched up the phone and stared at the time. In her mind, Shri'Ani exclaimed, "Avatars of Vishnu, I know the time was 7:45 . . . It's now 7:32! I've traveled 13 minutes 'back" in time."

The impossible scene was complete as the lovely, dark-haired college professor fell backwards in the grass. The irony of her statement was comedy enough for one soul. The three women laughed hysterically.

Helen rose to her feet and reverently placed the magic green talisman in her pocket. Placing the twisted stick under her arm, she punched viciously at her phone. She muttered frantically, "Answer, Aaron. Answer now!"

The disheveled woman looked back at her house and began to walk swiftly towards the patio doors as a voice spoke out of the tiny speaker she held close to her face.

"Helen, what are you doing up so early on a Saturday morning?"

Helen shouted frantically, "Get over here! It's happened. Get over here! I need you, now!"

The time traveler stood at the deck table, stiff-backed, legs spread, as she poured the hot coffee eagerly through her lips. She exclaimed. "It's hot! I am 13 minutes in the past! I had to have just set this coffee on the table."

Sliding the patio door open, she entered her den and sat down at the computer. Remembering Aaron's warning, she reached down and disabled the WIFI adapter. Helen's sparkling green eyes appeared frantic as she considered the formidable task. *I have less than 21 minutes.* Multiple minds agreed. *I'll start with my childhood in India.* The English professor considered her considerable typing skills. *Let's see . . . 110 words a minute, times two. Okay, I'll have to pace 300 years to the most pertinent issues in each life.*

The "total mind" state allows consummate focus. Helen and Molly smiled wryly as the eidetic memory of Shri'Ani flowed seamlessly through Helen's fingertips. *Molly must be given extra time for Yeat's tutelage.* Three souls nodded approval in corporeal forms beyond visual reality. Molly's mind slowed when the lifespan entered the Nuremberg rallies of 1933.

The machine gun resonance of Helen's dexterous keystrokes continued uninterrupted as the sliding glass door opened. Aaron stood quietly as he studied Helen's motile autistic trance. Glancing at his watch, he knew that she must be approaching the temporal limit. Suddenly, Helen's chair spun around and the aging physics professor was greeted with a rapturous smile and piercing, jade-green eyes. The energized woman leaped to her feet and grabbed Aaron's head, drawing his face to hers.

"Oh Francois, main tumse pyar karthee hoon!"

Aaron's soft brown eyes began to water as the harmonic energy of Helen's rapture seemed to pierce his soul. For just the instant, he steadied himself as his mind flooded with ancient memories. Gazing back into the sparkling green eyes, Aaron's focus fell to the eternally distinct snowflake in Shri'Ani's chin. The most enduring memory of the human mind filled his senses. The intense smell of the Indian girl's floral parfum melted Francois's soul. Reaching around his teenage bride, the 25-year-old French scientist consumed the lips of his true love. He realized, at that instant, that 300 years could not erase the eternal waters. Three minds held the fountainhead of his one true adoration.

(circa June 2015, Sunday [Y] time line)

Aaron reached out and pulled in the mounds of colorful chips. A side-long glance at the professor's gaming partner was met with a sardonic comment, "I still don't accept that there is any advantage in that sequence."

Professor LaSalle retorted, "Well, if you go back to the database, you'll see that out of your 646 shoes, that multiple combination only goes 'back to back' two times."

The sophisticated, mixed Italian smirked. "There are what, three of those sets in each shoe?"

Aaron stacked his chips as he answered confidently, "Guido, do you really want to win or just verify the notion of what is impossible? I told you mathematical Invariance is wrong. The combinations are permuting around the even/odd sets."

"Can I get you another Heineken, sir?" The scantily clad

hostess was obviously quite proud of her natural endowments as she leaned forward, asking the question.

At that same instant, Guido also posed a question, "Are you going to say yes, or no, when Bob gets back?"

Aaron pivoted from his companion and tried to keep his gaze upward into the eyes of the waitress. "Okay, that's perfect!"

Gazing suspiciously at his longstanding casino acquaintance, the ancient mathematician responded, "Look Guido, here's the deal. I'll redo the three files with the final method. I'll also include the new fourth file. When it's done, I'll bring it up on zip drive and review it—only with you. I will not leave you with any copies. If that's not agreeable, then there's your answer." Aaron leaned down, and pulled in another win as he peered upwards at his friend.

Guido smiled, "I already know that that should work."

(circa June 2015, Monday [Y]time line)

Aaron sat quietly at the side desk in his office. The distinctive sounds of key strokes coming from Bailey's corner desk seemed to compete with the ticking of the omnipresent wall clock. Aaron turned the typed page of Helen's diary as he raised his head to the approach of his fellow early bird.

The hot cup of tea was matched with a pleasant smile as Bailey commented, "Well, here it is Monday, 6:30 in the morning, and it's finally happened!"

A thin smile crept across Aaron's face as he quipped, "Yes, it was a full weekend. The only issue is why were we given more questions than answers two days ago?"

The vitality in Bailey's facial expression remained as she ran her right hand over her protuberant abdomen. "Well, (Y) sent her back for some reason. I guess the answer has to be in those pages."

Aaron drank deeply from the hot Earl Grey as he set the cup down and commented. "Yesterday, I was reminded of the curious and sometimes costly relationship in single and multiple sequences. The worlds of science and religion are oblivious to the 'loophole' that exists in all random events."

The thoughtful scientist continued, "Are you aware of Freud's three states of mental progression?"

Bailey leaned into the table as she answered, "Probably not. I heard your question earlier. Does that explain why the Unsinkable Molly Brown was 24 years younger in the (S) time line?"

Aaron continued, "Freud spoke of the Id, the Ego, and the Super-Ego. All three of us have had three lives. The first and the last we were all together, but in the second one, we were in completely separate realities."

Bailey grimaced as she stood patiently.

Aaron smiled and quipped, "Haldane's Dilemma speaks of a speed limit in the rate of change in evolution. It's asymptotic, like time dilation."

Bailey studied her mentor's pause; she knew that he was deeply absorbed in thought. She also knew that he needed as much help with the conundrum as he could find.

She spoke quietly, "Aaron, I'm still waiting."

The distracted mind of the thoughtful man returned to the moment. "A geneticist, J.B.S. Haldane, posed a paradox. He said, 'The universe is not only stranger than we imagine, it is stranger than we *can* imagine.'"

Bailey's left eyebrow rose as a perplexed expression spread across her face. She remarked, "Well, you always say that there is no such thing as a coincidence. There has to be some greater reason that your macro-quantum entanglement is at work with us."

The intense moment of contemplation was broken as the office door swung open. "Tweet, tweet . . . There's another 'early bird' in the nest!"

Helen's vivacious presence was met with broad smiles, if albeit curious expressions. Helen smiled as she set her purse down on Aaron's desk. She peered at the open pages of her diary.

Her eyebrows lifted as she remarked, "Well, I know why you two have been so intense these many months. Time-slip is not an experience for the faint of heart."

Bailey stood wide-eyed, staring at Helen. She hesitantly remarked, "Helen, you look beautiful this morning. That's a silk blouse. That color, it's cyan, I think?"

Helen's smile widened, her bright crimson lip gloss framing a perfect set of pearly white enamel. "Well, I don't know how to explain it. Since Saturday morning, I feel, well . . . so alive!"

Bailey's study of the English professor remained focused as she continued, "I've never seen your hair like that. It's perfect for you! Wait, I've seen Bekah wear her hair like that. It's like, really European."

Helen ran her right hand back along her face and raised the thickness of the coiffure. She smiled as she jiggled its mass and responded, "It's called a French braid. I don't know if I've ever worn it like this, at least not in this lifetime."

Aaron meekly responded, "Shri' kept her hair like that most of the time. She'd smack me gently in the face with it when she wanted some attention."

Bailey's left hand unconsciously capped her mouth as her grey eyes grew wide. Her eyes darted from one to the other as she heard herself mutter the words to the couple, "You two were married. Of course! I guess when Helen experienced the total mind, she was Shri'Ani, and the energy resonance produced, voila', Francois! After all, I guess we knew there had to be a Frenchman in Aaron, somewhere."

The two women laughed unashamedly as the physics professor returned to his reading. Aaron sat patiently, allowing the frivolous feminine behavior to run its course. Peering upwards from the diary, he spoke up, assertively, "Bailey, dear, would you like to get mom and dad and yourself some coffee and tea? We have 300 years to catch up with and only about one hour to do it."

The three time travelers sat quietly around the table. Aaron shuffled through the stacks of paper and set the new diary in front of Helen. He queried, "Helen, what do you make of the entry for the year 1933?"

Helen shook her head as she responded, quizzically, "I don't know! It happened in Nuremberg, Germany. I guess you see who I met at that moment? It ended abruptly. It's the single event that worries me the most."

Bailey interjected, "Well, fill me in! I haven't seen any of it."

Helen replied, "Bailey, I was the Unsinkable Molly Brown, you know, the heroine that picked up passengers from the freezing water."

Bailey's eyes grew wide as she asked, "You mean, like on the Titanic?"

Helen continued, "Exactly, but my consciousness was taken to the (S) time line; there was a lot that was different. I Googled Margaret Brown. She was born on July 18, 1867. She was a socialite and a women's activist."

Bailey smiled wryly as she agreed, "That's you, all right."

Helen continued, "She made the crew on lifeboat no. 6 return to the sinking ship and pick up people. The thinking, at that time, was that the swell from the sinking ship would pull the boats under. I have a vague impression of it from the (Y) time line. I couldn't find this in the historical record, but I think I actually had to make them do it at gun point!"

Bailey leaned into the table and inquired anxiously, "But the Titanic didn't sink in the (S) time line! Aaron and I have wondered about that. We didn't record it in our diaries. How did it keep from sinking?"

Aaron interrupted, "You're not going to believe this."

Helen continued, "Well, we all know that people are much more psychic in the (S) time line. I was a 3rd-degree card-carrying (psy). I went to Captain Edward Smith and pulled rank. I made him take the ship out of the North Atlantic ice fields!"

Bailey's eyes grew wide as she stared at Aaron, speaking quietly. "Now, I know why you haven't even texted me this weekend. This whole thing just gets weirder and weirder. We'll never get this figured out!"

Aaron looked at Helen and asked, "What year did Molly Brown die in our time line?"

Helen responded, "She died October 26th, 1932."

Aaron pursed his lips in a ponderous expression. He looked at Helen and asked, "Do you think you succeeded on that day in 1933?"

Helen shook her head from left to right as she timidly answered, "I don't know? I don't know what any of it means."

Bailey responded in total exasperation, "Give me that diary. If I don't read this, I'll bust!" She reached across the table, took Helen's diary, and began to read silently.

Aaron continued, "Do you know about the Kabbalah Tree of Life?" Helen shook her head. Aaron went on, "Do you remember? We discussed dimensional expansion. The current sophistry is that everything is physical. Matter equals energy is about as far as the wisdom cares to reach. In the ancient Hebrew mysticism, there is a numerological construct which contains eleven steps. One interpretation speaks of number-word equivalence. The Hebrew alphabet is both numbers and letters. The 22 letters contain no vowels."

The English professor smirked as she listened intently. Aaron continued, "Here's the point. Two times eleven is twenty-two." Helen's look turned to complete bewilderment. "Stay with me," Aaron implored. "You'll understand where I'm going with this in just a moment."

"Letters are information," he went on. "The words they make comprise knowledge, but the meaning the words create is something extra, something not contained on the paper they're written—wisdom. Numbers are dimensionally distinct from alphabet symbols, but they operate the same way. Counting numbers provides useful information and the mathematics can prescribe wonderful sequences and events. But we find that the numbers reach limits that cannot be surpassed, like the speed of light or the time barrier. Here's the point. Minds that are attuned to the spiritual or paranormal phenomenon realize that words and numbers can be viewed as the same axis of information. If we think of the physical reality of time and space as the x axis, the y axis is the mind. There is a convergence of self-awareness."

Helen looked up at Bailey, and the two exchanged a grin.

Bailey interjected, "What Professor LaSalle is saying is that we don't simply seem to experience love and hate. We *are* love and hate! The mind is a little time-traveling space ship. Inside, there aren't any mirrors. The only way we know that we exist is to fly around the time:space universe and bump into one another." Bailey beamed as she completed her comment, "You know, like you and Aaron did on Saturday! Yes, I'm jealous. I waited my whole life to get married and experience the rapture of physical union. And now I know I'll die for the third time without getting to experience it even once, since I'll never get married."

Aaron grimaced sorely as he went on, "There are three tiers of three. The first tier is Truth, Faith and Hope. The second is Deceit, Contempt and Betrayal. The third is Victory, Virtue and Bliss. I call this the Three Rules of mind. It relates to many spiritual canons. The point is the 'links' I've seen in my tumbler and gaming experiments are reaching across negative time. If biological mechanisms are interacting with themselves across time, then there is a point to existence. That purpose can be loving or hateful. In many ways, it's much easier to believe that evil really doesn't exist than to embrace the idea that there is a good God."

Helen remarked, "So why is Molly so much younger in the (S) time line?"

Aaron said, "So you would be given the chance to kill the man Nostradamus called the second anti-Christ."

Bailey interjected, "Yeah, I just read that. You met Adolf Hitler in Nuremberg in 1933!"

(circa May 2015 [Y] time line)

The physics professor peered around the open door of Professor Helen Lovelace's office. The sound of rapid typing greeted Aaron's ears. Walking up to the busy academic's desk, he smiled broadly. Helen responded. "Well, hi! I haven't seen you in some time. It's just our mails passing in the ether."

Aaron responded, "I wanted to tell you in person that I think our expectations are about to occur."

Looking up from the computer, Helen relaxed in her desk chair and returned the stoic expression of her visitor. She spoke quietly, "I've received your mails. Do you think something wicked, this way cometh?"

Aaron nodded, agreeably. "I keep dreaming of cities being

consumed in blood and terror, many blood moons. But there's something I want you to Google. The first letter in the Tetragrammaton is the 10th letter in the Hebrew alphabet. It's the smallest letter. It looks like a small (y). There is going to be a city taken over by ISIS in Iraq. There is a river by the city. It forks into the shape of the first letter in the name of Yahweh."

Helen's expression remained calm as she answered, "The Administration says that the terrorist conflict is under control."

Aaron grimaced sorely as he spoke, "Recall our conversations about the 'collectivists.' It's in the interest of the left to rationalize their story line. The bloodshed has only begun. And it will proliferate primarily because of this current regime's 'globalist' agenda. The simple-minded pay little attention to the credulous and find prurient pleasure in the cynical."

Helen sat quietly for a moment, before speaking, "I had another dream about the students missing from the classrooms. I feel strongly that we've been together before this life. I want to believe you, but I still don't understand the importance of my involvement."

Aaron responded, "Bailey is torn with the issue of a fatherless child. For her, such progressive mores are not academic." Smiling softly, he added, "You'll receive the proof very soon."

Helen smiled curiously as Aaron turned and left the office.

(circa June 2015 [Y] time line)

Bailey interjected, "Yeah, I just read that. You met Adolf Hitler in Nuremberg in 1933."

Helen sat quietly as her thoughts returned to the moment. The visitation by Aaron, a month earlier, suddenly made sense.

Aaron studied her stoic demeanor as he queried, "What have you figured out?"

Helen drew a deep breath, before speaking, "You were right. (Y) has been brought down to the sands of the Middle-East. The Caliphate wants to destroy the Hebrew God. I think we're all here because of the sacred relationship of each family. It's been eroded by the falsehood of moral equivalence."

Aaron responded, "Bailey has demonstrated virtue under surreal circumstance. Our second lives must demonstrate sacrifice for the correction in 1703 to take place. This means that at least three time slips must still occur. But what I deeply fear is that, if the refracted time lines can be returned to their original state, it all represents some kind of preview of what is still inevitable."

Helen retorted, "No, I'm sure that the Holocaust will not occur. The religious conflict will not take place in the (Y) time line!"

Aaron leaned into the table as he spoke assertively, "Helen, we've discussed profound issues in extreme, albeit elementary, terms. The reality of good and evil is all about subtle deception and distraction. Elie Wiesel survived the Nazi Holocaust. He reminds us, 'The opposite of love is not hate; it's indifference.' The pendulum of deception pivots like a serpent. The deceitful few can dupe the naive with a litany of indulgence as easily as storm troopers can lull a nation into tyranny."

Helen grimaced as she responded, "I've started reading your mails more carefully, Aaron. It's incredible to think that 42% of the millennials actually believe that George Bush is responsible for more deaths than Stalin."

The professor of physical science chuckled as he replied, "Yeah, the socialist was responsible for the greatest number of mass murders in history, more than one hundred million people. The childish double standard is ceaseless. Many believe that Bush conspired to destroy the Twin Trade Towers and mankind never set foot on the moon."

The professor of fine arts enquired, "How do you explain it?"

Aaron retorted, "Helen, you know the answer! You just experienced it. There is a positive influence in each of our minds, and there is a negative voice perpetually reminding us to accept deceit. The presence of authority is ubiquitous. If you take a large glass jar and fill it with rocks, smaller stones, pebbles and sand, in that order and begin to shake it vigorously, you'll see the magic. The sand will fall to the bottom. The pebbles will sit on the sand. The stones will rest nicely on the pebbles and the largest rocks will always rise to the top."

Helen grimaced as she replied, "I guess that makes sense. We really are more what we're born to be than what we learn to be. But the trick is we're given a chance to truly improve our souls."

Aaron continued, "Plato discussed the issue 2400 years ago. In the Cave allegory in the 7th book of the Republic, he described the reality of knowledge and experience figuratively.   "Prisoners are chained in a dark cave. They watch shadows on the wall from events outside the cave. They have no knowledge of the outside world. Little information is obtained from the shadows.

"One prisoner is freed. At first, the light hurts his eyes. Real things seem false. Only their shadows seem real and clear. In time, the freed man's eyes adjust and he sees the truth of the world as something far more complex. He returns to share the knowledge with those still chained in the cave. They curse and reject his message.

"Plato described the masses as stubborn and ignorant. Few among them struggle towards the light and truth, choosing to remain in the shadow of half-truths and indulgence. The theory of forms suggests that physical reality is flawed. Only the mind can achieve the ultimate justice, truth, and beauty, which must be inseparably linked to creativity. The only hope for the government of man is Plato's concept of the philosopher king."

CHAPTER EIGHT

Ashes to Ashes

The steaming hot cocoa was like family to Helen. The familiar fragrance, in her sleepy eyes, was the kiss of nighttime elves. The literary scholar thought of the poem she once had written concerning such a mythical notion. Helen scanned the expanse of her California King bed. She pursed her lips as her expression turned sour. She muttered to herself, "I could have taken a Caribbean cruise for what I spent on this."

Running her left hand across the empty left side of the bed, she peered at the three copies of diaries. Her mind considered the curious reality of three lives times three lifetimes. The last bit of the wasted energy of the day welled up in her hips as she deliberately bounced up and down on the bed. She attempted a thin smile as she considered the hours spent in her throne just a week earlier. Errant thoughts of Clark Gable flirted with her attention. She muttered, "The breathtaking image of Rhett Butler carrying Scarlet O'Hara up that magnificent staircase finally came to pass."

The thin smile became a livid grin as she considered. *I never thought of Aaron LaSalle as magnificent, but I realize now he does have the eyes of Clark Gable.* She frowned as she realized something else she had not considered. *Clark Gable, Omar Sharif. . . Of, course! Aaron and Ibrahim—they all have the same eyes.*

Helen's own eyes opened wide as she retrieved Bailey's diary. Peering at it, she spoke softly, "Bailey's in love with Aaron. That's why Pyara's diary contains so much reference to him when she reached Bar Mitzvah age. I couldn't keep her out of our bed. Well, of course, there was only one fireplace, and it got very cold in Switzerland!"

Helen blinked as she picked up Aaron's diary and continued conversing with her inner selves, "Maybe it's only pragmatic. That man can't know everything. Well, maybe? He might have said it right. 'Every thought, every idea begins with misconceptions. We must admit that our attitudes are flawed before we learn anything.' Bailey won't marry anyone and she desperately needs a father for the child. Maybe that could work. She knows now that he loves me . . . I think she does. But there was that statement she made, 'We're all just little spaceships bumping into each other!' And she even admitted she was jealous."

Helen's heavy eyelids closed for a moment as she fought back the sleep. Turning to the Francois lifetime, she turned to the dog-eared page and read:

"Looking up at Shri'Ani, I smiled and spoke tenderly, 'I love you so much.' Shri's fiery jade eyes sparkled as her supple lips turned to a broad smile. 'You want to love Shri' now? Yes?'"

A pleasant sensation filled the woman's mind as she turned and tapped the light off. The frenzy of thoughts, both prurient and sublime, melted away as blissful sleep washed across 300 years of vitality and passion.

Hours later, from above the room, Helen's ageless, closed lids were seen to conceal her rapid eye movement—left to right and right to left.

(circa 1933, Dublin, Ireland [S]time line)

The ship sat pristinely at the dock, its towering presence filling the spring morning sky. Surely, the flawless scene stood etched eternally replete, with the ubiquitous chirps of sea gulls and the brisk scent of salt air.

The dock master bellowed into the megaphone: "All passengers disembarking the RMS Titanic to Dublin take Track 4. Track 4 to Dublin!"

Molly Brown disregarded the assistance; she knew that her dearest friend would probably beat her to the discovery of one another in the throngs of people.

The American celebrity scanned the rows of faces as, suddenly, her vivid green eyes closed tightly, and her face wrenched in discomfort. The image of the lady passenger, teetering on the verge of collapse, her right hand furiously clawing at her left wrist went unnoticed as hapless souls passed by. Helen embraced the total mind of three lives as she frantically urged complete cooperation. The 21st Century interloper cried out, "If we fall . . . I could be trampled. I must not fall! I'm better. Yes, I'm coming out of it. I'm steady now. I made it!"

"Molly, Molly!" Over her right shoulder, the interloper in time and space could hear the voice of one of the most important persons in her life.

The handsome woman, still youthful at 42 years of age, began to cry as she grabbed at her friend. "Oh, my beloved Gertrudt. I can't believe it! I'm finally here with you again."

The Bavarian German betrayed her ladylike rearing and clutched at the bourgeois, boisterous American. "Dear Lord, you art a beautiful vision." The two stood hugging one another as many years of separation melted away.

Stepping back at arm's length, staring at one another, Gertrudt Cohen spoke first. "For a moment, I thought we were back on this ship's maiden voyage. If not for that deck railing and you catching me, we wouldn't know each other even now."

Molly spoke briskly, catching her breath and nearly shouting,

"You crazy Kraut! If I hadn't pulled you off that railing, you would have fallen to your death."

Gertrudt shrugged. "I know, I know. Rube speaks of that day we all met, often. The picture of the two of us, next to that rail, will have to be interned with him. It was a special moment, and where it sits is proof of that. When I dust, first it's the menorah on the mantle, and then, it's that picture."

"Girls, Girls!" Ruben Cohen shouted. "This way, girls! We have to meet the taxi man. All the luggage is waiting."

Molly, Helen, and Shri'Ani stared up at the beautiful bilious white clouds and the vivid blue of the ocean-side sky of Ireland. One right hand grasped a left as the women who survived April 15th, 1912, ran to meet Gertrudt's husband. Rube stood waiting as the vision of the two friends was somehow detached from the tether of the moment. They ran from that instant twenty-one years earlier, catching up to that modern moment in the year 1933.

The train's horn blasted. The opulent train car rumbled along, climbing its way through the Bavarian Highlands.

"Oh, I thought for a moment dear Rube was going to wake up. That poor man needs his rest. The mills are finally working all shifts, and he works all the time." Gertrudt spoke quietly as she threw down the Rook game card, "Ya, I told you I would beat you, Molly!"

Molly smiled across the table and took out her pack of Camels. Molly sat back in the coach seat as she tamped her last cigarette. "Gertrudt," she said assertively, "I want to hear about this Adolf Hitler. You and Rube seem quite enthralled with him"

Gertrudt took a sip of Chianti from her goblet before she answered. "Oh Molly, I know this man is controversial, but look at the 20th Century. The Great Religious War of 1914 nearly destroyed Germany. You know there are those who want to blame the Jews for that disastrous Treaty at Versailles, France, but Heir Hitler is maintaining that it was, in fact, the Communist Bolsheviks. Rube says that Adolf is a friend to all Germans, including Catholics, Lutherans, and even Jews!" Gertrudt smirked with her statement and toasted herself with the last sip of wine. The crystal glass seemed to ring-out as she deliberately smacked it to rest on the table.

Molly blew out a huge exhaust of smoke, her head poised and tilted back. She leaned forward and gave her friend her patented "listen carefully" look.

"Gertrudt, you know I'm a licensed psychic."

Gertrudt guffawed. "I will never forget the time you told me and that Irish poet about the look on Captain Smith's face, when he asked, 'How do you know the latitude of our crossing?' And then you brandished your (psy) credentials. Oh, I know about the controversy. But with you on board the Titanic, it was unsinkable Molly Brown. You were destined to save all of our lives."

Molly spoke softly, "Listen dear, please listen. I have had dreams about this scantily mustachioed Corporal. He is not to be trusted!" Molly drew another puff from her Camel and waited for her companion's response.

Gertrudt spoke coyly, "Well, you're going to meet him, you know that. And I want you to behave yourself. If you break out and start one of your famous flapper dances with all those dignitaries present, I will never get over it." Smiling, Gertrudt exclaimed, "Oh, dear (Y) it's almost midnight, it will be 7:00 A.M. before you know it. We must pull down these berths and get some sleep."

Molly pulled up the covers and reached into her satchel purse. It was an expensive Spanish detailed design, made from durable suede. The special compartment at the bottom was custom designed, and its contents were guaranteed to always pass through

Customs. She tamped at the contents and placed the purse at her feet as she often did on trips.

The open field Rally events were ceaseless, the Nuremberg Nazi minions, endless. Gertrudt, Ruben, and Molly were in the long greeting line as it approached the political dignitaries and the military ensemble.

Molly spoke little and tried to appear formal, something she always experienced with dread.

She leaned towards Gertrudt and whispered, "Gertrudt, do you remember the time we sat talking with the poet Yeats about the Book of Kells?"

Gertrudt replied, "Of course. I mentioned that the other day."

Molly responded, "Something very strange happened to me at that moment. I've spent all these years trying to focus on something I can't understand. It's as if I was someone else, but I don't know who or when . . ." The American entertainer shared this idea with some emphasis to her friend.

Gertrudt looked at Molly and said, "Molly, you're a New York dancer, a women's rights activist, a card-carrying psychic, and you saved the Titanic. You art more people than anyone has the right to be!"

The greeting line proceeded as Molly continued, "Gertrudt, I dreamed I died."

Gertrudt looked at Molly with a disconcerted sidelong glance. "Please Molly, don't scare me, not now please."

Molly continued, "It was October 26, 1932."

Gertrudt answered, gleefully, "Thank you, dear. Even psychics have normal dreams. You can't die in your past. No more talking; we're being ushered directly before Der Fuhrer."

The open air podium rose before the troop of important

citizens. The German icon graced the parade of dignitaries with the obligatory Nazi salute. Molly looked up at the granite-eyed stare of the man she knew would massacre millions. At that moment, she recalled the dreams of the fire and the wailing, the cacophonous roar of explosion and smoke. She did not know her own precious mind any longer; she no longer loved life. She only feared the death.

The quick shot marksman of the Hannibal, Missouri Handgun Association stood erect, legs spread, and back arched, her left eye closed, her predatory right eye focused like a bird of prey on its next meal. The Colt 45 revolver felt like family in her hand. The years of target practice with her father was about to pay off. The gun's sight was aimed precisely on the bullseye of Adolf's be-smirked mustache.

"Die you piece . . ." Molly felt the pressure of the trigger beneath her index finger as the shot rang out.

"Molly, Molly!!" Gertrudt knelt over the collapsed form of her beloved friend, her eyes so filled with tears she could barely see the vision of horror that was before her. Molly's thick auburn hair seemed to be expanding as if some huge red octopus was unfurling beneath her head. As she nestled her dying friend's head in her lap, torrents of blood poured onto Gertrudt's dress.

Gertrudt screeched, her wails even causing the attending Luftwaffe Major to take notice from the melee.

Molly spoke in short gasps, "Is he dead? The shot sounds funny. I only hear it in my left ear."

Gertrudt rocked with a back and forth motion. "Oh, dear Lord, please take care of this wonderful soul. Please care for her."

Molly opened her eyes and peered upwards to the sky, over Gertrudt's shoulder. "Look, a Black Forest eagle has come to talk to us. Look, it's there, circling."

Molly's left arm struggled in its movement, finally grasping her right wrist. She gasped, "It's tingling, Gertrudt. I'm cold. I remember now. This is how it happened."

The Luftwaffe Major looked down at the two crouched figures and shouted, "It's the head wound. She's hallucinating. She's Kaput!"

Gertrudt looked upwards at the uncaring figure and wiped her eyes. Above the intimidating stature of the uniform, the Major's face was blocked by the sunlight coming around from behind. The medals twinkled and glistened. As she tried to make out the figure, the swooping of a huge eagle caught her attention. It circled, nearly forming a halo above the towering German's head. Its presence was pleasant for the distressed woman. It was a reminder that a world existed outside of the horror chamber which she had suddenly been thrust into. For just an instant, she saw the sun glint in the eye of the soaring creature.

Looking down at Molly, Gertrudt heard the fallen woman muttering, "Aaron's right, he's right."

Gertrudt's look of distress returned. "What? What are you saying Molly?" Gertrudt stopped her gentle rocking as she realized she would not be receiving a response. The most special woman she had ever known, the woman who had saved her life, lay dead in her arms.

Gertrudt dried her eyes once again as she sat up straight and looked at the beautiful face of Margaret Brown. She muttered woefully, "Oh Molly, what are they going to say now in Hannibal Missouri?"

As Molly lay lifeless, eyes closed, with her left hand still clasping her right wrist, she seemed to possess a thin smile. At just the instant Gertrudt noticed the smile, the vivid green eyes of Molly Brown reopened.

Gertrudt gasped as she raised her left hand, covering her mouth. With her right hand, she softly closed the eyelids of her lifeless friend.

Molly felt her eyelids drawn down. She resisted the darkness. The imposed pressure ceased as three souls found themselves standing in a beautiful pastoral scene. The lovely song of the wren and pastoral sounds seemed to hover—at once heard and, yet, as an echo. Molly's vivid green eyes mirrored the rich green fields of soybeans reaching to the farthest distance on the horizon. Helen spun around full circle, gazing at the azure sky.

She muttered, "It's more than blue. It's blue on blue, but there's a harmony with the color jade that I can almost hear."

Molly spoke to the total mind. "This is Hannibal, Missouri. My parent's home is just along this road."

Standing on the neatly-packed gravel road, Shri'Ani could see a figure approach. She squinted slightly as the image appeared to jump closer and closer, in quick motion. In an instant, a young girl stood just in front of the Hindu princess. Shri'Ani drew a deep breath as a solitary tear fell down her left cheek. She hugged the girl tightly as she exclaimed. "Praise Vishnu! Oh, my precious Pyara! Oh darling, how I've missed you!"

Pyara smiled broadly as she delicately wiped the tear from Shri's face. She leaned forward and kissed her tenderly before speaking, "We're together now, Mother, and we always will be." The heaviness in Shri's heart lifted as a cup held in the hand, one instant empty and then instantly full.

The grey eyes of the teenaged girl sparkled as Helen's jade eyes spoke through them. "Yes, Bailey! I see the paradox. It's the similarity of extremes. The heavy cup is full. The heavy heart is emptied."

Pyara reached over with her right hand and held her mother's left hand as she spoke out. "Walk with me a few steps. There's someone who wants to meet with us."

Molly spoke up, "This is my home."

Shri' queried, "Are we going Switzerland, sweetheart?"

Pyara looked up at Shri'Ani as they walked. "No, Mother. Not right now. Right now, I'm just helping you to get familiar with your total mind. It's harder for you because you can't stay. There are really big things going on. We all know that everything should be all right. But our total family seems to be involved."

In the distance, along the road, another figure approached. Shri'Ani smiled as the same stuttering motion brought the figure to within arm's reach.

Helen drew a deep breath as she exclaimed, "You're Thelma! We met just that once at lunch."

The warmth and tenderness of the woman's face contained a voice. It seemed to Helen that perhaps twenty-one minutes of conversation had occurred before she heard the first spoken words.

Thelma said, "Yes, it was so painful for him. But I've been allowed to reach out to him several times."

A tear ran down Helen's right cheek as she responded. "It's hard for me to think of Aaron as a little boy. I dare not let my mind go there. I couldn't bear the weight of losing him."

Thelma continued, "Even when we know that we'll be together again, it does not help to ease the pain of separation. I'm afraid, dear, that both pain and pleasure must be experienced."

Helen looked deeply into Thelma's soft brown eyes as she spoke tenderly, "You and Aaron have the same heart and the same eyes."

Aaron LaSalle's mother grinned broadly as she replied, "He was always so annoyed when someone would tell him that. He'd snap back, 'I look more like my dad.' There's no greater joy in

Paradise than the love of family."

Helen's expression grew stern as she timidly spoke, "I think I understand what Pyara and Bailey were telling me. Family is the real target of evil, isn't it?"

Thelma nodded in agreement as she answered, "You'll be very confused with what's about to be required of you. You've paid your penitence of sacrifice, but we've been called upon to do even more."

Helen's face appeared blank as Thelma continued, "I love you, dear, and I can't wait until you return, but there's someone else to take you on the last part of your visit. All I can tell you is you must follow your heart and try and stay faithful to the instruction of the Authority. Bye, Helen."

Helen reached out to the fading image of the tender smile of Aaron's mother as another image replaced her. Helen's eyes fell to the eager voice of a child standing before her. She grimaced at the sight of a rambunctious little boy, fully attired in his baseball uniform. The boy's broad smile was, at once, charming and anxious.

He spoke enthusiastically, "Hi, I'm Gary. And you are? Well, it's Helen I need to talk to!"

Helen's expression beamed back at the ostentatious child as she spoke, "Well, that would be me! And I'm really glad to make your acquaintance." Helen extended her right hand to shake the little boy's right hand. He shuffled his catcher's mitt as he reached out and shook hands vigorously.

Gary returned his mitt to his right hand as he reached up and took Helen's right hand with his left. He looked up and spoke eagerly, "I'm supposed to tell you some things, while we walk to the great hall."

Helen began stepping forward as the gravel road turned to a

polished golden avenue. In the distance, she could see the base of the brilliant blue sky begin to turn amber red.

She puzzled out loud, "Is sunset coming?"

Gary answered, "Oh no, there's no time here, unless you want there to be. When I go on vacation with Mom and Dad, we always like the sunsets."

Helen's expression grew stern as she spoke softly to the child, "Gary, it seems like I should know this, but I think I really am just Helen, now. And I'm curious. Would you like to tell me why you're so young?"

The little boy looked up and spoke enthusiastically, "Boy, I'm glad you finally asked. I was one of the children who died. I know it's really hard to understand. But Mom was here to meet me when I arrived. You see, there's really no such thing as time. Aaron can explain it to you when you get back home."

Helen stopped walking and turned to the child as she implored, "How do you know about Aaron?"

Gary answered with great distinction. "Helen, he's the reason all this is happening! Well, that's not right either. I told you this was a little confusing." The ostentatious child continued, "I asked Mom if it was painful to wait all those years to see me again. She tries not to cry when I talk about it, so I don't ask anymore." Gary reached up and took Helen's hand as they continued to walk. He instructed, "We're supposed to walk as we talk."

Helen looked ahead and saw that the horizon seemed to be filled with a thick red ring which butted up distinctly to the blue sky.

Gary continued talking as they walked, "I know you're curious. Yes, I go to school. Most people do. Mom makes my lunch each morning, and I go to school with my friends." The pert youth beamed as he spoke up loudly, "I'm the best center field catcher, in the whole Galaxy!"

Helen smiled broadly as she watched the scene before her transform. The amber red horizon and the deep blue sky seemed to elevate the world on its side. She blurted out, "Gary, what's happening?"

"Yeah," he answered, "it's kinda scary isn't it? Just look at the road until it stops. It always makes me dizzy. Mom says it's to remind us that humility is an important virtue."

Helen averted her eyes downward as she felt Gary release her right hand. Looking up, she saw that the entire sky was a deep red to the left and a deep blue to the right. Down the center, a perfect partition appeared. The image stood like a huge double door, one door red and one blue. Helen spun full circle to see that the sky's perfect part followed her viewpoint. As she returned to the forward path, along the avenue, a handsome young man stood in front of her. She gazed at him curiously, taking in the impressive sight of the man in full dress military uniform.

Helen blurted out, "Where's Gary!?"

The young man smiled broadly as he quietly answered, "I'm Gary."

Helen's jade eyes grew wide as she responded, "You've grown into a beautiful man Gary."

The young soldier reached out and, with each hand, took hold of both of Helen's shoulders as he spoke tenderly, "We're all very proud of you and your family. Do what you know is right, and remember, the Authority must be obeyed."

Helen reached out to the fading smile as the bifurcated doors opened and a voice was heard. "Child, step forward on the golden avenue. Enter the gates of the Authority with a humble heart."

Helen walked forward courageously as the binary reality filled all the space around her. Looking down to her feet, she saw that she stood barefoot. The parting line that split the universe into two parts even followed along the floor upon which she stood. The self-reliant woman tried to step left, but the split in the colored luminescent universe remained perfectly centered between her legs and above her head. She stepped to the right, but the universe remained polarized. She spun around in a complete circle, and the entire world followed the rotation as it remained a vivid red on the left side of her body and a deep blue on the right side.

From the left side, an image approached. It stuttered close, in rapid jumps. Helen blinked as an impressive individual stood in front of her. Helen's expression grew bemused as the person walked around her in a rather large circle. She wanted to turn and face the being, but she found that step as she might, she could not outpace the circling form.

Suddenly, the Entity appeared in front of Helen again as she heard a voice. "Do you recognize me?"

Helen's bemused expression turned intense as she spoke, "Well, no! I'm not quite sure what I'm seeing. Are you a man or a woman? I think you appear quite beautiful, but I can't quite be sure if you're attractive or frightening?"

The creature spoke again, "I will appear in a form you will recognize."

Instantly, the individual became the image of Aaron LaSalle. Helen shrieked, "Remove that image! I will not have a demon mimic one of the most wonderful people in the entire world!"

A cacophonous laughter was heard as the image turned to a dazzling winged angelic form. Helen covered her eyes as the intense beauty seemed to take the form of a painful blinding light.

Helen closed her eyes tightly as she insisted, "I will leave my eyes closed until I am removed from your presence!"

The laughter became softer as the Entity spoke, "You can open your eyes. I've tired of the trickery."

Helen cautiously opened her eyes to the presence of a crimson flame. She stood stoically, refusing to give the evil incarnation any opportunity to taunt her emotions.

Some moments passed before the Being spoke again, "You are indeed a formidable spirit. I commend your effort to destroy my earthly Avatar. You may speak; I'll play no more children's games with you."

Helen knew that she must not redress the being with empathy. She spoke assertively, "When will I be returned to my home?"

Beelzebub spoke crisply, "You know that wasn't the correct question, but it is not lacking insight. Ask, again."

Helen blinked as she considered the convoluted statement, "All right, I understand that you, at least, operate logically, so I will entertain the situation. Obviously, there is something I am supposed to learn and take back with me to earth." Helen watched as the flickering red flame seemed to slow and cool in its intensity.

Abaddon spoke in a soothing tone, "Yes, that is an entertaining notion. What do you suppose the message is?"

"You must wish to prevent the removal of the (S) time line," Helen replied, tentatively.

The flame flickered vividly as the Accuser spoke, "That is correct, but your heart is in denial of the direct cause of the reality."

Helen knew that the being wanted her to condemn Aaron's Reveal. She posed a quandary, "Regardless of our attempt to prevent atrocity, we are not the energy which fuels the acts of evil." Helen stepped back one step as the flame's heat suddenly made itself known.

Belial spoke harshly, the voice echoed in Helen's mind, "You are No One to judge the eternal workings of the Universe! You are here to answer for your hubris. Your efforts to aid the fool you love are of no merit."

Helen knew subterfuge when she heard it. She spoke demandingly, "You speak in riddles. I now understand the words spoken, when the gates of the Authority allowed my admittance."

The flame cooled again as Helen continued, "Upon entrance, a well-intended person will expect to be greeted by Yahweh, and humility is proper. That same soul greeted by the 'Father of Lies,' for whatever dubious reason, will follow the instruction and help to condemn their own soul." Helen took two steps back as the flame before her began to rage.

Lucifer's Word became as a thunderous clap of thunder, "Yours is a species of children! I will hold the reins of the Authority, and those that follow my influence will rule on earth."

Helen spoke bravely, "You can kill helpless children, but they will be saved by the one true God!"

The heat from the Thief of Souls became fierce as Helen stepped back in a constant retreat.

Satan's voice echoed, "That child's life would have amounted to nothing; he would have killed and been killed in warfare!"

Helen stopped her retreat. Her fiery jade eyes reflected the evil flames as she walked directly into them.

Helen's heart roared as she shouted fiercely, "I met that child, man, and soldier, and I tell you this, you demon from Hell. You can Not steal the 'duty, diligence and dignity' from that young man. You can Not steal his honor and virtue! You are 'deceit, contempt and betrayal.' I will march into Hell to destroy you!"

The Beast's incandescent flame cooled as Helen's mind slowed to the reality of the moment. The sound of her own thunderous heartbeat was met with the odd scent of her own singed hair.

The Tempter spoke softly, "Bravo, that was impressive. And yes, your last statement was quite correct. You have earned my commandment. Your hubris will test the soul of the man that tests my purposes, most sorely. Helen, if any accounts of the events that have transpired in this passage from your earthly life are conveyed to Aaron LaSalle, he will meet with death within a short passage of time. Further, neither of you will ever be together again, on earth or in eternity. I shall see if the fear of the loss of your one eternal and true love can muster such arrogance and bravery. You will now be returned to earth."

Helen blinked rapidly as she jostled upright in her bed. The effort was made all the more difficult by the wrenching grip of her left hand on her right wrist. She rolled over onto her belly as she caught sight of the red letters on the bedside clock. She jostled frantically as her feet finally hit the floor.

She muttered, "Oh, dear (Y)! It's 3:45 in the morning." The sleepless woman stumbled to her feet as she began the heroic trek to the computer in her den.

([Y] time line)

Helen stood next to her printer and took a deep drink of her coffee. She pondered her next move as she muttered to herself, "I can't waste any time. If there's some trick to be found to escape this Hell on earth, I've got to keep working."

She set down the half-empty cup, and picked up her phone. Punching the familiar number, she spoke out loud, "Come on early bird; show me what you're made of!"

A voice boomed through the tiny speaker on Helen's phone, "What the Hell are you doing up this early?"

Helen's bright green eyes sparkled as she queried into the faithful device, "Would you like another Heineken, Sir?" A paced chuckle emerged from the phone as Helen continued, "Well, yesterday was field research day, wasn't it?"

On the phone's speaker, Aaron's voice spoke out, quietly, "Yeah, that's right. I collected and picked up a lot of data."

Helen waited during what seemed to be a deliberate pause, then a sudden surge of Aaron's voice, a bit louder, made her jump. "Helen! Did it happen?"

Helen responded, softly, "You mean did I have a slip?"

Aaron's voice bordered on shouting, "Well, yes, of course!"

Helen smiled at the device and continued her mystery, "I want to meet you at your office at 6:00 A.M. I know it's Monday, and that's a little earlier then you normally get there, but I've had a strange dream. I need to talk to you. Is that okay?"

The small square of technology spoke assertively, "I'll be there at 6:00." Helen stared at her phone as she stacked her diary sheets from the printer tray.

Helen shouted at the phone, now sitting past arm's reach. "I'll see you then, okay? Bye!"

***

The door handle turned in Helen's right hand. She pushed the door open slowly as she peered around the vertical wall of brown wood and stared at the object of her interest. Professor Aaron LaSalle sat studying at his side table. His perpetual stacks of papers were in attendance. Aaron jumped as he looked up, his distracted attention instantly returned to the moment. A thin smile formed as his soft brown eyes grew wide.

Helen walked up to the seated man as she set her large and heavy satchel down on his table. She stood so close that Aaron needed to wrench his face vertically upwards to look into her eyes. The beautiful woman stood as a fragrant object of feminine perfection. Helen's jade eyes sparkled as she peered down into Aaron's soft brown eyes. The middle-aged man quietly muttered, "You look beautiful. This silk blouse, it's fabulous. The emerald color is breathtaking."

Aaron stood up, took a deep breath and took the eternal object of his passion in his arms. The kiss was the final wakeup call from his newly-rediscovered soul mate. Helen savored the vice-like embrace for some moments, until the urgency of the visit negotiated its way back into her mind. Helen pushed back, grudgingly, against the embrace she so desperately desired.

She spoke up, plaintively, "Aaron, I need for you to explain the Jungle Hypothesis."

Aaron laughed uproariously as he stared back at Helen with great exasperation. He anxiously retorted, "Are you trying to give this old scholar a heart attack!?"

Helen leaned forward and smiled wryly as she responded, coyly, "Well, maybe I'm trying to suggest that you could find your way to my field and do some experimenting with me a bit more frequently."

Aaron smiled broadly as he shook his head, agreeably, and nearly shouted, "Done! I promise. Is tomorrow night all right? I'll make dinner!"

Helen smiled broadly as she spoke up, "Make me some room, while I get my coffee, and please, start talking. I want to know why the diaries from our second lives are so important, and I want to know what kind of Universe I really live in. Start talking."

Aaron leaned back in his chair and with a defeated posture, he retorted, "Well, how much time do you have?"

Helen returned, sat down, and continued, "All right, you and I and our almost-daughter had second lives where we sacrificed ourselves for some greater good, right?"

Aaron shook his head, agreeably, as he responded, "Yes, I'm quite certain that's what happened. We need the exact details shared on paper. Then, our minds will act to focus the Super-consciousness into reenacting the total mind. That should return me to 1703. I'll know to lose the duel and the (S) time line will be erased."

Helen's expression grew stern as she spoke out, "Aaron, is the expanded mind of each living being and the total mind of the Universe, one single thing or a multiple of things?"

Aaron shook his head curiously as he answered, "How do you know to ask that question? I mean I know I go on about this stuff all the time, but I never imagined you would really get it!"

Helen grimaced as she urged, "Talk, Aaron, talk! I have to figure something out before Bailey gets here!"

Aaron continued, "Arthur C. Clark said, 'Any sufficiently advanced technology is indistinguishable from magic.' If the universe evolves to create second generation stars, heavier elements, the DNA molecule, and the minds that result, then entropy doesn't have the final say."

Helen nodded her head as Aaron continued, "Time is not a one way street. So our awareness doesn't cease with death. Our lives are imprinted on some type of continuum. Information, knowledge, and wisdom exist in a dimensional construct of numbers, words, and geometry. Form is the real foundation of existence. 'The shape of water is the vessel which holds it.'"

Helen interrupted, "So there is a new ongoing and cumulative mind that the Hindus refer to as the Akashic record. And like all your weird science suggests, there has to be a twin hemisphere to this mind."

Aaron sat quietly for a moment, gazing into Helen's intense stare. He rose from his chair and stepped to his desk as he began to rifle though its drawers. Sitting back in place with his companion he placed an aged, manila envelope between them. "Helen, this large envelope contains artifacts that stretch back for decades of my life. Its contents are a subtle proof that existence is far more complicated than we naked apes fear to consider."

Helen's gaze intensified. "Why haven't I been shown this before?"

Aaron spoke out gently, "I don't remind myself of some of the things in here, Helen. To be honest, much of it is confusing until certain things happen." Aaron pulled loose papers, odd fragments of notes and inexplicable items from the large envelope, as he held the folded pages of "Sandcastles" in the air. "You recognize this. I hadn't looked at it myself for decades before the day I brought it for you to see." Sorting through the morass of papers, he stopped and appeared frozen in time, as Helen noticed his eyes begin to glisten. "The terrifying dreams occurred over several years and seemed to end in 1988 with the vision of the attack by three planes on the towers and the Pentagon. In the years before these images, I saw an even more horrific destruction of the city. I see things, but I'm not given the dates. Oddly, those earlier visions appeared to be validated in part by this document. I was involved in a computer project many years ahead of its time. There were political forces that didn't want this project to succeed. This remarkable brochure was produced to market the company." Aaron opened the vividly colored brochure in front of Helen and sat quietly.

Helen stared at the page and commented, "I see the silhouette of a city across the bottom of the page and across the page above it in dark blue, perhaps the sky at night or on a dark day. There are these wondrous shapes, like Chicklets falling on the city."

Aaron laid an aged and tattered paper next to it and again sat silently.

Helen studied the paper. "This must be the rough sketch the artist gave to the typesetters to lay out the brochure."

Aaron's misted eyes never left Helen's gaze. "Do you notice

that even the orientation of the Chicklets is perfectly duplicated?"

Helen rebuffed, "Well, of course, the typesetter set them perfectly!"

A thin smile crept across Aaron's face. "Turn the drawing over, see the date, and read the words."

Helen followed the instruction and read aloud, "'June 21, 1984, psychic vision by Thelma LaSalle, two weeks before seeing this.'"

Her jade eyes grew wide with understanding as she retorted, "Psychic abilities run in families!"

Aaron began to speak quite intently, "That date is the summer solstice. My mother drew that while living in another state. She was a very powerful psychic. She was capable of the highest form of the transcendental abilities. She was capable of Remote Viewing. Here's the point. Two days before I saw that brochure, I had the DV in which the city was destroyed in the nuclear holocaust. In that vision, I saw myself stepping into an octagonal shaped time machine. In the vision, I saw the radiation falling down like fat Chicklets on the city on the darkest day. But again, I saw no date, only the woman I'd never met standing beside me. And I was given even more proof. The same morning of the dream, I was scheduled to be in a video production for the project. I was completely unaware that the script called for me to step into an octagonal shaped time machine. I actually experienced the dream within hours of having it."

Helen's green orbs grew wet as she stretched out her hand and clasped Aaron's wrist. "We must prevent this. How is such a thing even possible?"

Aaron spoke up adroitly, "In the early 1950's, experiments were performed by an obscure scientist named John Hammond. He set up a multi-layered Faraday cage in which psychics were tested to see if they could still perform telepathy, remote viewings, and so forth. The point is, if they could perform inside the cage—which would prevent any electro-magnetic conveyance of information—then our minds exist outside the physical universe."

Helen smiled broadly. "It proves that all life is intertwined like a kaleidoscope. We exist outside of time and space."

Aaron continued, "That's right. There's a dimensional construct that we are unaware of. The simple experiment proves that all life, no matter how small, is linked to some sort of super-consciousness. The self-evident truth says there must be some sort of deity. My work validates that it must be a binomial divinity. There was a mysterious US Army project set up in 1978 called Stargate in which psychics, mostly remote viewers, would attempt to see foreign military efforts. When I was a child, my mother told me about the project. She told me about Remote Viewers* that could look at a map and be shown a picture of, perhaps, a Russian scientist and see what they were working on."

Helen and Aaron both sat shaking their heads resonantly as the door to the office opened abruptly.

"Well, this is wonderful! We're all together." Bailey grinned broadly as she walked up to the full table and searched for a spot to drop her materials. Finally depositing her goods, she leaned down, carefully holding her basketball-sized abdomen, and kissed Helen on the forehead. The young, attractive woman seemed to waddle as she stepped over to Aaron and wrapped her arms around him. She smiled ecstatically as she gazed at Helen and spoke out, "Well, Daddy, did you tell Helen our good news?"

The blank expression on Helen's face belied the gut-wrenching emotion stirring in her bowels. Her mind returned to the jealous moments, just hours earlier, when she realized that Bailey was in love with the idol of her many lives. The memory of Molly tamping her last Camel and listening to the crap about Adolf Hitler being a "good guy" flirted past her neurons. The vivid recall of the comfortable feel of a Colt 45 in her fist suddenly seemed quite tangible.

Helen smiled fallaciously as she tersely commented, "Well, no, darling. He didn't tell me anything. He knows how much I love surprises. I can hardly wait . . ."

Bailey turned and kissed Aaron on the cheek as she whispered something in his ear. Helen's breathing deepened as Molly's childhood memories of the endless hours of target practice with her father erupted in her mind. Helen's crossed leg began to bounce rhythmically as she parsed her thoughts and queried, "Well, is anybody going to tell me what's happening here?"

Bailey stood upright as her left arm remained solidly wrapped around Aaron's left shoulder. She muttered encouragingly, "Go ahead, Aaron. You tell her."

Aaron grimaced as he begrudgingly spoke. "Well, Helen, something wonderful has happened. There's a solution to Bailey's trouble."

Helen's right leg, bouncing on her left knee, increased rapidly. Molly's obscure childhood question to her father blurted out of Helen's mouth, "Daddy, I'd like to shoot the target with a machine gun!" The tears fell like an unexpected spring rainstorm from Helen's eyes. The pitiful woman lurched over the table as she began to wail loudly.

Bailey looked at Aaron and nearly screeched, "What have we done!?" The frantic girl dropped to her knees, and clawed at Helen's left arm as she pleaded. "Helen! It's all right. Helen! Ibrahim is going to convert!"

Helen's face snapped back to the desperate young woman and smiled broadly, "What!? What did you say?"

Bailey smiled tenderly as she continued. "He came to me after class and said that he's been reading the King James Version of the Bible."

Helen pawed at her tear soaked face as she repeated the words, "He's reading the Bible?!"

Bailey stood up and took a chair as she continued, "He said that he got to Genesis 18, where Abraham argued with God about not destroying the city, and he heard a voice in his ear."

Helen's expression turned to wonder as she listened intently.

Bailey's grey eyes remained riveted to Helen's sparkling green-eyed gaze as she spoke up, "He said he heard a man's voice speak to him in a perfect Arabic dialect. He said, 'Judge not, that ye be not judged.'"

The tears returned to Helen's face as she began to weep audibly. Aaron jumped from his seat and fell to her side. He held her closely in his arms as a solitary tear fell down his right cheek.

Helen looked up at Bailey and reached across the table, taking her left hand with her right as she asked, "Is he, well is he . . . ?"

Bailey finished the sentence. "He wants to get married at St Michael's Church."

([S] time line)

Bailey stood upright as her right arm remained solidly wrapped around Aaron's right shoulder. She muttered encouragingly, "Go ahead, Aaron, you tell her."

Aaron grimaced as he begrudgingly spoke up, "Well, Helen, something wonderful has happened. There's a solution to Bailey's problem."

Helen's left leg began bouncing rapidly as Bailey interrupted, "I asked Aaron if I could live with him. I mean like, I've never been alone, and I desperately need a father for the baby. Now, that I know we're all family, it just makes sense. Aaron said he'd do it, if you would live with us, too. I mean, I know you and Aaron are a couple! I just want us to be together."

Helen's eyes continued to tear up as memories of the argument with (S) flooded into her thoughts. She responded in a gentle tone, "Bailey, I love you. I know now, you are both Aaron's and my daughter. But I'm looking at a vitally beautiful, young woman that didn't spring from Aaron's loins. When I see you look at my Aaron, the look I see isn't a daughter looking at her father. And that's the problem."

Aaron grimaced as he began to speak. Helen leaned forward and interrupted, "Aaron, dear, I'm the English professor. I know about the Electra complex. And so did our shared favorite author. He wrote about it in *The Tempest*."

Omniscience

([Y] time line)

Bailey hugged Helen tightly and then held her at arm's length as she smiled broadly and repeated her urging. "It's going to be a beautiful wedding. I want you and Aaron to stand up with me and my parents."

Helen gave Aaron a sidelong glance as she grimaced sternly. "Well, that depends on your current parents, dear. But I'm sure we'll do whatever you want, sweetheart."

Helen glanced at Aaron's wall clock and gasped, "Oh my (Y)! I've got to get to my office. Oh, how I hate Mondays." Helen loaded up her materials as she took a moment to glance inside her satchel and confirm that the apocryphal contents were still in their slot. Hesitating at the door, she looked back and caught Aaron's attention. "I will plan on tomorrow night, and I will cook." She smiled broadly and hurried out Aaron's office door.

Bailey stood quietly for a moment and looked at Aaron, who was still sitting at the table attempting to read one of the diaries. She asked, softly, "Aaron, did Helen ask about the expected time-slips?"

Aaron raised his eyebrows and gazed up at his young grad student. He answered with a curious tone, "Well, yes, she did. She spoke about it rather a lot."

Bailey stood stoically. Her bemused expression caught Aaron's interest. He inquired, "What are you thinking?"

Bailey frowned. "It's not what I'm thinking. It's what I'm

feeling. Or maybe it's what I'm seeing. I don't know how to explain it, but I'm feeling like there is an influence on her." Bailey looked at Aaron and insisted, "Didn't you say that your dreams suggest that the slips should occur almost immediately? Aren't your dreams always right?"

Aaron nodded as he agreed. "I had one DV in which a red truck tried to smash me on the interstate. It brought me right out of my sleep. If I hadn't had that dream, I might have been killed driving back last night from Louisville. I was able to get behind the 'seen' truck before it ran off the Interstate. Helen had something like this happen, the last couple of weeks, when some crazy lady tried deliberately to run her off the road. I think it's happened to her two or three times."

Bailey frowned as she stared at Aaron curiously and asked, "And that somehow tells you that you're going to experience the time-slip?"

Aaron smiled wryly as he answered, "Don't you see? These aren't just excursions in time. They're an awakening to one's previous incarnation. It all has to do with the greatest binomial events the mind experiences: life and death."

Bailey's concerned expression remained. "If there's something Helen isn't telling us, she has a good reason."

Aaron shifted in his seat as a look of concern filled his face. "Bailey, now you've got me thinking. What are you trying to say?"

Bailey smiled wryly as she responded, "If there's anything to find, there might be a way to find it."

Aaron queried, "Well, I'm not usually the one begging for explanations. What are you talking about?"

Bailey continued, "Helen is just as OCD as you are. You know about her four-leaf clover obsession, right?"

Aaron nodded as Bailey continued, "If she's not sharing

something, I think I know how to find it."

Aaron grimaced sorely. "I'm not sure that's right. It may violate the Twin Law!"

Bailey pursed her lips as she muttered, "I guess it's just a girl thing, but somehow I feel like there's something I should do."

([S] time line)

Bekah pulled her car slowly to a stop in front of Bailey's house. Sitting for moment, the young Swedish grad student honked twice. Seconds later, the front door swung open and Bailey raced breathlessly from the house.

The door slammed tightly as Bailey jumped into the car and beamed at her friend, "Bekah! Are you getting used to driving on the right side of the road? Is it harder to drive here than in Sweden?"

The white blond beauty brandished a cover girl smile as she shook her head briskly. Her thick accent bore an almost musical quality. "Bailey, a Viking is born to navigate. I've been driving since I was twelve years old."

Bailey leaned forward as she jostled her abdomen to a comfortable position. Leaning back upright, she turned to her friend and smiled broadly, her grey eyes beaming. "Bekah, take us to the English Department!"

Bekah checked her mirrors as she put the car into drive. "I knew you had something else in mind. You 'psychic' types are always coming up with a mystery. But I want to go to the mall!"

Bailey opened her coat and pulled out a Dr. Pepper. "Want a drink?"

Bekah gave Bailey a sidelong glance as she insisted, "Come on,

Bailey, it's Saturday! Why would you want to go to the University?"

Bailey took a drink and hesitated in her response, "I thought a European would know that International Law requires that a card-carrying psychic's instructions must be followed."

Bekah grimaced as she turned into traffic. "Well, I guess you've got me. Wait a minute! That only applies to a 3rd degree certified psychic, right?"

At that moment, Bekah stopped behind a line of cars at a stop light. Bailey peered at the foregoing car's license plate as she read silently, *On God We Depend.*

Bailey chuckled as she teased out an answer, "That's right. I'm only a second degree."

Bekah queried, "So most people don't have the abilities to make it to the 3rd degree, and many just don't want the responsibilities of being certified. Of course, Aaron LaSalle is a 3rd degree certified. Are you really that talented with your visions?"

Bailey turned to Bekah as the translucent blue eyes of the Swede seemed to hear the answer before the words were spoken. "Yes, I'm that talented, and your English professor is, too, just like my meta-physics instructor, Aaron."

Bekah felt a calming influence as she spied a parking spot quite close to the English department's entrance and spoke out, "I wish I could find parking this close during the week!" After pulling in and shutting off her car, Bekah turned to Bailey and calmly asked, "Okay, now tell me why we're at my department?"

Bailey studied her friend's face as she pursed her lips and smiled meekly. "We're here because I need for you to get us into Helen's office."

Bekah's soft azure colored eyes widened explosively. "What are you talking about? I'm not getting into trouble! I'm her assistant;

she trusts me."

Bailey settled into her seat, her grey eyes reaching out to her friend, soulfully. "Listen, this cannot be discussed with Helen . . . until I see if I find what I'm looking for."

Bekah guffawed. "Is that supposed to reassure me? What in the name of (S) are you talking about?"

Bailey responded, "You see why we're friends? You know more about meta-physical things than most people. There's an important paranormal reason for this."

Bekah's expression went blank. "Come on, Bailey. I guess I'm supposed to swoon and just go along with anything you have in mind. It reminds me of my ex-fiancé, Hans. This is the part in the scene where my panties end up in the backseat."

Bailey assumed her best pixie-like smile. "Well, yes, that's quite correct. But you want to keep the features of (S) correctly identified. The god (S) is not exactly oppressive. 'It' is passive-aggressive. Your consent is usually required."

Bekah smiled. "Oh my (Y), you really are a high-level psychic. Hans used to talk exactly like that. I guess a sexless semester in America has me wanting to get screwed. There's some Freudian psychology thrown in for good luck. Will you promise me that we won't get in any trouble?"

Bailey smiled broadly. "Professor Aaron LaSalle needs something from in there badly! He just doesn't know it yet."

The two conspirators smiled, one to the other, as they dashed from the car and made their way into the building.

([Y] time line)

Bekah smiled. "Oh, my God, you really are psychic. Hans used to talk exactly like that. I guess a sexless semester in America is about as long as I can make it, being good. If I have to do something bad, it might as well be for a good cause. There's some Freudian psychology thrown in for good luck. Will you promise me that we won't get in any trouble?"

Bailey smiled broadly. "Professor Aaron LaSalle needs something from in there badly! He just doesn't know it yet."

"Does it have to do with LaSalle's weird science?" Bekah queried. "I mean, I know you two are up to some strange stuff. Has Helen time-traveled, too?"

Bailey looked at her curious Swedish friend and replied, "Bekah, a few minutes ago you stopped at that stop light and I read the car's license plate in front of us. It read, 'In God We Trust.' It made me think of the subtle differences in the two time lines. Suppose I told you that when you drive in the (S) time line you'd hesitate for a moment when you make a left hand turn at the corners."

The blue-eyed blonde peered back with a bewildered stare at Bailey. Bailey continued, "In the alternate (S) time line, Sweden never switched from driving on the left side of the road. Before the day is over, I promise to explain what's going on."

The two conspirators dashed from the car and made their way into the university building.

Bailey and Bekah looked wide-eyed at one another. Bailey spoke calmly, "All right, as we make the turn down the far end of the hall, let's make sure nobody sees you unlock Helen's office. I don't want anyone to tell her that they saw us here over the weekend."

Bekah nodded her head. As the two students walked swiftly down the long hallway, Bekah gave Bailey a nervous sidelong glance. "Do you suppose any staff are in today?"

Bailey grimaced as she quipped, "You don't have to worry about that. The professors live for the weekend. Like, *nobody* should be around *today*."

Just as Bailey finished her comment, a student turned down the hall, coming from the opposing direction. Bailey noticed a rest room sign just ahead as she grabbed Bekah by the arm and quietly urged, "Come on, we don't want any notice or conversation."

([S] time line)

Washing her hands, Bekah took advantage of the moment. "Bailey, how did this other world happen? I never imagined such a thing."

Bailey leaned back against the sink and pulled the Dr. Pepper out of her pocket as she spoke calmly, "At 12:21, at noon on the 21st of December, do you stop whatever you're doing for the 'two minutes of silence' to honor the New York City Holocaust?"

Bekah responded, her voice quieted, "Well, of course. Besides, the phones and everything stop. A person doesn't have much choice."

Bailey took a drink from the Dr. Pepper and continued, "It's like 'the day the earth stood still' every year. Has it occurred to you that the Winter Solstice is the darkest day? It's the day with the longest night. Ancient people always considered it a sign from a loving God that warmth and life would begin to return to the world . . . after that day."

Bekah looked directly at Bailey. Her vivid blue eyes were on the verge of tears. "It was only two years ago! Zoe's gone. America carpet-bombed Tehran out of existence, millions are dead and the world is barely recovering. So you're saying there's a way to make it right again?"

Bailey reached out and gave Bekah a strong hug. "Do you pray to (Y) or to (S)?"

Bekah jerked back from Bailey's grip and grimaced. "That's a silly question! Of course, I pray to (Y). I'm not some atheist!"

Bailey took another drink from the Dr. Pepper, her eyes never leaving Bekah's stare. Pursing her lips and cocking her head in a slightly giddy fashion, Bailey spoke softly, "Suppose I told you that Helen and Aaron might know how to change history so that the Holocaust never happened."

Bekah pulled down a paper towel and wiped her eyes. "You can't get the twin Gods to change their minds. The Authority *is* the authority. The Judaeo-Christian and the Muslim deities have been at war for 1200 years."

Bailey took another drink, swallowing while nodding her head, slowly, up and down. "They are that psychic, Bekah."

The tall blonde Nordic beauty looked at herself and Bailey in the mirror. "Do I look like the Viking Goddess of the Stockholm Spring Festival?"

Bailey smiled. "Oh, yes, you are quite magnificent. If, like, I didn't have my gorgeous Ibrahim, I'd probably be madly in love with you."

Bekah continued, "I'm a student of Viking mythology. In Viking lore, Loki, the trickster God, could undo his destruction when Thor or Odin commanded it. Do you suppose (Y) could force the Muslim extremists to come to peace with their Koran and give up the violence?"

Bailey looked out the restroom door and motioned to Bekah, "Come on. The coast is clear."

Both girls moved in unison the short distance from the restroom across the divide to the faculty office suites hall.

Bekah gave a final glance down the hall before she closed Helen's office door behind her and spoke out, "It looks like we made it. Now, will you please tell me what we're looking for?"

Bailey pulled out a small stack of folded sheets from inside her coat. "This is Professor LaSalle's diary. It's time travel, Bekah. He's traveled through time, and this is his account."

Bekah stood with a distinctly incredulous expression. "Look, Bailey. I took meta-physics 101, and I never heard of such a thing!"

Bailey grimaced. "I'll explain it later! Helen also has a set of papers like this—in this office. We have to find them. Something's not adding up, and I have to find out why!"

Bekah took the papers and studied them for a moment as she answered, "I think I know where they are." Bekah walked over to Helen's kitchenette, and opening the cabinet, she reached high on the shelf and retrieved a small box. "I've seen Helen with this; she didn't think I noticed. And she trusts me not to be in things I don't have any business being in!"

Bailey took the box from Bekah and sat down at the small table by Helen's desk. "Make us some coffee, Bekah, while I get organized." Bailey set the two diaries side by side and began to read. "I know there's something missing; it's as if Helen has kept something from Aaron. I have to figure it out."

The coffee maker percolated in the background as Bekah spoke out, "Bailey, I just found another green and gold four-leaf clover cup high up in this cabinet!"

Bailey's focus seemed uninterrupted as she continued her study of the two diaries, but Bekah's near-shout startled her, and she looked up.

"Bailey!" Bekah insisted. "There's another sheet of typed paper, folded up in the second clover cup!"

As if she heard herself stutter or as though an echo had found its way back from a distant hard surface, Bekah experienced her own statement again: *Bailey, there's another sheet of typed paper folded up in the second clover cup!*

Bekah stood wide-eyed, her young face frozen in time. The

Nordic coed's expression might have been mistaken for a death mask. Bekah's mind raced—all the while, time stood still. She watched as Bailey arched upright in her chair, her right hand grasping her left wrist in a vice-like grip. The expression of pain in her friend's face sent a shockwave of terror through Bekah.

The image of Bailey falling from her chair seemed to occur in slow motion. It occurred to Bekah that it might have been a scene from the space station astronauts tumbling helplessly. Was gravity suspended? The scene seemed to telescope as if the distance to her friend became impossibly great. Could this explain why she was unable to move or take a step to catch her dearest friend before she struck the floor?

Bekah watched as Bailey's face fell softly, turned as it was. She stood helpless and could see her friend's soft grey eyes seeming to stare back. Ever so slowly, Bailey's grim expression began to fill with an inexplicable radiance. Images began to fill Bekah's mind.

The scene sped faster and faster—in reverse . . . Bekah could see herself and Bailey walking backwards, out the door of Helen's office . . . She saw a multitude of life "snapshots" as Bailey grew younger and younger. Pleasant scenes and painful scenes were somehow ordered, side by side. These appeared to rise above the mundane imagery of cutting fingernails and petting the dog. It occurred to Bekah that her friend placed little interest in life's comforts. Somehow, Bailey was predisposed with a fascination; it was some sort of internal contest. Her main concern was that of choosing between good and bad conduct.

In an instant, great distress filled Bailey and Bekah's mind. The frightful cold and wrenching pain of Bekah's first memories—first, the shock of air in her lungs, then the wailing—was replaced with the bliss and warmth of images reaching beyond and then back to this world. Wailing and distress had returned. The Kentucky rifle rose to Riley's shoulder. Bekah could see the red coat fall some distance through the smoke of the rifle's barrel. There was a shout from a figure astride a horse. Riley's memory filled Bekah's mind. "General Washington, this valley is cleared of British!"

The young Catholic-Hindu man, Riley, sat with Samuel Adams and handed him the document he had spent so much time composing. "This will be administered by the Judicial Branch. It will allow the citizenry to vote upon the Will of the Authority. Whether our laws and virtues are of (Y) or (S) will be determined by the fiber and character of a truly free and faithful people."

The thoughts were now no longer in English. The young Hindu girl held an ancient quill pen as she wrote feverishly. Somehow, the deep math and principles she recited in the letter were understood by the young Swedish student. The letter was a frantic warning to her mentor, Francois L'Hospital. Pyara felt the infinite blackness engulf her. The fiery furnace of her own flesh was beyond pain, beyond awareness. It reached throughout all of her lives. The combustion was the very essence of contradiction. The teenage Hindu girl's flesh, even her soul, became death. In that instant, Bailey heard the pivotal memory as she kissed her beloved Arab. "All right, Ibrahim, I'll convert to your faith."

Bekah watched as Bailey's image on the floor began to shiver as if it were being watched through a clear bowl of water. Bekah's blue eyes blinked as she saw Bailey's right hand become her left and her left wrist become her right . . . Suddenly free to move, Bekah outraced her tears as she lunged forward and gathered Bailey in her arms.

Bailey held her friend close as she spoke softly, "Oh! Dear Bekah, thank you so much for being with me through those years."

Bailey's numbness was intense as she allowed Bekah to help her return to her seat. She shook her head as if to clear it, then spoke, "Quick, get me a note pad and pen. We have 21 minutes, we won't speak until I'm done, and then, we'll go to Professor LaSalle's. See if you can text him while I write. Only tell him when we'll be there. Say only—'Bailey has the answers.'"

Bekah sat quietly in absolute amazement, her left hand covering her mouth. The blue-eyed European's expression might have been that of a helpless child watching as someone's home blazed in an inferno. It occurred to her that no human could write as quickly as the spectacle that she was observing. Bailey smiled as she stopped writing and looked up, speaking tenderly, "Whatever was hidden in that cup wasn't supposed to be seen by anyone."

Bekah slowly handed the folded sheet of paper to Bailey as she muttered, "Helen talked to Satan."

Bailey took the paper as she replied meekly, "Did you read all of it?"

Bekah's white-blonde hair seemed to shiver as she shook her head disagreeably. She spoke quietly, "I only read the first couple of sentences, and whatever just happened, happened."

Bailey grimaced as she unfolded the paper and began to read. Bekah nearly shouted, "No, don't read it! It might happen again!"

Bailey looked up and smiled tenderly as she encouraged, "It can't happen again. You haven't been through it. The power of the deity is embodied in the words, literally. This piece of paper is now linked to the evil god. You might have been killed just by reading it. That's why it triggered the total mind experience."

Bekah retorted. "What do you mean, 'I haven't been through it?'"

Bailey continued. "I've already time slipped. You just forced the energy to channel the consciousness back to me. Did you experience anything from any previous lives?"

Bekah's face turned sour as she replied disconcertedly, "I only got to the point where we were born!"

Bailey smiled as she responded. "Well, that's probably good. You're not ready to know anything else right now."

Bekah's bemused expression shifted to curiosity as she continued. "There was something very familiar to me about that fire thing, or whatever happened to you as a teenager. You were burned up, right?"

Bailey nodded as she answered, "Yeah, that was 300 years ago."

Bekah's bemused smile turned to wonder as she spoke, "Well, what was that? I mean, it wasn't like heat! I saw . . . I mean, you were looking at that piece of paper in your hand and it wasn't burning."

Bailey rose to her feet and gave her friend a loving hug. "Come on," she said. "Let's get over to Aaron's."

Bekah's car pulled slowly into Aaron LaSalle's driveway as Bailey removed her sunglasses and turned to her fellow time traveler. She spoke up cheerfully, "How can you stand to drive in the bright sun? I'd be blinded."

Bekah chuckled. "Oh my (Y), you mean the blonde Swede knows something that you American scientists don't? Blue eyes do not refract the sun's rays as readily as a dark iris."

Bailey picked up her packet of copies of both sets of diaries. "I don't know how I'm going to explain to Helen that I've stolen her most precious memories."

Bekah spoke timidly, "Ya. The hard part is you have to apologize to three different people and two of them aren't even alive!"

Bailey held the papers close to her chest and closed her eyes. "Oh dear (Y), if there is a way to prevent the holocaust of New

York City on 12/21/12, please help Aaron figure it out."

Looking at her friend, Bekah's intense stare never faltered as she replied, "One time, me and my friends sneaked into Hilga's dorm room and stole all of her panties. It's a tradition in Stockholm. We raid the drawers of the prettiest freshman and throw her panties down the halls of the boys' dormitory."

Bailey turned to her friend and grimaced. "You mean there's somebody in that country even prettier than you? I'm glad I'm an American!" Bailey's attention was drawn to the front of the house. "There's Aaron at the door! I guess we had better get this over with. I'm as scared as I was at the battle of Valley Forge. Three lifetimes, and it's one of my most vivid memories."

Bailey and Bekah hurriedly walked to the front door of the smiling meta-physics professor's home. Soft brown eyes tracked every facial nuance of the grey-eyed, dark-haired girl. Bailey lagged behind the scampering blonde, burdened as she was with an armful of papers and notebooks and her expectant condition.

Aaron held the door wide open as the duo of culprits crossed the threshold to his lair of paternal security. Bailey set her fistfuls of papers on the foyer table as mounds of thick brown hair bounced into Aaron's face. Throwing her arms around the wide-eyed man, the vivacious girl exclaimed, "Francois! Oh dear (Y), Francois. I love you so much!"

Aaron looked through Bailey's thick locks to see the blank expression of Bekah, staring back. The wide, blue azure eyes of the Swedish grad student were radiant. The total-mind experience with Bailey had left her with sporadic memories of the childhood years of the Frenchman's daughter.

Francois felt the loving warmth of his precious Shri'Ani holding him close. The cold black hair on his face seemed to shout for the need of another log on the fire. The thought of jumping out of the warm goose down bed was regrettable. Francois began to unravel himself from the nude feminine knot of his wife's flesh, when he heard an unexpected teenage voice. "I've got it." The aging French mathematician peered through Shri's thick locks to see Pyara jump from the bed as her lithe nude form leaned over the fireplace. In an instant, the young handmaiden, who was more an adopted daughter than a servant, snapped her head back to meet Francois's eyes. The young girl's Hindu accent was comforting. "It will be hot in a moment."

The young sprite flung herself back into the bed and the jostling for position began. Francois silently counted the arms around his neck as he felt cold hands kneading the warmth from his groin. Shri'Ani turned her face upwards to her beloved husband as she spoke quietly. "I told you she is almost 14 years old now! You must take her with us to meet boys her own age."

Aaron cupped Bailey's face and looked deeply into her soft grey eyes. He wiped a tear from under her left eye as he noticed that a tinge of green had appeared around the periphery of the iris. He spoke up tenderly, "Come on girls; let's go into the den and talk."

Reaching down, Bailey retrieved the stack of papers from the foyer table as the trio walked silently into Aaron's study. Seating themselves around the table, Bailey set the stack of papers in front of her mentor. "The top one is from the 'slip' I just experienced in Helen's office." Aaron's brown eyes grew wide as he gazed back at the expressive girl. Bailey continued, excitedly, "I know. It's unbelievable! But, that's only part of it. The next diary is another one you've never seen. Helen had a 'slip' she never shared with us!"

Aaron's blank stare moved slowly from Bailey to Bekah as he queried, "Did you witness this?" Bekah stared back silently as her head began to nod frantically. Aaron's expression remained fixed as he spoke up curiously, "Bekah, I'm sensing something I've never experienced. I see radiance in your eyes. Did you also undergo the rapture with Bailey?" Bekah's wide blue eyes sparkled and began to water as she again nodded her head up and down, frantically.

Aaron's soft brown eyes peered outward from the face of the frantic soldier. Yuri Vladiovich felt the intense heat inside the burning building. The thick black smoke threatened to steal the last bit of clean air from the inferno. The young Russian lieutenant knew that the terrified screams of the German girl were close. One more fiery door seemed to be the last obstacle between the frenzied man and the hysterical voice. Throwing all his weight into the door, the burning heat gave way to a shower of sparks and a torrent of blinding smoke. The child's desperate cries for help were finally connected to the embodiment of the torment. Peering from under a pile of blankets, Yuri saw the blackened face of the white haired girl.

In one swift motion, the resourceful soldier scooped up the pitiful scrap of humanity from the floor, covered her with the blanket, and headed back into the inferno. The roar of the fire almost squelched the sounds of the raging battle outside. Yuri knew that he must run as fast as possible, in the direction opposite to that from which he came. He closed his brown eyes tightly as he muttered, "Dear (Y), please grant this child salvation." Inhaling the last available breath of noxious air, the two souls burst forward into the flames. His pounding feet seemed to strike solid flooring. Yuri knew that was the key. He knew that the direction was right, and he knew that if he opened his eyes, the heat could overwhelm him.

As if time stood still, the dutiful man plowed forward. A recurring thought seemed to torment the ordeal. The beleaguered soul wondered if he might be fleeing in the wrong direction. His mind seemed to be fixated as the question kept repeating, *Is this the right direction?* As if running from a nightmare, the last step carried the sacred cargo from the fires of Hell to a world of cool fresh air. The Russian lieutenant set the child down as he fell to the ground, desperately gasping for air. Looking up, he saw the riveting blue eyes and white blond hair of the young girl's face.

Aaron understood that he must break the intense time sync that was raging in these two young women. The meta-physics professor understood that teenage girls evidence the greatest (psy) intensity. He also knew that the time-slip connectivity of all three of their lives was beyond improbable. The divine consciousness of the Authority had somehow brought all the participants to this moment.

Aaron demurred from Bekah's gaze as he drew a breath and muttered. "Girls! Why don't you go into the kitchen and make us some hot drinks? I need to get started on Helen's diary and somehow organize the last 300 years."

***

Aaron sat quietly working at his den table. The array of papers, notebooks, and his perpetually active pen were contrasted by a bowl of fast food condiments. Bailey stood peering in his direction down the hall as the tea kettle and kitchen sounds provided the background timbre.

She stood motionless as Bekah approached and queried, "What's he doing?"

Bailey spoke softly, "He's doing what he always does. He's sitting with his pen and paper, unraveling the secrets of the Universe."

The napkins were placed appropriately, and the tray of refreshments was set at the far end of the table. The girls scurried about pouring the tea, coffee, and hot cocoa as Aaron's focus remained uninterrupted. Seating themselves, each shared the impression that the serious moment should remain inviolate.

The chorus of Aaron LaSalle's handmade "ticking" clocks, ceaselessly announced the passing minutes. Sitting quietly, being careful not to disturb Aaron's concentration, both girls blinked as the scholarly man at last raised his head. Bailey felt her spirit lift as she saw the infrequent smile beaming across his face.

He spoke whimsically, "Who has the first question?"

Bekah turned to Bailey, raising her left eye brow, inquisitively. Bailey nodded as she asked Bekah, "Do you have a question?"

Bekah's Swedish accent was pronounced as she exclaimed, "Professor, what in the name of Odin is going on? Bailey calls me out, I steal into my dearest professor's office, and I see things that my eyes or mind or something could/should never see! Am I dreaming?"

Aaron and Bailey's eyes met as Bailey timidly smirked. Aaron's focus remained on Bailey as he reached across the table, retrieved one of the papers from Helen's stolen diary and held it up. "You dreamed this had occurred, didn't you?"

Bailey nodded as she replied, "Aaron, we've worked for months, trying to figure out how your one time-slip could have changed the entire world. It didn't make sense. You and I and Helen have each had one experience. We saw ourselves in our previous lives, but we didn't know there was an entirely different time line. You're the only one that knew the dollar bill is wrong."

Bekah's expression turned to that of confusion as she quietly opened her purse and began to dig.

Aaron responded, "When I did the 30 day Reveal for the 12/21/12 prophecy, I saw the Sandy Hook atrocity the morning of December 14th. I went to the computer and tried to contact Helen. She didn't respond, so I considered this a sign from the Authority. I sent the e-mail to the Newtown, Connecticut, authorities. That's when the rapture occurred—my mind was sent to my first incarnation in the year 1703, and I delivered the equations to myself, 300 years ago."

Bekah interrupted, "If this is supposed to answer my question, I see now why I'm studying literature. What are you talking about? What is a 'sandy hook'? And what is a 'reveal'?"

Aaron rubbed the palm of his hand across his face, blinked, and looked deeply into Bekah's vivid blue eyes. "Bekah, everything is broken into twos: high and low, up and down, men and women, night and day, (S) and (Y). You understand that, right?"

Bekah grimaced. "I'm blonde, Professor, but dumb and smart. I understand!"

Aaron smiled wryly, and continued, "The most important of these twins for humanity is a mother and a father."

Bekah blinked, questioningly, looked at Bailey's belly, and quipped, "That idea hasn't been real popular recently, has it?"

Aaron smiled and continued as he peered intently into Bekah's blue eyes. "Well, here's what only three people understand . . . now, there's four. There is also another entirely similar, but different, dimension. There are two time lines, actually three, but let's keep it simple and talk about just two. Have you ever heard of the Titanic disaster or the Sandy Hook massacre?"

Bekah's riveting blue eyed gaze went blank as she retorted, "No!"

Aaron replied, "In the one time line, the largest ship ever made—the Titanic—sank on its maiden voyage from Ireland to New York on April 15th, 1912."

Bekah grimaced. "That's ridiculous. What are the chances of that? And why would it sink?"

Aaron smirked as he wryly answered, "It hit an iceberg."

Both girls laughed loudly as Bekah retorted, "Oh, Professor, that is the funniest thing I've ever heard! It would take the depths of evil; only an atheist could come up with that. Even (S) itself could not dream up such an irony. And what is this sandy hook thing? It reminds me of the time I stepped on a fish hook as a child. I've half a notion to pull off my shoe and show you the scar."

Bailey covered her face with both hands and leaned into her elbows on the table as she mumbled, "Good luck, Professor!"

Aaron drew a deep breath and slouched back in his chair. His expression turned quite nonplussed as he spoke softly. "Bekah, you must hold a reverence for the inspired writer Samuel Clemens?"

Bekah's eyes sparkled as she smiled and replied, "Funny that you ask. Mark Twain is the topic of one of my papers."

Aaron's posture remained unchanged. "Did you know he was born the year Haley's comet appeared? He always said he rode in on its tail and would ride out on it?"

Bekah grimaced. "I suddenly see the dates of his birth and death in a new way."

Aaron leaned forward, reaching for the bowl of fast food condiments. The girls looked at one another as he began to pluck small packets of salt and pepper from the bowl. Concentrating on his search, he spoke quietly, "Well, my favorite Twain quote is 'Truth is stranger than fiction.' I think I know why this is happening. And maybe (Y) will have the last word. I need to explain a little more to you before I meet with Helen tomorrow. Another pertinent quote you may know, Bekah, is one of my favorites. Shakespeare modified an ancient Roman quotation—in Romeo and Juliet. The smitten Romeo said 'I am fortune's fool.' Captain James T. Kirk, of Star Trek fame, used a modification of this, 'Fortune favors the foolish.'"

Aaron smiled wryly as his focus rose to the level of eye contact with the girls. Briskly dumping out the miscellaneous contents of the large bowl onto the serving tray, he continued, "No self-respecting bachelor is without his hoard of ketchup, mustard, and salt and pepper packets. The fast food industry leaves the malnourished customer with a small bonus."

Bekah and Bailey gave one another a deliberately expressionless sidelong glance. Filling the empty bowl with the sizable mound of salt and pepper packets, Aaron reached in, fluffing and mixing the cauldron of checkered condiments. Holding the bowl above the girls' heads he spoke, "Let's do an experiment in probability science. Reach in and pull out one packet at a time and place them in order, in front of you. We'll go left to right. Bekah, you go first."

Bekah grimaced as she reached above and into the bowl. Looking at her catch, she replied, "Well, I got a white packet, salt."

Bailey reached in, grabbed a packet, and announced, "I got a pepper."

Bekah pulled another. "I got another salt."

Bailey pulled. "Well, does this have anything to do with our hair color? I got another black packet."

The girls pulled 6 times each and placed the packets in order on the table in front of themselves. Setting the bowl aside, Aaron leaned over the small rows of black and white squares, lined up before the girls. He looked up and instructed, "All right, Bailey, you pulled, in positive time order, black, black, white, black, white, white. Bekah, you pulled white, white, white, and white, black, white."

Aaron sat back in his chair expressionless, gazing at the girls. Some moments passed before Bekah finally looked at Bailey and spoke adroitly, "I liked the part about Shakespeare. But you two are the physics nerds. I don't get it!"

Aaron chuckled. "Well, curiosity is part of the point, isn't it?"

Bailey's soft grey eyes sparkled as she made eye contact with Aaron. "There are far fewer peppers in that bowl. That's right, isn't it?"

Aaron smiled as he lifted his hands from the table and began to clap. "I am constantly reminded why you are my favorite grad student."

Bekah grimaced and spoke abruptly, "Wait a minute. I got nothing but salt and she got mostly pepper. What makes you think there's far more salt?!"

Bailey spoke up, "Look, Bekah. There are eight salts and four peppers. Mine is one-half pepper, but there's more salt than pepper." Bailey peered up at Aaron. "Is that right?"

Aaron nodded his head, approvingly, as he responded. "It's actually . . . one in four is pepper."

Bekah's expression remained bemused. "Then, how did I get so many salts?"

Aaron leaned forward slightly and spoke very softly, "The Universe isn't fair, Bekah. There is an eternal contest between cosmos and chaos."

Bekah grimaced. "No, really, Professor! Now, I'm curious. How did that happen? Will it continue to give Bailey more pepper than me? I got mostly salt."

Aaron reached out and swept the packets into a pile, pushing them aside. Placing his note pad in front of the girls, he took his pen and wrote the numbers 1,2,3 across the pad. Directly under this row he wrote, 6,5,4. He then asked a question. "How many numbers do you see?"

The girls answered in unison, "Six."

Aaron continued, "Do you suppose I can turn the six numbers into seven without adding another number?"

The chorus was repeated, "NO!"

Aaron took his pen and pointing to the 1 above the 6, he asked, "How much is six plus one?"

Bailey answered, "Seven."

Aaron then took the pen and pointed to the 2 above the 5. "How much is five plus two?"

Both students answered, "Seven."

Finally, Aaron pointed at the 3 above the 4. "And how much is four plus three?

The cadence continued, "Seven."

Both girls chuckled as Bekah quipped, "Well, that's kinda interesting, but it's just numbers. What does that really mean?"

Aaron reached into the pile of spice and extracted 6 salt packets. Placing them in a row on the table, he inquired. "How many packets do you count?"

Bekah responded, "There're six."

Aaron looked at Bekah and said, "Take your finger and count them."

Bekah grimaced as she pointed at each packet in the row and began to count. "One - Two - Three - Four- Five – Six."

Aaron took the last 3 packets from the row and formed a column directly beneath the third packet. He queried. "Do you see the 'ell' shape? It looks like a seven, doesn't it?"

The girls nodded in agreement as Aaron continued, "Okay, Bekah, count the row and the column, start at the beginning in each case."

Bekah took her finger and counted the row of salt, "One - Two - Three." At the 3rd packet, she counted down the column, "Four - Five - Six - Seven."

Bailey's expression was nonplussed as she looked at Bekah. "If you are as under-whelmed as I was the first time I saw this, don't be afraid to say it."

Bekah began to laugh, nervously. "I love your American Twilight Zone! As a child in Stockholm, my parents actually asked the doctor about my fascination with macabre things. I had a huge insect collection. I still have nightmares about being pinned to a giant corrugated sheet of cardboard. I think I get it!"

Aaron smiled wryly and looked at Bailey as he spoke, "All right, tell us how the six became seven—without adding another number or another packet?!"

Bekah smiled with great confidence. "It's all perspective! There really are an infinite number of packets, if you close your eyes and just keep counting."

The meta-physics professor looked at Bailey and laughed. "She's smart, Bailey. I see why you like her so much."

Bailey retorted, "She's also the 'Spring Festival Viking Goddess' of Stockholm. I'm really not sure if I'm in love with her or I hate her. She's too smart and too beautiful!"

Bekah's tone became quite serious, "I want to know about this twin time line. And how are both of you able to make contact with your previous lives? I know it's in the meta-physics text books, but why is it happening to you, Professor, and Bailey and Helen, and now, me, somehow?"

Aaron responded, his tutorial tone was his comfort zone, "The (S) time line accepts the premise that consciousness is a natural physical property. Energy, mass, and the inherent information in permutable events are understood to be contained in some larger dimensional framework. What each of us observes is only partially the same as what someone else observes. Reality is not completely uniform. When probability is involved, which is pretty much everything, there is an odd multiple 'stutter' and a bias that occurs individually."

Bailey spoke out, "So I pulled the pepper packets predominately, and Bekah pulled the salt predominately, and that imbalance is actually expected."

Aaron nodded approvingly as he responded, "If you continued to record data for any binomial system, you'll find that you as the observer will experience an anomaly in the patterns. Following any improbable sequence, like Bekah's long run of salt packets, she will immediately tend to experience another improbable run. This occurrence should follow rates found by what's called logarithmic dampening. However, the phenomenon exceeds the rates that are expected. The mathematics comes from what is known as Bernoulli's Law of Large Numbers. The expected results follow a principle known as the Invariance principle." Aaron slowly shook his head, disapprovingly as he continued, "Francois L'Hospital ended up with the information that this isn't exactly happening. There's an extra Variant rate. That information changed all of science and religion."

Bekah asked, "So the Old Wives' Tale that lightning doesn't strike the same place twice is wrong?"

Bailey responded, "In fact, people who should never be struck by lightning, even once, like a sales clerk at the mall—not a forest ranger or a golfer—gets hit once, and then, it happens repeatedly. Today, we accept paranormal occurrences as real and do not overtly reject rare, albeit improbable, evidence. Aaron says that in this alternate time line they don't accept that there is some type of supra-natural reality."

Bekah interjected, "Everybody knows that each mind is like a cell in a larger body. That body has two hemispheres; the Super-consciousness has twin personalities: good and evil."

Aaron looked at Bekah, smiling as he asked, "You're Catholic, aren't you?" Both girls nodded in unison as Aaron continued,

"Suppose that this world has a slight bias for one or the other God. You just discovered that if you pull out too many high probability salt packets or too many low probability pepper packets that the bias will repeat. And this is independent for each unique participant. This time line, I now know, is the (S) time line; it has a mirrored counterpart, the (Y) time line. I saw you get out a dollar bill a while ago. Read the inscription."

Bekah retrieved the dollar bill from her purse and read, "'On God We Depend.'"

Aaron's expression remained blank as he spoke, "In the (Y) time line that bill says 'In God We Trust.'"

Bekah shook her head, smiling. "What does it all mean?"

"It has to do with perspective and attitude," Aaron replied. "In the (Y) time line, the Twin Law is obeyed more readily than it is here in the (S), even though they don't know the term. Individual free will isn't imposed upon, even by the omniscient deities. In the (Y) time line, the Great Religious Wars have still occurred, but they've been nation-state conflicts. The four-year vote on the Will of God, here in America, doesn't occur. The Constitution instructs a fully secular government."

Aaron smiled. "Bekah, it's like you said earlier. It is all a matter of perspective. If your eyes are open, you think you see six packets. If your eyes are closed, there are either no packets or an endless number of them. Only a mind can sort it out. I've discovered through my experiments that there is always something extra right before our eyes. We usually choose not to see it. Twenty five hundred years ago, a Greek philosopher named Democritus actually conceived of the atom. Supposedly, he cut an apple and asked himself a question, 'Are the two circular cut surfaces exactly the same size?' If they're not, then all things must be comprised of exceedingly small particles. He cut smaller and smaller slices and asked the same question. He conceived of the tiniest remaining speck of the surface of the ball-shaped fruit. He named this uncuttable component the 'atomos.' Democritus may have quoted something far more revealing about the mind. He said, 'Until a thing is named, it never existed. Until a thing is numbered, its value is never counted. Until this is understood, a person does not know himself.'"

Bekah queried, "All right, so both realms are almost identical, but there are small differences. You spoke of the world being influenced by the deities. What about this Titanic disaster? If I Google Titanic, there will be some really old ship somewhere. But in the (Y) time line, it sank 100 years ago. That seems like a pretty big difference!"

Aaron responded, "That's right, but the reality wraps itself around the events to bring the entire system back to roughly, a harmonic unison. For example, with the sinking ship, there was a woman who rowed a boat around in the freezing water and pulled as many people as she could into the boat. In our time line, this woman was an accepted psychic, so she went to the captain and showed her (psy) credentials. He took the ship out of the ice fields. You can Google it. Her name was Margaret Brown. She was known as the 'Unsinkable Molly Brown' in both time lines."

Bekah grimaced, "So I can Google this and it will tell me about her. So she's a heroine."

Bailey interjected, "Well, that depends on whether you're a Protestant or a Catholic. She was later killed trying to assassinate Adolf Hitler!"

Aaron interjected, "In the (S) time line, relatively small catastrophes, including mass murders don't tend to occur as much. The divine influence in our reality roughly follows the Twin Law, but in the (Y) time line, there are more isolated atrocities. One occurred in the (Y) reality at an elementary school known as Sandy Hook."

Bekah's expression became quite distressed as she nearly shouted, "Slow down! I'm getting really confused. Look, here's what just occurred to me. This heroine, who saved the ship, was she directed by (Y) or (S)?"

Aaron answered, "Well, in each time line, her actions affected many lives and affected history. So we can assume that she was participating in the Will of the Super-consciousness. This cumulative divine mind is known as the Authority."

Bekah continued, "So how does this work? Are we better off in the (S) reality?"

Aaron responded, "Well, you can answer that question for yourself. In the (Y) reality, New York City and Zoe are still with us."

Bekah grimaced. "What about this Molly Brown? Does her consciousness continue today?"

Bailey let out a small moan as she clasped her face with both hands and leaned onto the table. "I'm not even going there, you can explain it, Professor. Good luck!"

Aaron turned to Bekah, holding Bailey's hand written diary in his hand. "You haven't read any of this, right?"

Bekah's white blond hair spun back and forth around her face like snowflakes in a scenic snow globe. "I barely knew such things ever occurred!"

Aaron grimaced. "But you experienced Bailey's 'total-mind,' correct?"

Bekah nodded, her blizzard of follicles vibrating up and down.

Aaron leaned forward and spoke gently, "Tell me, how much do you remember about Bailey's lives?"

Bekah's fine Nordic features strained as her vivid blue eyes squinted, with a decidedly left sidelong glance towards Bailey. "I have two really painful images . . . no, three. I remember Bailey and myself being born. You Do Not want to relive that, believe me!" Bekah winced with the memory. "It's really cold. You never experienced cold before that instant! You can keep it!"

Aaron looked wide-eyed at Bailey as he spoke tenderly, "Oh, my poor child!"

Bekah nearly shouted, "Not so quick! That's only the beginning! The other memory, the one that really wants to stick, is Bailey burning up. I don't know how to explain even experiencing something like that. It's beyond pain. But here's why it's sticking in my mind. When Bailey and I first got here, and I looked into your eyes, Professor, I had a memory of being a child and being pinned under some kind of rubble in a burning house!"

Aaron's expression became most intense as Bekah continued, "This soldier, I think he was Russian, came in and pulled me out! I never experienced anything like that in this life! It was me, I look the same now, but it wasn't this life. It had to have been my previous life!"

Bekah's azure blue eyes grew wide as she looked deeply into Aaron's soft brown eyes. The blue of her eyes sparkled wet as she spoke adoringly, "It was you, Aaron, wasn't it? Tell me. It was you!"

Aaron's head nodded humbly as his stare dropped to the table. Bekah continued, "That's why I had the recurring dream as a child. I had a terrible fear of being pinned to this hard wooden floor and a fire raging around me. I can still feel the heat—just talking about it. I was always saved, at the last minute by my father. I think that's why I pinned all those poor bugs to the cardboard. I thought science would put my fear to rest."

Aaron spoke quietly, "Do you know much about Sigmund

Freud's work?"

Bekah shook her head, left to right. Aaron continued, "He talked about the development of the mind. We advance from the Id, to the Ego, to the Super-Ego. In the (Y) time line, such thinking is thought to explain all such psychological conditions. In the (S) time line, we know there is much more going on."

Bekah spoke timidly, "Were you my father, then?"

Yuri smiled as he spoke to the frail German blond girl in his arms. "I'm taking you with Sasha and me. You'll be safe with the two of us."

"Aaron," Bailey queried, "why is it that there seems to be less individual sacrifice in the (S) time line? Even the Twin Towers weren't destroyed until the 2012 Holocaust?"

Aaron looked slowly, left to right, first deeply into Bekah's teary blue eyes and then deeply into Bailey's grey orbs. "That seems to be the issue, dear! We can't avoid the disasters or the loss. Reality seems to be some kind of pressure cooker. (Y) lets the steam out slowly. (S) likes the catastrophes. Large. It's why the ecclesiastics talk about the Authority. The twin Gods seem to fight over which destiny prevails."

Bailey mused, "The Twin Law says 'Goodness is any act or intent that allows a separate thing to be all that it can be. Evil is any act or intent that impedes a separate thing from being all it can be.' The thing that's always been hard for me to understand is the paradox. If I eat a salad, I killed the lettuce. But I can't live without eating."

Aaron smiled; his humane expression spoke volumes. "The curious thing to me is that evil doesn't have a better way. It doesn't have a better idea. It wasn't trying to re-direct our actions or thoughts. It's Only intent is to destroy! How can something so dead exist in the same reality as life?"

The three sat quietly for a moment. Bekah spoke first. "I like Molly. I want to know about the Unsinkable Molly Brown." Aaron and Bailey's expressions turned to amazement as she continued, "Why, though, when I think of her, do my thoughts go to Helen?"

Aaron squinted slightly as he focused his attention on Bekah. "I want to clarify something. The reason Bailey got so many pepper packets stems from a mathematical curiosity. The greatest chance of a low probability event repeating is immediately after the event occurs. Can you wrap your mind around that?"

Bailey and Bekah gave one another a sidelong glance as Bekah quipped, "And you spend most of your time around this?"

Bailey shrugged as she smiled broadly and replied, "I can't help myself. If I ever get a straight answer, I start worrying if he cares!"

Bekah smirked and continued, "My aunt has been struck by lightning four times. It almost killed her the last time. It's not natural, I know that." Bekah looked up at Bailey and then Aaron as she queried, "Aaron, Bailey said that you and Helen might be able to prevent the Holocaust of New York City. Is that right?"

A timid expression filled Aaron's face as he responded, "Two out of three of our reincarnated family members died, by the Will of (S), in their second lives. If I'm taken back directly to that lifetime, and I can record what happened, then the written word in this reality should force the hand of the Authority."

Bekah asked, "Why can't (Y) just return you now?"

Aaron smiled wryly as he answered, "If the Authority doesn't perceive a reason to intervene, it won't act. The Super-consciousness is the genuine personality of the Universe. The creator and the destroyer parts of the issue are little different than our own indecision. We weigh the good and bad possibilities, which ultimately lead us to some sort of action. Humanity desperately needs to come to the realization that we can make enough mistakes to finally destroy even our greatest accomplishments."

Bekah grimaced as she asked, "But isn't (Y) like our father? I mean good and bad is relative. We're supposed to survive, right?"

Aaron chuckled as he retorted, "If you can get in some type of spaceship and go very nearly the speed of light, you can age maybe one day, but back on earth perhaps one thousand years has passed. You can turn the ship around, return to earth, and you've aged two days, while the earth is as far in the future as today is from ancient Rome. Can you wrap your mind around that?"

Bekah smiled. "I took physics. I don't really understand it, but I accept it."

Aaron smiled. "Okay, let's try this, then. If you can travel thousands of years into the future and still be you, the young woman I'm looking at, doesn't that mean that the future must already be there?"

Bekah grimaced. "So two thousand years for the world would be the day after tomorrow for me?"

Aaron began shaking his head, approvingly. "Yes, exactly! If you are still you, and your awareness is little different, then doesn't that mean the future is already there?"

Bekah smiled. "That's pretty deep!"

Aaron continued, "When you counted the salt packets stacked in rows and columns, you counted more than six packets. The 'shape' of the counting actually changes the numerical set of objects. That's the issue. Just as the future can be seen to already exist, the past can also be seen to be immutable. You're still getting out of bed this morning! The past doesn't disappear. Time and space are simply mental impressions of variant shapes. Our mind is adding up the construction, microsecond to microsecond, to produce what we call reality."

The three sat quietly for a moment as Bailey interjected, "So mankind isn't as important as we think we are. If something doesn't grow, it dies. Maybe our existence is all some sort illusion."

Aaron shook his head. "Oh, no, reality is quite explicitly real! Our perceptions are simply woefully inadequate. We're really just naked apes. We're simply ants in some vast jungle. There are creatures and consciousness that we can't even conceive. The one thing that is certain is that we are not simply 'self-deceived' computers."

A thin smile crept across Bekah's face. She turned her head slowly, looking directly at Bailey and then deeply into Aaron's eyes. "The Unsinkable Molly Brown *has* been reborn," Bekah stated matter-of-factly. "It's my English professor. It's Helen!"

Aaron and Bailey looked at one another in disbelief.

Bailey spoke first, "It must be the total mind we shared! I've never seen any sign of such psychic ability in Bekah."

Aaron stood up from the table and walked over to his desk. He returned and reseated himself. A large smacking sound was heard as he dropped a brick sized stack of one hundred dollar bills on the table. The mound of money was held together by a set of strained rubber bands. Aaron beamed ear to ear as he spoke, "My grandfather used to say, 'The proof of the pudding is in the tasting.' I've done things with L'Hospital's 300 year old science that the Vegas statisticians do not know is possible. It's curious to me, that so many implications are currently being missed. It's almost as if there is some greater agenda that each of us is compelled to obey."

Bailey beamed as she spoke up, "Combinations do, in fact, permute."

Aaron smiled wryly. "The given probability rate in Baccarat is devilish. It disguises the variant rates which are drastically exaggerated at the permuted sequences. The card game has the lowest house advantage. I beat it easily. The even/odd sets are variant at reversed rates, compressed rates, and dilated rates. Bailey, I'm going to give you a way to get into my safe, if the time comes that you need to do so. There's approximately one million dollars in there. You and Bekah are to share it equally."

Bailey's grey eyes became wet as she muttered meekly, "What do you mean, 'If I need to get into the safe'?"

Aaron peeled off several sheets of legal tender and handed it to the smiling, young college-aged girls as he instructed them, "Helen and I are going to be called upon to risk everything."

Bailey's words fell plaintively from her lips, "You'll succeed, won't you!?"

The smiling professor of physical reality spoke assertively "It's Saturday, and I want you two to go where all young people love to go on the weekend."

Bailey and Bekah finished Aaron's sentence, in unison, "The shopping mall!!!"

Aaron stood at the door watching his two wards, one straggling behind, make their way down his sidewalk to Bekah's car. He called out loudly, "Please drive carefully and text me when you get to the mall!"

Bailey snapped her head back and shouted, "You don't have to worry. No one can navigate the roadways better than this Viking princess!"

Aaron stood watching until the car was out of sight. Returning to his desk he thought to himself. *I have to put all this in the right order. That's the key. (Y) took Bailey back in the last time-slip. He must be willing to set things right. Perhaps he can break His own rule and intervene in the 2012 Holocaust. My meeting with Helen must be perfect. I have to get this right.*

Looking over at the sofa in the den, Aaron's eye was drawn to his comfy blanket and mumbled to the empty room, "Maybe a nap will get me on track. It's Saturday, and I have nothing to do but rest for a moment."

The aging professor lay beneath his plaid quilt, his eyelids closed tightly. Beneath them his eyes darted left to right and right to left. Beneath the blanket, Aaron's right hand clasped his left wrist fiercely.

From high in the square room, the sleeping man appeared quite small. Above the rectangular house, and the triangular rooftop, a gentle rain could be seen to fall across the countryside. High above the thick, white cotton clouds, the burning intensity of sunlight beat down on the billowy haze of the circular world.

From an ethereal viewpoint, which no earthly eye can see, a hand rocked the globe of the earth from left to right and right to left. The ivory sheets of haze danced in an aura of bright pin pricks, golden sparkles in the mist. And high above this grasp of flesh, a wry smile formed in a solitary place.

Desperation

(circa December 1944, [S] time line)

The young Russian lieutenant sat close to the burning embers of the sparsely lit fireplace. The flickering light provided pitiful illumination to the furious scrawls of the soldier's penmanship. The hand of Yuri Vladiovich could not write with such speed. The scratching sound of the coarse pencil against the thick paper of the military log might have been confused with that of a wild animal ensnared in a cruel trap. Again, the pencil dulled as yet another page filled with the apocryphal text of a mind held vice-like in desperate and impossible circumstances.

The talented and experienced grasp of the razor-sharp military dagger, raised by the officer's right hand, brought an immediate response to the dull writing utensil held by his left. In an instant, the pencil was again sharp. Aaron LaSalle blinked repeatedly as a tiny brown wooden shaving flew from the pencil into his left eye. Suddenly, the rough hand of a man hardened in desperate combat swung too rapidly and nearly scratched the academic's most important tool.

Francois L'Hospital blinked hard and concentrated as he drew a deep breath and slowed the thoughts of his total mind. He muttered to himself, "We must calm down. The diary is nearly finished. I must remain focused. The twenty-one minutes must be nearing its end. I must remain focused. The child's life must be preserved. I must not give in to the fear. I feel it returning. I must keep the talent of three lives to survive the next few hours!"

Francois's focus returned to the image of the diary held in his left hand and the blurred speed of his writing hand. He knew that the split instant of discomfort had distracted the crucial text. Yuri Vladiovich would not be able to translate the diary from French to Russian. There was not enough time. Francois immediately began to transpose his written account and the remaining text into Russian. The mind of the total man focused on the important words now transcribed in the foreign language. Yuri knew that he must remember the sentences now written in French.

Suddenly, the door to the small cottage-bunker burst open to the bluster of snow and the numbing cold of the winter storm. The Russian soldier instinctively emptied his hands and reached for his rifle as a frozen form seemed to step in slow motion through a portal in time from some frigid Hell.

A fierce voice rang out through the howling wind, from the rip in time, into the tiny warm space of the time traveler. "Comrade Lieutenant! The German bastards are stirring. On the hill, I see motion. They'll send another child out. I know it's about to happen again!"

Pushing the door closed, the Russian Sergeant urged his superior, "Come to the window! Look across the ravine. It's only a child! The damn Nazis are shooting at a child!"

Yuri lurched forward with his Tokarev rifle and opened the door to the blast of the freezing winter snow and wind. The Russian platoon leader called out at the top of his voice, "All of you, on your feet! If you are not out this door and behind me before I take twenty steps, I will shoot you dead as you stand. By comrade Stalin, I swear it! I will eat your livers with these bastard Germans before they murder another Russian child! On your feet, NOW!"

The young Russian soldier ran out from the farm house, racing to intercept the child in the howling winter storm. In Yuri's mind, it seemed as if he were the child, somehow being chased by a demon creature as fast as a wolf. Feeling the blood and adrenaline course through his veins, he knew it would take his best tricks to save this victim from predation.

The experienced fighter began to repeat his mantra, "My pockets are filled with seeds of the fern; no bullet can reach me . . . My pockets are filled with the summer spirit; the warmth fills me . . ."

The young soldier fought back the fear as the cracking whiplash of shots neared. His mind repeated his comforting words, *My pockets are filled with seeds of the fern; no bullet can reach me . . . My pockets are filled with the summer spirit; the warmth fills me . . .*

Yuri's psychic ability began to surge. It was an odd sensation. The young man's legs were pounding the deep snow of the Budapest hillside in the endless December snowstorm of 1944. The rifle strapped across his back slapped in unison with each surge of his frozen breath. And yet, his mind became one with the snow blurred image of a solitary human being, desperately running on the hill's ridge.

Yuri's thoughts merged with the terrified child. He heard her call out her name, in the eternal cruelty of the moment. She cried out, "I can't make it. I'm going to die!

The adrenaline surged in the soldier's legs as he screeched across time and space. "Tonia, it's just fifteen more yards. If we can run just fifteen more yards, you can make it over that ridge! The snow isn't so deep across the ridge. We can make it!"

The child's mind detached from the savage pain of her furious flight. Tonia felt renewed courage as the moment seemed to loop in time. The Einsatzgruppen SS commander's grip suddenly disappeared from the 6-year-old's scantily clad shoulder. Tonia was tall for her age and had already lived perhaps an entire lifetime in her few precious years. She watched as the other Waffen SS soldiers began to step from the house where she and others had been detained.

In that instant, both Yuri and Tonia heard a very calm and clear voice. It spoke without the howling wind or freezing pain of the winter storm, "Run child! Run straight ahead!"

The two young souls ran with a fury. Their legs pounded the ice covered ridge, beating like the hooves of wild horses. Yuri's breath seemed frozen before his face as he called out in native Russian, "Fall as we top the ridge! Fall, Tonia! I'm right on you!"

Yuri heard the bullwhip crack of the German Mauser round as it narrowly missed his ear. Several shots began to chorus from the distance. He knew that his Russian comrades were close behind him. In perfect unison, Yuri's arms wrapped around the child as they peaked the ridge. Rolling his body into a ball, he let gravity perform its magic as both rolled down the ravine, out of the German gun fire for just the moment.

Yuri released his grip from the child as she rolled just beyond him, coming to rest against a snow drift. For the briefest instant, the two stared wild-eyed at one another. Yuri was reminded of the wild fierceness he had seen many times in the black eyes of forest wolves.

Yuri's order seemed to spin from his mouth as he rolled over on his back and up the ridge. "Don't move, Tonia! Stay down!"

As if a contortionist had magically appeared from some traveling gypsies' band, Yuri pulled the Tokarev rifle from his shoulder, in his first roll. In the next roll, he chambered the shell with the tilting bolt action. On the third roll, flat on his back at the top of the ravine he looked up, over his prone body to see the German Waffen SS Colonel, perhaps fifteen yards away, running like a threatening demon towards him.

Time seemed to stop as the German officer planted his feet in the snow and made eye contact with Yuri. It occurred to the experienced Russian that the grim face of the SS soldier appeared quite relaxed. Yuri wondered if his small target, which he knew was what the German must be seeing, might appear unarmed. Perhaps he couldn't see the rifle, which had begun to levitate in Yuri's grip to set its sights, downwards between his legs on the Einsatzgruppen murderer's mustache.

The snow and wind seemed more intense as the Russian and German—one flat on the ground, the other standing looking down to the distance—seemed frozen in time. Both opponents raised their rifles in what appeared to be perfect cadence as if the entire scene was some surreal bit of military parade ground choreography.

The SS Colonel's face leaned right and over into his sights as Yuri tilted his head just slightly to the left into the rifle sight 'V', which was his rifle and the greater 'V', which was his booted feet he had just parted to clear the shot.

Yuri was familiar with the odd paranormal events which filled his life. Once as a child, he had heard the same wonderful voice which he knew Tonia had heard only minutes earlier. It was a voice like his father rousting him from his warm bed at home during the winter months deep in the Urals.

His psychic abilities had, no doubt, saved Yuri from the cannon fodder battles, which massacred so many millions of Russian youth. His odd talents had earned him a 3rd degree certification and the rank of lieutenant in Russian Intelligence. He wondered if his ability to see the future would leave him alive at the end of the Great Religious War.

The white snowflakes settling across the sights of the Russian rifle seemed to flicker in an intense pin prick of red light. A grotesque blood red image erupted from the face of the German target. Perhaps the frozen moment, of the life and death conflict, was in fear of losing its own existence.

Yuri was a superb marksman, but the impossible image held his shot. The vision which had become the face of his target was horrifying in its form. It was as if some demonic creature had eaten its way upwards from the German's body and had regurgitated itself from his shoulders. The glowing red corporeal flesh seemed to dance back and forth across the image that had been the man's face. Red eyes spoke to Yuri's mind, "You have no ability to kill me. You have no desire to kill me. Death will be your only companion."

Yuri held his nerve, and his aim, fast. He squeezed off the shot. In the Russian's rifle sight, he saw the snow erupt in an intense red mist. The snowflakes themselves seemed painted rouge in the eruption, which was the Waffen SS colonel's head.

The eternity of the dark moment was shattered by an uproarious shout, "Comrade Lieutenant, we've done it!"

The Russian Sergeant came running towards his commander who was walking towards the scene with a child in his arms. "Comrade, there was no one at the machine gun nest! The child must have escaped before they manned the guns. We've taken the German squad!"

Yuri continued to walk with Tonia in his arms. He understood, for the first time, what had just occurred as he muttered to Sergeant Gorgi, "God was not going to allow these murderers to send any more Jewish women and children out to be shot dead in front of us."

The Russian Sergeant lowered his head. "They've killed countless Russian soldiers trying to get at their bunker, taunting us to come and save these children." Gorgi reached over and took the child from Yuri's arms as he shouted, "You will be called Sasha, and we will take you with us to the heart of Germany! You are a lucky child, Sasha! Child, you are God's helper—sent to defend!" Gorgi danced in a circle with the smiling girl held high above his head.

Yuri continued a few more steps and stopped, looking down at the dead SS colonel. "Gorgi, did you see my shot that killed this German?"

Gorgi responded, "Comrade, I was only ten or so yards behind you. The other men charged the bunker. I wasn't going to leave your side." Gorgi stood looking down at the dead German, his head split down the center like fire kindling. He held Sasha just behind himself.

Yuri asked again, "Did you see anything unusual?"

The Russian soldier laughed as he spoke, "Comrade Lieutenant, I have never seen such a shot! I once saw the Turkish whirling dervish! Their bodies danced like flaming swords. It was as if you handled your rifle like a sword. It happened faster than I could raise my rifle to shoot."

Yuri took Sasha's hand as the men walked back towards their cottage. "Sasha, I have a magic talisman in my pocket. I want you to keep it with you from now on. Tell me you will. Promise me!"

The child looked up at the Russian. "I promise I will Yuie, and I promise I will always love you."

Yuri smiled to himself. He knew that Sasha had just answered the question. She had not heard his name mentioned. He knew that he had just shared "total-mind" with the child. She was now his family and must be protected at all costs from the evil force that had broken the peace with goodness itself.

(circa June 2015 [Y] time-line)

Helen dug furiously at the thick auburn locks of her wet hair. The terry cloth towel soaked up the shower water as she turned the towel, wrapping it around her head. Rearing back and staring into the bathroom mirror, the terry cloth white robe fell open to her nude, lithe form. The youthful, green-eyed professor leaned into the mirror and stared into her wide-open eyes. She smiled wryly at herself and muttered, "That Aaron doesn't need to do his field work every Sunday. Imagine the nerve of making me set an appointment for a nice Sunday afternoon together!"

Stepping back and holding the robe wide open, she gazed at herself and quipped, "I'm as beautiful as any of those half-naked cocktail waitresses at the casinos. I think he's up to something." Wrapping the belt of her robe back tightly around herself, the perturbed professor leaned back into the mirror and spoke directly into her green-eyed image. "It would be just like that eccentric to get rich and fly off to Vegas with one of those young half-naked casino girls!"

At that instant, the dinging sound of the coffee maker interrupted the lonely professor's rant. Helen ran down the hallway as the aroma of her omnipresent libation spoke out to her senses. Helen drank deeply as her mind began to ponder her day's solitary activities. She suddenly stood dumbfounded and motionless, her hair a wet, frenzied mess, the cup hot in her hands as she listened intently. She put the cup on the foyer table as though doing so might assist her hearing. Helen's expression turned to bewilderment as she confirmed to herself that indeed she had just heard the doorbell ringing.

Creeping up to the peephole of her front door, she peered out meekly as her expression turned to complete amazement with the image of Aaron LaSalle standing timidly on the front porch.

Throwing the door open, Helen leaped into the shocked professor's arms and shouted loudly, "Aaron, I love you so much! I knew you were up to something. You planned this surprise! Didn't you!"

The surprised professor returned the wet kiss of his dearest companion and held her smiling face a reasonable distance from his thinly smiling expression. "Helen, you and I truly know that we love each other. But I'm afraid we have work to do."

Helen's joyous demeanor turned a bit sour as she turned and walked back into the house. She picked up her coffee cup from the foyer table and turned back abruptly to the man she had spent the morning pining for. She spoke disconcertedly, "You are here, and I will not entertain any notion that you are here, for any reason, except that you came here to surprise me and prove that you love me!"

Aaron's thin smile remained as he demurred from Helen's nonchalant gaze. He spoke up tenderly, "Well, I'm not sure which one of us will be dismayed the most. But I'm afraid this Sunday is probably not going to be a beautiful summer day having a picnic."

Helen's eyes fell to Aaron's omnipresent satchel hanging from his right hand. She retorted sharply, "Go into the den, and I'll get your tea."

Returning from the kitchen, Helen saw that the seated professor of physics had dutifully arrayed her office table with several copies of the apocryphal work of the couple's transcendent identities. Helen seated herself as she gazed back starkly at Aaron. "Well, I finally get you to show up and surprise me and just look at me! I just got out of the shower!"

Aaron ran his right hand over his face and blinked hard as he answered timidly, "That's a very good point. I'm really not thinking quite right, I guess. Only a few hours ago, I returned from 1944." Aaron's stare became quite adroit as he peered back at the subject of the issue.

Helen's expression turned blank as her words fell disjointedly from her lips. "But you said that I needed to time-slip first. You said you needed the details from Molly before you would be sent back . . . How, I mean why would (Y) send you back without the information?"

The aging professor leaned into the table, picked up a stack of papers, and held them motionless in the air in front of Helen's face. He spoke sternly, "This is your diary from 1933. It's quite fabulous! I have no idea how the woman who has entranced my very soul for 300 years could be so incredibly brave and yet keep this huge divine event a secret from me!"

Helen's expression burned fierce as her jade eyes turned to flame as she nearly shrieked, "Satan himself told me you would die! I don't care about the truth anymore. I can't lose the only man I've waited my entire life for!"

Aaron stared back meekly as he watched the fire in Helen's eyes turn to a doused ember. The tears slipping down her cheeks neatly resonated in the window of his soul. He looked away and knew that the incredible complexity of what needed to be figured out and what must come to pass may well be beyond their earthly abilities.

The beleaguered scientist set Helen's diary back down and retrieved his 1944 account. He meekly peered back into Helen's gaze, handing her the work. He spoke softly, "You'll see why we must succeed when you read this. Your bravery will ensure that this child will be with us to prevent the future catastrophe."

Helen pursed her lips and frowned sorely as she snatched the diary from Aaron's hand, snapping back at his words, "If this means you die, I'm going to kill you myself!"

Aaron chuckled nervously as he queried, "You do realize that we're in the (Y) time-line and we're now waiting to be returned to 1703 to stop the dissemination of the Variance equations?"

Helen responded timidly, "Well, yes, of course."

Aaron continued, "So tell me what the main point is."

Helen guffawed. "It's to prevent New York City from being nuked in 2012."

Aaron smiled broadly. "Has it ever occurred to you as strange that we exist in a world where New York City is still sitting there undisturbed, that is to say, with the exception of the World Trade Center!?"

Helen set the diary in front of her and leaned into Aaron's gaze. She responded curiously, "I know these diaries are real. I know that Zoe and Balto won't leave me alone. I mean, yeah, the memories are curiously vague. But you say the same thing in your diaries that I'm saying in mine. So it all must be real."

Aaron replied. "So if the world is intact and (Y) is in charge of the Authority, where is Zoe?"

Helen grimaced as she replied, "You're not supposed to be a meta-physics professor in this time line. Is this a test? I remember you said there was a separate (Y) time line where everything was truly undisturbed by the 1703 event. You said that your hubris created some kind of . . . what did you call it? Yes, I remember . . . you called it a 'temporal refraction.'"

Aaron leaned forward and peered deeply into Helen's eyes as he calmly responded, "Dear, Satan's threat is quite hollow. Now that we've gotten this far, you need to understand just how complicated all this truly is."

Helen stared back stoically as Aaron continued, "We're probably going to return to 1703 before this day is out. But that's only the end of the first trick of evil. Satan's greatest trick is that he doesn't even exist."

Helen nearly shouted, "What in the Hell are you talking about?"

Aaron replied quietly, "Today is Sunday. I'm talking about the world being returned to this almost-correct world, saying what the dollar bill is supposed to say, and Zoe and Balto coming back to your classes tomorrow. The religious wars that we've prevented are going to manifest themselves again. New York City will be destined to nuclear annihilation at some date in the near future which you alone will know."

The curious and beautiful green eyes of the woman who sat completely befuddled began to grow wet with tears again as she muttered her words in quiet desperation, "Can't we simply argue like normal beings? I'm not done being mad at you. And I want to know how you got my diary."

Aaron sat stoically, gazing at the pensive expression of the most impressive woman he had ever known. His eyes might have been a dried sponge eagerly soaking up the mottled detail of Helen's darkened, still-wet auburn locks. He was certain that he must not express the absolute titillation filling his mind. The aging professor of academics threw caution to the wind as his gaze fell from the lady's exquisitely carved features, following her nude form wrapped tightly in the bleached-white terry cloth robe.

Aaron's wide-eyed stare suddenly looked past the focus of his eternally responsive mate as an intense feeling of déjà vu overwhelmed him. He smiled warmly as he remarked, "Your hair was jet black, but it had the same body and the same frolicking curls." A sparkling wide-eyed gaze instantly replaced Helen's sad look as she responded with a capricious grin. Aaron continued his thought-filled comments, "I just realized that you had an enormous wardrobe of saris and robes—I never saw you in pants—but not one of them was white. It suits you. It's eternally vibrant and young."

Her robe loosened as Helen stood up and leaned over Aaron's face. She kissed him on the forehead and deeply drank in his lips. A vivid jade fire pierced the handsome brown orbs of Helen's one true love.

She spoke tersely, "I want you to freshen your tea and give me time to read your diary from 1944. I'm not sure if I can hold the hot passion boiling up inside me, so you'd better be the strong one and do it. I know you're right. We have work to do, and I have to know what happened to you in WWII."

Helen hugged him, and Aaron breathed in the fresh clean scent of the nape of Helen's neck as he pecked at it with a wet kiss. He stood up and held her close as he spoke out dutifully, "You sit down, and I'll get some hot tea. We have something absolutely wondrous to share."

Professor Aaron LaSalle sat in his perpetual pose. The swift dance of his pencil sketched cryptically across the blank sheets of paper. He blinked as the pencil stopped abruptly. Frozen in the instant, his soft brown eyes raised from their focus to the wry smile of Helen Lovelace. The professor of literary arts queried, "You felt my stare, didn't you?"

Aaron grimaced as he meekly replied. "Yes, I suppose I did. How long have you been finished reading?"

Helen picked up her coffee and drank deeply; her eyes never left the object of her interest. She spoke in a matter-of-fact tone, "Aaron doesn't all of this terrify you?"

Aaron sat back and toasted Helen's libation with his matching tea cup as he slowly responded, "It doesn't matter if I'm scared. We have no choice."

Helen guffawed. "Look, we're dealing with the impossible. There's some kind of multi-layered reality which we just aren't sure of." Helen picked up a dollar bill from among the diaries sitting before her on the table, and spoke assertively, "I've been sitting here for some minutes trying to figure out what I just read. This says, 'In God We Trust.' The only thing that tells us that there is another reality are all of these diaries."

Aaron remained mute as he nodded approvingly. Helen rebuked, "Do you remember the time we had lunch and you told me that I could watch the sun rising and setting from the back of my house, even though you had never been here?"

Aaron smiled and answered abruptly, "Yes, of course! Both the Summer and the Fall Solstices are tied to your Karma."

Helen leaned into the table and insistently continued, "Then, you gave me five hundred dollars because you said I needed it for the charity event you saw in a dream."

Aaron chuckled nervously. "I told you it was from the casino; you didn't have any choice but to take it."

Helen crossed her right leg over her left and began to bounce it vigorously as her signature pensive expression returned.

Several seconds passed before Aaron spoke up meekly, "All right, I know it's an odd set of parlor tricks, but you must tell me what you're thinking."

Helen's voice crackled. "Yuri Vladiovich died so young. Those children's lives were meaningless to those predators. Now you tell me that even if the (S) time-line is eliminated, this secondary reality we live in will also be replaced by a new threat. It's all insane!"

Aaron pursed his lips and adjusted himself in his seat as he responded, "I needed your diary to find out about Gertrudt Cohen. Yuri ended up with Sasha and Rebekka. If I hadn't known about Gertrudt, the children would not have been in the right hands when my time came."

A bewildered look filled Helen's face as she exclaimed, "How do you keep figuring all this out?! It scares me senseless! Look, we know that Rebekka died pretty young because she's only around twenty years old now. And she has the same name and looks exactly like she did in the 1940's."

Aaron interrupted, "You see how sensitive your abilities are? Biblically, Rivkah is a very important feminine name. Remember what Democritus said. Until a thing is named, it never existed."

Helen's jade eyes went wide as she nearly shouted, "I know you, Francois L'Hospital! You're trying to confuse me. You're evading the point!"

The master swordsman knew he had his adversary in an appropriately defensive stance.

Aaron spoke out in a matter of fact tone. "Let me explain the 'We have no choice part.' You were once a 'so-called' political progressive. You've come to see a much larger picture. Are you aware of the fact that there are 61 million 'left behind children' in China? These children see their parents two or three times a year. They live with grandparents, strangers, and sometimes they live with no supervision at all. The parents are off working 60 to 70 hours a week in 'sweat shops', living in barracks. Do you know how much they make an hour?" Helen's expression remained stoic as Aaron continued, "They make between 75 cents an hour to one dollar and 25 cents an hour. That number of children without parents in China is about the same as the number of children in America."

Helen spoke out meekly, "It's the crab allegory. The wage-slaves of the 19th Century have returned so we can live cheaply. The indulgent masses accept the fantasy that the government can legislate morality and prosperity."

Aaron smiled broadly and continued, "All this so-called

'political correctness' accomplishes nothing! Interesting how the collectivists never see the Big Picture, but they're quick to promote new trade agreements. It's no coincidence that the balance of the family has been sacrificed. It's no accident that an agenda for children without a mother and a father is the by-product of economic imbalance and the rich-elite simply getting richer!"

Helen replied softly, "So the world wars never really ended. World War I and World War II was the same war separated by a 20-year armistice. And your time refraction will make World War III a religious war."

Aaron continued, "Helen, the reason that Balto loves Zoe so much is revealing. Wolves were domesticated 50,000 years ago. All canine varieties are wolves at their core. They love us and we love them because they think like we do. They're pack animals, just like primates. We've survived because we cooperate. Matthew 10:29-30 reveals that all species of life is shared in love and not a piece of it is lost. But the sublime issue is problematic. We've evolved to cooperate in the hunt. We're predators! The naked ape hasn't learned to move past this and the Twin Law will not allow the Super-consciousness to let us escape the consequences of our shortcomings. The machine-like intent of a predator implies something quite subtle. Sometimes we conduct ourselves like divinely loving beings; sometimes we act like cannibalistic crabs."

Helen smiled thoughtfully as she replied, "I love Bekah like a daughter. She was your daughter. It's too weird to be a coincidence."

Aaron answered enthusiastically, "That's right! Sasha is her sister and is now about 77 years old. She will become involved with us to somehow prevent a second annihilation of New York City."

Helen queried, "So my diary gave you the way to connect both girls with my German friend, Gertrudt, but how does that lead up to an intervention for World War III?"

Aaron responded eagerly, "Helen, the intense political conflict in America is no coincidence. The Twin Gods are at war. It is no accident that the coming titanic conflict of the candidates is between a man and a woman. This is the sublime 'extra' reality that the deities are always using to test humanity."

Helen grimaced sorely as she retorted, "What can we possibly do to prevent Armageddon!?"

Aaron replied quietly, "I have to know what will happen. You must know when it will happen!"

Helen's green eyes grew wide as Aaron's words slowed and seemed to repeat in her mind. She watched helplessly as the dignified professor's face wrenched in pain. Twin right hands grasped vice-like grips on matching left wrists. The duo fell from their seats in perfect unison as soft brown eyes and desperate jade orbs screeched silently, one to the other.

(circa December 1703 Switzerland [S]time-line)

Francois L'Hospital lurched straight up out of his goose-down-filled 17th Century bed and muttered frantically in his colloquial French dialect, "Oh, dear (Y), where is Shri'Ani?"

A familiar voice rang out with a thick Indian accent as Francois's young wife ran into the bedroom. "There's no time for the diaries! We only have 21 minutes to make this happen. Get dressed fast!" The young and beautiful green-eyed Hindu lady steadied herself at the doorway. "I'm still getting over the dizziness." Shri'Ani set down the fencing foil and silken gloves of the master swordsman on their bed. "Hurry, hurry Francois! That is the challenge, we must arrive at the duel and you must find a way to lose quickly."

Soft brown eyes blinked hard as the aging Frenchman clamored to the nightstand's shallow water bowl and splashed his face with the frigid water. Aaron LaSalle turned to the rapturous sight of Helen Lovelace adorned in jet black curly hair, a vivid azure Hindu sari and her familiar blazing green eyes. The 62-year-old scientist spoke out hesitantly as he clumsily stepped into pantaloons and buttoned his shirt. "I have so many questions, Helen. So it was the contest that led to the work being published? This must happen perfectly. There's no second chance! Has Miller arrived with the carriage?"

Francois stepped close to his beloved wife and spoke up, loudly, "You look so beautiful!" He took a step back as Yuri Vladiovich and Aaron LaSalle gazed in wonder. The azure silk sari garment appeared on the young woman as superbly wrapped as a fine glove on a delicate hand.

The French sabreist reached out and lifted his dueling vestment from Shri's arms as a crumpled sheet of hand written paper fell from her hand. Francois noticed an odd blackened stain appearing on one side of the page as it hit the floor. He queried nervously, "Qu'est-ce que c'est? Is that a note or what?"

Shri' quickly leaned over and swiped the slip of paper off the floor, crumpling it in her hand. Scolding her husband, she nearly screeched, "In exactly 30 seconds, we are marching straight out the front door. I have everything you need from the library. Please, please, Aaron, we will not be given another chance!"

Before Shri'Ani, Molly and Helen finished their entreaty, Francois snatched the sword and items from the bed and shouted, "Let's go! Run, Helen, run!!"

The last thing Francois L'Hospital did as he hurried from his Swiss abode was to glance at the hand built pendulum clock he had painstakingly constructed. The two time travelers rushed from the door and stepped into the waiting carriage.

Francois shouted loudly to the driver, "Miller, there are triple wages coming, Monsieur, if you get us to Potter's field in half the time! You must get us there in less than five minutes. Whip the horses, Miller! It's of great urgency!"

The carriage door slammed shut, and the two people who were, in fact, many more looked at one to the other. Shri'Ani looked at the bedraggled love of her many lives. For the briefest moment, Helen nearly fell victim to an intense urge to tear up. She fought back the impulse. The lives of millions hung in the balance. The beautiful Hindu princess leaned forward and with Molly's most delicate voice asked, "How much time will you have once the contest begins?"

Aaron LaSalle demurred from Shri's gaze as he spoke up over the raucous sounds of hooves and the clamoring wooden carriage, "I'm only going to have about 10 minutes; then, I'll only be Francois, I won't know that I must lose!" Yuri grimaced as he stared back at his eternally faithful comrade.

Helen wiped her eyes and stared out the window of the shaking carriage as it bounded past the snow covered woodlands of the Swiss countryside. Francois gazed at the distracted image of his loving wife and muttered solemnly, "These fights can last an hour!"

Shri' turned directly to Francois and implored frantically, "Dear (Y), will this nightmare never end? How will you appear to lose convincingly?"

Shri'Ani leaned forward from her seat into Francois's detached expression. It occurred to her total-mind that he looked as if not the sword fight, but the real fight, was already lost.

Suddenly, the carriage took a sharp turn, and both passengers nearly fell from their seats.

Helen shouted back assertively, "We have but a moment. You must know why I hid your diary. It has to do with this very moment."

The Frenchman's face turned from its grim contours to an intense focus, "I'm at a loss, Helen."

The windows of the same soul sparkled as she fought for the best way to describe the impossible events which had conflicted her actions. "When I was taken from my backyard, a 'y-shaped' stick nearly poked my eye out. You had discussed the mass death that occurred in Ramadi, Iraq. You had told me about the symbol of the 10th letter in the Hebrew alphabet. You said that the sacred name of Yahweh would be brought down to the waters of the 'sands' of Iraq. Aaron, in our time the dollar bill has changed. The time line will have returned from this moment to the time line of (Y)."

The terse confused look on Francois's face frightened Shri'. The young Hindu shrieked at the dignified European, "Francois, you've never truly believed in the mystical! You've spent your life trying to connect your science to the supernatural. I am telling you that all of this isn't your fault. You didn't change the time line. You didn't destroy New York City! It was Satan! I was taken at that moment from our future and told by the demon to keep you from the truth of it. You've read it in the Sandy Hook diary . . . It wasn't you. It's us."

The masculine total-mind absorbed every nuance of his feminine counterpart. The truth of Helen's words seemed to be spoken simultaneously in three languages. "We're somehow the avatars in this war between the light and the darkness," she continued. "I hid the diary because I knew that the city would be saved. I hid it because I knew you and (Y) would figure out a way to save humanity. I hid it because I was still being deceived by the commandment to be humble. Damn humility and damn the Gods! You and I are all that matter. I'm not talking to the Gods. I'm talking to the only being I love. And I know I'm about to see you solve this problem!"

The carriage ground to a jarring stop as tears poured from the vivid green, pleading eyes of Francois's beloved wife. "Hurry, Francois, hurry! You can do it. There's no problem you can't solve. You will win—win by outwitting the Devil."

Sword and garb in hand, the Frenchman jumped from the carriage and looked at his wife for just an instant. "I love you more than life itself."

Shri'Ani, Molly, and Helen watched as her dearest friend, the dearest soul she had ever known—her husband—ran pall mall through the rough field towards three gentleman standing and watching from the field of honor. In truth, her heart was filled with total doubt. Only minutes remained to return an eternity to its proper destiny. And yet, her "total-mind" saw the future both ways. In her mind's eye, she saw the phrase "In God we Trust." Helen muttered, "If anyone can do it, this soul will . . ."

From the carriage, the dutiful vessel of feminine hope and faith watched the two opponents stand stiff back, one to the other, and raise their swords in salute. Shri'Ani muttered quietly, "Remember Francois, you mustn't win. You must also convince this man that you've lost fairly."

Francois L'Hospital was a master of the nobleman's game. He knew that both the academic premise of his game theory and his gentleman's diligence were superior to the haughty skills of Jakob Bernoulli. The complex treatise of the brachistochrone problem was far more sublime than the "Apple of Discord." It involved future physical concepts beyond his opponent's earthly convictions. Few minutes remained before the implacable twenty-one minutes of total consciousness would expire.

Francois fought excellently. Jakob Bernoulli had been on the defense for the majority of the fight. Francois drew his stance and his sword to an erect salute, announcing commandingly, "You will necessarily publish my Treatise; your honor requires it." At that instant, Jakob Bernoulli mocked his opponent with a "chicken wing" torso, dipping his stance to the unsightly 45-degree taunt. Francois took the bait and advanced with a textbook kick and lunge. Outflanking his opponent, their swords connected with a counter thrust snap as vicious as any thus seen.

As Francois straightened to draw his foil to salute and renew the en guarde stance, his face drew taut and he desperately grasped his right wrist with his left hand. The glistening steel foil, used as skillfully as the finest stroke of pen and ink, toppled to the ground, followed by the master swordsman himself.

Henri, Francois's trusted second, rested his master's head in his hands and turned his body around from the wet grass to rest his face upwards. Jakob Bernoulli and his second stood motionless as Francois returned to consciousness.

Jakob's second entreated, "Does your master still breathe?"

Henri responded requisitely, "He does! He has merely succumbed to the exposure. He has nearly regained himself from the momentary vapors."

Francois opened his eyes and spoke out assertively, "I'm fine, just fine! We shall now resume our contest!" Francois sat upright and cautiously moved to his feet, sword in hand, as he attempted to re-posture himself.

"Au contraire, mon amie!" The confident voice of Jakob's second shouted out. "You have forfeited this contest. If you have outpaced yourself, the indignity rests with your poor judgment!"

Jacob Bernoulli stood silently, his sword grasped and lowered before him, both hands firmly coupling the hilt.

Henri began to interject, "The match will continue! This lapse cannot be viewed as a departure from neither skill nor honor!"

Francois was still struggling with the loss of his total-mind. He could remember the conversation that occurred in the last span of time with Shri'Ani, but it was difficult to place it in the same reality. His thoughts were hard to focus. He wondered if he might be suffering some sort of delusion from his momentary palsy.

The 17th Century swordsman fought his instincts, struggling to remember the mantra which he had silently repeated all during the fight. With a most gallant bow, Francois rose up before his opponent and recited, "I have been too anxious. You, Sir, have bested yours truly."

Jakob Bernoulli snapped to the en guarde pose and, with a salute of his foil, spoke out, "I accept your forfeiture, Francois, and your glove. This contest is finished. Providence has decided the outcome. I will see to it that your papers are returned to you."

Jakob and his second turned, walking from the field as Francois looked past them to see Shri'Ani running fast. The vision of the breathless lady in her fine azure sari appeared dreamlike as her loving mate watched her approach through the snowy white field. "Oh, Francois, my dear! Are you alright?"

Francois caught the slight, angel-like form of his young wife in his arms and kissed her deeply. "I think it's been made right, Shri'! Do you have the same memory?"

Shri' smiled broadly, her eyes gleaming as she replied in a curious tone. "Yes, yes, Francois, I do. You lost then?"

Francois smirked, "Yes, dear, I lost."

The French gentleman turned to his faithful second, Henri, and thanked him for his service as the two partners in love and destiny began walking slowly back across the snowy field to the awaiting carriage. Shri' reached into her pocket and retrieved a tattered, oily, soot-stained note. She spoke quietly and mournfully, "Something most terrible and painful has happened to our beloved Pyara, Francois. I do not know if we will ever understand. It must have to do with all this, somehow; it can only be the work of Kala."

Francois held the note in his right hand and began to read as he walked, holding Shri' about the waist with his left arm.

From above the scene, there came a distinct shriek. Shri' looked upwards above her husband's head, and when his eyes followed, he could make out the circling and circling of a huge Black Forest eagle. She spoke out joyously, "Francois, Vishnu is speaking to us! The God paints a picture above us. It forms a Halo above our heads."

A Shade Approaches

(circa 2015 June [Y]time line)

The breathtaking blue sky was subdued by the allure of the rich brown eyes returning her gaze. Shri'Ani's focus fell to the blinding snow as the steam of her own freezing breath marred the image. Looking down as her husband's grip held her close, Helen Lovelace studied the intricate fabric of the divinely woven, matching intensity, of the colorful azure silk sari.

***

The college professor's closed eyelids fluttered from left to right and right to left as Helen Lovelace's left hand groped across her California King bed. A wry smile returned to the eternal features of a woman whose mind simultaneously contained an instant in time and centuries of reality. Joy became the moment as Helen's fingertips proved the memories real and traced the length of Aaron LaSalle's nude torso.

Turning to the stalwart fixture of Helen's somnolent world, she saw the curious and coincidental details of time and space. The clock's bright red letters beheld the moment, 4:44 a.m. The teacher of young minds knew that the magical moment must soon end. It was the most difficult of days, Monday morning.

Helen sat straight up in bed to the faint sounds of canine conversation in the distance. Pulling the comfy blanket from her sleeping mate, she exclaimed, "Aaron, do you hear that dog!? I've discovered another (Y) time line shift! I always knew the neighbors were supposed to have a dog. I've been awakened by a real dog!

And now, I remember talking to Bekah and precious Zoe Blankenship at school last Friday!"

Helen rolled over, straddling the wide-eyed counterpart of her flesh-and-blood reality. The impassioned professor of Fine Arts ground her body onto the surprised participant as she shouted wildly at the bemused facial expression of one Aaron LaSalle. "We really are back! The world's almost perfect again!"

Tightly robed and standing in her kitchen, Helen dutifully poured hot coffee and hot water into the matched set of her home edition, gold four-leaf clover cups. She had purposefully bought two boxes of Earl Grey tea bags, in the largest commercial size possible, and left them sitting conspicuously on the counter.

Waiting patiently, she knew that one Aaron LaSalle would be walking into the confines of her domestic setting any moment. She watched as the distracted professor made his way down the hall, fully-dressed, phone in hand, punching a text as he made his entrance.

Helen focused stoically, tea cup with bag inserted as she stood silently with the cup held high awaiting its recipient. Presenting himself before the smiling gaze of his benefactor, Aaron pressed the send key on his phone and rose up with a mirror image of the broad beaming grin.

Taking the hot cup, the dutiful professor of time and space managed a few words as he began to sip his obligatory nectar, "I just texted Bailey and told her that her fellow 'early bird' was going to be a little late this morning."

Helen stood quietly, green eyes peering through the steam of her glittering gold crucible as she considered every nuance of Aaron's expression. A moment of curious tension seemed to manifest itself as Aaron set the cup down and renewed his shy grin.

Helen shifted her stance and coyly responded, "Did you tell

Bailey why you were going to be late?"

Aaron's expression became nonplussed as he quipped, "Well no, of course not! She won't concern herself with what I'm doing."

Helen chuckled sorely as she retorted, "Men! I'm going to demonstrate some psychic ability that doesn't require your hefty abilities, Professor. I will bet you, before we finish our morning libation, that 21st Century enemy of privacy in your left hand will be asking you a question."

Aaron guffawed as he lifted his teacup for another sip. Helen tilted her head as her jade orbs began to sparkle and she remarked, "You really don't see it, do you?"

Aaron smirked as he retorted, "See what, Helen?"

The professor of literary exactitude laughingly replied, "She's had you to herself for years. She hovers over you like a cross between a mother hen and Juliet pining for Romeo."

Aaron began laughing and shaking his head as he rebuked, "Oh, Helen! Bailey is our daughter! She's here because of some divine coincidence."

Helen interrupted, "Oh, now, I've really got you! Bailey being here for you is a coincidence? I have never heard that word fall from your lips! She may be our most precious 300-year-old memory, but she's not your daughter in the flesh."

At that instant, Aaron's face whitened then flushed as his phone began to chime. The bemused expression on Helen's face was indeed rapturous.

"Oh, let me guess," Helen mused. "Forsooth, should it be the despairing Juliet?"

Helen held her right hand out as she stood arrogantly in a pseudo-demanding stance. "I'll write the text. Don't worry. I'll let you see it before I send it." Aaron pursed his lips as he begrudgingly handed over the phone. Helen spoke out the text as she typed,

> *Bailey, Helen and I have a new set of diaries. Yes, dear, we are now in the final (Y) time-line. You may be experiencing some déjà vu episodes. I'm with Helen now, and she says to tell you how much she loves you. See you in a bit.*

Helen waggled the phone above her head as she taunted Aaron. "She'll get used to it. She has to come to terms with it, Aaron. She has a wonderful husband now, and she needs to let go. Her mind won't let her stop obsessing over you because she thinks you're all alone. Now, she knows better." A stern grimace filled Aaron's face as he silently nodded his head. Helen returned the phone to eye level and punched "send."

Aaron turned from Helen's open door, satchel in hand, and pecked her lips softly with a quick kiss. "Let's have lunch at the Red Dragon at 1:00; I'm good then until my afternoon class."

Helen smiled broadly and replied, "That's just perfect! I'll be there."

***

Professor Aaron LaSalle peered at Bailey Smith with a disconcerted sidelong glance. The four-top restaurant table remained decidedly asymmetric, with only the two inhabitants squeezed into seats at one corner of the dining table. Bailey held onto Aaron's left arm with both hands as she leaned into his left shoulder. Aaron gazed at the curly, dark hair of the young physics instructor as she continued to prattle.

Bailey spoke lyrically, in a whimsical tone, "Oh, Aaron, I'm so glad that you and Helen are finally an item. Bekah and Zoe have been going on about it for years! They kept at me to try and act like some kind of Saint Valentine to bring the two of you together. Can you believe that?"

Suddenly, Bailey popped up onto her knees in the seat and

gazed briefly into Aaron's soft brown eyes. Aaron's expression responded to the dreamy, grey-eyed gaze with a thin smile as the young woman returned to her inquiry. "Sometimes, I think Ibrahim is jealous of you. I've reassured him that our relationship has always been like family. He's constantly asking me if I think he's as handsome as you. I've told him that Helen thinks the two of you have the same eyes. Aaron, do you think that we can have some sort of party or something at Helen's? I'm dying to see her home. I mean, I just know it's like gorgeous or something. I bet her bedroom looks like something out of *Gone With the Wind*!"

Bailey stared wide-eyed at Aaron as her demeanor became quiet and self-reflective. Her right hand clapped over the front of her mouth nervously as she spoke out cautiously, "Aaron, I'm being horrible aren't I!? You're right; I've been inundated with déjà vu images. One minute, my mind flashes to scenes of a horrible Revolutionary battle, in the next, Shri' and I are talking about how much we both love you, and then I'm ripped from my life with you and I remember my spontaneous incineration."

Bailey slowed for the moment as she continued to look deeply into the man's eyes who, in fact, had been the most important soul in her many incarnations. Aaron peered back intently as he considered the delicate response which he must tender. "Bailey, if any human being ever had a reason to feel some doubt about their purpose in life, I suppose you would certainly have to be forgiven for that. But I will never leave you. We have to learn to be a family again. I must return to being your father, and you must be the wife and mother who's been ordained. Many people need you and love you, Bailey." The young, damp-eyed woman leaned into Aaron's lips and kissed him sweetly.

"Well, aren't Mondays just the most annoying!" Helen Lovelace stood wide-eyed and smiling tersely as Bailey abruptly returned to her seated position. The young woman quickly withdrew her grasp of Professor LaSalle as she covered her lips with her right hand.

Taking the seat to the right of Aaron, Helen picked up the menu and began to study it as she inched her way closely to him. She spoke adroitly as her focus remained consumed in the open booklet, "Well, I'm glad our family is back together. What a difference 300 years makes."

Several tense moments passed before Bailey finally uttered the first words, "Helen, I've been experiencing a troubling set of flashbacks. This morning, I read both Aaron's and your diaries from Francois's duel. I almost 'slipped' again! Okay, I'm going to admit it. I'm sure it will settle down, but I actually 'saw' an iteration where New York City was annihilated again. I resisted the 'slip.' It was very frightening! In one instant of the vision, only Aaron and I survived together all alone."

Helen set the menu down and took a deep breath as she turned to her left and leaned past Aaron, speaking quietly, "You're going to be all right, Bailey. Reading my diaries appears to affect you in odd ways. I've been odd myself since we returned from the 1700s. Sometimes we just have to remind ourselves of what's normal and what's expected. You are our daughter, and we will defeat whatever is sent against us. It's harder for you because now you have to be both our child and a mother yourself."

Helen hesitated as she intentionally awaited Bailey's direct eye contact. "We both have our insecurities, darling, but I will never mistrust you or Aaron. I think we're feeling Satan's fury over being displaced." Helen smiled knowingly as she peered agreeably into Bailey's responsive gaze. "The demon is scratching at our libidos, darling. Believe me; I couldn't keep my hands off him this morning either!"

Suddenly, the group turned its attention towards the entrance of the Red Dragon restaurant. The smiling image of a young woman appeared to approach in slow motion. Her bright, hazel-colored eyes radiated a joy and an almost effervescent love of life.

The petite Zoe Blankenship flashed a wave as the dark-haired, pixie-like beauty reached the table and spoke up, "Hi, everybody! Bekah said I could find you all here and I'm supposed to meet you for lunch. I guess she's not here yet."

Aaron muttered quietly into Helen's ear, "It's overwhelming. I can see us all sitting in my office while I recite the 23rd Psalm. We mustn't let on. Remember, she doesn't know that anything's happened. Bekah and Bailey will have to talk to her about it slowly, but only if she has any residual memories."

Helen rose from her seat and ran around to her dearest grad student and hugged her intensely. Zoe smiled back curiously as she queried, "Yeah, I know it's been a long break, but I just saw you last Friday." A chorus of laughter emerged from the table as Helen pulled a chair from the table for the young girl to be seated.

As the dignified English teacher turned from the chair, the room itself appeared to shatter with the chaos of a bounding canine. The barking and wagging tail of the Siberian husky were followed with the hapless licks and grasping paws of the loving animal.

Helen shouted out in delight, "Balto! Oh, you beautiful creature!" The smiling woman knelt down and held the pet closely in her arms as she spoke directly to him, "You know, don't you? You remember me, don't you?" Helen eyes filled with tears as she buried her head in the licking animal's fur.

At the same moment, Hannah Blankenship caught up with the rollicking animal and spoke out. "I've never seen him do that before! He never disobeys like that! The door opened, and I couldn't stop him."

Helen stood up and looked into the mirror image of Zoe's twin. Reaching out, Helen hugged Hannah tightly and nearly shouted, "Oh, this is just the most wonderful moment!"

Hannah looked at the table full of smiling faces and explained, "I've been visiting Zoe this summer. I brought Balto with me from New York. I'll get back outside and wait for her until everybody's done eating."

And then, in a stern but loving voice, Hannah commanded the dog, "Come on, Balto! Yield, Balto!" Zoe's doppelganger and her obedient, albeit hesitant, charge walked from the table as Zoe and Helen returned to their seats.

Looking across the table, an intense childlike expression fell across the face of Helen's grad student. Zoe inquired gently, "How do you know my dog? I don't think anybody sitting here knows his name." The young student appeared nearly flabbergasted as she queried, "Helen, that was really kinda wonderful. Can you explain it?"

Helen leaned into the table as she reached out and took hold of Aaron's right hand with her left. Glancing over Zoe's shoulder, she brought Aaron's attention to the commanding approach of Bekah. The tall Swedish beauty, with her striking white blond hair and riveting sky-blue eyes might have been walking onto a Hollywood movie set.

Helen looked around the table and laughed heartily as she said, "Who planned this beauty contest? All I have to say is Aaron LaSalle you are one seriously lucky man."

Aaron smiled broadly at Bekah as she pulled up a chair, remarking to her, "Bekah, Helen decided that I have a much lovelier group of lunch companions than my humble presence deserves."

Bekah smiled timidly as she remarked, "Bailey has discussed

the issue with me over the last two years. I'm not as psychic as the three of you. But I know that it involves Zoe. I also know something has happened since Bailey and I took the diary to Aaron's on Saturday. So I took it on myself to invite Zoe and myself to lunch today."

The meek expression in Zoe's hazel-colored eyes turned to a sharp focus. "Bekah and I have talked a little this morning. Aaron, there's been a rumor around campus for years that you have a time machine. Is it true?"

Bailey covered her face with both hands and leaned into the table as she muttered, "What are we doing?"

Aaron looked across the table and asked Zoe directly, "Have you ever had any dreams that seem to have come true or experienced what people call déjà vu?"

Zoe smiled wryly as she quipped. "Well, I do have déjà vu. But I had a really strange dream a couple of years ago. It was as if Balto and I, and I guess my entire family, were running from some kind of terrible storm. I had it again Saturday night. But this time in the dream, Balto ran into Helen's arms and she knew his name. That dream just came true."

Bekah smirked as she commented, "See, I told you there was a reason for us being here."

Aaron spoke up in his tutorial fashion. "Girls, let me explain something to you. In the (S) time line, people are more psychic and religious. In the (Y) time line, people are less psychic, but more tolerant of spiritual views. The shortcomings of this are that they're collectively less attuned to social injustice. The place that reality has just returned to is the world I left on December 14th, 2012. I suppose that this (Y) time line is perhaps the most balanced, in some respects, but I now perceive several oddities."

Zoe remarked curiously, "So you do have a time machine!"

Helen responded, "Zoe, it's a little more complicated than that. But yes, sweetheart, there is a way to travel through time."

Aaron continued, "Our awareness of these psychical oddities will settle down, but here's an example. The entropy side of the divinity is now working in its traditional method. It will seek to undermine the rational balance of society and the family unit. Sexual procreation is time travel. The ecstasy given to us at the moment of climax is an amplification of the instantaneous time-loop we all experience in our consciousness. We're not self-deceived computers. Our minds have the unique ability to slip in the time continuum. It's the real reason we have emotions and are self-aware. All random systems tend to an 'extra' bit of order. It's the reason genes are successfully modified with infinite variation throughout the ages."

Bailey and Helen turned to Aaron and blurted out in unison, "That's why I'm acting like this!"

A wave of thin smiles traveled synchronously around the table as the waitress approached. "I guess we're all here," she said, eyeing the table's occupants in one sweep. "Are we ready to order?"

(circa 2016 June (y)time-line))

The smell of bacon and eggs completed the Sunday morning ambiance as Aaron LaSalle sat in Helen's den working intently on her computer. Through the hallway, the sound of the literary academic's voice could be heard with the subtle inflection of the happy domestic, "Breakfast is ready!"

Aaron sat quietly as he buttered his toast and smiled approvingly at his mate. Helen inquired, "What are you working on?"

Aaron grimaced as he answered, "Today is the one year anniversary since we 'slipped' and corrected the time lines. I've been accessing my mails to you. Did you realize that the frequency of our dreams regarding worldwide disaster is increasing?"

Helen quipped, "Is that the reason you're my part-time roommate? We have to make sure we document the dreams and remain apart?"

Aaron peered back at Helen meekly, his right hand pausing with a forkful of bacon still in his mouth. He smiled nervously before chewing and washing the tasty morsel down with his obligatory drink of hot Earl Grey tea. Leaning forward, he spoke out tenderly, "Do you remember the conversation with the girls at the Red Dragon restaurant a year ago?"

Helen retorted, "Well, it was the most emotional experience of my life! Zoe, Hannah and Balto might as well have been angels sent from heaven."

Aaron continued, "Has Zoe ever said much about the conversation?"

Helen quietly replied, "No, and Bekah has said that she's been careful not to discuss it with her again."

Aaron nodded his head agreeably as he concurred, "Exactly, and Bailey's said the same thing!"

Helen responded whimsically, "Okay, I'm at a loss. What are you saying?"

Aaron continued. "Something very special is happening with us, Helen. People are mildly psychic. They experience déjà vu and so forth. But very few people are given the knowledge of their previous incarnations. And I'm not sure anyone has ever been able to change history."

Helen replied thoughtfully, "So as far as Zoe's concerned, she and her family truly never died in 2012."

Aaron smiled broadly and replied enthusiastically, "Exactly, and that's wonderful. The ancient Greek that intuitionalized the atom was right. If something isn't known to us, it truly never existed. Each mind is its own reality. Here's the point. Pyara did not live out her life. Bailey is still aware of this. We are aware of this. The diaries prove it. So we know something that is infinitely frightening. The entire world is in the throngs of some kind of test."

Helen drank deeply from her gleaming golden artifact as she studied Aaron's words. "So we're not supposed to be too content are we?"

Aaron grimaced sorely as he nodded his head in agreement. "In Genesis 2:17, mankind was warned not to eat from the tree of the knowledge of good and evil. 'In the day you eat of it, you shall surely die.'"

Helen mused, "It reminds me of your Twin Law. Do you suppose the verse is suggesting that intolerance is the essence of evil?"

Aaron smiled as he remarked, "It doesn't take much imagination to realize that the conflict between science and spirituality is extremely dangerous. But I think the verse has a more esoteric meaning. Mankind is teetering on an evolutionary cliff. Either we become a truly psychic species or we annihilate ourselves. It's no coincidence that the established earthly powers deny the obvious realities of paranormal events."

Helen sat quietly and muttered, "Life is infinitely more complicated than people want to accept."

"I've tracked the frequency of our mails," Aaron replied intently. "Do you remember a few years ago when we, separately, were almost killed in car accidents? I was warned of the red semi-tractor trailer. You had some maniac in a white SUV repeatedly trying to run you off the road. It just happened again, didn't it?"

Helen pursed her lips and nodded her head. Aaron continued, "In the dreams of 1988, I saw you long before we ever met, correct?"

Helen nodded and replied, "I'm the Woman from your short story, 'Sandcastles.' You've proven that, definitively."

Aaron peered intently and responded. "Okay, the politics in this country are insane. We've turned into the United States of Anarchy. We have either the Wicked Witch or the bombastic billionaire Truth Warrior being handed the destiny of the world. On your computer, you can find the mail regarding the 'butterflies' dream vision which I mailed you just months before the November 8, 2016, elections. I saw you painting two plaster of Paris butterflies. The one on the left, you painted blue. The one on the right, you painted red. The left one had a long pin stuck through it, half way down. The one on the right sat neatly on top of the pin."

Helen smiled wryly as she replied, "Yeah, that's often how the visions work. You 'saw' me helping my niece work on her hobby crafts. You said this meant an unexpected result for the Republicans. The scandals of Hillary Clinton would impale the Democrats (blue) and the Republican (red) victory would allow Donald Trump to rise from the election and fly into the White House. The party of the right would win the presidential election."

Aaron smiled and spoke up, "If that were not the case, there would be no chance of preventing the nuclear annihilation of a major city. In this time line, Yahweh is trying to balance mankind's destiny. It's a tough job. Satan is working with whatever he can manipulate. If the religious terrorism succeeds in one nuclear blast, World War III will last one hundred years and there will be dozens of nuclear battles. The (yud) is the 10th letter in the Hebrew alphabet. It's the smallest letter. It's like the lower case (y). In this time line, people are given the greatest opportunity for free will.

But evil turns subtle things into disasters. Natural sexual attraction has been turned into a war with women. The youthful vote is turned into a childish 'hissy fit' for 'free stuff'. The presidency is turned into a pulpit for racial activism. People aren't genuinely this stupid. The human race is oblivious to the influence of an external Super-consciousness."

Helen spoke up gingerly, "All right, I know what's coming. We have to perform the tandem Reveal. That's where this conversation is headed, isn't it?" Aaron nodded, approvingly.

Helen continued, "I knew I couldn't prevent this. I'm scared, Aaron! I've had dreams. I can't get the demon's threat out of my mind. I know we have no choice, but I'm afraid something will happen to you." Helen leaned into Aaron's gaze, as she spoke intently, "I try not to bring it up very often, but you seem to forget I am quite liberal in my political persuasions. I don't think I like this Donald Trump. No, I can tell you quite honestly. I abhor Donald Trump!"

Brown eyes sparkled, as Aaron replied. "I still love my left hand. I've grown accustomed to the knowledge that the only hand I can perpetually shake is the one hand diametrically opposed to my own."

Helen continued, "There's something that I've never spoken of. Many years ago I had a horrible nightmare. It's peculiar because I can't explain why it terrifies me like it does. In the dream, I saw a huge grey and tarnished nickel high in the sky. It seemed to vibrate and almost hum with some deeply, throttled voice. But, it was only a nickel. Just last week, I walked into the academic lounge and when I sat down I saw two nickels resting by my feet, one heads up and one heads down. I felt oddly afraid. I don't understand!"

Aaron's expression grew stern. "The second Tier of the Trinity is the bad one {4,5,6}, {Deceit, Contempt, Betrayal}. Notice the contra-positive to the first Tier {1,2,3}, {Truth, Faith, Hope}. The third {7,8,9}, {Victory, Virtue, Bliss}, three squared takes us to the 9th Realm, Paradise. Here's the point. The Hall of the Authority stands in contrast to even the ninth level. The Tenth is the letter/number in the aleph-bet. The Hebrew alphabet avoids the vowels. It is divined deliberately that the number/name of Yahweh is the atom of the 22 letters. The tiniest, most demure, the 10th. Its appearance is as "an arm and a hand". How do we travel in time? What overwhelming impulse thrusts our opposing (left/right) (backwards/forwards in time) (hand/arm) death grip in response to the rapture of the infinite energy displacing our minds through time:space? (y) intercedes as little as possible, it's the Twin Law. I now know that we must return to the (Y) time-line. The Tetragrammaton will return us to the time-line of His Will."

Helen stared at Aaron in a confused daze. "Aaron you're scaring me as much as the nickels. What are you talking about. How does a physicist know so much about religion?"

Aaron rebuked, "It's not religion Helen, It's meta-physics. It's why all this is happening. You and I are the right hand and the left of a divine purpose. You really don't understand what you saw do you!?"

Helen's jade fire erupted, "Of course, I don't understand! Why else would it terrify me?"

Aaron leaned across the table and spoke softly, "I see the future and you see the dates. (Y) has given you a sign. The doubling of the {FIVE} is symptomatic of the one true God's power over evil. If deserved, even the consummate, irrevocable destructive force of {Contempt} can be converted to the word/number of (y). Your wren and your horrid DV with the huge nickel in the sky are the total-mind counterparts to yours truly. You saw the answer to the divine riddle. You've seen the Holocaust I saw. Your mind holds the dates. We cannot escape the Word of (Y). You have now been given a sign for our success. The Authority represents both sides of the same coin. You are blessed my dear Woman."

Helen gazed at Aaron curiously. "I have reasons to think that the city might be destroyed on the Solstice of the year 2021. Yes, the horrifying nickel in the sky has always brought numbers to my mind. It's as if it's spinning or recycling somehow, as if in a mirror. It's definitely tied to the Solstice, 12/21. The date of December 21st, 2021, must be the date. But, there's something ominous about the Solstice from that point forward."

Aaron smiled broadly as he exclaimed, "That's unbelievable! It fits. The date is the mirror image of 12/21/2012. We'll get prepared, and that date will guide the ritual. December 21st, 2021, will be our destination."

Helen spoke out, chiding the suggestion, "Aaron, the total mind is not controllable. We assume that the links to our previous incarnations have been allowed by the hand of deities. Are you saying there is a way for us to make contact with ourselves at that future date?"

Aaron smiled broadly. "Of course, all we've had to do is get sufficient information to know what can occur and it has occurred. Not knowing is not an option. Einstein pondered positive time displacement when the inviolate speed of light was proven. This principle of Physics has been labeled, Relativity. My research proves that negative time displacement is concurrently influencing real time events. The connection of events across time infers a 'memory or shadow' which lingers outside the three physical dimensions, space:time:mind. It appears undeniable that from the atomic to the galactic, even the wave:particle nature of light itself must be participating 'entirely' in this geometry. We should be able to contact ourselves in the future."

Helen retorted, "Aaron, I have to admit something to you. I have to spend hours mulling everything you say to me over and over in my mind. I usually don't have a clue what you're talking about." Helen's green eyed stare sparkled as she sat smiling broadly at the physicist. "There's nothing you can say that I don't believe. Just tell me what to do and we'll get started. We have all of this Sunday to ourselves."

***

Hands were cleansed and the sacred ritual was followed as the two time travelers sat across from one another at the table. Twin Bibles lay open before each as Aaron began the instruction. "There are 1549 instances in the King James Version of the Bible in which the left hand is referenced. Open to Matthew 25:32-33 and then Genesis 48:13."

Reaching across the table, Aaron took hold of Helen's right wrist with his left hand and spoke out, "Now, we each recite our individual prayer silently."

Moments passed before Aaron spoke out again, "This is the beginning. Together, let's read the verses from Matthew and Genesis."

"32) All the nations will be gathered before Him, and He will separate the people one from another as a shepherd separates the sheep from the goats. 33) He will place the sheep* on His right and the goats on His left."

Hardly a breath passed between them before they again joined voices and read.

"13) Joseph took them both, Ephraim with his right hand toward Israel's left, and Manasseh with his left hand toward Israel's right, and brought them close to him."

Helen picked up the die. "I'm ready."

The dice jostled in the free hands of the duo, rolling out of the open hands in near unison. Helen called out "6." Aaron also called out "6." Holding the Bibles in their left hands along the spine, the pages of the sacred book fanned out. Each studied the width of the pages and ran their finger to the 6th section of the scripture. Pinching this sixth block of pages of the book between the index finger and thumb of their left hand, each rolled the die again with their right hands.

Helen called out "5." Aaron called out "6." Studying the width of the block in their left hands, each opened to their respective fraction of the bundle.

The bibles lay open on the table to the 6th Chapter of Revelations for each. The die was tossed again. A throw of 1, 2 or 3 meant that the selection would lie on the left page. A throw of 4, 5 or 6 meant that the selection would lie on the right side of the open Books.

Helen called out "4." Aaron called out"6." The final roll would position the selection from the top of the left column to the bottom, breaking this into thirds and then the right column from top to bottom, also into thirds. This would act to see the left column of the page as area 1,2,3, top to bottom, and the right column of the page as area 4,5,6, top to bottom.

Helen called out "3." Aaron called out "5." Aaron looked up at Helen and smiled. "It's happened! We've been guided to the exact same Book and Chapter."

Both closed their eyes and repeated their silent prayer. Each then brought their right index finger down, eyes still closed to the approximate area that the last random number indicated.

Helen spoke first, "I'm on Revelations Chapter 6, verse 1, exactly."

Aaron spoke next. "I'm on Revelations Chapter 6, verse 8, exactly."

Helen felt an odd sensitivity. The music, which she would always play during the sessions, seemed to suddenly play a bit louder. The beautiful symphonic and classical sounds of the modern group "Hybrid" seemed very crisp in its lyrics.

"Sometimes, I run away. Sometimes, I just want to stay. Sometimes, just one day where I'm watching every word you say. Straight ahead as fast as I can run, wild horses beckon me to come. Open the door and let the wind blow in, finding the place I've always been. Sometimes I run away. Sometimes I just want to stay. Lately, I'm watching every word you say."

The look of malaise seemed to also fill Aaron's gaze as Helen looked up at her partner. "It's time." The two reached around the Bibles. Aaron's right hand grasped Helen's left wrist as Helen's right hand grasped Aaron's left wrist.

Helen and Aaron began to read in unison. The voluminous candle light seemed to dance in cadence with the words.

"And I saw, when the lamb opened One of the seals, and I heard as it were the noise of thunder, one of the four beasts saying Come and See."

"And I saw, and behold a white horse and he that sat on him had a bow, and a Crown was given unto him: and he went forth conquering, and to conquer."

(Helen seemed to feel the rapture as pins and needles; Aaron had described it as numbness. Each could feel something happening, but knew that no matter what, the reading must be enunciated without interruption.)

"And when he had opened the second seal, I heard the second beast say, Come and see."

"And there went out another horse that was red: and power was given to him that sat thereon to take peace from the earth, and that they should kill one another: and there was given unto him a great sword."

"And when he had opened the third seal, I heard the third beast say, Come and see. And I beheld, and lo a black horse; and he that sat on him had a pair of balances in his hand."

(The energy of the presence was producing a slight vertigo in both Helen and Aaron. It was as if each knew with certainty, the discomfort the other was feeling.)

"And I heard a voice in the midst of the four beasts say, A measure of wheat for a penny, and three measures of barley for a penny, and see thou hurt not the oil and the wine."

"And when he had opened the fourth seal, I heard the voice of the fourth beast say, Come and see."

(The room began to spin for each of the readers. It was as if the distance between Helen and Aaron was becoming telescoped. The grasp on one to the other's wrist was permanent as was the position of the scriptures before them, but the room and each reader seemed farther and farther away.)

"And I looked, and behold a pale horse: and his name that sat on him was Death, and Hell followed with him. And power was given unto them over the fourth part of the earth, to kill with sword, and with hunger, and with death, and with the beasts of the earth."

(Aaron and Helen stood within a spinning vortex; the only solidity was their grasp on one to the other. A spinning cloud of dim light, which might be experienced on a mountaintop in an early morning mist, seemed to have engulfed the now standing and dizzied couple.)

Helen asked, "Aaron where are we? This has never happened before!"

Aaron responded, "Do you feel the total mind?"

Helen shouted, "No! I'm still just Helen. What's happening?!"

As the two held each other close, the nearly terrified explorers saw that the cloud surrounding them was beginning to brighten and clear. They realized that they were high in the sky. Behind them, both could see a vast expanding city and a clear blue sky above. Before them, an unspeakable terror was at work. A vast wall of billowing flame and blast appeared to be retreating. The houses and buildings beneath the holocaust seemed to be returning from flame and destruction, jumping to their original pristine state.

The huge towering mushroom cloud shrank quite quickly to a smaller and smaller size. An entire metropolis was springing back into reality. A vast expanse of skyscrapers jumped from the ground up to claw at the beautifully clear winter sky.

It was as if the couple was chasing the Genie back into the bottle. The green expanse of Central Park appeared, and in the distance, One World Trade Center stood again. The blast shrunk down to the size of a building and then a house and finally seemed to emerge from the corner of a thoroughfare that made its way around the Manhattan Park.

At that instant, an intense pure white light burst out from a single point on the street. It was as if 10,000 Suns burned in that small spot. Aaron spoke out, "It's amazing. We can look right into it and there's no discomfort whatsoever!"

Helen grabbed tightly onto Aaron. "Do you hear it!? It's growling! It's as if it were something living!"

In just an instant, a white Chevrolet van sat at the point from where the light had emanated. The couple saw men in protective garments. One was closing the van's back door and began walking backwards towards two other men. All the men stood together briefly and the two men dressed in suits also began to walk backwards to a black vehicle.

Helen shrieked, "Oh, dear God! It's you, Aaron! It's you and some military General!"

Aaron steadied Helen in his arms. "Helen, you must have faith in (Y). We're being shown this for a reason. I think I understand!"

At that instant, the couple was sped along the streets and thoroughfares of New York City. Both marveled at the traffic and pedestrians as they went about their business, all completely oblivious to the fact that their lives were stuck in complete reverse. The docks and warehouses along the waterfront came into view as the couple was brought down close to the dock. In the scene, a tall blonde woman closed the door of a white Chevrolet van and a man closed the door of a black Chevrolet van. The two then ambulated in reverse back to a black car; it appeared that it was the same type of vehicle as the one that the General and Aaron had returned to.

The candlelight flickered strongly in Aaron's eyes. He watched as Helen lifted her head and stared back at him. Suddenly, Shri'Ani shrieked at Francois in colloquial French, "Ou etais-je!? Where was I!? This is not going to happen again. I will not lose you again!"

Francois skirted around the table to the feet of his beloved child-wife. "Oh, darling, you must be strong. Please, be strong for me!"

The tears poured from the wide green eyes of the teenage Hindu princess. "Where was I?" The woman sitting above the Frenchman was in a frantic state, the likes of which Francois had never experienced. Shri'Ani looked down at Francois. "I know what you've done, you've outwitted me. You're going to do something to keep me out of Ground Zero!"

The Hindu wife spoke with a demanding intensity, "I will not be disgraced with your sacrifice again; Vishnu will damn me for eternity if I leave you solitary on this funeral pyre!"

Aaron knew that both he and Helen were deep in a spiritual energy that mere mortals should not experience. He screeched,

"Helen! Helen, snap out of it! No one is going to die. Yahweh has shown us how to prevent it!"

The daze on Shri'Ani's face was absolute. Francois knew that only a 17th Century cure would break the spell. The sound of the slap across the Indian girl's face returned a sharp report. Helen held her hand to her face and for an instant looked quite surprised. She spoke calmly as she rose to her feet. "I'm all right now. Aaron or Francois, please, will someone please explain to me what is happening!"

Aaron rose to his feet and began to speak with confidence. "Remember, anything that (Y) knows, so does (S). The only thing that Satan can't manipulate is the future. He/She needs to absorb our free will to control that. Yahweh showed us the events in negative time. (S) hasn't seen it at this moment, and He/She can't see through the cloud of it in our minds. Don't you get it? We've been given a power to prevent this over Satan. Somehow, you were left out of the picture, so that we can undo the Apocalypse from the end unto the beginning."

Helen's expression was thoughtful. "You mean whatever we come up with, (S) can't prevent our intervention?"

Aaron smiled broadly. "That's right. (Y) can't intervene. Mankind has disabled his shepherding. Only a couple mere humans can prevent this now."

Helen looked perplexed. "Can't (S) intercede when we figure out what to do?"

Aaron laughed heartily. "Oh, Helen, the only thing the evil being does worse than see the future is to determine our choices! The dumb sycophants in our human heritage hand that over on a silver platter. We saw it in reverse, because that is the only future that (S) sees. The clever twist that you and I are going to figure out hasn't occurred yet. Yahweh is truly the Creator God!"

Helen walked to the wall and switched on the light switch. She shouted out, "Aaron, there's no power. Oh, dear (Y)! Aaron, don't you understand what just happened? I am Shri'Ani and Molly! We're in a total-mind state. Think, Aaron, think! It's December 23rd, 2021! We've 'linked' with our future minds. And we only have twenty-one minutes to find out what needs to be done!"

Molly's mind seemed to hold sway at the moment. "Aaron, you've done it. We're one mind. It should be just another Thursday, two days after the Solstice. I know everything throughout these ages. And nothing's changed. I feel the same world shaking terror I felt on April 15th, 1912."

Francois lurched to the beloved soul which (Y) in his wisdom had held in a grip of love and destiny for 300 years. The two stood in the flickering candlelight with tears falling from each face. Separating from the breathless kiss that was an eternity in the making, Aaron almost whimpered, "Oh, dear God, I love you so preciously. How can the world be in such a mess, Century after Century?"

Helen spoke out assertively, "Aaron, we only have twenty-one minutes to return the information to 2016. We don't have it. The computers are out. Marshall Law is in effect. Two days ago, New York City was obliterated. We've accomplished nothing without the exact location of Ground Zero, the exact minute the blast occurred and someone to contact."

Aaron spoke out with renewed strength. "The newspapers are supposed to come out today with the information. They'll be at the stores. We have to drive there now. My watch shows it's 7:00 a.m. The papers will be there."

Molly nearly shouted, "Are you serious? The military has orders to shoot to kill. We can't go out!"

Aaron grabbed his keys and headed for the door. "It's two

minutes to the Minute Mart. All we have to do is read one paragraph before we slip back. Are you coming!?"

Helen blew out the candles and scrambled out of her office den. Pulling the sliding door shut, she stepped across the concrete patio where so many odd events had occurred, toward Aaron's car. After fastening their seatbelts in unison, the duo gave one another one last brave sidelong glance as they screamed out onto the barren Mid West's morning roads.

Molly exclaimed, "Aaron, are you going to kill us before we reach the store!?"

Aaron's eyes never left the road as he replied, "It's simple logic. There will be neither the constabulary nor the populace on these thoroughfares."

Helen rebuffed with calming conversation, "I want you to know, Aaron, that I've come to a certain wisdom concerning the 'left and right' politics. The globalists that have left America defenseless may not be easily turned." Helen's mind had wandered to the simpler time as Shri'Ani, when she had spent an entire lifetime with her adoring Frenchman.

Aaron spoke intently, "The New York City holocaust happened again because of that. Listen carefully; I had a dream 3 nights ago. This happened twice, then in 2015, and in this time-frame. I was keeping a pack of wolves away from you while you were reading something. It didn't go well."

The solitary soul of three lives focused intently as Helen's face went blank. "What are you saying?"

Yuri Vladiovich's eyes never left the road. "The wolves are behind us, Helen, coming on us quickly."

Molly spun around to see a rapidly approaching pack of lights in the distance. Yuri continued, "I'm almost at the Minute Mart. When I stop, you stay in the car. Do not get out. Lock the doors. I'll slip the paper through the window. Whatever happens, Do Not Stop reading! I'll keep them off you until we slip. We've got about 10 minutes left."

Screeching to a halt, Aaron jumped from the car and ran to the bundle of newspapers sitting on the sidewalk in front of the store. Brandishing a small pocket knife, he cut the strapping and pulled out a copy of the crucial account of the national disaster.

Racing back to the car, the aging professor slipped the prize through the car window, just as he heard the officer shout. "Freeze and drop! You, in the car, get out—NOW!"

Aaron watched as Helen rustled the paper into position. Her focus remained intact. She was following the plan: doors locked, she heard nothing, saw nothing, and she was absorbing only the written information in front of her.

The frantic academic turned from the car to see an army lieutenant with both hands on his pistol, the barrel of the gun nearly blocking his face. "I told you to drop! Do it *now*!"

Aaron's face went blank; he had frozen in his tracks, unable to even blink. Suddenly, he felt the heavy thud of something against his back. He knew that there must be someone else on the scene. This occurred to him as he felt the first pain, the same instant he felt the ground hit his face.

The two soldiers began to toss around the sophisticated man like so much fare at a fishmonger's market. Aaron felt the cuffs clamp tight on his wrists; he wasn't sure if his arms would remain in their sockets, twisted as severely behind his back as they were.

Suddenly, the multiple minds of several lives were being instantly levitated from the ground. The frail body of one lone man was easily jerked viciously upright to the same foreboding face, which moments earlier had hidden cowardly behind steel and gunpowder.

The sneer and words projecting from the mouth of the inquirer somehow appeared quite perfidious to the keen intellect of the assailed academic. Aaron gasped, struggling to take a breath as he barely managed to speak, "We only need a newspaper."

The sneer returned to the face of the young lieutenant. "You only need a newspaper!?" The questioning tone of the statement was matched with a disrespectful intensity. "New York City is a 10-mile diameter hole in the ground. The Muslim marauders are butchering women and children, every city in this country is aflame, but you only need a newspaper!" The soldier's retort was stinging.

The two men stood a few feet apart. Aaron stood transfixed as the rank soldier held him in place. The staring contest seemed odd to Francois. He knew that most duels began with a moment of mutual respect. The young man's tone worried the skilled swordsman. He sensed that his opponent was inexperienced. This suggested a lack of confidence. This meant he was truly dangerous.

The officer stepped forward, unblinking, his eye contact never veered from Aaron's gaze. The granite expression belied a worrisome uncertainty. A few inches from Aaron's face, the soldier spoke with derision, "I'm going to ask you one last time . . . What are you doing here?!"

Aaron's jaw had barely opened to speak when the soldier, who had demanded a response, dropped from Aaron's sight. Leaning down in front of Aaron, the curious assailant picked up an object from the ground. Returning to his stance, the officer held up the tiny pocket knife used by Aaron a few minutes earlier. It seemed to Francois that perhaps an hour had transpired since the two or three minutes had lapsed when the small tool had been in his grasp.

Aaron managed a response, "I used that to cut the strap for the newspaper." The look on his face was relaxed and sincere as he spoke.

A curious expression crept across the stone face of Francois's opponent. "What's going on in that car?"

Aaron suddenly realized that the restraint from his back was no longer present. He spun around, hands still cuffed from behind, to see Helen still reading. The only motion to be seen in the car was the subtle rotation of her head scanning the pages.

Francois considered his words as he spoke out with a tone of sincerity, "The woman in the car is a fellow professor from the University. We had to find out about the destruction in New York City."

The sneer on the soldier's face returned. "Well, I'll be damned, Doc. You smart types are just so curious you couldn't wait until noon to come out of your hole and be legal. There's no decal on that car. You're not a 'need to be' traveler. If this were a major city, I would have shot first and not had to hear this crap!"

Francois took one step forward as his pleaded, "Listen, I know this is hard to understand, but we only need about one or two more minutes. Please, let the lady finish what she's doing. She'll step out on her own and you can arrest us peacefully!"

Francois recognized the expected thrust-parry of his opponent. "Doc, who the hell do you think I am? Rod Serling? Is this the goddamned *Twilight Zone*? If she doesn't get out of that car with her hands in the air, and I mean right now, you're not going to like what's about to happen!"

Francois realized that his move had been outstepped. The high ground was held by his opponent. A look of disbelief covered Aaron's face as he saw a figure come into his peripheral view. The soldier, who had overwhelmed him so effectively, was standing next to the car window with a metal tool ready to strike. "Tell me when, Sir!"

Inside the car, Helen was beginning to focus on the tension outside. She knew that Aaron could not delay the aggravated dilettante much longer. The arrogant tone returned to the officer's voice, "Get her out of that car!"

Francois had been trained by the finest Swiss swordsmen. He knew that he must now do the single most dangerous thing he could possibly do. The 17th Century gentleman lunged forward as the soldier drew back to strike the car window.

Molly's hand reached for the door handle. For the first time, she saw the tumultuous scene that was unfolding. Time seemed to slow before her eyes. She pushed the car door open against the tumbling bodies of men she did not recognize. A vague glimpse of a uniformed man pulling a revolver from his side holster seemed to appear before her. The wrestling men on the ground seemed to include Aaron. The shouting was indecipherable until it was instantly silenced by the cacophony of a gunshot.

Molly Brown wasn't sure if it was her being held by Gertrudt Cohen or perhaps that was Aaron LaSalle in her lap. The scene was blurred by the tears and screaming, a sound that she suddenly realized was her own voice.

The soft brown eyes of her dearest love lay looking up at the true center of his eternal worship. Molly pleaded softly, "Lay still, darling. Lay still. We'll get help here."

Molly's look at the officer standing above her was scathing. "What have you done, you damned fool! You have no idea what evil you have served!"

The tears poured like an open spigot onto Aaron's face. Helen reached down to dry his face, only to see that she was smearing Aaron's face red with her blood-drenched hand. Molly looked up at the officer again, just as the pain of rapture began. At that instant, she felt Gertrudt's soul speak to her from within.

The man looking down was the same officer standing above them both on that terrible day in 1933. In the fraction of a second which was that moment, Molly saw the uniform transform to that of the German officer. She saw the Black Forest eagle circling above the scene. She knew that Gertrudt was telling her to remain strong.

Looking down at Aaron, Molly saw that he was struggling to grasp his left wrist with his right hand from behind his back. She watched the handcuffed man's hands clamor successfully as Helen's right hand tightly grasped her left wrist. She smiled down at her beloved and pleaded, "Hang on, darling. We'll be home in just a moment."

Francois struggled to speak as a thin smile crept across his face. "Did you get what we need?" As the last words fell from his lips, Aaron's soft brown eyes closed gently, and he lay quite still . . .

The last thought in the year 2021, in the mind of Helen Lovelace, was how impossibly tragic and how ceaselessly eternal is the repetition of death.

Flight of the Valkyries

(circa August 2016 [Y]time line)

The green eyes of more than one soul opened to the dim flicker of candlelight. Helen Lovelace inhaled the fragrant scent of her sandstone candles and absorbed the melodic companionship of the music. Shri'Ani studied the length of the many burning candles. She could read time as accurately from spent wax as Francois could from his ticking clocks. Molly Brown knew that little had changed. The time-slip had required little, if any, time at all.

Helen spoke softly to herself, "Oh, thank you, (Y). We're back . . ." Lifting her head from the table, she saw that her tingling right wrist was being held 'as in a mirror' by her left hand. Sitting quietly for several seconds, the professor's mind drifted back to the curiosity of the issue. *I see the question now. If the phenomenon only involves our mind, how does the hand:wrist grasp reverse itself, physically?*

Several women thought to pose the question to their eternal mate as fear riveted through the bowels of Helen Lovelace. The fire returned to her jade orbs as she dashed around the table to the still unresponsive flesh and blood of Aaron LaSalle, now sprawled, half on his back and half on his side on the floor—arms behind him, his left hand firmly encircling his right wrist. She dropped next to him and implored, "Francois! Francois, are you back? Please, speak to me!"

Shri'Ani's plea echoed in Helen's ears as the unified mind of one desperate woman pulled the limp form of her only reason for existence into her arms. Tears poured from Helen's face as the total-mind of the horrific experience appeared ready to repeat itself across time and space. Molly spoke out to the single soul of the woman. *Remember, Bailey didn't return to consciousness quickly. Aaron thought to dampen a cloth and try to stimulate her back to the current time. Give it a few minutes. Both Pyara and I returned from death. We must stay calm; (Y) will not leave his children alone!*

Sitting flat on the floor, Helen gathered Aaron's body in her arms and rocked to the rhythm of her music as the flickering image of the candles seemed to burn in slow motion. Through tear-blurred eyes, 300 years of life and death could be reviewed literally in the blink of an eye. The pain of the aging Hindu woman's lonely decade without Francois and Pyara tormented her mind. Helen blinked hard as she focused on the infinite joy of their centuries-old embrace in the 9th realm. Helen worried for a moment as the tears poured too rapidly from the window of her soul. She wondered, *Could this be physically threatening? I'm not sure!*

A vague sensation of wetness and pressure against her right cheek seemed to distract the torrents of desperation. The mind itself, of a nearly eternal being, blinked to the image of the smiling man's face.

Helen gazed at the everlasting male image, now bestowed with the odd smirk, which she instantly recognized as that of her beloved Frenchman. Francois rolled over And seemingly in one move, rose to his feet and defied the laws of gravity as he deftly levitated Helen Lovelace from the floor and cradled her entire body in his arms. Snuggling him close to her face, Helen kissed and cooed as she covered his face with a rapid fire of wet kisses.

Separating from the tears and sweet endearment, Francois softly muttered, "How can hundreds of years be so stingy and grant us only these few moments to share our love?"

Helen pushed from the loving embrace and fell to her feet as she ran to the light switch. "Aaron, quick, now! Grab the notepads and pens. We've got perhaps eighteen or nineteen minutes before we fade out of total-awareness. I'll get my computer fixed. We must hurry, Aaron. You're not going to believe what the newspaper said. Boy, it just amazes me how right you always are. The minions of leftist crabs have left the country almost defenseless!" Perhaps a minute passed as the resonance of Helen's rapid-fire typing was complemented with a loud remark, "A General James King with the Pentagon died at Ground Zero."

A pale expression covered Aaron's face as he looked up from his writing, "Did you say King?"

Helen's response was terse, "I knew better than to say anything! Yes, I said 'King.' Now, don't talk. Just write!"

Perhaps fifteen seconds passed. Helen's typing never broke its rhythm as she quietly asked, "Why?"

Aaron looked up, stopped writing, and nervously answered, "I recognize this General King. He's the one I saw in the Pentagon, circa 1988. He's the last paragraph in 'Sandcastles.'"

Helen's lips pursed tightly as several minds decided instantly on the appropriate retort, "Keep writing, Aaron! If we don't get the right plan to your General, he's going to die, and so is the love of all my lives in just a little more than five years."

(circa September 2016 [Y]time line)

The handsome couple stepped through Helen's front door as the smiling professor of literature remarked, "I just love a beautiful fall Saturday."

Helen leaned over and gave Aaron LaSalle a wet smack on his right cheek as the professor of natural science smiled wryly. "Hey, that's not fair. My hands are busy!" Aaron messed with his hair for a moment as he removed his Yamaka.

Helen stepped ahead as she called back, "I'm going to get our refreshments. I know where to find you."

The dutiful professor-turned-domestic set the tray of hot drinks down on the den table as she remarked, "Remember, you promised me you would attend Sunday services with me. I know how much you truly revere the New Testament."

Aaron peered upwards from his pen and paper as he replied quietly, "Oh, I'm glad you reminded me. I told Bailey that we would attend Catholic services next Sunday."

Helen beamed broadly as she spoke out, "Well, that will get us to the newer scripture anyway. What's the occasion?"

Aaron sat back and brought his hands together behind his head as he spoke whimsically, "I think Bailey wants our advice on Jeshua Abraham Abdulaziz. He's going to give an invocation."

Helen grimaced as she queried, "What? Jeshua isn't two years old. Are you serious?"

Aaron continued writing as he replied, "Bailey says he can read and write Biblical verse flawlessly."

Helen blinked hard as she sat at her computer and began typing. Speaking quietly, the master of language arts knew that the possibility of an answer was as improbable as the question even being heard, "Have you figured out what to do about 2021?"

The scratching sound of the physics professor's pen never ceased as the incongruous reply was made, "Yeah, I've got mail from General James King."

Helen jumped to her feet and turned indignantly to the unexpected response. "Oh, and just *when* were you planning on telling me about this?"

Aaron walked towards the computer and his distressed mate as he instructed, "Sit back down and punch up my mail. You'll understand when you read this."

Helen sat impatiently as she read the rather lengthy response. Her expression grew intense, and she began to speak out loud, "He's saying that he appreciates your concerns and he finds the details of bombs being shipped in by clandestine means on sea shipments as plausible, but he's not in any position 'to comment on security matters or the given date.' Blah, blah, blah."

Helen spun around and exclaimed, "Did you tell the famous General that only 5% of ocean bearing cargo is even inspected?!"

Aaron chuckled as he replied, "I think he probably knows that, dear."

Helen continued. "Well, he was very nice, but he obviously doesn't know what to do with the cryptic nature of the information you provided."

Aaron reached across Helen and punched in a more recent sent mail. He smiled wryly as he quipped, "I think you'll understand why we had to get around (S) with the Yuri Vladiovich lifetime when you read this."

A broad smile and wondrous expression filled Helen's face as she read out loud:

Dear General King,

I want to thank you for the courteous and personal response to my mails. I think it is now time for me to take us past our remedial introductions. I think the following phrase will not press your security restrictions too greatly, but I suspect you will want to establish a safer means of transcribing our conversations, when I repeat the following suggestion.

I would like for you to ask 'Sasha' – "Do you know Yuri Vladiovich?"

Yours truly,

Helen spun around in her chair with her jaw wide open and her sparkling green eyes filled with a total look of disbelief. "Sasha is still alive and in American government intelligence!"

A thin smile formed as Aaron meekly replied, "I always told you (Y) doesn't operate on the basis of coincidence."

(circa October 2016 [Y]time line)

"I hope you've got some tricks up your sleeve." The brilliant academic stood in her home-office and wondered if anyone truly deserved the knowledge which justified the question. Helen silently pondered, *What is it that makes me this special?* It occurred to her that something new had been introduced into the never-ending saga. The future 'link' had not brought either of them to the total mind of the future. Instead, it was as if both she and Aaron were teetering back and forth between the different lives.

Helen thought to herself, *Two months ago I was momentarily stuck as Shri'Ani. Now, I can almost remember the person that I was. It's as if the past total mind is trying to stay with me.*

Shri'Ani stood looking at Francois, the 17th Century quill pen dashing about the page. Helen realized that she had stood and admired her husband at that beautiful French-crafted desk in their Swiss home for thousands of hours. Helen held her left hand before her face. The tactile experience rushed into the woman's mind as she ran her thumb across the tips of her fingers. The teenage girl was left breathless as her coy suggestions had finally had their way with her husband in his 20's, leaving her splay legged across the desk's elegant surface, papers and pantaloons tossed.

Helen set the obligatory mugs down on the den table and took her opposing seat. "Well, we've got a few hours before 3:30

arrives. Have you come up with anything?"

Aaron smiled wryly. "Well, yes I have, but I can't tell you."

The abrupt comment was matched with a deep drink from the scientist's teacup. The steam roiled across his eyes as he peered back into Helen's abject stare.

Helen nearly shouted, "What?! Did I hear you just say - You can't tell me!?"

Aaron set the cup down on the table, avoiding Helen's stare. Sitting sideways in his chair, he crossed his legs, pre-World War I style, and turned his head back to his perturbed partner. "I can't tell you. If I tell you, then (S) will know. You have the privilege of knowing that you are the nexus of this entire situation."

Smiling wryly, soft brown eyes studied the image of the perplexed woman. An unexpected shriek instantly filled the air. Helen's tone was startling, "If you don't stop kidding around, I'm going to knock you flat over this table!"

Aaron began to chuckle nervously. "Helen, I'm serious. You are the hub of the issue. You are the one that will stop the bomb and the terrorists. I know how you're going to do it." Aaron returned to his composed state and took another drink.

Helen knew that the cryptic scientist, sitting before her, was expecting her to sufficiently connect the dots as she scolded, "You can't know exactly how I'm going to do it. You've ascertained with sufficient certainty that exceeds, we'll say, a 10 million-to-one probability. Let's hope it's at least as certain as the number of people that will die."

Francois looked around to his left to see the rapturous form of his Hindu princess leaning nude over the finery of the dark wood of his French desk. The dignified Frenchman squinted and looked again. He stood up and took a deep breath, giving the surge of adrenaline and blood in his loins a chance to exhale.

Aaron set the tea cup down and inquired timidly, "Helen, I have something important to ask. Are you having flashes of total-mind memory? And are some of them filled with, well, youthful prurient thoughts?"

Helen smiled broadly. "Boy, am I glad to hear you ask that! I thought maybe I was still stuck in my teenage years in the 17th Century!" Helen's frustrated expression remained as she picked up her gold four-leaf clover cup, replete with steam, and walked to her computer desk.

Aaron moved to Helen's side and continued, "Do you remember me telling everyone at the Red Dragon that the divinities influence our thoughts?" Helen turned to her mate and nodded agreeably. Aaron continued, "The national security codes that we've been given and the secure line that was set up on this computer are only earthly defenses. At 3:30 today, I'm going to receive the first message from Sasha. Have you wondered why she hasn't contacted me at all? You know how much she loved Yuri. You also know that love is the most pervasive emotion across time."

Helen grimaced as she replied, "Well, I guess I just thought that my computer had to be modified first."

Aaron responded, "The morning that I saved Sasha in 1944, I completed the diary from the time-slip as myself, Aaron LaSalle. I was returned there by (Y) for multiple purposes. We exist on a linear plane. You and I and Bailey have been concerned with retrieving the math from 1703. The deities are not three-dimensional. When I was taken back to the incarnation, during World War II, the future religious war was already taking place. New York City was blown up on the Solstice of 2021 the instant that it was saved in 2012."

Helen's jade orbs stood transfixed with the words emerging

from the face of the man who had held her passion and admiration for 300 years. Aaron sat silently, drinking his tea. The 17th Century swordsman held sway. The master of the duel knew that his opponent often must make the first move.

The professor of Literature grimaced as she thoughtfully responded, "You left Sasha with the diary, didn't you?"

Aaron's beaming smile and sparkling eyes provided the reply. Helen returned a thin smile as she remained thoughtful. "You told her something in the diary that no one else can know. I just figured something out. All of these diaries are like the scripture. They touch the very mind that experienced the reality. When Bailey read your diary, she was sent to her previous incarnations. When Bekah read just a little of my diary from the Hall of the Authority, it almost killed her. The biblical scriptures hold a piece of the minds of those inspired by God."

Aaron leaned forward enthusiastically as he finished Helen's thought, "Sasha is telling me something by not speaking to us directly. She's telling me that she holds a piece of the answer, and we must be careful how we share it. Satan must be outwitted, and that's not easy. The deity works through our minds. What each of us know, 'It' will know."

Helen guffawed abruptly. "There's no way to do it then! If the city's destruction was only delayed for nine years, we can't outwit the future!"

Aaron held his hands out and fanned slowly against Helen's frustration. "Helen, you're the key. Sasha would have slipped to a time after our slips. She wasn't concerned with saving the city in 2012. She'll know about problems we haven't experienced yet."

Helen's expression became more distressed. "Problems we haven't experienced! The damn city and the only reason for me to exist are going to get blown up in five years. How can she know about problems that we haven't experienced?"

She gazed intently as Aaron smiled knowingly. "You are the only one involved that hasn't killed anyone, Helen! Think about it. Bailey and I have been involved in war. You not only failed at taking a life, but you were killed by quintessential evil. Sasha knows about you from Yuri's diary of 1944. She's confirming that you are the only one destined to stop the terrorists in 2021. Don't you get it!? It's how you knew the date. I knew you knew it in 1988—before we ever met."

Silence returned to the conversation for some moments as Helen sat dumbfounded. She spoke out timidly, "Satan manipulates everything possible to distract our focus, doesn't he?"

Aaron nodded his head as Shri'Ani's eyes twinkled. "We still have more than an hour before the weekly correspondence with the government contacts. Let's let Beelzebub have his way one last time. If Francois doesn't take me in his arms and rip my clothes off, I'm never going to have the energy to get through this!"

***

Helen typed the secure codes into the computer as she turned smiling at Aaron. "It's a good thing this is just mail. I wouldn't want any video involved at this point."

The aging academic turned to his feminine counterpart and quipped, "I'm not so sure. I think we look rather Avant Garde, sitting here in our robes talking to the Washington intelligentsia."

Helen spoke out, "Here it is. It's coded as military security clearance. That's the same as General King's. Sasha's some type of military officer. It's coming up. I'll read it out loud for us."

Dearest Yuri,

I have lived these 77 years waiting for this moment. My love for and memories of you reach across all of time. I understand that you are a vital and successful man in this life. I know from my experience with time-slip that your mind is returning to the brave and tragic times of the Great Patriotic War. I see it in both time lines, which I know you understand.

It is truly a blessing from Yahweh that Helen is with you. I have seen her in the visions and know how beautiful and loving she is. You deserve the rich and full life that she has brought to you more than anyone living will ever know. The sacrifices you made in the war to save so many are remembered.

I know that you are wondering about Gertrudt and Rebekka. Tell Helen that my beloved mother and Molly's eternal friend lived a long and blessed life. Thanks to both her and you, Yuri, Rebekka and I made it to America. We obtained the very best education.

It is a tragic thing to report that my dear sister died at an early age of a sudden and inexplicable illness. I dream of her often and know that she is content with our mother in Heaven.

Now, onto the current conflict with today's evil. Sadly, much of the populace of this country has fallen into a deep abyss of self-deception. I have lived a very long time and have seen the catastrophic results of a society which falls into the childish and politically convenient Marxist agenda.

The leftist elitists have all the banners and proclamations of modernism and self-righteousness, but totalitarianism can work from either direction. Fascism and globalism are a matched set. I'm taking this moment to remind you of the wisdom which you shared with me 61 years ago. We now exist in a completely unrealistic time. The worst is yet to come.

I also have the same date in mind for the apocalyptic event we all fear. The diary that I have reflects facts that I cannot share with you now. But everything that you now believe is correct. Of the coming years, I can only tell you the diary speaks of death and chaos from the outset of the 20's decade. * *I want you and Helen to* *send any additional information you can, perhaps once a month, until the approaching date.*

I know from the diary that both you and Helen will be required to come to us and assist in the final efforts to prevent the terrorist strike. We must not see each other, and I will most likely not respond to any information that you send. That will rest in the operational arm of the military.

You will be contacted.

I live for the next five years to pass so that I can be held in the arms of my father once again.

Your loving daughter,

Sasha Cohen

Aaron sat looking downwards at his hands. Helen watched as he pressed them together, as in prayer, holding them to his chin. In the next moments, he seemed to repeatedly bounce them together like a five-sided spring. Then, he smacked both fists together like a "high five."

Through teary eyes, Helen gave her best friend a curious sidelong glance as she spoke out, "Please, you dear man, would you tell me what you're doing?"

Aaron peered timidly back at Helen, through moist and strained eyes. "Most of the horrid conflict in battle is spent in the torment of thinking about the fear and death. In simpler times, we still must learn to somehow cope with the incongruous emotion that existence forces upon us."

Helen entreated quietly, "I've never experienced death and war. You were right. Sasha is your daughter. She knows the pain and suffering. She validates your soul."

A single tear fell down Aaron's right cheek as he gazed at Helen silently. Helen's jade orbs flashed brightly as she muttered softly, "A human being drove a truck this summer in Nice, France, through other human beings for over a mile. Nearly one hundred human lives were forced into a meat grinder, and the collectivists still seek their selfish and deceit-filled agendas. Can the human race consider any part of itself divine?"

Aaron seemed to almost whisper, "The silver-back gorilla forces young males into the jungle, away from his harem. The hummingbird displaces the bumble bee. Territories are essential to existence. When a mother weans a child with hunger, the child drinks on his own."

Helen replied, "The Zoo hypothesis is right; 10 million advanced civilizations want no part of us. We are just ants in the jungle; it would require a divinity to even fool with us."

Aaron smiled wryly. "Well, if you have eternity to deal with, you're not very interested in anything that's easy. The impossible simply requires more time."

***

Helen hit the pause button as she wiggled her toes in Aaron's lap. "I adore the weekends, but I need for you to give me a lesson in your 'weird science.' I want you to explain something. You said a month ago that it didn't matter what (S) knows. Now, you say you can't meet with Sasha for 5 years because her diary says that's when she 'sees' you for the first time. And you say you can't tell me what you know about my part. And you can't tell Sasha that Rebekka has been reborn and even has the same name."

Aaron turned to his lover and quipped, "I know you've waited until we were on your comfy couch because you thought I might be more vulnerable to your wiles."

Helen smiled seductively. "I told you I have to mull these things over. So I'm sneaking up on you in our favorite spot because, yes, you're exactly right. You always are!"

Aaron leaned back. "All right, there's a lot to explain. So I'll see if you stay awake. To begin with, probability science is quite imponderable in many respects. The contained random generators I've experimented with produce varied series of binomial results. If you take say 3 red cards out of a deck of 52 cards and do a little exercise in probabilities you'll observe something quite weird. I used 8 decks and shuffled them very consistently for the experiment. I shuffled and flipped the cards 50,000 times. Yes, it took several months. I recorded the reds as an X and the blacks as an O. The string of hugs and kisses filled 50 sheets of paper. Here's the point. When I began to look for patterns, the fancy term is permutations, I found something quite impossible. When a single X is followed by a single O and then followed by two or more multiple X's, which is then followed by the high rate Q card, an O, the next card should be an X only about 47% of the time. Do you think that sounds right?"

Helen smiled upwards at Aaron and quipped, "Darling, I really like the symbolism—fifty thousand hugs and kisses is what I'm pondering—but yes, it should be a black card 53% of the time. Keep going I like the anticipation."

Aaron continued, "There were a couple thousand of these sequences and here's the quandary. Each time that sequence occurs, the red card, the X, the low probability card occurs at almost the high rate. It occurs at 51%! I worked with this extensively, and it occurs consistently. The cards are not coming up with the expected invariant black bias with each outcome. The rate has 'flipped'. In fact, I've observed three types of variant permutations, rate compression, dilation and the flips. I know this sounds ridiculous, but if the cards are remembering the pattern, then the cards know what color they are. Simple, mixed, randomizing systems possess a mind of their own."

Helen frowned. "How is that possible?"

Aaron smirked as he replied, "In every physics text, there is a reference to Newton's 1st Law. It is said that one explanation for momentum and inertia is that the Universe is Lazy. Do you see much difference in my personification? I built a four foot tall vertical tumbler that uses ping pong balls and saw the same rate flip. I did experiments with a roulette wheel so that I could look at the effect under different geometries. The different systems are all permuting, not simply producing combinations at the geometrically expanding rates. Combinations do, in fact, permute."

Shri'Ani smiled broadly as she peered upwards at Francois L'Hospital. "I'll try and explain this to you later, but I really do grasp what you're saying."

Aaron continued, "This varied rate provides information. In the circumference of the wheel tumbler, you can plot the data across time in the horizontal and displacement in the vertical and you can see the results peak backwards in time." Aaron grimaced sorely as he continued, "I guess we've talked about this. But I don't think I really ever thought you got this far with it."

Helen continued, "The data points prove there is a distinct real-world phenomenon unique to each observer. The peaks, backwards across time in the wheel, suggest that atoms and much of the discounted events that are considered paranormal are real."

Aaron replied, "I couldn't have said it any better. The 'Halo' graph proves that there's a connection across time. It's evidence that there is some type of information dimension beyond our senses. We're still getting out of bed this morning. The past doesn't disappear."

Helen sat up and mused, "So each mind is its own reality."

Aaron replied, "There are three huge mysteries in science. Gravity is not sufficiently explained by General Relativity. Science doesn't have a clue. Human memory is inexplicable. There are around 200 billion neurons in our skulls. Coincidentally, the same number as the stars in the Milky Way galaxy. There is no way to explain our memories or emotion. The last is the DNA molecule itself. Geneticists know that natural selection doesn't remotely explain its existence. We've talked about the cyanobacteria. It cleansed the atmosphere and oceans with oxygen. There is no way the immense coding in the molecule occurred by accident, and there was nothing before it to mutate or naturally select its code."

Helen replied, "So you've discovered a connection between events and, therefore, objects themselves, which means there is some type of magical and unexpected reality."

A thin smile formed on the physicist's face as he commented, "It means that matter:energy:mind coexist. We're not just self-deceived computers."

Helen nodded her head. "I like that phrase. I understand it more and more. But let's get back to the original question. Why can't we see Sasha now? Why can't we share everything around the issues?"

"One of the thought experiments that blocked the idea of time travel is called the 'Grandfather Paradox,'" Aaron replied. "If I get in a time machine and go back 50 years and kill my grandfather, I could never be born and go back to kill my grandfather. I now know that I could get in a space ship, which is surrounded by a material of hybridized matter, and by traveling nearly the speed of light, I would travel to the past. I could in fact kill my grandfather and it would create a parallel reality. I would not exist in one and I would be a murderer in the other."

Helen thoughtfully replied, "So if we know about the future events, we could end up with multiple time lines again just like you created in 1703."

Aaron smiled broadly as he nodded agreeably. Helen remarked,

"You just told me something you never admitted. You've said that the Kepler satellite has provided data which says that there are 100 million Earth-type planets in our galaxy alone, in the habitable 'Goldilocks' zones." Aaron nodded again as Helen continued, "You've just told me that UFO's are real. The aliens get here with time travel just like Luke Skywalker. George Lucas of Star Wars knows that must be the answer to star travel."

Aaron smiled broadly. "And Gene Roddenberry, the creator of Star Trek conceived of space warp to travel to the stars, but we will probably never warp space."

Helen pursed her lips as she grimaced. "All right, I've got one more question about time-travel. Why have the grey hairs I pluck out of my eye brows disappeared? Every few weeks, I had to pluck 'em out. I haven't had any since we linked with ourselves five years from now. And there are other things." Helen's eyes dropped to Aaron's lap as she continued, "I'm sure you've noticed that we both seem to have an inordinate amount of youthful vitality."

Aaron grinned broadly as he replied, "I've been wondering if you noticed. I don't think we're aging like we were before the 'slip.' The physics shouldn't work like this. I can only think that it comes from a higher power. We have to be as young as we are now in five years. I suppose we should look back to scripture and see if we can get a clue from the biblical patriarch Methuselah." Helen grimaced sorely as Aaron continued, "He was 969 years old, and we've seen that the mind exists beyond the body."

(circa October 2021 [Y]time line)

Helen's robe and slippers flapped comically as she hoisted and plopped the last open suitcase onto her king-size bed. She immediately turned and exclaimed loudly, "It's a good thing you packed last night. I can't believe all of this. We only get to take two suitcases and one carry-on each. How are we to get along for nearly two months?"

Aaron chuckled to himself as Helen watched his reaction disconcertingly. Her wet curly locks shivered as she entreated, "What's so funny!?"

The calm and patient mathematician replied, "I'm only taking one suitcase! How can you not have enough clothes with three large suitcases?"

Helen retorted as she continued her frenzied efforts, "Men! I will never understand how you think!" Suddenly, the frantic woman let out a shriek, "I almost closed the last fly of summer into my dress suitcase. I would have had fly droppings all over my silk blouses!"

Aaron quipped, "It could be worse. They could have evolved without wings and then we'd have to call them 'walks.' You'd have tiny footprints all over your clothes."

Helen looked over her shoulder, standing erect with her back arched as she calmly scolded her fully-dressed and seated partner, "That's really quite funny. And yes, it reminds me why I love you, until I'm also reminded of how annoying your efficiency can be. It's 2:22 a.m.! How did you get ready in less than an hour?"

Aaron sat quietly and only responded with a wry smirk on his face. Helen continued, "Why were we only given two days' notice for this and why are we being picked up in the parking lot of the Red Dragon restaurant at 4:30 in the morning?"

The professor of physical science replied curiously, "I've wondered about that, too."

Helen turned and looked at Aaron for several seconds and, setting her chin defiantly, demanded, "Yes? I'm waiting for a logical explanation!"

Aaron raised his eyebrows and softly replied, "It's quite

mysterious isn't it?"

Helen rebuked, "Well, the world is blowing up! Airports have been terrorized. The Middle-East is a war zone. Iran just got decimated by Israel. America carpet-bombed their military installations. And France and Germany might as well have time-slipped back to World War II. And you just sit there all calm, ready to jump right into the frying pan." Helen's fiery jade orbs began to water up as she completed her indictment, "We don't even know where we're going and why can't we just drive ourselves to the airport!?"

Aaron sat patiently punching into his phone as he responded, "Bailey just texted me. She said that Bekah just texted her and said she would be here at 3:30. Bailey says that she will check on the house tomorrow and make sure that everything is secure. She also says that both of them will take care of our classes and not to worry. She's going to let Bekah take care of getting us to the rendezvous site. She loves us and demands that we keep her informed, daily."

Helen shrieked as she became even more frantic, "Oh, my (Y), I only have one hour to get ready. You've got to help me!"

Aaron began toting designated feminine items from closets and drawers as he began to prattle, "Have you ever wondered how half the country could buy into the leftist agenda? The current administration may not get our defenses back in place."

Helen continued to scuttle about as she called out, "Follow me into the bathroom. Look, it's like your geneticist hero, J.B.S. Haldane said, 'The Universe is not only stranger than we know, it's stranger than we can know.'"

Francois watched as his teenage bride readied herself in the 17th Century mirror. Aaron smiled, knowingly and spoke out, "I figured out why we haven't aged a day in five years."

Helen snapped back, "It's gotten a little difficult. Bekah said that she's overheard people in the department getting quizzical."

Aaron continued, "In Genesis 5 there is a verse. 'His death will bring judgment.' Methuselah lived to be 969 years old and preserve his people!"

Helen turned to Aaron sternly and retorted, "Don't you dare do this to me now! You better have a hopeful algorithm for that comment, Professor."

Aaron smiled and replied, "Darling, it is hopeful. When we slipped to ourselves, five years later, we have remained ourselves from the past until that moment."

The professor of literature turned and inquired, "Does that mean we'll survive past that moment!?"

Aaron grimaced, shrugged and responded, "I hope so. I mean, it proves that we 'slipped' by the Will of (Y). (S) wouldn't have left us with any advantage, with what's coming."

Helen turned to Aaron and spoke intently. "I remember our lunch that one time with your dear mother, Thelma. She told me of that remarkable episode when she stepped into the dark room as you lay in your crib, only a babe, and the morning light streamed through the curtains and fell upon your chest. Neither you nor her ever told me what it meant."

Aaron peered back into Helen's gaze adroitly. "I've felt you caress the unique birthmark I bear on my right chest. It's odd that it appears as if someone's thumbprint had been dipped in blood and pressed onto my body." Helen's green eyes widened as Aaron continued, "My mother told me the white light appeared to condense and touch my chest at exactly the location of the port wine mark."

Helen retorted, "Yes, but what does it mean!?"

Aaron replied, "It has to do with messages from beyond Helen.

Humanity is involved in an ongoing relationship with a higher consciousness. Those who have faith will witness signs and wonders. Birthmarks such as this often reflect a pre-life trauma, often the trauma from the cause of death or great hardship during that life."

Helen asked, "Does this have to do with your last life as a Russian soldier"?

Aaron smiled agreeably as he began to speak softly. "It has to do with the fact that I was shot through the chest during the Battle of Stalingrad in World War II. It has to do with the fact that only you know the date which will begin the next great war. It has to do with a riddle I ponder continually. What is the significance of the mirrored date of the Winter Solstice, 12/21, and will the year 2021 you selected truly end the ominous threat or will it perhaps repeat on that date each year throughout that decade?"

***

Helen and Aaron stood in their home's driveway surrounded by a flotilla of suitcases as Aaron spoke up, "Well, It's 3:28. Yuri's reincarnated daughter and your fellow literature department's professor should be here in two minutes."

Shri'Ani spoke out as she hesitated to translate into English, "Francois, I'm scared to death. I need to remember how brave I was as Molly. I can't keep it in my mind. Why?"

Aaron replied softly, "Remember our conversations about the divine influence. How can people throughout the Ages be so naive and obtuse when helpless human beings are being slaughtered?"

Helen's green eyes sparkled in the moonlight as she peered back at her eternal partner. "Whatever you say, I know it will be encouraging."

Aaron responded calmly, "Have you ever wondered why people look like their pets?"

Helen's expression turned nonplussed as she retorted, "I get it. When you're nervous you make jokes."

Aaron grimaced and replied, "No! I'm serious. It's true, Helen. The human mind transposes its world-view. We want the world to reflect our own identities. The less experienced the mind, the more one simply disregards the pain of others. It's the old story. 'Don't confuse me with the facts; my mind's already made up.'"

Bekah swung into the driveway and popped her trunk as Helen turned to Aaron and had the last word, "I hope Yuri or Francois kicks in. We're going to need more than Aaron's dry humor to defeat Satan and his minions."

***

Three figures stood in the dark parking lot of the familiar college restaurant. The green glow of the streetlights could not drown out the vivid stars shining in the early morning sky.

Aaron looked at the feminine image of his dearest friend and lover. "I hope a cop doesn't come up and ask if we're going to break into the Red Dragon restaurant and steal breakfast."

Helen chuckled. "I just hope no one sees three people standing in an empty parking lot with enough luggage for a long trip on a luxury cruise line."

Aaron looked over at the statuesque white-blonde-haired young woman standing next to Helen. "So Bekah, I understand you were the Spring Festival Queen of the fjords!"

The young Swedish beauty answered with a broad percolating smile. "Oh yes, Professor. I was the youngest winner of the contest!"

Aaron could not help but drink in the vivid blue eyes that seemed to twinkle at him in the dim light. Francois looked at Shri'Ani standing next to Bekah. The sensual contrast between the jet black hair of the teenaged, green-eyed Hindu princess and the nubile Nordic beauty was truly rapturous.

Helen's voice came to Aaron's mind as he caught her sidelong glance. "For just a moment, I thought perhaps you were back at your French desk, professor."

Aaron looked at Bekah almost timidly as he thought to himself, *Do these two both know something the one shouldn't know?*

The outnumbered man felt a sensation travel through his lower extremities. He suddenly realized that the ground beneath his feet seemed to be pounding rhythmically. The physicist immediately turned to study the glass windows of the Red Dragon restaurant. The same vibration was visibly shaking the glass.

At that instant, the air itself seemed too thick to breath as an intense "whoosh, whoosh" sound filled the air. The scene was suddenly awash with a tremendous wind. The trio grabbed for one another as the stars above them disappeared. The sky was suddenly filled with a black object, which appeared cast in a green glow in the morning street lights.

A dozen yards away, the unmarked helicopter sat down in the open parking lot. The trio steadied themselves and watched as three men dressed in completely black outfits came running towards the group. Helen grabbed onto Aaron's arm as the men grabbed bags and suitcases and the arms of the two professors.

Bekah stood open-mouthed. She could scarcely believe the scene she had just witnessed. The young Swede stood dumbfounded as the craft lifted from the ground and streaked directly into the early morning sky towards the vivid glow of the moon. Looking at her watch, she realized that the entire event had occurred in less than two minutes.

The young student of Viking lore quietly muttered to herself, "I'm standing in front of one Red Dragon and another green dragon grabs my American professors and flies away with them into the night sky. They are truly special. But no, it was not a dragon. They fly to Valhalla with the Valkyries!"

***

Both Helen and Aaron seemed to be thrown by the dutiful airmen into the plush tandem seats of the craft. Huge headphones were clamped onto their heads and seat belts snapped in place as smiling faces seemed to be carefully attending to their needs.

Each passenger looked at one to the other and wondered if the same thought was being shared. Helen spoke first. Her voice was conveyed perfectly over the headgear. "You look like Mickey Mouse!"

Aaron retorted, "The irony does not escape me, Minnie. There are some pretty big cats throwing this party. I just hope we can build the best mouse trap."

The conversation was interrupted by another voice, "This is Captain Reynolds. Welcome aboard! I am instructed to inform you that your next stop is Langley, Virginia. Your ETA is 07:30 Eastern time. General King will meet you there. So sit back and enjoy the ride."

Aaron looked out the cabin window and studied the landscape racing away below the craft. Several minutes passed, before he commented, "We're doing in excess of 250 MPH. I had no idea the military had such a craft!"

Helen replied whimsically as she leaned into Aaron's left shoulder and closed her eyes to take a nap, "Well, the morning is proving productive. I've lived to experience the moment when not even 'one of you' knows something!"

Belly of the Beast

(circa October 2021 [Y]time line)

Helen's words echoed in the multiple mind of the man who loved her more than life itself but never knew her. *I've lived long enough to experience the moment when not even the "one of you" knows something.* Yuri Vladiovich heard the words which he knew held the darkest secrets of all. His eyelids grew heavy as the deep almost embryonic rhythm of the speeding super copter overwhelmed his weary flesh.

(circa December 1945 [S]time line)

The Russian lieutenant spoke casually, "Wait here, comrade. I will interrogate this household on my own." Sergeant Gorgi nodded to his superior and sat patiently in the armored German Volksvagen. Yuri Vladiovich threaded his way up the East Berlin wooded path to the bedraggled German home.

The knock at the door was intense, but the Russian Intelligence officer waited patiently before rapping a second time. The door opened slowly to the presence of a dignified lady who produced a thin smile which, in fact, belied much concern. "Yes, what do you want?"

The young Russian's gaze dropped to his file's picture of the woman. He considered that it must have been taken some years before the date stamp it bore. "Fraulein Cohen. Are you Gertrudt Cohen?"

The response gave witness to High German breeding and social station, "Ya, I am Fraulein Cohen."

The Lieutenant spoke respectfully, "I am Russian (psy) Intelligence Lieutenant Yuri Vladiovich. I would like to speak with you, Fraulein."

Gertrudt's trepidation seemed to fade as she studied the smile and soft brown eyes of the handsome young man. Yuri removed his officer's cap as the door swung open for him to enter the dwelling.

The timid lady spoke out courteously, "I have very little, but I may be able to boil some tea."

The graciousness of the lady who stood before him was precisely that of the recent dream vision he had experienced. He responded with a slight bow and spoke softly, "Da, I would find that most appealing."

Left to his own discretion, the young man looked about the room. Stepping up to the mantle over the small fireplace, the Russian saw the menorah. His mind wandered to the thought of how precious few Jews were able to escape the Fundamentalist Nazi destruction. He knew that practical management of a factory could sometimes be more important than theocratic rhetoric.

Next to the sacred Jewish symbol of Grace, Yuri saw the picture which had burned its way into his dreams for so many years. His eyes would sometimes tear up as he would read the frantically scrawled words in his aging diary, *"Could all this be real?"* As he held in his hands the image of the two whimsical girls leaning against the shipboard railing, a sudden dizziness overcame him. He focused on the image of the girl whose two-dimensional black and white face suddenly sprang to life. Smiling broadly, vivid green eyes shouted to his mind. Yuri heard the pounding of his own heart as the voice worked its way into his mind. *"Sasha and Rebekka must remain with Gertrudt!"*

"Leftenant, Sir, your tea is hot!" Gertrudt's expression was palpable as the young Russian turned to see the curious German lady standing transfixed with the tray of drinks and cups.

Gertrudt's expression was curious as she saw the picture of herself and her truly unsinkable friend, Molly Brown, held quite delicately in the young Russian's hand. "Please come over and sit with me."

The young man belied a slightly feeble appearance as he sat on the small settee. Gertrudt sat in the chair next to the young man and poured the tea. It occurred to her that it had been a very long time since she had witnessed such distracted behavior. Yuri sat with the picture of young Molly and Gertrudt cupped in both hands, his gaze never leaving the picture.

Gertrudt spoke gently, "You're much too young to have known her, and I know we have never met."

Yuri's focus returned to the moment. "Is it true? Did she very nearly kill the German Wolf?"

Gertrudt's face lit up. "Do the Russians know this name? It seems to me that only a few Russians would know this name for Hitler, the Wolf." The smiling woman's eyes grew moist as her voice trembled slightly, "It was the saddest day of my life. I have not lived one day without her love in my heart. She did what she knew she had to do. She was one of those special people who know more than they should. She was so gifted." A tear fell down Gertrudt's cheek as she looked up at the young man, his gaze still transfixed on the picture in his hands.

She spoke softly, not sure if her words were being heard, "Molly was a 3rd degree (psy). She saved the RMS Titanic on April 15th, 1912. Do you know this? That picture was taken on April 16th. I have wondered if that picture is supposed to exist at all." Gertrudt began to feel a kinship for the lost soul still sitting silently. "You're a psychic, aren't you?"

Yuri looked up, responding to the entreaty, "I can feel why she loved you."

The two sat together silently for some moments, when Yuri finally reached out and took a drink of tea. Looking up at Gertrudt, he spoke with renewed energy, "There is a reason why I am here. There is a reason why I have never married. There is a reason why the Great Religious War, which has just devastated the world, is only of secondary consequence."

Gertrudt thought to herself that the young KGB Intelligence officer looked quite strong to her, suddenly. She was quite pleased as she spoke up. "If this involves Margaret Brown, you will succeed with your destiny. I can tell you that no stronger soul exists. Her strength is the only reason I continue to survive. I knew the day would come that she would return to my life."

The young soldier smiled, "I knew I could depend on you. I need your help with something that will not take place for many decades. If you will help me, we can put something in place that may save all of our eternal souls." Yuri looked at the aging German with a curious expression.

Gertrudt's face lit up as she spoke, "I don't know how many more years until I am back together with my dearest Molly and my beloved husband. But neither one will think much of me if I do not assist someone who obviously has been sent by (Y). How can I help you, Yuri?"

(circa October 2021 07:31 ET Langley, Virginia [Y]time-line)

Helen and Aaron stood holding onto one another as the crisp morning air filled their lungs. The physicist turned to watch the levitating craft steady its vertical ascent, rotate in place, and streak off towards the horizon. He held Helen close as he spoke out, "I didn't know the military had craft with such extreme design parameters."

Helen stared meekly at the man who represented her only attachment to reality as she muttered, "Please Aaron, if there's anything else you don't know, don't tell me."

At that moment, the duo of temporal interlopers watched as a solitary tram rolled away with their assortment of bags and suitcases. Aaron looked bemused as he quipped, "These people must get paid in reverse, the more quickly something happens, the better. Helen watched as a solitary figure dressed in a well-fitted black suit and tie approached from an adjoining building to the heliport. She quipped, "Oh, my (Y). I wonder where his dark sunglasses and the companion Grey Alien are!?"

The smiling figure stopped a few feet from the embraced couple and spoke confidently, "Good morning, Professors. I hope you had a good flight!"

Standing with their arms wrapped around one another, the pair stood as if the voice might not be quite real. Aaron spoke out shyly, "We're just a little tired. Our sleep's been pretty disrupted this morning."

The smiling figure motioned and began to walk as he spoke, "Breakfast is waiting. There's freshly ground Colombian coffee and hot Earl Grey tea."

(October 2021 08:30 hours)

The door opened with an unexpected swiftness. In itself, such a response, even by inanimate objects spoke of the imminence of military brass. The 4-Star monolith, which towered before the humble intelligence officer, sent a shot of adrenaline through the middle-aged naval 'lifer.'

The middle-aged colonel blasted from his desk chair. Standing erect, back arched, with his right hand to forehead in a salute, the dutiful marine spoke out, "Colonel Paul Bush, Special Deep Operations Coordinator, Sir." Looking straight ahead, the instantaneous flash of the last few seconds seem to extend forwards into negative time. The mental tumblers of a mind used to telescoping all events in over-thought scenarios wondered if he had responded too officiously.

General James King saluted and smiled. "At ease, Colonel. These are Professors Aaron LaSalle and Helen Lovelace. They will be the operations Chief Adjuncts for the "Deep Vision Operation."

Col. Bush came around his desk and began shaking hands. "Please, let's have a seat at my table." The morass of incomprehensible papers, preponderances, and files on the table were nearly swept onto the floor as the colonel made room for the group.

Gen. King placed a briefcase on the table and pulled out a file. Sorting through the papers, he retrieved a picture of an Iranian and another picture of a Russian. Placing them on the table, he said, "These are our unit targets. It is believed that these are the two directly in charge of the Syrian, Iraq, and Iran unification. They direct all military and civilian activities. Their true boss appears to be one Russian President Putin. They're the direct puppet masters for the Shia plot against New York City."

Col. Bush spoke out, "I've read the dossier on the professors. May I call you Aaron?"

Aaron replied. "That's fine. And may I call you Paul?"

Paul looked both to Helen and Aaron as he spoke out, "Your psychical awareness is unprecedented. There are several thousand questions I would like to ask both of you." Looking at Aaron, the composure of Paul returned to that of the instinctive problem solver. Paul studied Aaron's dignified features, looking him directly in the eyes as he spoke, "May I give you a brief 'psy' exam this morning? I have some understanding of the negative time 'kaleidoscope' which you have introduced with your mathematical work. I need to know what your wakened state 'remote viewing' abilities are."

Gen. King spoke up. "In fact, Colonel, I want you to test both of them. Helen may not be involved directly with your team, but we need the results for her assignment."

Aaron interceded, "Paul, Helen and I don't really have any idea what this test involves."

Gen. King responded, "Sometimes, in the heat of battle, field promotions are made on the fly, Professor. I just showed you the pictures of the main suspects in the terrorist plot you described to me five years ago. Paul has sat here studying your response. He is a very talented psychic."

Col. Bush explained, "In 1978, at Ft. Meade, Maryland, the Defense Intelligence Agency set up an investigative body to consider psychic abilities to 'see' events, individuals, and sites relevant to national security. This involved a lieutenant "Skip" Atwater and Major Albert Stubblebine. The Stargate Project was officially declassified in 1995, and it was tactically asserted that it provided no useful information."

Gen. King continued, "Paul, you have Aaron and Helen until 1100 hours. I'll need all of you at the field operatives conference at 13:30 hours. We will conference on the current intervention stratagem."

(circa October 2021 1600 hours)

The meeting had been long and filled with an enormous amount of National and International information pertaining to national security. Aaron looked at Helen sitting next to him and asked, "Well, there are thirty-two people at this conference whom we haven't even met. Do you suppose anyone can figure out this riddle?!"

The room lights brightened as Gen. King rose to his feet and began to speak, "I want to introduce the two new members of our team. Please stand for us. This is Professor Aaron LaSalle and Professor Helen Lovelace. They're new admissions to the 'remote viewing' contingent."

The tall, 30-something woman who next rose for an introduction was a striking image with her tightly-wrapped, white-blonde hair and piercing black eyes. "I am Marguerite Cohen. I am known as the 'Wolf.' I want to address you, Professor Lovelace."

Helen gave Aaron a timid sidelong glance as she rose to respond, "Yes, I am Helen Lovelace." Her green eyes widened, as she noticed the jade amulet on the blonde's right wrist.

A thin smile crept across the Wolf's face. "I want to ask you an impossible question. Did you know my grandmother? Her name was Gertrudt Cohen? If you say yes, we have a chance of preventing this attack!"

Helen stood at the opposite end of the main conference table, transfixed as the statuesque blonde walked in her direction. The feminine beauty of the intimidating woman was only outmatched by her strength and confidence, both of which flowed from every pore of her being. Helen's wide-eyed trance followed Marguerite's feet, crossing the carpeted floor. Each step towards Helen suddenly slowed in time. The image became visceral as if some pacing, predatory animal was stalking Helen's mind.

***

Molly Brown watched as her feet lifted from the ship's deck, laughing hysterically as both girls leaned back on the ship's railing. Gertrudt yelled, "Careful, or you'll pull us both overboard!"

The young and outlandish American smiled and turned her

head skyward. "Don't you see that beautiful blue sky, Gertrudt? Such a magnificent memory can never disappear! I will never leave this day, April 16th, 1912."

Molly and her dear German friend were filled with vigor and rapture. The moment was one of the most delightful memories of their lives. The two turned and smiled, holding each other against the railing of the RMS Titanic as Ruben Cohen snapped the camera shutter.

***

Helen stood face to face with the Wolf. The intimidating, hypnotic trance testified to the power of the inquisitor. The CIA operative stood in perfect choreography with the very soul of the college professor. Marguerite studied the contours of Helen's face, her fascination pausing as she appeared consumed in the fire of the academic's green-eyed gaze. The Wolf stood quietly, awaiting an answer.

Helen peered directly into the Wolf's penetrating black eyes. She nodded an affirmation.

Marguerite's tone and expression remained blank. "I would like for you and Aaron to accompany me; there is someone I need for both of you to meet"

The three traveled for several minutes down the corridors of the National Intelligence complex. Badges were swiped, and a maze of passages threaded as the final door was opened to a small meeting room. The party entered to the presence of a solitary figure sitting at the end of a long table. The aging woman sat with a small, plain box resting before her.

The Wolf spoke out, pleasantly, "Mamma, they're here."

The woman who rose to her feet might have been mistaken for an older clone of the Wolf. She spoke up with a quiet, but confident tone, "I am Sasha Cohen and you are Molly Brown and

Yuri Vladiovich."

Sasha's gaze fell upon Aaron as the aging college professor's brown eyes began to water. Helen's hand covered her mouth as she watched the dignified man lurch forward, snatching the smiling woman into the air and into his arms. "Oh, my blessed Sasha! We have been resurrected!"

The scene was sacred as the two refugees in time and sacrifice stood gazing at one another. Helen stood transfixed as her green orbs blurred. She entreated, "Speak to me, Aaron! I must know Sasha."

The aging lady held open her arms as Helen raced into the grasp of the daughter of Yuri Vladiovich. The American immigrant spoke out joyously, "Oh, dear lord, you are more beautiful than I imagined."

The miraculous reunion was validated as the mysterious lady picked up a box from the table to reveal a number of aged, hand-written pages inside a very old military log. Helen recognized the writing as that of perhaps Russian in origin.

The Russian Lieutenant took the papers reverently in his hand and recited a phrase, speaking in perfect Russian dialect, "The magnificence of our memories can never disappear." Aaron's head shook slowly as he spoke, "You've done it. I have the diary from 1944 in my hand!"

Sasha wailed and burst into tears, wrapping her arms around Aaron's waist. "Oh, my blessed Yuey. You have returned to me!"

Helen spoke timidly as she asked, "What does all this mean?"

Helen watched in abject fascination as she made out the traces of the first smile she had witnessed from the Wolf. The elderly woman's truly surreal daughter nearly shouted, "It means that we have everything we need to beat the damned Devil!"

(0600 hours)

The ringing phone brought Helen's senses to the moment as her now awakened state flooded in from both her ears and her suddenly wide open eyes. Smacking at the phone and finally managing the receiver to her ear, she succeeded in silencing its urgency, "Hello?"

A vibrant voice spoke up as if it had never known sleep, "Good morning, Commander. Have you chosen your breakfast option this morning?"

Helen spoke out vaguely. "Oh, that's right. There are four standard options. I guess we'd like "B," and you know the drinks."

The voice continued its encouraging tone, "Yes, ma'am! It will be there in 20 minutes or less. Thank you, ma'am!"

Helen sat up in the king-size bed which had provided her with a much-needed rest as comfortably as her very own. Patting with her left arm, she felt the one article which truly brought life into her soul. Pulling down the comfy covers, the woman who had not aged one minute in over five years mounted the multiple loves of her life.

Francois's eyes grew wide as the deep snores were replaced by a quiet and encouraging voice, "Shri', you always wake up before me."

The young Frenchman's wife leaned down from her lofty stance and kissed her lover as she sang out, "No, Francois! I was sure you were up first this morning."

The couple lay embraced quite still for some minutes when Helen looked back at the large red digits of the hotel room clock. "In less than five minutes, breakfast will be here. I have to meet the Wolf at 0800 hours."

***

Aaron walked from the adjoining bath, fully dressed and sipping his Earl Grey as he sat and watched Helen, wrapped tightly in her obligatory white robe, leaning into the mirror. The dutiful man gazed at her distractedly as he spoke up, "Well, I guess we just call and the transport service will be waiting for us. I'm not sure how much we'll see each other today."

Helen remarked, "I'm wearing my dress pants suit for training with the Wolf today. I dreamed of myself as Molly last night. I'm glad she was an expert marksman. It's funny to think that a dyed-in-the-wool 'progressive' is supposed to be capable of military skills. I've never had a gun in my hand."

A sheepish expression filled the science professor's face as he remarked, "I remember our early conversations. God, guns, guts was some extinct and ridiculed mistake of antiquity."

Helen was relaxed, but answered reflexively, "I'm going to a briefing and a gun range with the Wolf. I've rethought my paradigm. 'The Universe is stranger than I can know.' Now, I know the bad things can't be wished away."

Aaron smiled warmly as Helen turned to his response. "(Y) put us here for a reason. The good will defeat the evil only if the good is very prepared, and even then, it's an eternal battle."

Aaron tried not to expose his thoughts with his expression. "When the Wolf spoke to you alone yesterday, were there any discussions about your psychic abilities?"

Helen tucked the finery of the white silk blouse into the worsted wool slacks as she retorted, "Not a word. The woman is a robot. I thought there was only one robot in your science fiction allegory."

The professor of all things science smiled. "That was one of our first epiphanies. I asked you to pick a name if you and I wrote a story about science and mysticism. You said that you always thought Patricia would be perfect. The 1950's classic, *The Day the Earth Stood Still*, required Helen to save the earth from the infinite power of the robot Gort. It starred Patricia Neal. You agreed that the name for the woman and even the tie-in with her last name was too much to be coincidence."

Helen stood in front of Aaron with a girlish, somewhat nervous, expression. The thick furls of her Irish auburn hair, vivid green eyes, and deliberately whorish rouge lipstick sent a shot of adrenaline through the energetic professor. Aaron tried to remember that they were still both in their 21st Century roles. He fought back the 17th Century French urges.

Helen quipped, "You can't kiss me. You'll mess up my Wolf impersonation. This is the most intimidating I can be."

Aaron smiled broadly as Helen queried, "I want to know what you're thinking about the science fiction movie. I know you saw me in the 1988 visions, and yes, I do resemble the actress Patricia Neal, but are you saying you also actually knew my name would be Helen?"

A wry smile formed on Aaron's face as he quipped, "Do you find it curious that you just put that together? The information that can be shown to us can be absolute."

Helen looked pensively at Aaron as she commented, "I've been reading the commentaries of one of your heroes. William F. Buckley said, 'The best defense against usurpatory government is an assertive citizenry.'"

The professor of natural science smiled broadly as he responded, "I won't insult your intelligence by suggesting that you really believe what you just said."

Jade fire returned Aaron's gaze as Molly Brown spoke up,

"Helen and I might disagree in our preference for a President, but don't confuse me with the facts; my mind's already made up. We're more what we're born to be than what we learn to be. I know what needs to be done; those who don't had better get out of the way."

The strained look on the ravishing woman's face turned to smiles as she grabbed Aaron's arm and spoke out, "You call the transport, and I'll get your satchel and my purse. Let's be early and win the 'War of the Worlds.'"

(1500 hours)

General James King, Colonel Paul Bush, and Professor Aaron LaSalle sat at the side table in the general's office. The large room had the appearance of a war museum. The general spoke out, "I'm sure you understand that the duo will be the final two that will stand between the city and its destruction."

Col. Paul Bush added, "I've read all the diaries from 1944. Sasha's and Aaron's fit together like pieces of a puzzle. If we didn't have this, we'd never have known."

Gen. King queried, "We have most of what is going on, but we don't have the name of who's heading up the contraband."

At that instant, the intercom's feminine voice announced, "Sir, I have two field agents to see you."

Gen. King's commanding voice sent trepidation through the bemused physics professor, "Send them in!"

Aaron sat at the conference table with a clear view of the door to the general's impressively large office. The door opened, and the two entering appeared somehow unfamiliar. Helen entered first and stopped a few feet from the door, and with a blank expression, she turned and looked towards the three seated men. The Wolf entered next and also turned to look at the group seated at the table. Closing the door behind them, the two women began to approach

322 ❦

in unison.

Aaron's mind focused on the ambulating duo. He watched as each step for both appeared to synchronously strike the wooden inlay of the floor. Aaron thought it curious that he had not noticed the rich inlay of the solidly built floor. Behind the slow motion of the two women, he also noticed, for the first time, a 19th Century Gatling gun on display. It occurred to him that he was indeed sitting in a war museum. The two approaching in perfect cadence could just as easily have been marching in a finely choreographed military review or executing a battle field maneuver.

Gen. King rose from the table; Aaron realized he was the last to react. The group returned to their seats as the general spoke, "Welcome, ladies. Have you had a productive morning?"

Sitting next to one another, Aaron wondered if Helen would speak or wait for the Wolf to acknowledge the group. Helen sat quietly as the military commander spoke, "We have gone through a checklist of handgun certification." It occurred to Aaron that the Wolf had the appearance of someone who had reported on such test results many times before.

Gen. King smiled casually and asked, "Did you find some skill in our new associate?"

Aaron felt a slight uneasiness as he awaited the Wolf's answer. "Helen's firing range marksmanship scores are nearly perfect. She is a natural."

The table was silent for several seconds as the general began to shuffle through a stack of papers on the table. Leaning across the table, Gen. King placed a paper in front of Col. Bush and spoke quietly, "Paul, did you see this?"

Col. Bush also spoke quietly, "I've set up a new category on the secure servers, General. I've created a new paranormal listing; it's titled 'Life Iterations.'"

Gen. King looked at Helen and calmly spoke, "Helen, I see in the files that you report never having fired a gun of any type."

Helen leaned forward in her chair slightly and smiled wryly. "That's correct, General."

Aaron suddenly felt the eyes of everyone at the table turn to him. He responded in an uncharacteristically nervous tone, "Well, as we've discussed, this phenomenon is something quite new. And it appears to be morphing in unexpected ways. Helen and I are experiencing aspects of this in our memories, our emotions, and our physical inclinations."

Aaron caught Helen's eye for the first time during the meeting. He hoped that his comments had not exposed the insecure feelings he had experienced since she walked into the room.

Gen. King passed around a stack of files to all at the table and spoke, "You will notice that the file you are holding is labeled 'Deep Vision.' Everyone here will also notice the phrase on the Top Secret Seal, and you will recall the signed National Security process, which you have each executed. Please open to the cover letter."

Aaron read the Intelligence Brief intently. Glancing at Helen to reassure himself that she was also on the same page, his feelings of insecurity returned. The discussions with Helen regarding the idea that Gen. King's group possessed too much information appeared to be confirmed.

Aaron looked up as the group seemed to finish reading. Gen. King spoke up, "Colonel Bush, you and Professor LaSalle will comprise the team's mission intelligence executives. You will remain at Central Base. Your group will process all information and planning for the New York City activities. Operations from civilian authorities, national security, and military activities will be processed by my executive team and filtered to you. Rear Admiral

Sasha Cohen, Commander Marguerite Cohen, and Professor Helen Lovelace will represent the spearhead of the field investigations team. Again, your activities will be directly coordinated by my executive team."

Col. Bush spoke up, "I have a question for Professor LaSalle."

Gen. King nodded. "Go ahead, Paul."

The military psychic leaned forward. Aaron had noticed that a kindred spirit seemed to exist within the man. When he appeared to ponder a question or doubt an answer, a curious expression would belie the naval officer's emotion.

Paul's eyes squinted and his head shook slightly as he began his question. With lips pursed tightly, he said, "When the previous life memory comes to you, how does this impact your current awareness? Do you feel like another person, or is it simply like remembering, say, what you ate for breakfast?"

Aaron looked up at Col. Paul Bush and smiled. "Well, we're going to have a lot of time to discuss the implications of a world where science and magic are seen as the same thing. I don't really have a quick answer."

Gen. King spoke up, "All right, let's all turn to the brief titled 'Foreign Contingents.' I want to begin to outline what we know as of this moment."

Leaning over, the general pressed a remote keypad sitting on the table. A large screen began to drop from the ceiling, covering the entire wall adjacent to the table. At the same instant, the intercom spoke out, "Yes, General."

Gen. King again spoke up, "Bridgette, we need a tray of coffee and hot Earl Grey tea!"

(October 2021 14:30 hours 3rd day at Langley, Virginia)

General James King tapped his table top remote again as the

lights in his office brightened and he spoke out, "What is known by combined resources of National Intelligence is now known by all in this room. You have your files, key codes, contacts, and itinerary. I will meet with you again at Central Headquarters in New York City at 07:30 hours the day after tomorrow."

The four men and women seated before the general glanced at one another. The penetrating black eyes of the Wolf met the jade fire of Helen's green orbs. Each in turn met with the soft brown wisdom of Aaron's gaze. Looking at Paul, Helen noticed that he had resumed his endearing squint; it passed through her mind that this charming man must be perpetually embraced in prayer.

Gen. King again spoke out, "If no one has any additions, I would like to take a moment and lead us in a prayer."

The general looked around the table and smiled. It occurred to Helen as curious that she had not considered the deep spiritualism that must thrive within a warrior. She watched in amazement as the towering man quickly and reverently wiped his hands with a quick wipe and opened the KJV bible to a bookmarked page.

"I will speak a verse which has led me to Victory in many battles. I will read from Ephesians chapter 6, verses 13-14: 'Wherefore take unto you the whole armor of God, that ye may be able to withstand in the evil day, and having done all, to stand. Stand therefore, having your loins girt about with truth, and having on the breastplate of righteousness.'"

Helen and Aaron stared, each to the other, wide-eyed and startled. Helen's left hand rose to cover her mouth in fear that she might gasp. The room seemed to spin around the duo. *"Helen, it's as if I can hear your voice through your eyes."*

"Aaron, I hear you, too! How is it possible? That was the last entry from the Reveal. The entry was from 12.21.12. It was the passage that showed the hand of (Y) had intervened to save the

city. It was also the passage which showed the fight was not ended without sacrifice."

(06:30 hours)

The clatter of bags and bustling was typical of two people hustling about, ready to leave a hotel room. Helen stood at the door, looking at her watch. The aging professor clattered to the door, his hands and arms filled with bags and satchels.

Looking up at Helen, Aaron smiled deliberately with the special smile which always worked for Francois. Stopping in front of Helen, he dropped his bags and spoke brusquely, "All I can say is, I'm glad I didn't get any older in the last five years. I wonder if the same Men in Black that swept us from the streets of the Mid-West are going to swoop in here and take us to New York City!"

Helen smiled tenderly and framed both of Aaron's shoulders with her hands. "I . . . need to share something with you." Helen dropped her hands to her side and paced for a moment. "I need to tell you something that happened three days ago at the target range."

Aaron stood, blank-faced, and timidly answered, "What? Tell me quick! I can't stand much more suspense these days. I should be 25 years old again. I might find all this exciting."

Shri'Ani, the teenaged bride, leaned forward and gave her adoring husband a truly breathtaking French kiss. She pulled back and peered into the young man's eyes as she muttered. "We have time, and remember, Francois, you are only 25 years old."

Aaron's face turned seriously red as the adrenalin and heat filled the entirety of his body. "For the love of (Y), how did you do that? Helen, I'm getting concerned about the overlap of the 'slips'! We must maintain control of ourselves. There are going to be people here any minute!"

Helen covered her mouth as she laughed almost hysterically. Aaron also began to smile as he spoke up, "I've spent these half dozen years playing various rhetorical tricks on you to always make you answer my queries first. There's one thing I intend to always say first to you." Aaron's eyes began to water as he continued, "I don't want to live this or any other life without you. I love you more than life itself."

Helen covered her face and turned quickly with her back to Aaron. Wiping a tear from her cheek, she stood steadfast with her back to her beloved. "Remember when the Wolf said my marksmanship was nearly perfect?"

Aaron nodded as he spoke, "Yes, you're totally perfect, Helen!"

Molly spun back around and looked deeply into Aaron's eyes. I hit the bull's eye on the cusp, on the last shot of the rapid fire exercise."

Aaron grimaced, "Well, Annie Oakley, I repeat myself you're perfect!"

Helen smiled. "You don't understand. Half was in, and half was out. Rapid fire is what Molly does best. I'm a pressure performer!"

Francois understood what he was hearing. "Something happened. There was something that interfered with your focus!"

Helen smiled. "I have loved your genius for 300 years. But what fell in my sights for that split instant was *much* older, much more terrifying. I have never felt such terror in *All* my lives."

Aaron stood steadfast as the terrified woman lunged into his arms; her tears covered his face as she kissed him deeply. "I won't leave you, Aaron." She drew a jerky breath and continued, "I saw a red-blazed creature that flashed in my pistol sights, a creature which must be destroyed, but I'm not sure I have the ability!"

The rap at the door was abrupt and sobering. Aaron shouted,

"Give us a moment! We'll be right there!"

(07:30 hours)

Aaron closed the overhead and looked down at the brave woman staring out the plane's window. He stood for a moment, allowing his gaze to trace along the long contour of Helen's leg. The topaz-colored suit was indeed skirted. It occurred to Aaron that he hadn't seen her legs in a skirt for some days.

The dignified academic plopped down on the seat and lowered the arm rest between the two lone passengers. "Well, we know there's somebody in the cockpit, but the MIB's got us here in typically rapid order, and I guess they've left the plane."

Helen's crossed leg began to rock methodically as she turned and leaned into Aaron's gaze. Smiling, she spoke up enthusiastically, "Thank you for our conversation this morning. I feel much better." Helen turned back to the window, and then quickly reaching back into Aaron's lap, she grabbed his right hand with her left and nearly dragged him from his seat toward the window. "Look at the trolleys coming across the tarmac! One, two, three, four; how many people are on this private flight with us!"

Aaron spoke assertively, "There's another L10 sitting just port and aft of our plane. Maybe, that's where they're going."

Helen pulled on Aaron's hand, drawing him close as her jade eyes seemed to swallow the essence of the moment. "How do you know so many things? I mean, really, Aaron; will you ever really tell me what you know?"

Aaron's stare returned to the bare white limb rocking just below him. For the first time, he noticed a tiny pinpoint jet black freckle on her inner thigh, just at the skirt line. The tiny blemish had an almost deliberate appearance as if someone had taken a quill pen and, with the black ink from the mortar, dotted the "i."

The ravishing white skin of the Hindu princess lay across the Swiss mathematician's dark, finely-crafted French wooden inlay of his desk. Shri'Ani instructed, "I am your wife! I get no attention! Now write, 'I love Shri'. Do it now, Francois! I mean it."

The teenaged bride of the 17th Century Frenchman lay flat, the papers she had thrown from his desk lay scattered on the floor. Francois watched as she traced her fingertips upwards along her torso. Peering up over her shoulder from the facedown prone position, she tormented him; he watched as each of her hands squeezed the respective white mounds of posterior flesh. Shri's voice became lyrical as she nearly sung her plea, "Do it now! Please, Francois. Write here. 'I love Shri'Ani.'"

Aaron blinked; his face flushed beat red as Helen barely restrained her laughter. Aaron looked down and noticed that her leg was rocking even more rapidly. Aaron drew a deep breath, rose to his feet, and grimaced sternly at his seated companion. "You have to stop that. It's easy for you. Now, I have to go to the lavatory to clean up!"

Aaron turned his back to Helen and marched down the aisle as she began to implore, "Francois, I love you! I'm nervous, and I can't help myself. I need you sometimes. Please, don't be mad!"

Some time passed before the dignified aging physicist stepped from the jet plane's cramped accommodations. The scene that greeted him was not the solitary cerebral scene he expected. Seated along the aisle was an array of smiling and waving men and women. Aaron wormed his way around the stampede of uniformed and casually attired passengers.

Returning to his seat, Aaron was greeted by warm smiles from Paul and Sasha, seated in the opposing two seats. Sasha spoke with vigor, "Oh, I just love these mission flights!"

Aaron looked at Paul as he was receiving the glasses for champagne and passing them to the group. The powerful psychic produced his signature squinty-eyed smile as he spoke out, "You didn't know that Rear Admiral Sasha Cohen can drink any sailor on this ship under their seat!"

Aaron glanced at the 82-year-old woman, who had the appearance of a well-kept 50-year-old. He wondered for a moment if he was on the same plane or even in the same time line. Helen's left hand felt comforting as she turned with a grin. She answered quietly, "Don't worry. I just checked. It still says 'In God We Trust.'"

Soft brown eyes widened instinctively as the statuesque form of the Wolf approached the seated foursome. The lithe, tightly-wrapped, blonde-haired, 6 foot, exquisitely feminine form of the military's premier assassin demanded attention in any crowd. Aaron felt the characteristic mixed emotion of fear and wonder as the huge predatory ebony eyes, which were the very image of her face, caught his stare. His expression went blank as he realized that she was actually smiling in response to his attention.

"Sasha, here comes your daughter." Aaron watched as the Naval officer emptied her glass of champagne in one swill. Sasha jumped from her seat and embraced the Wolf. Aaron chuckled to himself at the wonder of the scene. It was like something from a Twilight Zone child's book. Perhaps, the title would be *Granny and the Big Bad Wolf Party down at Valhalla.*

A hand suddenly thrust a glass of champagne in Aaron's face. Taking the libation in his hand Aaron looked up to see a shoulder clad with a Naval Captain's epaulets. Looking up a bit farther, Aaron heard the man speak. "I'm Herbert Potter."

Aaron knew there was no way he could stand, so he simply

looked up and returned the smile as he offered his left hand. Aaron studied the contours of the officer's face. It appeared, for all the world, that President Ronald Reagan had been reincarnated as a distinguished white-haired black man. The straight, yet curly, locks and the impressive Russian widow's peak pompadour were dead-on.

Sasha suddenly shouted, "Herbert, it's Yuri! I told you he would return."

The President that neutered the last Russian invasion spoke eagerly, "I am so proud to meet you. Tonia's husband said it would happen!" Herbert's shaking hand sent a sinusoidal waveform through the physicist's champagne glass.

Sasha's giddy face kissed Herbert on the cheek and leaned over Aaron. "Herbert and my husband served together for forty years. Oh, if only Robert could be here now!" Sasha held her glass out for a refill as she shouted, "But this special group all knows he really is!"

It seemed to Aaron that everybody on the plane laughed, quite loudly and in perfect unison, at that moment. A call for a toast was given. Aaron turned towards Helen who was sitting back with a precocious smile and asked, "Does everybody know about this?"

Helen emptied her glass, leaned forward, and with a giddy shrug, kissed Aaron on the lips. "How do I know? The only mind I can read is yours."

Several toasts to victory were placed as the time passed and the plane's flight continued.

The low frequency hum of the plane's engines filled Aaron's ears as he looked about the plane and saw a quiet and mostly napping group of passengers. The plane banked hard to starboard enabling Aaron to see the New York City skyline through Helen's window. One World Trade Center stood impressively against the shoreline. Aaron studied Helen's face, realizing that she was fast asleep. Hearing the sudden gasp of a snoring man, he looked directly across from her to see Paul Bush, replete in his endearing squinty eyed pose.

"Aaron." The voice snapped his attention to that of Sasha sitting quietly, directly across from him. The smiling face of someone that reached across an eternity of time and space spoke quietly. Aaron noticed that she held some sort of plastic covered package in her lap. "We need to talk, while we have a few minutes to ourselves." Sasha pulled the plastic from the box on her lap to expose the coiled leaves of a young fiddlehead fern. Leaning forward, Sasha Cohen held her gaze on Aaron's face as she placed the plant in his lap. "Do you recognize it, Yuri?"

Aaron's face was blank as he smiled and peered back at Sasha. "I noticed that Herbert called you Tonia. It sounded right to me, but it's as if my mind doesn't want to go there. How does he know your birth name?"

Sasha smiled vibrantly. "Because I told him!"

Aaron grimaced. "Dear, dear Sasha I hoped that a 6-year-old would never remember such things."

Sasha spoke quietly and methodically, "Do you remember how you would read to me? The seeds from the coiled ferns will make you invisible, child. Place them in your pockets and no one can see you. The seeds ripen on the Summer Solstice when it is warm and the intruders will be overcome by lightning and thunder or fall helplessly asleep by their spell. You and I are going to the Thuringian forest. The fern is called the irrkraut, and no one can violate them. Whoever tramples them will lose their identity and will lose their way."

Aaron's eyes began to water as he looked at the ageless woman. "I feel so much love for you, Sasha. It's as if I'm terrified to go back there with you."

Sasha continued, "Do you remember? You would read your Russian translation of your beloved Shakespeare. I remember the verse in *Henry IV*. 'We have the receipt of fern seeds, we walk invisible.' That plant is one of hundreds. I grow them, Yuri. They have been raised generation after generation from the seeds you placed in my pockets. The child you saved has never forgotten or stopped loving you."

(circa December 1944 [S]time-line)

"Comrade-lieutenant! Wake up; the Germans are firing at something. Come to the window! Look across the ravine. It's only a child! The damn Nazis are shooting at a child!"

Yuri grabbed his Tokarev rifle and opened the door to the blast of freezing winter snow and wind. "All of you, on your feet! If you are not out this door and behind me before I take twenty steps, I will shoot you dead as you stand. By Comrade Stalin, I swear it! I will eat your livers with these bastard Germans before they murder another Russian child! On your feet, NOW!"

The young Russian soldier ran out from the farm house racing to intercept the child in the howling winter storm. In Yuri's mind, it seemed as if he were the child, somehow being chased by a demon creature as fast as a wolf. Feeling the blood adrenaline course through his veins, he knew it would take his best tricks to save the child.

In his mind, the experienced fighter began to repeat his mantra, *My pockets are filled with seeds of the fern, no bullet can reach me . . . My pockets are filled with the summer spirit, the warmth fills me . . . My pockets are filled with the seeds of the fern . . .*

Yuri took Sasha's hand as the men walked back towards their cottage. "Sasha, I have a magic talisman in my pocket. I want you to keep it with you from now on. Tell me you will. Promise me!"

The fearful black eyes of the freezing child peered upwards at the strong young Russian as her gaze softened. "I promise I will, Yuie, and I promise I will always love you."

Yuri smiled to himself. He knew that Sasha had just answered the question. She had not heard his name mentioned. He knew that he had just shared "total-mind" with the child. She was now his family and must be protected at all costs from the evil force that had broken the peace with goodness, itself.

(circa 1946 December East Germany [S]time-line)

Gertrudt called out, enthusiastically. "Girls, it's Yuri. He's coming up the walk."

The three sets of smiling eyes mirrored the broad smile of the Russian lieutenant who had saved the lives of both the innocent and the helpless. Sasha and Rebekka rushed from the door, stopping the soldier in his tracks as he knelt to embrace the frenzied hugs, wet eyes, and wails of the children.

In a broken German dialect, the (psy) Intelligence officer struggled to speak of his love and his heartfelt tenderness, "Oh, my little children! You know that Yuri's heart is yours. You never leave my thoughts."

Yuri Vladiovich returned to his feet, holding the girls and a large package close. Walking through the door, the warmth of Gertrudt Cohen's face was greeted with a loving kiss to her cheek. Yuri's smile spoke of pride in his foster family. "Gertrudt, I have a small assortment of surprises for you and the girls. Make us some tea and I'll open up my cornucopia."

Yuri gazed into the vivid blue eyes of Rebekka. "For you my

beautiful blonde daughter, I bring you the precious Matryoshka doll. It is a wonder of the Soviet craftsman. It is like you, my precious child. It is one miracle child within each child. And I have brought my tall daughter a new and beautiful coat to hold your warm heart."

The strong young Russian picked up the much younger, dark-eyed, blonde-haired Sasha and set her on his knee. "For you, my mysterious child, I bring you new shoes. You are growing so swiftly, child. And I have the famed white Russian bear for you, my darling. This is the softest, most cuddly creature in all of Siberia. It will hug you dearly while I am away."

Gertrudt returned to the moment and set the hot drinks for all on the table. Yuri peered upwards into the dear woman's gaze. "For you, my mamochka, I have bacon and cheese and many more ration coupons. And for all of us, I have chocolate!"

The wet eyes of the German lady grew close to Yuri's stare as she kissed him dearly on his cheek. "You are a wonderful man. You have brought joy to the hopeless. May God in heaven reward you eternally."

Yuri looked at the children and coaxed. "Run to the table, girls, and explore your gifts. Eat the delicacy very slowly. You will cry if its sweetness is lost from your tummies."

Walking to the fireplace mantle, Yuri picked up the revered picture of the young Molly Brown and Gertrudt Cohen. Returning and sitting down beside her, he spoke quietly, "I must now show you a bit of my magic. I have spoken to you of the things which will come. I must now give you a proof, which comes from your beloved Molly." From his pocket, he pulled a soldier's thick log of handwritten pages. "In this log, you will read of the life to come for your friend. You will read of a message from her and what we must do to insure that the victory of the true God succeeds."

Gertrudt's dark eyes began to grow moist as she studied every word. Yuri held the picture from April 16, 1912, in front of them both. "Gertrudt, look how both of you girls are holding your feet in the air as you hang upon the Titanic's railing." The aging lady's hand moved swiftly to cover her lips as Yuri continued, "Your secret was never betrayed by your sacred friendship. The trip was made safely to transport the fortune to New York City. You and Ruben were very wise to get the rough cut diamonds to the safety of America. The shoes were made most carefully as were other items, like yours and Molly's purses. The contraband was never discovered."

The shocked woman nearly collapsed into the soldier's arms as she began to cry and wail.

"Mama! Mamochka! What is it?! What is wrong, Yuey!" The girls ran up to their elders as they pleaded.

Gertrudt reached out and took the girls in her arms as she spoke to comfort them, "Nothing is wrong, my darlings. Yuri's power has brought a beloved voice from mama's past. The goodness of God is with us, children! Run back and play, children. Mama will have us a fine dinner, soon."

Yuri leaned into Gertrudt's gaze and spoke confidently, "I've found a way to get you and the girls out of East Berlin."

The stoic face of the German lady grew stern as she replied, "You did not say all of us, Yuri. You must not remain behind. Do not let me hear that your plan is to leave us!"

The strong and reassuring soldier entreated, "I will try to make it out with all of you. But I will not subject any of you to danger. If I can make it safe for all of us, I will be with you. If I cannot make it safely with you, you will care for the children. There is only a 50:50 chance."

Gertrudt turned back to the picture of Molly Brown. "I can feel her spirit. I must do what is ordained."

Yuri spoke out. "There are fellow (psy) contacts on the American side. They are going to help us. I must now explain to you the most important part."

The wide-eyed stare of Gertrudt Cohen returned to the warm smile of the young Russian. Yuri spoke softly, "I'll return in a few days. It will be at night. Now, promise me that you will follow all instructions, and when you reach America, you must do what I am now going to share."

Gertrudt nodded approvingly as she listened intently. Yuri spoke quite deliberately, "If I don't make it through the checkpoints with the three of you, there will be a psychic to guide you to America. When you make it to New York City, there will be people to provide you and the girls with swift American citizenship. There will be some cost to this, but it will not be too great." Yuri's words were received agreeably as he continued, "Now comes the most important part. You must promise me that you will obtain the very best education for the girls, and they must be enrolled in American military academies. They must become American military officers. When you read the diary from the future, you will understand their destiny."

Gertrudt wrapped her arms around her beloved friend as she whispered, "On my soul, I will do what you have asked. I told you before, my precious Molly and my beloved Ruben will not rest if I refuse to do this thing."

***

The somnolent drone of the jet engines suddenly pitched. Helen's eyes opened to the rolling view of the New York City skyline. In that instant, the bright sun reached through her window. Closing her eyes again, she turned her face into its warmth. The bright red blood of her own eyelids cast a kaleidoscope of designs. It seemed, if even for the moment, there was a promise of goodness and hope which somehow must last, eternally.

Helen reached behind herself for Aaron's hand. Patting about, she felt his left hand wrenched tightly to his right wrist. With a wide-eyed gasp, she turned to see both Aaron and Sasha, seated across from one another, each rubbing and squeezing their right arms. Helen's right hand quickly covered her mouth as she looked directly into Aaron's eyes.

The "total-mind" experience, which washed over Helen, was breathtaking, literally. In an instant, she was standing in the Budapest countryside and simultaneously in the bone freezing wind tunnel of a blizzard. She looked down and saw the shivering, sparsely-dressed child she knew was Sasha.

Helen knew that she was "linked" with Yuri, and this was the year 1944. The tumbling memories, which were in fact the reality of the moment, were leaking forwards and backwards in time. Helen struggled to keep the time images moving forward. Was the running child before this moment or after this moment? The spinning images, the fear and fury, is this a sword? No, it's a rifle. This must be Yuri in battle!

Helen experienced horror as she had never conceived of it. The same hideous creature which had filled her own gun sights three days earlier, now challenged Yuri. She struggled to hold a thought. *Time must possess some meaning which escapes the mere mortal. Words and time, reality and memory are somehow—one.* She felt the blast-furnace intensity as the vision of red eyes became words: *"You have no ability to kill me. You have no desire to kill me. Death will be your only companion."*

"Helen, Aaron, come back!" Helen's head shook as her vision focused on Paul's face. "Are you all right?" Helen opened her eyes to see Sasha and Paul frantically working to snap both Aaron and Helen back to consciousness.

Helen calmly responded, "I'm all right. I'm back." Giving Aaron a sidelong glance, being careful to avoid direct eye contact, Helen queried, "Are you all right, Aaron?"

Aaron took hold of Helen's left hand and smiled. "I'm okay. I've never experienced anything quite like that. There are intense forces involved in this!"

Sasha spoke up loudly, "Wolf, get us two Chiantis before the landing begins. No make it three. I need to get the chill out of my old bones!"

Aaron took Helen by her left arm as both stepped from the jet fuselage onto the deck of the passenger boarding stairs, his left hand loaded with carryon luggage. Aaron spoke to his fellow Mid-West colleague, "It's chilly here for late October."

Helen heard the thud of the aluminum platform beneath her step, her hands also filled with luggage and satchels. She squinted as she raised her head looking to the bright sunny morning sky. "Look, Aaron, you can see the New York City skyline in the distance."

A small fleet of trams sat in a line just beneath the disembarking passengers. Just ahead of the duo, Colonel Bush held the Rear Admiral by her left arm as all stepped in unison. Sasha turned briefly and shouted, "Don't worry, Yuri. I've got your fiddlehead ferns!"

Helen smiled as she saw the plastic bag fluttering in the wind. It struck Helen as genuinely touching, watching the dignified woman holding the tray of greenhouse goods as if their value was truly limitless. It occurred to Helen that Aaron had been right all along; there was someone else with foreknowledge of the earthshaking challenge ahead.

The troop quickly began stepping downward as Helen called out, "I guess we're following you two, right!" Paul Bush answered, "You two stay on our aft. We're on that first Tram!"

Aaron leaned into Helen's ear and spoke softly, "Do you see the Wolf and Captain Potter at that far Tram?"

Helen leaned back and answered, "What are they doing?"

Aaron spoke tersely, "Look. That uniformed man is snapping a handcuffed satchel onto the Wolf's left wrist, and Herbert Potter is signing something."

Helen responded, "Now, the Wolf is signing, too. That must be the off-line server. Just think; all the files to stop the holocaust are in that bag."

The entire plane seemed to empty as quickly and orderly as a well-choreographed Broadway Hit. The trams sped quickly across the tarmac in single file. In the distance, a small flotilla of twin blade BV 107 helicopters sat awaiting the onslaught of passengers.

Paul Bush leaned across the Tram seating aisle, smiling to Helen and Aaron. "Once again, stay with Sasha and me. We're on the same bus!"

The window view from the levitating aircraft was surreal as the G force pressed down on the passengers. Helen looked out to see a sky filled with huge twin propped copters, the ground beneath them disappearing in an instant. Leaning into the window, Helen pressed her cheek into the cold glass, struggling to see the fleet's destination. It was mesmerizing to see the splendor of the greatest metropolis on earth, steadily filling the horizon.

At that moment, Sasha leaned forward and called out to Helen, "We're staying at the Algonquin Hotel in Mid-Town Manhattan! You and Aaron have the same style tandem suite like you had at

Langley. The Wolf and I have one just like it. Our crew has the top two floors. You'll love Times Square!"

Helen looked at Aaron, smiling. "It just occurred to me," she said softly. "She's been waiting for this moment her whole life. You're her father. She knew this day would come. It was written. You've come back from the grave to take your little girl to the Big City!"

Aaron returned the smile, looking into Helen's sparkling jade eyes. "I know! It's truly magnificent. Now, we just have to figure out how to keep the Big City intact."

CHAPTER FOURTEEN

Convergence

(circa November 2021 [Y]time-line)

The Algonquin dining room was a scene from a more dignified time. The linen napkins and silverware settings spoke to the patronage of a world which must ultimately be orderly and sated.

Aaron and Helen stood looking back toward the elevators. Helen looked at her phone. "Wolf just texted me. They're on their way."

The dining room host spoke to the two guests, "Monsieur, Madam, I have your table for four."

Aaron spoke up, "Our companions will emerge from that elevator in just a moment."

The host spoke officiously, "Oui, Monsieur, I await your discretion."

Sasha and the Wolf stepped into the large and elegantly marbled hall at that moment. Walking in unison, the image slowed for Helen. It occurred to her that Sasha was only a bit shorter than Marguerite. The two would have been spotted as mother and daughter by anyone who saw them. Perhaps even as sisters. The flawless bone structure, identical eyes of glimmering coal, the genetic architecture of health and form, even the fledgling artisan would be inspired with the image of the walking portrait.

The waiter was as fast and efficient as Helen's perfect dining experience required. It occurred to her that she had waited her whole life to participate in such a social occasion. The intrigue and backbiting of the collegiate world wasn't at all what the uninitiated was inclined to think.

Helen spoke up, "I have never had Oysters Rockefeller or Beef Wellington! I feel like life is giving me so many unexpected presents"

A moment later, two waiters appeared with a cart. The choreographed scene was a delight. "Mademoiselle, would you prefer the' or cafe'?"

Helen responded, "Coffee, please."

"Would you prefer a dry Cabernet or perhaps a Sherry?"

Helen smiled, "The Cabernet, please."

Helen looked across the table setting to see Sasha studying her. Helen smiled back. "Sasha, I must seem like a wide-eyed child!"

Sasha smiled broadly. "I know what you're thinking. You think the Wolf and I must be quite accustomed to such elegance."

Sasha and Marguerite turned to one another and chuckled. Marguerite spoke out, "Since papa's death, we have a number of dates during the year in which we meet and have a fine meal."

Helen looked at Aaron who sat quietly and merely responded with a meek grin. Helen replied, "It's terrible to lose the ones we love. Knowing that you will be together again in the realm of the Authority doesn't remove the currency of separation."

Sasha spoke out, "Robert visits me on occasion."

Aaron smiled and queried, "Sasha, after all we've shared, please forgive my question. Do you mean as an apparition?"

Sasha and the Wolf broke into a loud laughter. Sasha retorted, "No, you silly Russian! He comes to me in the dreams. I won't hold court to any damn specters! If they can't wait 'til I get to the next world, they have no business haunting me in this one."

All four laughed deeply as the cart of entrees arrived.

Sasha leaned across the table and quietly spoke to Helen as she took a bite of the chilled radish dipped prawn, "Helen, I have the dream visions. You know what I'm talking about. I mean real experiences!"

Helen smiled and answered, "It's very satisfying to know that all these things are not lost."

Sasha took a drink of her chardonnay; the fine crystal resonated as she set the glass down, tapping the plate of entrees with the glass. Sasha leaned even further forward and whispered, "No silly. I mean Robert comes to me in my dreams and really does 'satisfy' me!"

The Wolf grimaced and looked at Helen. "Forgive Mamma; she really doesn't get out that much anymore."

Sasha sat back and spoke tersely, "Wolf, you know as well as I do we must all become family. We can't have too many secrets. I want you to tell Aaron and Helen about Michael."

The Wolf sat quietly, looking down at her plate as she took a drink of coffee. "It was the Iraq war. I was shipboard coordinator for Navy assault missions. Michael was a Seal. We fell in love; he died. His birthday was March 13th. Mamma and I meet each year on his birthday and light a candle during dinner."

Helen gave Aaron a sidelong glance as she spoke up, "I'm so sorry. Have you and Sasha worked through it all right?"

Sasha spoke quietly, "I have never seen my Marguerite so devastated. I tell her that (Y) can only do so much. She must be strong and patient."

The Wolf spoke up, "I experienced the weakest time of my life for about two years. I began drinking. It was not to the point where it was debilitating, but it was affecting my focus."

Aaron softly queried, "What brought you out of it?"

The Wolf looked at Aaron, her jet black eyes seemed to radiate as she spoke, "I have the dreams as all of you. But Mamma says I'm a younger spirit. Thirty-one days before Bar Mitzvah, I did the

Reveal. Mamma says I have lived only once before."

Sasha chimed in, "I think Marguerite wants me to tell you. She has 'awakened visions.' I'm not sure any of us have that psychic sense. She doesn't see the future. She is able to 'know' danger and can move just ahead of it."

The Wolf smiled wryly as she spoke, "Mamma, don't parse words. Like you said, we all have to get to know one another. I am a natural born predator. I have an uncanny survival instinct. The closest I get to the sublime spiritual realm that all of you are on is when the occasional dream directs me to my target. I am the Wolf!" The steam from the Wolf's coffee cup danced through her ebony eyes as she swallowed deeply, her gaze never leaving her dinner companions.

Sasha smiled and laughed. It occurred to Helen that it was a very good thing that this powerful life force was on their side. "Sasha, you must be very proud of your beautiful daughter."

Sasha reached over with her right hand and grabbed Aaron by his left wrist. At the same instant, she grabbed the Wolf's right wrist with her left hand. A strength and confidence filled her voice. "These two are the reason that I am alive, Helen." She looked Helen right in the eyes as she continued, "And you, my enchantingly beautiful woman, are the reason that we will all survive next month." Sasha sat back and hesitated for a moment, before continuing, "There is an important paranormal event that has been kept from the prying eyes of the military 'straights.' We know how to do something that was lost for thousands of years." Helen and Aaron looked at one to the other curiously as Sasha continued, "You know what I'm talking about! I can see auras. Both of you and I have re-discovered what Methuselah knew."

Aaron smiled wryly as he nearly shouted, "Sasha, you've 'linked' with your future self, like Helen and I did!"

Sasha took a deep swig of white wine as she retorted, "Oh, I've got some fantastic genes, but do you think anyone would look like this at my age! Twenty-five years ago I 'synced' with myself to the same date you two did next month, the 23rd. I haven't aged a day!"

Aaron spoke reverently, "Praise (Y)! He works in mysterious ways. The toughest battles are saved for His strongest warriors. The ancient Kabbalah texts reflect the ten steps in the Tree of Life."

Sasha stood up, holding her crystal glass in her hand as she spoke out, "Wolf, I want to toast our family."

The four stood and in unison shouted, "L'chaim!"

The Wolf and Helen stared, one to the other, eyes of jade fire almost challenging the other's black eternal abyss. The four crystal wine glasses were heartily drained.

Smiling and in good cheer, the group took their seats as the service carts arrived. The scene was filled with delightful aromas and wondrous dining presentation.

(Central Command, New York City 07:30 hours)

The Wolf stared at the itinerary with an experienced eye. She raised her head and looked curiously at Colonel Paul Bush. "Paul, I've spent months working with the New York/ New Jersey Port Authority. This 'viewing' suggests undocumented cargo near the Bayonne bridge route. I need specific information on the method of concealment."

Bush leaned forward in his seat and looked at the team of field agents as he spoke up urgently, "We know that less than 5% of the arriving sea cargo is inspected. The team of 'remote viewers' says that the Syrian-ISIS connection is filtering the shipments through this waterway. They have time of day, the route, and the 'image' connection to the main terror suspect. If you cross reference the

Port database, you should be able to link the suspect to all the given commercial cargo for the data points."

The Wolf's expression remained stoic as she remarked, "This is new information, but we'll need a serious bit of good luck for all these pieces to fit. And we'll have to intercept the contraband before it's off-loaded. Can your new team tell us where it's hidden?"

Paul Bush grimaced sorely as he handed out copies of a cryptic drawing. "This is what the focus 'viewing' has produced." The squinting psychic officer handed around copies of the hand-drawn image to the two dozen cleared Port Authority officers and military inspectors.

The psychic spoke up, almost whimsically, "All right, here's what the team thinks you're looking at. The team says it's definitely just one of three possibilities. Number one, you could be looking at an engine compartment of some type of diesel truck or large machine. This would mean that you need to check the database for heavy equipment shipments. Number two, this drawing might represent some aspect of the crew's galley on one of the containerized cargo ships. The heavy vertical lines in the drawing are thought by two of the 'viewers' to be some type of shelves used by the infiltrated crewman. And the number three option is thought to be the actual engine room of the ship. The dials and instruments, next to the shelves in the picture, are made small by the large pistons you see at the top of the drawing."

The sidelong glances and chuckles in the room were met with looks of concern from both Commander Cohen and Helen. The Wolf rose to her feet and spoke up assertively, "Ladies and gentleman, if we have to search 24/7, that. is. what. will. happen!" The towering blonde commander turned around to the Intelligence advisor. "Paul, you said you had an equalizer. I'm hoping you're saving the good news for last."

Paul's eyes squinted intently as he smiled and replied, "Yes, we have a new image associated with the target suspect."

The "Deep Vision" commander passed around another drawing. "This is an artist's rendering of the suspect believed to be coordinating the on-board contraband. The 'viewing' team has 'seen' him with the main suspect on multiple occasions when the undocumented cargo is handed off to the domestic conspirators."

Still standing, the Wolf studied the picture intently as she calmly inquired, "There must be something you can tell us about this face."

The "Deep Vision" commander's eyes widened for the first time as he smiled broadly and replied, "Yes, we have 100% agreement from the 'viewers'. This man works on the vessels and holds Libyan International and Merchant Mariner credentials."

The roomful of dedicated government officers lurched from their seats as the group shouted uproariously. The Wolf stared down stoically at Helen as the timid professor of Fine Arts gazed back timidly. Helen asked meekly, "Does this mean we have places to look, now?"

(New Jersey docks, 1200 hours)

The Wolf scanned the ship's manifesto. "I want to see these engine refit dockets."

The foreign petty officer leaned over the handheld clipboard of the American naval officer as the ship's escort nervously fingered the clumsy list of print-outs. Pointing to the entry, he answered in a thick North African accent, "That dolly has already been taken below."

The Wolf gave the New York Homeland Security Officer, Hassan Rahami, a sidelong glance as she turned and looked the

Libyan directly in the eyes and spoke up, "Then, lead on. That's where we're going, crewman."

The team of port inspectors split up as the Wolf, Helen, Herbert, and Hassan followed the nervous young man through a maze of stairwells and ship's corridors. The sounds and smell of the machinery filled their senses as they threaded their way into the bowels of the city-sized sea-faring vessel.

The Wolf stepped up to Helen and turned for a moment to catch her attention. "Helen, I had a fearsome dream last night. Do not get separated from me. I've got an idea that our hunt is about to yield some results."

Helen felt her adrenaline pulse as she strode up a set of steps into the ominous cave-like vista of the ship's engine room. Feeling through her suit coat, the drafted warrior checked the snugness of her shoulder holster fit.

   ***

Helen's thick auburn hair fluffed sopping wet in the white terry cloth bath towel as she squeegeed it to a manageable wetness. Luxuriating in the Algonquin Hotel's fine bath appointments had become a pleasant ending to daily tensions.

The youthful green-eyed college professor arched upright vigorously, wrapping the warmed terry cloth towel about her head. Pausing long enough to lean into the mirrored wall above the bath counter, she gazed closely into her own green eyes. Then, began to comb through her wet, naturally curly hair.

Wrapping the bath robe belt tightly, she peered out the door to see if Aaron was still seated in the common room. "Do you want some company?"

Aaron looked up from the large table and turned, smiling. "I've been waiting all day to see you!"

Stopping at the service cart to pour herself a hot cup of coffee, she walked across the sizable room to see her eternal companion writing vigorously, with pen and pad. Helen seated herself across from him and watched as he almost comically popped his gaze upward, smiling broadly as he spoke, "Well, I've got my tea ready. Are we going to take our synchronized sips? Tradition requires it, you know!"

Helen found herself actually chuckling as she tipped her coffee cup in perfect cadence with the opposing tea cup salute. Aaron continued writing; Helen could almost see the dancing feather of the 17th Century quill pen. "Aaron, you don't see the humorous aspect in this scene at all, do you?"

Aaron spoke timidly as he took another drink of hot tea. "Well, there's probably no limit to the fantastical ironies involved. But I'm just happy to have time with you. I'm not used to having you taken from me day and night. It's pretty rare for both of us to be in this hotel suite at the same time, isn't it, darling?"

Helen's lips pursed as her face went taut and her eyes widened. "Do you realize that no one uses paper and pencil any longer? I don't even need partial memories of previous lives to see a 300-year-old man sitting there writing."

Aaron knew the tone and timbre of Helen's voice. "How's your team doing?"

Helen retorted, "My team? I don't have a clue about any of it. We travel to these odd locations, like something from an old movie, and I watch while all these official types tear through paperwork, computer screens and crates. Even the Wolf doesn't say much to me all day long. Have you ever seen the old movie *On the Waterfront* with Marlon Brando?"

Aaron grinned and looked at Helen warmly, waving his hands like an excited Italian. "I could'a been somebody! You should'a looked out for me a little bit. I was your brotha!"

Helen folded her hands across her lap, leaning back into her chair. "Dear (Y), how I wish I could hate you!"

Aaron smirked and mimicked Helen's pose. "Okay, I'll bite. What's really bugging you?"

Helen took a deep drink of her hot coffee, gazing at Aaron through the steam. Setting the cup down, she leaned forward as the heavy terry cloth robe cleaved from her shoulders. "Do you really trust all these people? You and I have never trusted governments. All these people Are the Government!"

Aaron's focus on the rapturous, nearly-nude woman sitting a few feet from him had genuinely impacted his concentration. Aaron slowly raised his gaze to Helen's fiery jade stare as he spoke out, "You remember all our arguments about the left and the right? You remember our discussions about conservatives seeking the truth and the, so-called, progressives are really just masquerading as sympathetic, when, in fact, there's always some selfish agenda."

Aaron paused, awaiting the expected retort.

Helen sat back upright in her chair, the fire in her eyes increased, "Like I said, I wish I could hate you! I had a nearly normal, boring life. You walk into my life, and I find out that everything I ever thought about everything in the Universe is All wrong!"

Helen's wide eyed gaze never ceased as her vibrant green eyes began to water. Aaron knew that the assignment his "remote vision" team had handed down to the "Wolf pack" was being executed in the morning. In his heart, he yearned to reach across the table and savagely cleave his passion with the multiple souls of this one exquisite female, which in truth was his only reason to exist. He knew that his response must impart candor.

The skilled swordsman determined the thrust. "Do you trust the Wolf's instincts?"

Helen stood upright from her chair, coffee cup in hand, as she walked to the service cart. Returning without taking a sip, she re-seated herself and looked at Aaron with a confused expression as she spoke out, "I can't read the situation. I've had No dreams. But I don't trust Hassan!"

Aaron felt more confident as Helen's tone became more relaxed. He peered upwards from his writing, for just an instant, to absorb Helen's expression. The thoughtful academic spoke up. "Under the Obama Administration, the spin of destiny was primed for religious conflict. Hassan Rahami, an Egyptian, was placed into his lofty position because of the accepted influence of the Muslim Brotherhood. Two Administrations later, and the chaos that resulted in Egypt, Libya, and the whole Mid-East war zone is still biting at our heels."

Aaron continued his writing as he refrained from eye contact with the white-robed object of his every thought.

Helen spoke up with more energy, "We get a daily itinerary. You know all about those. Your Deep Vision team prepares a lot of it. Sometimes, it identifies target inspections that are to occur the next day. Twice, the Wolf has, inadvertently, let Hassan see the itinerary. No one but she and I can see that! Why has she let that happen?"

Aaron retorted, "Ask her about it!"

Helen's voice peaked, "I did! She dismissed it as insignificant. She was pulling rank on me. I've got news for that lupine goddess; I'm not in her damn Navy!"

Helen's eyes began to water again as Aaron queried, "Do you remember, now years ago, when I told you I couldn't tell you everything I knew about the means that you would use to defeat the terrorists?"

Helen's focus returned as she stared intently at the 17th Century swordsman. Her lips parted deliberately as she hesitated in her words, "What are you saying!?"

The obligatory smile of Francois L'Hospital greeted the jade fire of Shri'Ani. The master swordsman knew he had his opponent precisely in his stride. The Frenchman knew that distraction sometimes led to renewed clarity. "Helen, this is no time to engage in the passion that would genuinely soothe the savage beast percolating in both of us."

Helen gazed curiously as Aaron spoke quietly, "Tomorrow night, Sasha is coming up here for dinner with us. She loves room service! She says she has something very important to show both of us."

Helen's expression remained blank as she appeared to hang on Aaron's verbal thrusts. The 300-year-old dialectic continued, "She's going to tell us something that she says both of us must know."

Aaron sat quietly, waiting to see if Helen would take the idea as sufficient succor for the important night's rest. Helen stood up as her robe fell open about her hips. "Aaron, come here."

The classic intellectual fought back the flush of adrenaline as the single body filled with multiple passions struggled to remain innocuous. Aaron LaSalle rose from his seat as he walked into Helen's open arms. The passion in Helen's radiant eyes was riveting as she muttered quietly, "I know you would sacrifice yourself if it meant you could tell me what you know. I want you to kiss me, like you, Aaron, have never kissed me before."

***

Feeling through her suit coat, the drafted warrior felt the snugness of her shoulder holster fit.

Stepping up next to the Wolf and Hassan, Helen heard the Wolf order the Libyan petty officer, "Tell everyone in this compartment to step out here onto this spot and identify themselves. Tell them in all languages. Do it now!"

Helen watched as the Wolf turned to Hassan and asked, "Hassan, will you be able to understand his instructions?"

Hassan answered, "I'm Egyptian. If he tells them in Libyan, I can probably make it out."

Helen heard the quick orders bleat from the ship's petty officer. The professor of language could make out the foreign command as validly containing a subject and a verb, but there was one other syllable – "Moh." It occurred to Helen that this could possibly be a name or a nickname or a code.

Helen listened as the Wolf quietly spoke to Hassan, "Did he say anything besides the instruction to come to this spot?"

Hassan calmly responded, "No, he spoke just as you ordered."

The engine room began to fill with many men. Some were obviously laborers, their sweaty shirts betraying their roles; others were more composed in their appearance; these were the brains of this realm.

The Wolf shouted, "I want all you men to sit down flat on your butts. Do it now! Do not move from this area until you are instructed. Is that understood?" The congregation began to drop to the floor, sitting close to one another. The Wolf spoke to the Libyan crewman, "Is this everyone?"

The Libyan looked down at the group of confused expressions. In his thick North African accent, he repeated the question, and then turned back to the Wolf, "I believe this is all."

Helen could not help but detect a slightly pernicious tone in the crewman's voice. She wondered if the Wolf was thinking so as well. The Wolf continued her instructions to the petty officer. "All right, take me to the original palate indicated on this manifest." Helen could not help but be impressed with the commanding presence of this woman, bringing this hapless group of capable men to their knees.

Helen stood motionless, watching the tall, tightly wrapped, blonde haired woman follow the guide to a set of distinctly heavy vertical racks and crates, some ten yards from her purview. The thought passed through the novice field officer's mind as a wry smile formed on her lips. Helen muttered to herself, "The drawing at the field ops meeting was my 17th Century lover's penmanship."

The drafted warrior watched as the Wolf shuffled through the clipboard of papers and appeared to point at one large crate resting high above them in the shelves. The scene continued as the unheard conversation between the Wolf and the Libyan appeared to result in an order being given to one of the crewman seated on the floor. Helen watched as the crewman jumped up and returned in a short time driving a fork lift. She turned to gauge the position of Hassan and Captain Herbert Potter, still standing strategically around the room. The distinguished, grey-haired, black naval officer turned to Helen and smiled reassuringly. The newly recruited officer returned the smile and responded with a strong nod.

The crate had just reached the floor when Helen first heard the shuffle of rapid footsteps coming up from behind. The wrenching arm around Helen's neck instantly cut off her breathing. She felt herself arch forward as the painful push of something metallic dug into her back.

The screaming in Helen's ear was that of the same North African heritage as the Libyan crewman, "All of you, put you hands up! Any bad moves, this woman dies!"

Helen felt herself being pushed as she struggled to waddle forward into the middle of the room. The horrible voice continued, "I have hostage. Do you hear me? I will kill her! I'm taking her up to the deck. I want a helicopter when we get there! Do you hear me, blonde lady? No funny business!"

The Wolf began to turn towards the screaming over her shoulder. As she turned, she felt a numbness creep through her body. The effort to turn became increasingly difficult as she forced her muscles to resist the rapture. In the Wolf's eyes, the spinning room began to slow and then stop as the vision filled her sight.

The wide-eyed and terrified face of Helen was wrenched backward by the man's arm. It occurred to the Wolf that she may not have drawn a breath in many seconds. The Wolf stood directly in front of the assailant as she studied the words being spit silently from the dark features of the Middle Eastern face. The image seemed almost comical to the trained American assassin as the pistol filled the ugly features of the man's suddenly wide-eyed expression.

At that instant, the most terrifying image appeared between the Wolf's gun and the frantic face. The man stood frozen in time as some hideous red-eyed creature appeared to erupt from his shoulders.

The Wolf turned to the foreign crewman's shouts and saw Helen being throttled by someone new on the scene. The intimidating woman raised her arms and began to walk the significant distance between herself and the pair. As she walked, the assailant continued to scream incoherently.

Helen wondered if she would remain conscious much longer. She watched as the Wolf's approach began to slow before her. She was reminded of the first day she ever set eyes on this powerful woman. Helen's focus dropped to the slow rhythmic motion of the predator's steps. It occurred to her total mind that she had seen this image, once before, when she stood with her dearest friend on the deck of the RMS Titanic, so many years prior. Was she about to be reunited with her beloved Gertrudt? It would not be so bad.

***

Helen looked into Aaron's smiling face as he announced, "There's the knock. I'll get it!"

The still-distressed academic watched as Aaron opened the door and hugged his loving child from another time. Sasha shouted, "Helen, you little hero, get over here and hug me! Oh dear (Y), I was so frantic when the Wolf texted me!"

Helen ran to Sasha and hugged her tightly as tears began to fall from her sparkling green eyes. Sasha reassured her, quietly, "Oh, I love you so much, dear. It's all going to be all right." The mirror image of the tall blonde warrior who had cleaved the skull of Helen's assailant, held the meek academic at arm's length and smiled. "You had a memorable day! Come on; let's go check our makeup while the men get the dinner table ready."

Sasha and Helen left the common suite as Herbert Potter and the flotilla of service trays entered the room.

A wry smile filled the face of the distinguished woman who had lived long enough to witness two world wars. Sasha Cohen poured the Sauvignon blanc into both her and Helen's glasses as she spoke out. "Isn't this poached salmon simply to die for!?"

Helen looked up, with the fork pausing in her lips as she moaned rapturously.

Aaron looked up from his plate and eagerly asked Herbert Potter, "How's your prime rib?"

The smiling features of one of the Twentieth Century's most beloved presidents peered up from his meal and spoke out heartily, "You can't beat the Algonquin Hotel's kitchen. They have the best prime rib in all of New York City!"

Helen smiled broadly as she quipped, "Well, come to think of it. The meals here might just be our last supper."

Sasha interjected, "I got the salmon for us Helen. And not simply because it's delicious, but I knew you preferred the white wine. I knew you had to have the Cabernet with the Beef Wellington the other night."

The professor of Fine Arts spoke out, "That's really perceptive of you Sasha. How did you put that all together?"

Helen gave Aaron a sidelong glance as the four seated diners broke into uproarious laughter, at the same instant. Helen spoke up timidly, "Well, I guess that is a silly question, isn't it? But, yes, thank you. Sasha. I just love a truly fine clear wine."

Sasha spoke again, "I remember once when Yuri and I and the Russian troops had nothing to sustain us but home-brewed vodka. It was quite a challenge to stay focused when all you've eaten for days was snow and clear liquor."

Helen looked up with a startled stare as she meekly replied, "Thank you for that, darling. I've been trying to come to terms with my heartfelt cowardice."

Sasha raised her head quickly and looked directly at the stern expression which filled Aaron's face. She spoke up, brusquely, "Lieutenant Vladiovich, I once saw you knock a soldier from his seat for such a comment. I am waiting, Commander!"

The Russian soldier leaned close to the freshly-blooded recruit as he instructed, "You must learn quickly that those who live and those who die are all cowards. The warrior that acts quickly and properly in the face of terror simply survives. Bravery simply means outliving fear!"

Helen looked directly into Sasha's coal black eyes as they began to glisten moistly. The eternal lady spoke up, prideful, "If the horrors I have witnessed in my long life have ever led me to doubt a loving God, I have only to think of the many lives my Yuri saved in his time."

Reaching from beneath her seat, Sasha retrieved the cardboard shoe box which she had produced on her first meeting. She set the top next to her and pulled several very old pictures from its depths. She spoke up quietly, "This is a picture of your dearest friend, my true mother, Gertrudt Cohen. Standing next to her is Margaret Brown. It's you, Molly."

Helen and Aaron's eyes grew wide as each exclaimed, "What! How is that possible?"

Sasha held the antique picture before them both as she explained, "This was taken by Ruben Cohen on April 16th, 1912 on board the USS Carpathia. Notice how much older you are, Molly, in the (Y) time line. Gertrudt and Ruben survived because of you. The Unsinkable Molly Brown and my mother saved many from the freezing waters that night, including Ruben. I remember the story of how narrowly Ruben was saved. He had a whistle and you and Gertrudt rowed to him and others with him."

Helen spoke up, "That makes sense. I knew I was much younger in the (S) time line. Aaron said that the Authority chose that reality because I needed to be tested."

Sasha smiled broadly as she replied, "That's right! Your bravery has already been proven. That's why you are the only one to kill the root demon this time around."

Aaron spoke up "So Gertrudt and Molly were involved in carrying the diamonds to New York City, even in the current (Y) time line."

Sasha guffawed. "Of course, money is the root of all evil in all time lines. Even the twin Gods can't figure out how to motivate their children with any other currency. Love works wonders in the afterlife, but it doesn't motivate much effort here on earth, unless you consider the benefits of procreation."

Aaron studied Sasha's expression for some moments as she

smiled at him and pulled another picture from her stores. She spoke up, wondrously, "And here is the love of our many lives, Helen. Here is your lover at the age of 25, in the year 1946."

Helen lurched from her chair as her hands covered her dropped jaw. Aaron watched as Sasha reverently handed the aged picture to the wide-eyed woman. Helen nearly shrieked, "But I thought you died getting the girls to the West! Aaron, you said no pictures survived."

The teary-eyed, but smiling, officer of Naval Intelligence spoke up eagerly, "He did die, Helen. I have memories of him from both time lines," Sasha continued. "In the current (Y) time-line, our beloved Lord left him with me for many more years. Yuri Vladiovich helped defeat many communist plots. We may not have been victorious in the Korean War if it were not for this modest-looking Russian soldier. But he still died young, and I waited a lifetime for him and Molly Brown to return us."

Sasha sat quite still for some moments as she peered at Helen and spoke up calmly, "I'm afraid I have some troubling information about the contraband that was seized at the ship today. The container from the racks in the engine room contained drugs. It's pretty obvious that the Libyan group have been bringing in all sorts of illegitimate cargo. The consensus is that the bombs have already been delivered to our shores."

A pensive expression filled Helen's gaze as she spoke up plaintively, "Sasha, I've been reading your translation of Yuri Vladiovich's 1944 diary. I remember reading Aaron's diary when he returned from the 'slip.' There's a portion in Yuri's account where he stopped writing in Russian and, for a few paragraphs, wrote in French. I'm truly amazed with the message that Francois gave to Yuri. Aaron's 2015 diary made no reference to the curious words."

A blank expression filled both Aaron's and Sasha's faces as they turned silently one to the other. Aaron's expression turned to a thin smile as he turned to Helen and reflected, "Helen, the Twin Law is a paradox. Existence is a paradox. Francois and the intellectuals of the time knew much more than our 21st Century science gives them credit for. Yuri was told about the existence of the multiple levels of the conscious mind. Mankind is considered just a step above the other animals. The higher aliens are called Beb's, or biological entities from beyond. The Extraterrestrial term implies life forms from other planets. In fact, advanced life forms travel to earth in ships using time travel. Their worlds don't view time the same way we do."

Helen's expression remained calm as she queried, "But the message sent by Francois was intense; he urgently told Yuri to 'attend' to the matter and also instructed something vague about the Biblical verses in the Book of Esther."

Aaron continued, "The total-mind in the 1944 diary knew that (S) might try another means to reinstate the evil time line. If mankind knows too much he corrupts himself. Remember our discussions, Genesis 2:17. If we eat of the tree of the knowledge of good and evil, we shall surely die."

Helen grimaced as she retorted, "Are you saying that ancient prophets knew about aliens?"

Sasha responded, "Helen, it will be hundreds of years before society catches up with the wisdom of the ancients. Yuri became involved in national security issues. He was instrumental in establishing the policies to conceal alien existence."

The curious expression remained on the face of the beleaguered professor of Fine Arts as Aaron chimed in, "If knowledge of the lesser aliens were generally known, knowledge of the cumulative higher consciousness would be assumed. Mankind was not supposed to have definitive proof that God exists. It messes with our free will; again the Twin Law is therefore broken."

Helen's jade eyes sparkled as she eagerly queried, "What is the Book of Esther doing with Yuri's instructions about mankind being kept ignorant about alien worlds?"

Sasha smiled warmly as she replied, "Esther was raised by Mordecai, a Jew. An evil man named Haman used an ancient technique called the 'pur,' which means 'lot' as in lottery, to determine a date in the reign of King Xerxes to destroy all the Jewish people. The date was given in the 12th year of his reign and was instructed for the 13th of the 12th month. Esther interceded by her power to usurp one-half of Xerxes power. She saved the Jewish people, and we celebrate the Days of Purim for this reason."

Helen sat quite still as she responded quietly, "I've had a recurring memory from the (S) time line. I remember telling Aaron and Bailey Smith that the two must be a couple Jedi Knights and I wasn't up to it."

Aaron beamed broadly, "Don't you get it? The Reveal is a reversal of the evil use of the pur. It will be used to save all peoples this time. Francois gave a message to Yuri to give to us directly that a gentile would repeat the miraculous salvation from evil."

A bemused expression filled Helen's face as she reached around her back with her left hand and rubbed the bruised spot. "Did Esther almost get skewered?"

Captain Herbert Potter and Aaron looked quietly at one to the other. Herbert smiled approvingly as he spoke up, "I remember when I first heard of these wondrous things from Commander Robert Jenkins. That's the other half of Sasha's hyphenated last name."

Aaron, Sasha and Helen smiled curiously as they turned intently to listen. "The Commander and I were on board a heavy cruiser, and we had been in a North Atlantic storm for almost two days. It was one of the worst storms I ever experienced. Anyway, here's the point. Robert was as calm as he could be, and I was scared to death. I mean that ship was listing 20 degrees and more. Now, I'm here to tell you that when a vessel that size heels that much, you're in trouble. I asked the Commander why he wasn't scared, and he gave me a letter from Sasha."

The two academics smiled pleasingly as they awaited the completion of Herbert's story.

The handsome and dignified grey-haired man continued, quite deliberately, "I'm going to tell you something remarkable. I read Sasha's letter, which had been written over a week earlier, and guess what? This magical woman sitting right here told her husband that he would be in that storm. She told him the date, the magnitude, and the degree to which the ship would list. She also told him that she would have dinner waiting for him on the exact date that the ship was due back at port! I have never doubted the power that you folks seem to possess. I'm a believer!"

Helen smiled encouragingly as she grasped Herbert's left wrist with her right hand.

Herbert shouted out, "No, don't do that Helen! I believe, but I don't want to go where all of you have been. I just want to be there when you need me. I'm a second stringer!"

The table laughed in unison at the humor of Sasha's dearest friend.

Helen spoke out with a sense of calm, "Here's the curious aspect to all of this. There's some odd set of rules that humanity seems to have to second guess. The Angel of Light is the highest type of Nine Levels in the ranks of spiritual beings. But he isn't a he; angels aren't supposed to be either sex. There seems to be some kind of conflict over procreation itself. And then there's the

Genesis 2:17 'Tree of Knowledge' conflict. It just goes on and on."

Aaron looked at Sasha as he responded, "Helen is curious about the connected information which she knows we hold about her final conflict with the main suspect in the terrorist plot."

Herbert watched Sasha as she grimaced and hesitated. He spoke up assertively, "I've been around the 'remote viewing' team for some time. I go where Sasha goes. That's my blessing. So I'm going to bring up an idea that I think is all right to discuss." The presidential expression returned to the distinguished military man as he awaited a sign of approval from his superior officer and dearest friend.

Sasha nodded approvingly; then, Herbert continued, "There's a Haitian seer on the team. This psychic is a black man who reportedly was an Ethiopian shaman many hundreds of years ago. Now, there are a variety of religions represented on Aaron's and Paul Bush's team. Sometimes, even Sasha focuses on the tough subjects. This 'viewer' is reportedly an expert on the African mysticism of Voodoo. I think that the team should hold a convergent reveal. Here's my point, sometimes you've got to get real close to a problem to solve it. Now, I've always considered Voodoo just about as close to the devil as you can get without being truly evil. I think you'll agree, Sasha, that Jean Preval is a good man. If you can all get together and do your stuff, he might just add that extra push to get one over on this evil plot."

(07:30 hours)

"Let me begin by congratulating each of you individually and the 'Deep Vision' team as a whole. Yesterday, the first definitive breakthrough was made by the Investigative Officers and Military Intercession Corp. This was a successful capture of contraband resulting from your paranormal team's efforts." A resounding cheer filled the conference room as Rear Admiral Sasha Cohen-Jenkins spoke.

Dressed in full naval whites, the highest level Intelligence officer in charge of Selective Naval Intelligence Operations continued, "I have here, with us today, Adjunct Commander Helen Lovelace and Captain Herbert Potter. These two were on the four-man intercession team responsible for the capture of several suspects and the elimination of one felonious assailant to the team. Commander Lovelace has received a field commendation for bravery and conduct resulting in the termination of a dangerous combatant. Please stand, Commander, and receive your medallion and pumpkin patch for the operation."

Helen Lovelace's expression turned to shock as she turned with sparkling green eyes to Aaron LaSalle, who smiled broadly as she rose and approached the Admiral. Helen stared wide-eyed into the smiling face of Sasha Cohen-Jenkins as she heard the strong words announced to the group, "Well done, Commander."

The drafted warrior returned to her seat as the military decorum continued, "Commander Marguerite Cohen-Jenkins will now proceed to the podium for her medal and patch." The maternal pride was assumed as the formidable warrior stepped before her commanding officer to receive her commendation. "Captain Herbert Potter and Civilian Adjunct Hassan Rahami will now proceed to the podium to receive the commendation and patch."

The group returned to their seats as the Admiral continued, "Each member of the Deep Vision team has been processed for a full Naval Intelligence commendation. This will appear on military records and duty files. On behalf of the United States Navy and the Government of the United States of America, I am authorized to extend a hearty well done to each and every one of you. I invite you now to rise and join me for a well-deserved round of applause."

Helen reached for Aaron's hand and smiled broadly, looking into his moist eyes as he stole a quick kiss from her cheek.

The dozens of men and women returned to their seat as the Admiral continued, "We have less than one month to intercede in the plot to inflict great harm on our American city. It is my duty to inform you that as a result of the intervention team, it is now assumed that the weapons of mass destruction are currently located on American shores. I want to leave you today with a few words of confidence and certainty. There are those of us who have been blessed with an up-close and personal experience with the power of the one true God. I am here to tell you that our creator saves the hardest battles for his strongest and bravest warriors. Colonel Paul Bush and Adjunct Commander Aaron LaSalle will lead the 'Deep Vision' team in our current mission to locate and destroy the evil forces at work against our country, its people, and our faith. I have absolute faith that on December 22nd, 2021, I will be standing at this podium in this city and handing out additional commendations. I know that not one of you in this room will disappoint me."

The Admiral, along with the Wolf and Hassan Rahami, stepped quickly and directly to the meeting Hall's doors and exited.

Colonel Paul Bush rose to the podium and addressed the group, "I need for the 'Deep Vision' team and Commander Helen Lovelace to report to the operations center at 08:30 hours. Thank you."

(18:30 hours)

The knock at the commanding officer's hotel door was crisp. Helen stood wide-eyed and confused with her own mind. The door opened to the immediate smiling face of the academic's best friend.

Sasha spoke up, warmly, "Molly, you get in here! I'm so glad you came by. How'd you like my General Patton impersonation today? Here, get over to my service cart. I've got a vintage Sauvinon blanc for you."

Helen took the fine crystal glass as she implored, "I caught your chopper pilot back for transit, tonight. I hope you'll forgive the infraction. I asked him if you had returned to quarters."

The relaxed lady of many years and more experiences retorted, "You're figuring out how the military works, just fine. Thinking on your feet is what we need desperately. Now, come over to my comfy couch and talk to me for hours." The distinguished woman pouted sorely as she gazed into Molly Brown's jade orbs.

Helen sipped the savory nectar as she spoke out softly, "I'm so very proud of the honor you paid me, today." The strong woman of many lives and many roles peered back into the striking jet black eyes of the formidable personality. "I have a question, Sasha. The 'remote viewing' team is organizing for the convergent Reveal, the day after tomorrow. They want me there. And Aaron and I agree that we must bring Bailey Smith into the meeting. We need all the power we can muster to locate the bombs. She'll be at the Red Dragon departure site tomorrow morning at 04:30 hours."

Sasha smiled broadly as she nodded in agreement. "I've read your daughter's diaries from the three Centuries. She holds karma from the inception of the American Republic. That makes her crucial and she holds an extra demand note with Satan. That demon might have gone too far with what He did to your precious Pyara."

Helen sat shaking her head in agreement as she queried, "Sasha, I have to ask about Bekah." Helen sipped her nectar as she peered into Sasha's gaze. The woman familiar with the most subtle nuance in the written word awaited the response to the difficult question.

Sasha demurred as she considered the unexpected question. "I loved my sister as desperately as I loved Yuri and Gertrudt. My life was slaughtered before my very own eyes. (Y) has blessed me with the love of my foster family. I know that my birth family are well cared for and await my reunion."

Helen's courage softened as she embraced the numbing reality of the questions she knew she must ask. "Sasha, we are family. There exists a special embrace of minor miracles which cannot be denied. The realities of the relentless brutality of this world require such exploration."

Sasha peered at the gentle being sitting beside her as she reached out with her hand and gently lifted Molly's gaze to her own. "Molly, speak the words you need for me to hear."

Molly Brown spoke up, "I had a dream last night and Gertrudt asked me a question, 'Why do the children argue so?'"

Admiral Sasha Cohen's eyes began to water as she gazed past Molly's eyes and began to speak, "It was the Cold War. The last time I saw my beloved sister, she was shipped out to the blockade in Cuba. We had had an argument. It really had nothing to do with anything, but it troubles me that that was the last time we spoke. Oh, Molly! You have never met a more beautiful soul than Rebekka Cohen!"

Molly Brown sat quietly as she struggled with her words, "Did she keep the Matryoshka doll that Yuri gave her?"

The tears flowed like water as Sasha struggled to answer, "It was a shrine to her. All her pictures and the dolls are now with her son in New Jersey. He loves them as dearly as his mother did."

Helen sat starkly as an errant thought, no a de'ja vu, filled her being. "It's Bekah! She's the final key. Sasha, you and everyone around this are Jewish. That's the key. You and Aaron have kept it from me to press the Authority. You are demanding that Yahweh Himself step in and give us the answer."

The gracious lady sat dumbfounded, with her left hand

covering her mouth. She lowered her hand slowly as she began to speak, "You and Bekah don' know about the wife of Isaac. Rivka was most beautiful and she held two sons in her womb, Esau and Jacob. They argued, even as they grew within her flesh. It is the very crux of the issue, Molly. Mankind should be loving brothers, but the evil one has created penury and derision throughout the ages."

Helen turned from her friend as she pondered, "The deities work through man slowly throughout the eons. We don't see their tests and influence because their works are the smallest things. The hand of God is like the gentlest breeze. The mightiest tree is toppled when its time has come."

Sasha sat thoughtfully as she replied, "You now know half of what Yuri and I was shown regarding this final battle. We need a sign . . . for you to be taken the final distance."

Into the Breech

Bailey sipped her hot tea and nestled into the deck chair, a blanket tucked around her legs. She watched as a cardinal pecked about the patio. The perfect winter day was truly memorable. The blue sky, calm air, and Ibrahim, little Abraham and the precious gift.

Bailey pondered the wonder of Ibrahim's grace. She recalled the intense conversation and the descriptions of the desperate childhood of the Middle-Eastern man. It had touched her deeply that so many lives could exist without the memory of the simplest of nurturing joys.

Grey eyes blinked hard, as the young woman's right hand scratched along the length of her left arm. The moment of desperation passed as she felt relief that the forewarning of the slip seemed to pass. What was the reason behind the momentary trauma?

Bailey felt an effervescence as the kaleidoscope of life memories washed across her mind. The Hindu child looked up to her beloved mother image, the most precious woman she had ever known in an eternity of lifetimes. "Shri', why do I have to sleep alone? It's warm in your bed. Can't you just hold me until I fall asleep?"

Life images sped forward. The weight of the canon ball seemed heavier in the winter. 'Could the frozen glaze of ice be the reason?' Grey eyes grew wide, as the red coated warrior charged forward. The young American revolutionary took heed amidst the cacophony of battle. "Riley! On your left soldier!"

Bailey Smith-Abdulaziz blinked hard, as the Siberian Husky barked playfully. A smile filled her face as Ibrahim tossed the ball and the puppy and Abraham, bundled like a delicate package, toddled after it. The young wife studied the contours of her tall and handsome young husband. She knew that she indeed held a prize that any woman would cherish. Her right hand again clasped her left arm. This time, for the briefest moment, the scratching became that of an intensely burning sensation. How could such a thing be possible. Grey eyes looked upward towards the crisp winter sky and the happy sounds of her husband, son, and their new pet. Riley O'Riley stood frozen in absolute terror at the image of the soldier burnt beyond recognition. *How could human flesh burn spontaneously and so completely?* Bailey's cognition returned to Pyara's fierce refusal to burn the written warning. *No! Francois must read this. This future must not become reality!*

Bailey watched as Ibrahim studied the play of his young child and the hapless antics of the pedigreed pet. It occurred to her that this man had also transcended Hell. Not the Hell of the classics, but perhaps a childhood without love is the worst Hell.

Bailey knew that the gift of the greater mind held dangers. She and Helen and Aaron were more than family or perhaps even people. They were the solitary soul of what Riley and Pyara had died for. Grey eyes blinked hard, as a rich and broad smile covered the young girl's face. *I've been angry at this man. I've blamed him for 300 years of torment. He's converted his soul for Yahweh and the love of the Word whispered in his ear. And yet, I've clung to some ancient jealousy over another woman's man. I will allow that man to be my father and I will show this man how much I love him. I'm going to tell Aaron about the pet and ask to tell Ibrahim the whole truth about all of us. Ibrahim's precious gift to our son is more than beautiful. He knows nothing about any of this and yet he named this beautiful Siberian Husky - Patriot. Yes, it's a sign and I will call the fuzzy little girl Patty.*

Bailey gazed at her husband intently. "I promise to love you as much as you truly love me."

(0400 hours, 1st week of December 2021 [Y]time line)

The young Swedish man's car sat in his friend's driveway as Bekah sat peering out the passenger window towards the home's front door. She perked up as the porch light came on, and Bailey Smith opened the door, waving at her two close friends.

Bekah spoke up eagerly, "Hans, pop the trunk and help get her luggage."

Bailey Smith-Abdulaziz quickly pecked Ibrahim on the lips as she spoke out, "Tell Jeshua that Mommy promises to be back in just a few days. I love you both!"

Bailey's bright grey eyes sparkled curiously as she climbed into the back seat of the car and urged, "All right, let's hurry! It should take less than fifteen minutes." She sat quietly, awaiting some comment regarding the extra luggage in the trunk.

Bekah turned to Bailey's gaze, smirking affectionately, as she said, "I hope you want some company?"

Bailey spoke up, quizzically, "Well, I don't understand. Aaron's and Helen's text didn't mention you, Bekah. I mean, it's all right with me. But what did I miss!?"

***

Bailey peered up at the greenish cast of the streetlights as she gazed at the closed Red Dragon restaurant. She spoke out comically, "Well, I hope some traffic cop doesn't come by and ask if we're going to break in and steal breakfast!"

Bekah laughed out loud as she nearly shouted, "Oh, my (Y)!

That's exactly what Aaron said when we stood here weeks ago!"

Bailey pursed her lips before speaking up insistently, "All right, Bekah, you said we'd talk about it when we got here. Well, you sent your sweet Swede on his way, and we're standing here in an empty parking lot with half a dozen bags of luggage. What are you doing?"

Bekah peered wide-eyed at her friend as her blue eyes sparkled in the early morning light. She parted her lips as the words appeared to stick in her throat.

Bailey peered back at her silent friend and nearly shouted, "Bekah! I need for you to talk to me! I've never seen you act like this before. Please talk to me!"

Bekah appeared sheepish as she replied, "I don't really know how to explain it. I saw things when we met with Professor LaSalle those years ago, but you know I don't have your psychic abilities."

Bailey glanced over Bekah's shoulder as an intense pinpoint of distant light began to grow much larger. "Bekah, you had a dream and you were told to go with me, right!?"

The exquisite features of the European beauty erupted in a broad smile as she nodded her head. Bailey continued, "You somehow know what to say that will get you on this flight, right?" Bekah nodded her head even more vigorously as Bailey smiled and spoke comfortingly, "Well, that intensely deep vibration in the air tells me that you and I will find out shortly if you're right!"

The descendant of ancient Vikings shouted out, smiling wildly, as the black craft filled the sky and began its descent in the near distance. "I'm going to fly with the Valkyries! I have the ticket for the flight."

Bailey grimaced sorely as the men began grabbing luggage and the girls' shoulders. "What do you mean by 'ticket'?"

Bekah shouted back as the duo ran pall-mall to the pulsing

craft, "All I have to say is Admiral Sasha Cohen!"

(0800 hours New York City, Central Command Headquarters)

Helen and Aaron stood silently in the breaking morning light, watching the small dot against the horizon growing large. Helen's sparkling eyes seemed to convey more vigor than her words as she shivered and said, "Aaron, it's freezing this morning."

Aaron instantly replied, "We're thirty stories above the city! It's much colder and windier than the Algonquin's heliport."

Helen punched at her phone as she muttered, "Operations confirm the flight's blackout. But it's responding with 'Vision flight verified.' That approaching copter must be the MIB's." Then, Helen jumped up and down, childlike, as she nearly shouted, "Oh, I can't wait to hear Bailey's voice. I can hear her now, 'Oh, my (Y)! It's like something out of Star Wars. Why can't they just put us on like a plane or something!?'"

Short moments passed as the patriarchs of three centuries stood breathless, and the surreal craft rotated in an elegant arc and touched down almost silently. The two stood in place, remaining stationary, awaiting the embrace of their shared progeny.

Helen's expression turned to amazement as she gazed upwards to the matching look of bewilderment. "Aaron, that's Bailey *and* Bekah stepping out!"

Aaron grabbed Helen's arm as he spoke out, "Wait here! You know the drill. We have to wait for them to be escorted past the debarkation markings!"

Bekah and Bailey ran out of the reach of their two escorts as the shrieks of joy began. Bekah shouted over Bailey as she ran into Helen's arms, "I did it! I flew with Odin's winged horses. I'm now a Valkyrie!"

Bailey threw herself into Aaron's arms, smothering him with

kisses as she screeched, "Oh, I've missed you two—SOO much!"

Helen and Aaron stood transfixed as the two girls 'high-fived' one another and switched positions, smothering the next recipient with loving joy.

Aaron's expression returned to that of the dignified academic as he queried, "Bekah! I'm happy to see you, but what's going on?"

Bekah turned timidly and gazed at the three sets of inquisitive faces before she meekly replied, "I know about Sasha Cohen, but I didn't know she was an Admiral!"

Helen gazed at the tall, blonde-haired, blue-eyed Swede and queried, "I know you like my own daughter, instead of just Aaron's, but I don't get it!"

Bailey looked at Helen and quipped, "She dreamed it last night. She was told to be on the flight and what to say to make sure she'd be here!"

The four family members, reunited across time and space, turned towards the building's doorway as Bailey hesitated and spoke out, "What about our luggage?"

Helen turned to Aaron's gaze and nearly chuckled. "They don't know about this place, do they?"

Aaron spoke up as the group walked to the first elevator, "Your luggage is already on another chopper and on its way to the Algonquin Hotel in Manhattan. It'll be there when we all return this afternoon."

Helen watched the bemused expression fill the young girls' faces as the elevator doors closed and the machine began to move. Helen stared stoically as the numbers on the panel counted downwards and her mind traced backwards to the meeting with Sasha Cohen, just twelve hours earlier.

Sasha's words repeated over and over, in the multiple memories of the one woman's curious mind, *"You now know half of what Yuri and I was shown regarding this final battle. We need a sign . . . for you to be taken the final distance."*

The foursome walked through the maze of corridors and work stations, until finally arriving at an unassuming corner door. Aaron spoke up, modestly, "I share this office with Colonel Paul Bush. Everybody have a seat at our conference table." The field-commissioned officer hit a small remote on his desk.

The reply was immediate, "Yes, Sir."

Commander LaSalle responded, "Corissa, would you get us a cart of the Columbian and my tea, and if we've got any of those good croissants, I'll love you forever!"

The intercom spoke out, loudly, "I'll hold you to that. Give me four minutes."

Bailey and Helen looked rather abruptly, one to the other, as Bailey studied Helen's nonplussed expression. She noticed Helen's signature pursed lips as the tell-tale pilot light of her jade orbs that might have flickered, ever so slightly.

Aaron returned to his seat and smiled affectionately at the fountainhead of his visceral passions. "Bailey will assist me as I discuss the fundamental physical concept of energy. It can generally be broken into the twin dynamical states of potential energy and kinetic energy. A roller coaster at the top of the hill is absolute potential energy. The speeding cart at the bottom of the hill is absolute kinetic energy. The word potential has the same origin as the 'pot' we boil water in. It is a container that holds a volume of energy. This room is a pot very nearly ready to boil over, and our beloved Helen Lovelace must ride the cart to all of our destinies."

Bekah sat quietly as the moments passed. She watched as Bailey's eyes remained transfixed on the unchanging expression on Helen's face. It occurred to the rapturous young Swede that either

Helen was upset about the curious familiarity evidenced by Aaron with his secretary, or if the gaze from the professor of Fine Arts reflected an interest in Aaron's somewhat interesting physics allegory.

Bailey drank her coffee with cream, no sugar. She smiled and spoke up, "Bekah, did you notice that Helen and Aaron drink their tea and coffee without any sweeteners or additives?"

The girlish Swede chewed the peach croissant as she mused and swallowed. "Well, I know Helen likes her coffee black, but I never noticed Aaron was also such a purist."

Helen's blank stare turned to a wry smile as she quipped, "Oh, dear (Y), I toy with the desperate attachment I have with this man, but he never ceases to amazes me." She looked at Bailey and asked, "You've already figured out Aaron's riddle haven't you!?"

Riley O'Riley spoke out. "The coaster is the mind. In the case of everyone at this table, there are several people taking the ride. More importantly, the events in life are very much a roller coaster ride. But here's the real point. The stored energy turns to experience and then returns to the next set of memories. The riders can only be added; the memories can't be lost. Energy can only be transformed; it can't be created or destroyed."

Molly Brown queried, "So if I question the feelings of another, am I really in doubt of my own feelings? Does it mean if someone's love is pure, it can't be altered and it's eternal?"

Francois L'Hospital smiled meekly as he interjected, "If I lived another life, (S) could not deny me the company of this family. The deity's curiosity would remain unfulfilled. The doubt is not the power of love. The doubt is our own self-image. Am I worthy of the power of the passion of love, its rapture? The shape of water is the vessel which holds it. The strength of our love is the faithful mind which holds it."

Bekah smiled curiously as she mused aloud, "I remember when I experienced just a small piece of what Helen experienced on the other side. If it weren't for Bailey's mind, I might have been killed. I'm also a professor of literature, but I'm not on the same level as all of you."

Aaron's soft brown eyes caught the immediate gaze from the jade fire in Helen's soul. Shri'Ani spoke slowly as she searched for her words, "Bekah couldn't slip past her own birth; she traveled along with Bailey's total-mind to the destruction of Pyara. The constancy of Bekah's appearance, her name, and even her age, which is the same as it was when she departed from Sasha, there's something we're missing. The power of something very ancient is at work. My mind returns to the memories of Shiva."

At that moment, the intercom spoke out, "Sir, Admiral Cohen and the Wolf are here to see you."

A bemused expression filled both Bailey and Bekah as they turned one to the other in a matched chorus, "Did she just say, 'the Wolf!?'"

***

The early morning sunlight shown through the window blinds of Aaron's office and illuminated the nearly six foot tall, white-blonde-haired, black-eyed women stepping through the doorway. It occurred to Helen that the broad swath of shaded horizontal light was somehow annotating the commanding presence of the two vertical, sleek and feminine forms.

Bekah, Bailey, and Helen rose respectfully as Commander Aaron LaSalle introduced the two naval officers. "Admiral Sasha Cohen, Commander Marguerite Cohen, these are our daughters, Bekah and Bailey. Helen leaned left and took hold of Aaron's right hand as the girls stepped up to shake the officer's hands.

Bailey stepped first to the Admiral as she noticed the epaulets of her casual attire. She smiled broadly as she held her hand out to the officer. "May I call you Sasha?" The ageless woman reached out and hugged the surprised young, dark-haired woman. Bailey's grey eyes sparkled brightly.

Turning to the Commander, Bailey repeated her question, "May I call you Marguerite?"

The statuesque creature standing before the smiling young woman responded with a thin smile as she retorted, "That name is rarely used. I've grown accustomed to my moniker; you may call me 'Wolf.'"

Bekah trailed the greeting procession and, at last, spoke up, "It's amazing to look at you both and see you as mother and daughter. You really appear more like sisters, perhaps twins."

Helen gazed at the women standing before her and chuckled wryly as she turned to Aaron to see if he had also caught the irony of Bekah's statement. Helen spoke out, whimsically, "Bekah, as I stand here watching you shake hands with the Wolf, it's as if I'm watching you shake hands with your own clone. The only real difference between you and the other two beautiful blondes is the color of your eyes."

Seated across from Sasha, Bekah sat with a meek expression as the older, but nonetheless vibrant, woman inquired, "Do you have any impressions of me, my beautiful Rebekka?"

Bekah demurred slightly as she responded, "I had a brief 'slip' with Aaron just once. I remember being saved as a child by him as Yuri, the Russian soldier." The blue eyes of the Swede sparkled as she inquired, "I've read all the diaries. Were you my sister?"

The rigid, yet sensitive features of a woman whose life could fill countless journals, responded softly, "For you, I might be a remnant of some forgotten dream. But for me, I'm sitting here looking at the young woman who shared the most devastating times of my life and the lives of everyone who once lived on this planet."

Bekah's sky blue eyes appeared to almost leap from the exquisitely carved features of her own face as she appeared at once both pensive and enlightened. "Sasha, I just experienced an intense Déjà vu. As a child, I had an odd recurring dream. I would stand in front of a mirror, and I would see myself with dark eyes, not blue. I tried desperately to claw through the glass and hug myself. I would wake up screaming, and I knew that my life as an only child wasn't right. I knew that someone was missing."

Bekah stood up as a torrent of tears flushed from the blue pools of her soul. "Oh, Sasha! Dear God, you've returned to me." The young woman cried out pitifully, "Liebe schwester!"

Helen's eyes began to tear and she lurched into Aaron's arms and began to sob woefully. Aaron gazed at Bailey and the Wolf, who sat quietly and respectfully, watching the scene. The professor of physics considered the mirror image of the two women embraced in the teary-eyed 50-year reunion and the resonating woman in his arms.

Some time passed and the intense group finally settled into seats to discuss the important meeting set for the following day.

Aaron explained, "There are an unknown number of nuclear devices that are now on American soil. The Deep Vision team has a number of insights into the locations and itinerary. (H) day is the 21st of this month. The real issue is the internal conspiracy. We know that there is an individual who is walking a fine line between the terrorists and the authorities. This individual is known to us. We can't say more right now."

Bekah spoke up, "So we're all going to sit in some type of group Reveal and attempt to 'see' what? a name? a device? Just what are we searching for?"

Aaron continued, "At 1000 hours, you will be introduced to the group. There are 12 psychics. There are several religions represented. We'll discuss the technique, we envision, at that time. But what we need are names and images - pictures and renderings of the individuals involved. We had one breakthrough with this when the Wolf and Helen captured one terrorist cell."

Bailey's eyes grew wide as she nearly shouted, "What do you mean, the Wolf and Helen?"

Helen smiled wryly as she peered at her curly haired daughter from three centuries past and lifted her suit coat to reveal the neatly tucked shoulder holster and its formidable contents. Bailey and Bekah sat quite still and dumbfounded as the demur chiming and ring tones began.

They watched as their elders began to grope and punch, in a marvelous choreography, at their phones and devices. All four military officers lurched to their feet as they seemed to shout out both discordantly, but also with a singular unity, "They've got one! It's along the Jersey docks. The Port Authority and the Intervention team are waiting on us!"

The Admiral shouted out, "I'll be downstairs at the 'conn' with Aaron. Wolf, Helen—get upstairs. I'm notifying the choppers. We'll contact the assault team on the waterfront. Move, now! Don't think! Just Act!"

Bailey and Bekah sat frozen to their seats as the room itself seemed to fly apart faster than the Admiral's voice demanded. Exasperated expressions lingered in their wide blue and grey eyes as Bailey muttered, "They forgot about us!"

A moment later, an attractive and disembodied voice filled the room, "Girls, come out to the reception desk. I'm to escort you to Colonel Bush."

The Bell copter roared across the low level environs of the New York City/New Jersey coastline. Helen and the Wolf sat on the edge of their seats listening to cross-talk in their headphones. The Wolf spoke out, "Pilot, what's the ETA, now?"

The pilot responded as the two command officers listened, "I've got the 'crow fly' bearings set. We're less than two minutes out."

The Wolf spoke up, "Helen, you know the drill. I'm trying to get Hassan to text me back. The assault team shows they're stationed and presumed undetected. Stay by my side!"

Helen peered below the speeding craft, allowing her mind to escape from the intense moment in the blurred image of the homes, buildings and humanity rushing by.

Molly Brown stood on the windy Hannibal, Missouri, hillside, with her left eye closed. The 10-year-old girl knew that the five tin cans would fall, but she intended to hit all five by merely grazing the very top of each can. The words of her father traced through her mind, *"The gun must become an extension of your hand. It must feel like family."*

Helen's head lurched towards the Wolf as the voice exploded in her headphones, "There's the '20.' They're going in! Something's happened! Pilot! Get us down, now! Get us in that parking lot, behind the building. There . . . there . . . Set us down between those cars."

Helen tossed off the headphones and pulled hard on the side door handle. She watched the approaching concrete and knew that she must jump to meet a distance not exceeding three feet. Running into the leap, Helen could hear the voice of the Wolf as she instinctively maintained a pounding run in her direction.

Helen blinked hard as she watched the Wolf live up to her

name. She experienced the odd thought, *How can that crazy blonde run so damn fast!* The teenaged mind of the Hindu princess realized that her Caucasian legs were not going to do any better. Helen reached the doorway, perhaps only one second behind her partner. They stopped fast in their tracks as the vista of a huge and abandoned warehouse staging dock rose before them.

Breathing deeply, the two interlopers tried to muffle their frantic gasps for air as they listened closely for the direction of the assault. A moment passed as shouts and heavily muffled sounds emerged. Helen gave the Wolf a sidelong glance as, once again, she found herself in a dead heat chasing after the blonde-haired woodland creature.

Running just behind the Wolf, Helen's gaze fell upon an object lying ahead on the concrete central expanse of the warehouse thoroughfare. A small, but bright, image of the color red seemed to waft across its form. The drafted warrior reached beneath her suit coat and pulled hard on the revolver as the image of the Wolf brandishing her firearm caught up with Helen's mind.

The Wolf's voice appeared somehow unfamiliar as the shouts and "popping" sound of the guns overcame the academic. "Stay back! Take cover!"

Helen veered hard into a concealed spot, next to a heavy forklift. The machine sitting high on the concrete blocks afforded a good view of the fighting just a few yards ahead. The inexperienced but game participant watched as, high above the scene, the tall blonde predator stalked.

The wide jade eyes and grimaced expression stood frozen in time as Helen heard the rapid fire of shots ring out from the Wolf's gun. It occurred to her detail-oriented mind that the sounds were not quite in sync with the visual image. The errant thought passed through Helen's mind. *This couldn't be time-slip, nor could it be the difference in the speed of sound and light.*

In the split instant, between the moments the Wolf stood with both hands held out grasping her smoking pistol and the odd thought concerning the timing of the shots, Helen's focus turned to the opposite tier in the lofty room. Her eyes never left the image of the man standing erect and pulling the rifle to his shoulder as Helen stepped into the open thoroughfare.

In a fraction of a second, before the terrorist's rifle reached his shoulder, Helen Lovelace stood—legs spread, back arched—her Colt 45 revolver held high in both hands, her arms straight out. The new recruit to military maneuvers shouted to the man, "Drop the rifle. Drop it—*now*!"

Helen wondered about the oddity of time and motion that she seemed to be experiencing as the sharp, green eyes of the Missouri "crack shot" squeezed the trigger of her most familiar weapon. In slow motion, the 10-year-old watched as her five shots filled the scene with an accuracy that was not quite natural. The rifle barrel itself seemed to cleave as the first bullet carved into its length. Next, the second magnum round cleaved the tiny white space between the inattentive soul's eyes into the perfect image of freshly split kindling.

The Wolf stood the aerial distance, across from the target of the marksman, and lowered her piece as a wry smile traced her expression. The tall and otherwise feminine form stood, quite entertained, as she watched the "double tap" performance of Helen's oscillating shots. Even from the considerable distance to the target, the Wolf knew that she was witnessing a skill set far superior to her own. She stood enthralled as all five shots tore the man to bloody bits before the laws of gravity and humanity could intervene.

The Wolf approached Helen as she stood stoically. The

instinctive predator's gaze remained as a thin smile traced her lips. "That was quite impressive. But you haven't reloaded, and you made a severe tactical error calling out the warning. Next time, do not think. Just act."

(1800 hours)

"Aaron, I think it's the girls at the door." Helen peered from the bath to verify that her trusted half had heard her call. The suite of rooms was instantly filled with the cheery sounds of Helen Lovelace's dearest young companions. With a rapturous smile and wrapped tightly in her comfy white robe, a still-damp-from-the-shower-Helen reached out with open arms to her company.

Helen walked towards the wall of windows overlooking the greatest city on earth as she entreated, "Come over to the cart, girls. We've got coffee, tea, soft drinks, and some really fine wines. Dinner will be brought up after we order, so you've got to go through the menus pretty soon."

Bailey walked to the cart and examined the box of Earl Grey tea as she exclaimed, "Bekah and I are still pinching ourselves. Our suite is as big as my house. Helen, the bath towels are, like, heated! Bekah's scared to death that you and Aaron aren't going to want to come back home!"

The tall Swede chimed in, "Helen, I've never seen any place that has a restaurant like this. This is 5-star dining, *and* they bring it to the room!"

Aaron sat quietly at the conference table in the common suite as his pen swept its centuries old patterns. Peering upwards from his work, the faithful mate to the truly gentle woman studied her pleasing demeanor as he considered the joyous feelings their guests had produced. Some moments passed as the feminine triad approached the scientist's table and gazed skeptically at the sole proponent of the male member of the species.

Bailey hung on Aaron's shoulders as she queried from behind the seated man and gazed at the other two women, "Aaron, were you terrified when you heard about the military action today?"

Aaron took a deep breath as he looked up at the freshly-bathed woman standing before him, replete with her bath towel wrapped around her head. The thoughtful academic considered his company and spoke out casually, "Why don't you girls let Helen finish getting dressed and bring the menus over and sit with me for a while? Sasha and Herbert will be here before too long, and we have to place the room service orders by 06:30 hours."

Bekah closed the menu and spoke up excitedly, "I'm having the veal. I still cannot believe this wonderful hotel." The blue-eyed blonde glanced at Bailey studying her menu and then focused on Aaron. "Aaron, I want to ask you an important question."

Aaron stopped his writing and rested his chin upon his hands as he leaned into the table and replied, "Of course, dear, ask me anything."

Bekah hesitated for a moment, struggling with the thought, before she spoke up, "I've read all the diaries, except Sasha's, but I don't really understand why Helen is on the military assault team. I mean, she's definitely as psychic as you and Bailey. I know that paranormal abilities take different forms, but why did she have to, well . . ., eliminate a terrorist today?"

Bailey's expression formed a thin smile as her grey eyes met the soft brown depths of Aaron LaSalle's. Bailey nodded just slightly as Aaron considered the acknowledgment. He spoke up softly, "Bekah, you remember when you were a child and you outlived your beloved puppy?"

The delicate Norwegian features of the young blonde grimaced sorely as she nodded her affirmation. Aaron continued, "There are many ways I might answer your very sincere question, but I'll respond in the only way I know how. To the young mind, one that has never experienced the mindless horror of deliberate death and destruction, there is no way to understand the need for war or death or its pain."

Bekah sat quietly for a moment as she continued, "You and Bailey have glimpses of your prior incarnations. You both have killed in battle. I remember you saving me from the war. But Helen was killed trying to stop the man that caused the war. Is that why she's the only one who can prevent the attack on the city?"

Bailey looked at Aaron and hesitated before speaking up, "Yes, Bekah, that's exactly the reason. She could tell you about karma. She knows more than any of us. But there's something else. Aaron and Sasha were told something in 1946, and it's the key to the whole situation."

Aaron's eyes grew wide as he interjected, "Bekah, Helen will be back out here shortly. You mustn't repeat that to her! Bailey's quite correct. It has to do with things that are interwoven in all of our destinies. Sasha and I experienced a psychic event when she was only a child. We were given a vision, in which only Helen's mind can sort out the final solution to this terrifying threat to 10 million lives. You found out today that (H) day is the 21st of this month. One nuclear device was captured today. We now know that three bombs are in the city. Only Helen can unravel the Gordian Knot."

A perplexed expression filled Bekah's face as she pleaded, "Aaron, Bailey—aren't you terrified? The whole thing is impossible. How can this be happening!?"

Aaron leaned into his words as he spoke out, gently, "In 1st Corinthians 1:27, it says, 'God chose the weak things of the world to shame the strong.'"

Bailey continued, "Bekah, the world operates on a simplistic dogma. The academics like to think that all attitudes are based on cause and effect. We push the painful things like Aaron's question about your pet, out of our consciousness. But in fact, the connection to our attitudes and our abilities stem from prior experiences and incarnations. We're much more what we are born to be than what we learn to be. It's an almost incomprehensible kaleidoscope, but each of us in this room is somehow irreplaceable."

Blue eyes gazed past the professors of physical science as the pragmatism of an ancient warrior seemed to speak, "Winston Churchill said, 'I worry about the heart of anyone under 30 who isn't a liberal and I worry about the brain of anyone over 30 who isn't a conservative.'" Bekah smiled warmly as her focus returned to her companions. "I guess (Y) has chosen the right person to return balance to the world."

At that moment, Helen stepped from her bedroom. The group looked up, with broad smiles, at the smiling green-eyed beauty standing before them. Helen's dark hair was combed and pinned perfectly as she twirled before them, adorned in a magnificent azure-colored silk sari. Francois gazed at the eternal image of his inspired passion. The 25-year-old man-child was oblivious to the fact that the vision brightening his soul entered through portals far older.

Bailey nudged Bekah as she sat quietly beside her. The two exchanged wry smiles as they studied Aaron's enthralled gaze. Bekah whispered to Bailey, "That's the most romantic thing I've ever seen. If Hans ever looked at me like that, I wouldn't come down for weeks!"

At that instant, several knocks were heard at the door, and Helen stepped to open it. Cheerful greetings were heard as Sasha, the Wolf, Herbert, and Paul entered the room.

Helen called out. "Sasha, this is the most beautiful thing anyone ever gave me!"

Sasha replied, "It was Marguerite's idea. I can't take credit. You may not realize it, but the diaries are her favorite reading. She puts herself to sleep at night studying them."

The statuesque dark-eyed blonde smiled broadly as the group walked to the serving cart to retrieve drinks. Sitting at the large conference table, Sasha watched as Helen stood next to Aaron, embraced in his arms.

The Wolf sipped on a glass of white wine as she spoke up, "Helen, I want to thank you for your superb instincts today. I want you to know that I have never witnessed such speed and marksmanship. I believe your grouping of shots was made in less than three seconds. The head, chest accuracy and the unbelievable rifle barrel hit were truly incredible."

Helen's gaze fell to Aaron's soft brown eyes. She peered back at Sasha and the Wolf as she spoke up timidly, "Thank you, Marguerite. I'm truly honored by the gift and your words. I understand so much more about so many things now. I see that there is a place and a time for all types of expression and all types of feelings."

Sasha took a deep drink of her wine as she chimed in, "The Wolf and I have kept that garment for this moment for weeks. My Wolf knew this day would come."

Helen nearly blushed as she looked deeply into the softened black abyss of the Wolf's eyes. She spoke up meekly, "May I give you a hug, Sasha?"

The formidable woman stood erect and held out her arms as the moist-eyed lady scampered to her and embraced her warmly.

Aaron chewed slowly as his eyes rolled in utter delight. "This veal peppercorn is the most delightful thing I've ever tasted."

Bekah looked up at Helen and nearly shouted, "I've got Zoe Blankenship on the phone. Zoe, wave at Helen!"

Helen looked over at the phone and saw the smiling face of the dark-haired beauty. "Zoe! Oh, you beautiful doll! The girls and I are going to see about meeting you this Sunday at the Park. Can you be there with Hanna and your mom?"

Zoe's voice leaped from the phone, "Oh, we'll be there! And you should see Balto. He's going nuts just at the sound of your voice on the phone. Can you see him!?"

As Helen peered into the symbol of 21st Century sorcery, the barking crucible of love and dedication licked at the screen.

Zoe called out, "Balto! No lick!"

Herbert Potter smiled broadly at Aaron as he spoke up, "Aaron, I want you to teach me about dueling. I'm going to admit it. I can't put the diaries down either. Can you show me some moves pretty soon? You tell me what to order and it'll be here the next day!"

Aaron smiled broadly and nodded his head in agreement.

Paul Bush sipped his coffee and set the cup down as he interjected, "I want to get everyone's attention for a few minutes. I need to let everyone know that General King and I have discussed postponing the convergent Reveal for a few days. He wants Bailey and Bekah to sit in on the 'viewing' sessions. We must locate the remaining devices. And we must decide what to do with the main suspect."

Bailey's grey eyes sparkled as she turned to Bekah and spoke up, "Bekah has never slipped past this incarnation. She's not prepared for the intense concentration."

Sasha rang out, "Dear, we all have our breakthroughs. It may be the reason she's here. Don't you see? We represent Aaron's contained randomizing system. When she breaks through, we may all break through!"

Aaron chimed in, "Bailey's referring to things that only she and I have clear understandings of. It's quantum mechanical. The pinball machine can be observed to obtain an explicit outcome, but atomic-level events can only be studied though probabilities. Here's what I think she's saying: If Bekah doesn't enter into this with an understanding of her previous lives, she may not be able to contribute anything."

Sasha smiled broadly as she held her clear wine and glass above her head and announced heartily, "Then, I guess it's time to 'get real.' Yuri, have you ever wondered how your Jewish daughter can be a fair-haired blonde with jet-black eyes? The medical, so-called, experts say it's very rare. And then I turn out an exact replica. What do you suppose the chances are of that?"

Aaron sat stoically, gazing at Bekah as he replied, "Sasha, it connects doesn't it. We know that the link with Helen consolidates the biological aspect. It can't be a coincidence that Bekah is almost an exact copy of you and the Wolf, except for the blue eyes."

Helen nearly shouted, "I don't have a clue what you two are talking about. What do Bekah's blue eyes have to do with this?"

The Wolf spoke up, "I think I understand part of what you're saying. I know that, in truth, I may be a very attractive woman, but standing next to Helen, I feel like a newspaper next to a rainbow. She's beautiful with that auburn hair and raging green eyes. I'm just standing here with black ink for eyes and white paper for hair."

Helen stared back at the Wolf with a truly befuddled expression, "I've never considered that. I'm so intimidated by you I can barely stand to look at you. I mean you're a cross between Grace Kelly and Raquel Welch.

Sasha peered at Aaron and spoke out, "It's Genesis 2:17, isn't it?"

Aaron nodded approvingly as he spoke up, "There's something wrong with the human animal. We're not wholly formed. We're evolving into a varied species. Perhaps, it might be called Homo Psyche Sapien Sapien. Sasha and I are of Middle Eastern Semitic descent, but we both show more features of European genetics. Now, we have Bekah who doesn't even know the name Rivka."

Bekah stared back with an astonished look. "I know it's really odd that I had nearly the same name in both incarnations—Rebekka and Bekah—but who is Rivka?"

Sasha spoke up, "She was the beautiful wife of Isaac who bore the twin sons, sons who fought even in her womb." Bekah stared back silently in wonder.

Paul Bush interjected, "So Bekah was somebody much older than perhaps anybody in this room. And perhaps all our psychic abilities are slowly transforming our bodies across time. The shape of the shapeless substance is the vessel which holds it."

Aaron continued, "It's like I said earlier, 'We're more what we are born to be, than what we learn to be.' We're influenced by our previous incarnations. The greater mind is influenced by both sides of this paradox, (Y) and (S). How else do you explain the irrational and petulant attitudes, particularly the social attitudes of people? Look at the so-called liberal agenda; its hypocrisy has brought the world to the brink of nuclear war."

Victory

(0800 hours, 2nd week December 2021, Central Command [Y]time-line)

Bailey Smith grimaced as she turned to Colonel Paul Bush and inquired earnestly, "There is a practitioner of Voodoo on the remote viewing team?"

Paul grimaced with his patented squinty-eyed expression as he replied, "Jean Preval is Haitian. He has been in the employ of the CIA for almost 20 years. He's been very helpful with remote viewing programs. He even received a meritorious commendation. Lives were saved during the operation. But, there is something that's quite relevant. His family immigrated from Niger, they're Muslim, and I've been struck by a verse from the Koran which he's mentioned a number of times."

Grey eyes appeared strained, as conflicted memories of dealing with the ancient religion filled Bailey's mind, "You have no idea how curious I am to hear what you are about to say, Colonel."

Col. Paul Bush continued, "Jean has told me that he has studied mysticism and spiritual beliefs from all directions. He told me that there's a Koranic verse which compelled him to do so. Koran 13:22 says 'To repel evil with good, for those will have the good end.'"

Bailey retorted, "That's all well and good. I can understand that the 'viewing' activities are mostly independent focus sessions. And I understand enough about spiritual animism to believe that voodoo is not intrinsically evil. But I can't sit at the same table and perform the sacred biblical Reveal with artifacts of animal sacrifice and pagan talismans!"

Aaron leaned over the conference table and interjected, "We'll have to do this without any religious connotation. Paul's group of twelve viewers and I have worked pretty well together, but we've sat and reviewed the photos and locations and then gone to our separate focus locations. It hasn't been anything approaching the sanctity of the Reveal."

Bekah spoke out, "I've been sitting in on this for days. The closest I've come to achieving time-slip is when Bailey and I have tossed the die randomly and located biblical verse. I acquired intermittent visions from an ancient life when I was directed to Genesis 25:22."

Col. Bush replied to the group, "Here's what I suggest. Each morning we'll review the 'identified targets', including objects, locations, and persons of interest. We'll hold hands—left to right and right to left. I'll place the non-theological members between yours and Sasha's group and Jean Preval. We'll only have a pad and pens in front of each member. Let's see if we can locate the devices and acquire an image of the enemy operatives."

Aaron looked at Helen, Sasha, Bekah and Bailey as all nodded approvingly.

Sasha spoke up, "Paul is going to begin the visuals with the photo of the individual who is known by us to be collaborating with the ISIS infiltrators. The Shia divergence from al Qaeda must be understood."

The group peered around the table with an odd mixture of blank stares and surprised expressions as Bailey remarked, "Now, I understand! We're getting desperate. I'm not sure I even want to know how delicately the whole Intelligence community is hanging by a thread."

(1200 hours Sunday, 2nd week December 2021)

The bright blue winter sky contrasted the still green grass of New York City's Central Park. Helen Lovelace peered out the window of the twin blade, fifteen-passenger copter as she exclaimed, "There they are! Everybody's there by Balto's statue!"

Four smiling faces peered from the descending craft's windows as the NYPD officers waved the pilot onto the cordoned landing site of the park. Zoe, Hanna, and Balto came running across the grass as the officer turned back from the orange-coned area and held his arms high in the air.

Zoe stopped and reached out, gathering her precious pet in her arms as her four dear friends descended the copter's stairs. Zoe turned to the mirror image of her sparkling hazel eyes, and exclaimed, "Hannah, our professors are VIP's now!"

Bekah and Helen ran screaming to the group as Bailey and Aaron walked briskly behind them. Bailey turned to the dignified professor of physical sciences and remarked, "I'm glad to see her parents are going to dinner with us."

Aaron quipped, "I knew the FDNY Captain's curiosity would get him to take a copter ride to the Algonquin Hotel."

Zoe set Balto down as the frenzied Siberian husky ran to Helen. Helen, with a broad smile, greeted the faithful animal with open arms as the loving pet smothered the woman with wags and kisses. Zoe and Hanna ran to the professor's side as the girls shouted out, "Balto! No licks, Balto!"

The girls' mother and Captain Robert Blankenship stood by the bronze statue of the historic canine hero as Helen and Aaron approached with broad smiles. Aaron held out his hand to the Captain as he spoke up, "Captain, I'm so very glad to meet you!"

The smiling father of the twins replied, "Please call me Bob! Well, I'm impressed, Professor. You've sure figured out how to beat the New York City traffic!"

A short time later, Helen called out to Aaron as they captured a moment to themselves and walked towards Balto's bronze statue. Helen read aloud the dedication:

Dedicated to the indomitable spirit of the sled dogs

that relayed antitoxin over six hundred miles

over rough ice, across treacherous waters,

through arctic blizzards from Nenana

to the relief of stricken Nome in the winter of 1925.

ENDURANCE FIDELITY INTELLIGENCE

Helen turned to Aaron and spoke thoughtfully, "It's pretty strange to think of the mirrored irony of this moment. You'll end our glamorous lunch with an instruction to the fireman to take his family and flee the city on the 20th of the month."

Aaron pursed his lips as his soft brown eyes misted over. "I'd rather have them safe and be the one here in the city myself than to ever hear their voices again as they stood here awaiting nuclear incineration."

At that moment, Zoe and Hannah stepped up to the statue. Zoe addressed Aaron, "Professor, do you remember when we were back at school and Hannah asked you what the equations meant and I said, 'It meant that you would save us?'"

Helen fought back the intense emotion that wafted through her mind as she blinked hard and turned from the girls. "Aaron, I'm texting the pilot. Let's get everybody on the aerial tour and get back to the Algonquin."

(07:30 hours)

General James King looked up from his desk as Colonel Paul

Bush and Admiral Sasha Cohen entered his office. Gen. King picked up several files as he announced, "Welcome, welcome! Let's move over to the conference table. I have several things to discuss before the others arrive."

Admiral Sasha Cohen leaned into the table and spoke assertively, "We've got everyone settled down for the convergent Reveal. We're going to try and coordinate the field information with the viewings. I'll be sitting in and I'm sure that Jean Preval can bring the suppressed incarnation out of Bekah."

Paul Bush spoke out, "General, the timing will have to be perfect. What can you tell Sasha and me about the nukes?"

Gen. King sifted through the files and pulled out a document. "All Intelligence supports the findings from the disabled nuke captured on the New Jersey waterfront by the Wolf's assault team. We're dealing with three additional Russian-made, strategic miniaturized MIRV re-entry warheads."

The field-tested man of many years spoke tersely, "These are five-megaton thermo-nuclear weapons. They are easily transportable in any number of means, such as a van or even a pickup truck."

Sasha's dark eyes grew fierce as she responded, "How do you know they're all the same armament?"

Gen. King responded, "We've been trying to track down the weapons for three years. The four weapons came up missing from military audits in Russian, Georgia, and we've tracked them from Iran to Syria, and that's where the trail ended. Interrogations from the containerized cargo ship contraband capture verify that the remaining three are now on our shores."

Paul gazed at Sasha with an intense stare as he spoke out in earnest, "These weapons are going to be distributed about the city, possibly just driven to optimum locations for detonation, is that what you're saying?"

King replied, "We know from Aaron and Helen that one weapon will be parked in Central Park. I intend to be present when that weapon is captured. We've got several dozen vehicles with very sensitive gamma ray detectors and other sensors that will be on the roads on the 21st. But there's a wild card that may make capturing one of the bombs even easier. The arms experts tell me that at least one of the bombs will probably be smuggled to the top of one of the skyscrapers for maximum blast radius."

Paul Bush spoke out, "We've got 'viewings' that I'll provide to your teams. Several psychics have identified license plates, and I have a drawing from several 'views' showing towers being consumed by demons. One of them is the Empire State building."

King sat listening as he drank deeply from his Earl Grey cup of tea. He set the cup down as he peered timidly at the matched set of stares. "Yeah, I know! That charming couple of academics grows on you, don't they!? Now, look here. We all know that we can't move on any of the weapons when they're in the field. There's no way to know if there's some type of dead-man's switch. Your people will have to direct Helen and the Wolf's team to the precise moment that the control IED is set. We know from the interrogations that it will simply be a cell phone in the key man's hands."

At that moment, the receptionist's voice rang out. "General, Intelligence officer Jean Preval is here to see you."

The Haitian/American sat quietly as Gen. King spoke up, "I want to thank you for being here this morning. We haven't met directly before, and I'm pretty new to the paranormal. Can you tell me what the 'Deep Vision' team has in mind?"

The dark eyes of the jet-black face of the grey-haired man peered past the General's gaze as he slowly began to speak with a heavy Caribbean accent, "We have deep problems, General. Fierce demons seek to destroy this city."

Paul Bush's expression turned blank as he spoke up, "Jean, we've got to explain this to the General. You've got to help me explain the timing problem to him. Work with me now!"

Sasha studied the face, which she knew held deeply esoteric knowledge of the darker side of the Authority. She entreated, "Jean! Talk to us about Rebekka. King doesn't know about Rebekka. Explain to him about her importance!"

Gen. King's eyes grew wide as a look of amazement filled his face. Paul spoke up quietly, "It's all right, General. His eyes morph when he enters a trance. They'll white over like that for a while. He was a blind African shaman several incarnations back. He's entered a total-mind state. He should start talking in a moment."

The disembodied soul of Jean Preval spoke out softly, "I am Malatu Buhari. I know the struggle you face with these demons. I have seen this evil. There are three demons sent by the Angel of Light. Balaam, the Hebrew demon of avarice and greed. Damballa, the voodoo serpent God. And Dagon, the Philistine avenging devil of the sea. Such evil has not existed in this world for many decades."

Paul leaned into Jean's near comatose expression and entreated, "We know that Rebekka is somehow the key to stopping their power. What can you tell us?"

The glazed-eyed man spoke very quietly, "Sasha has seen the final victory. She knows most of the riddle. This is why she prayed to the Hebrew God to send the incarnation of the ancient Jewish woman."

King grimaced sorely as he leaned forward and spoke earnestly, "Yes, yes, we know that we have everybody we need. Can you tell us what we're looking for? We must reach the man with the trigger cell phone before he keys in the final code to coordinate the blasts."

Jean Preval sat upright in his chair as his dark eyes returned and he spoke out, "I can't reach the answer. The demons are too powerful! We can only hope that Rebekka can 'see' the terrorist's name during the group reveal." The grey-haired mystic breathed deeply as he muttered a final remark, "It has to do with the Muslim traitor. This government liaison, Hassan Rahami, he will give consent to the hand of Satan at the final moment."

(1100 hours)

Aaron sat peering at the white pad of paper and the assortment of pencils and pens. He turned to his right and smiled meekly at Helen. Looking up at Admiral Sasha Cohen and Bekah directly across the conference table from them, Helen looked to her right and smiled at Bailey. The intimate family, which spanned for Centuries across time and space turned and gazed at the long table filled with the diverse group of government employed psychics.

Helen whispered to Bailey, "I hope seventeen is a lucky number today."

At one end of the table sat Jean Preval and at the other end sat Colonel Paul Bush. Paul Bush rose to his feet and began to speak, "King says that the location of the enemy weapons will be at the 'imaged' locations that we've worked so hard to find. We have high probability that the intervention forces can capture the devices within minutes of the 'disabled' command. Today, we have the final piece of the puzzle to unravel. I'm going to spend some time reviewing the information around the main suspect. I'll begin by bringing up the photos and intel on the large screen behind me." Bush pressed a button on his remote, and instantly a face appeared on the screen.

"The individual you now see was assigned to the pentagon in

2015 by the Obama Administration. You will recall that, at this time, there was tremendous sequestration of US military influence abroad. This man was a member of the Muslim Brotherhood and was born in 1988 in Egypt. He and his family obtained American citizenship in 2012."

Helen drew a deep breath as she turned to Aaron and muttered quietly, "Oh dear (Y), that's Hassan Ramahi! I knew that traitor yelled some sort of code that day on the cargo ship. That bastard nearly got me skewered!"

Paul Bush spoke up with some hesitation, "We've maintained this operative at arm's length for some years. Sometimes, you must keep your enemies even closer than your friends. I'm going to have us all join hands, left to right and right to left. I'll put up 'trigger' images on the screen and we'll repeat until someone thinks they have something useful. We must locate the individual most closely tied to Hassan Rahami. We believe he will be the one to coordinate the three nuclear devices on the 21st."

(12:30 hours)

Jean Preval's eyes turn to bleach white as he arched upright in his seat and shattered the quiet in the room full of people all sitting silently and holding hands. He shouted out, loudly, "Jewish woman! Ancient Jewish woman!"

Aaron watched as Bekah's right hand clamped hard onto Sasha's left. He swung his focus to her and saw her arch upright, stiffly in the chair, with her eyes tightly closed.

Malatu Buhari called out in native Ethiopian. "Demon God, you cannot defile this soul. She holds the power to defeat you!"

Bekah sat stiffly, eyes closed as she shouted out, "Bitter struggle! Conflict in my womb! Children of Isaac! Your hatred disgraces your father and mother. As the foul battle between Isaac and Ishmael brought the prophets to war, my sons still fight. My love for Jacob, Isaac's love for Esau, this battle still wages. My loving son has shamed his mother. Esau's birthright curses the ages!"

The blonde Swede stared back at the group of silent attendants as she wiped the tears from her glistening blue eyes. Lurching into Sasha's arms, she wailed out loud, "Sister, the demons dwell in Hassan's brother! Hassan has a brother. He's been kept secret from all sources. He holds the devil's tail. He will enter the nine-digit code that will bring the new Holocaust."

(0700 hours 21st of December 2021)

Helen stood in the suite's bath, staring stoically into her green orbs as she rotated her face slowly left to right and right to left and whispered to herself, "This must be the final trick. I wonder if Aaron and Sasha even know."

Stepping from the bath with her cell phone, the drafted warrior stopped and gazed discordantly at Aaron seated at the suite's conference table. "I just got a text from Bailey. Bekah and Hans dropped her off late last night. Oh, dear (Y)! I've never cried so much in three lifetimes!"

Aaron looked up; his soft brown eyes appeared on the verge of more tears, "Has Zoe and her family sent any more texts?"

Helen sat down at the table and nodded. "They're an hour's drive upstate. Zoe said that her mom took the keys from the Captain. Hannah keeps telling him that he can't help until after it's over. She says that if we make it past noon that they're all coming over here tonight and nothing can stop them. She just keeps texting that she loves us more than life itself. And she says that Balto is acting 'very strangely.'"

Helen's hands flew to her face as she wailed out loud, "Is this what it's like to be in war!? It's impossible to remain in your own body. All I can think about is the pain that those you love will feel. I can't die today! It'll cause too much torment!"

Aaron held Helen close as he pulled his obligatory Kleenex from his pocket and wiped his eternal mate's eyes. "Let's go darling; the Wolf's transport should be up on deck waiting for us."

Helen stood at the door and gazed back at the suite of rooms where so many weeks had transpired. She hesitated for a moment as she quipped, "Now, I even love the damn Wolf, and I have to worry about her, too. She refuses to even wear a protective vest. I guess it doesn't matter. We'll either stop the Rahami demons or we won't."

Aaron cupped Helen's chin and held her gaze as he looked deeply into her saddened stare. "Do you remember the morning when I drew the same look in your eyes, the one I'm seeing now, staring through that giant '4' on your office door white board?"

Helen replied curiously, "Of course, that was my birthday— October 4th. It was a sign to me that we had to work together."

Aaron smiled wryly as he retorted, "No darling, I knew right then that there were several dates that the world could stand on the brink of nuclear devastation. I never explained this to you. I've tried to be as gentle as I can with such foreboding knowledge."

Helen grimaced sorely, "In less than six hours, New York City is going to be annihilated. If there's something you're keeping from me, talk fast!"

Aaron remained stoic as he spoke, "Helen, you've long-supposed that I was born to address this issue. Once again, darling, there's always something more. The Solstice and, unfortunately, several more dates are all represented in the exact numerology of your birthday."

Helen's Jade eyes went wide, "What the Hell are you talking

about?"

Aaron reached into his coat pocket and extracted a small spiral ring notepad. Helen's stare remained fixed as he scribbled and talked. "Suppose I hold out a rubber ball at arm's length and drop it. It'll bounce back nearly as high as my hand, the next return will be lower, and then lower, until the inertia is countered."

Helen's jade orbs strained as Aaron peered deeply into her gaze and said, "You and I are wedged deeply into some incomprehensible destiny." The professor of physical realities beyond any textbook turned the pad to his wife of three centuries. "What do you see?"

Helen looked at the twin set of hand written numbers on the small pad:

10/4

12/21

Helen's nonplussed response seemed almost defiant, "Aaron, please, the copters are waiting. What are you saying?"

Aaron grimaced. "You're the numerologist in the family. It's your birthday repeated and more times than I care to consider. It's how you knew the date, Helen!"

The annoyed countenance of the dignified literary academic immediately turned dumbfounded. "Oh, my (Y)! If you add zero to both sides of the 12:21, you get 01.22.10. It's my birthday forwards and backwards! The numerology for 01/22/10 adds to become 10/4 and 4/10."

Aaron's stare also went blank as he spoke comfortingly, "We have the divine code to unravel the evil plot, but the real question is whether the first bounce of the ball will be the last. There are four times each year that your 21's repeat significantly, twice on the Equinox and twice on the Solstice. It's why your house sits precariously to face both the summer Equinox and the winter

Solstice. The universe is an infinitely woven tapestry." Aaron smiled broadly, as he gazed into Helen's jade fire. "You haven't aged a day in so many years. And, I don't suppose you will for many more."

Helen smirked, "The Methuselah Effect should cease in two days. You said it runs out when we come to the date we slipped to, now, in the future."

Soft brown eyes glistened, "I'm going to enjoy remaining young with my Hindu bride a while longer, Shri'. How many years have passed since 2012?

Helen spoke, "Well, let's see. The Solstice of 2012 to the Solstice of 2021 is . . . nine years."

Aaron returned to his professorial tone. "Helen, World War One and World War Two were the same war separated by a 20 year armistice. The 'Roaring Twenties' ended in 9 years with the commencement of the Great Depression. It's the Trinity of Tiers, Helen, three squared. The greatest threat for mankind's undoing will last for nine years!"

Helen gasped, "Oh, Dear (Y), that can't be right! Tell me it'll end today, Aaron!"

Aaron replied, "We can't be sure how many years the nation state threat or the religious conflict will continue. But, the dreams have shown me that the Century of Warfare is repeating itself and the nine years commencing with your 2021 Solstice and the Darkest Day on each year thereafter will decide our fate."

Helen let out a deep breath and held her husband close as she pressed her face into his chest. "I can't think about it, Aaron. That's your job. Let's get upstairs to the copters and stop the first bounce."

Helen pulled the chopper's side door closed as she placed the head gear over her head and spoke into the microphone, "Are you reading me, Wolf?"

Peering out the opposite windows, the Wolf nodded her head. Some minutes passed as Helen once again spoke up, "Are we returning to Headquarters for Captain Potter and Hassan?"

Still peering out the window, the Wolf again nodded her head. Helen gazed out her side windows as she peered out at the approaching landing pads. She spoke up, with some emphasis, "Wolf! Say something. I need to hear your voice."

The wolf turned silently, with a brave and toothy smile as she answered, "I've been waiting for this for half a dozen years!"

Helen blinked hard as she considered the odd response. Stepping behind her commanding officer, Helen watched as the Wolf marched up to Hassan and Captain Herbert Potter. Stepping quickly to carry herself past the prop wash, Helen noticed that the Captain stepped just behind Hassan as the Wolf's pistol appeared in front of the surprised man's face.

Helen stepped up next to the Wolf as she heard the command. "Raise your hands, now!"

The bemused hesitation on the part of the Egyptian was met with a loud report as the Wolf immediately cracked the indignant man across the face with her weapon. The Wolf spoke in the same uncompromising voice which Helen had heard just moments before the last man standing within her gun's reach had returned to his maker.

It genuinely seemed to Helen that the same time slip analog, which had occurred at the warehouse, was repeating itself as she heard the Wolf's instruction, "When I say jump, you will be two steps ahead of my words, or you will be dead before I finish the sentence."

A pleasurable smile slid across Helen's face, nearly as quickly as the traitor's hands reached for the sky. She watched as Herbert pulled Hassan's cell phone from his pocket and reached beneath his jacket to extract his pistol. Helen stood quite impressed with Herbert's skill as the military man turned the Egyptian roundabout and thoroughly frisked the befuddled culprit.

The Wolf returned her weapon beneath her coat and again commanded the arrested man, "Let's go! Get in my chopper!"

Helen turned to Herbert and smiled thinly as the friend and fellow warrior smiled back warmly. It occurred to Helen that Hassan had not been cuffed. She knew that their destination must be the same location as the one Hassan had already planned on. It seemed apparent to the professor of details that the next stop would be an expected visit with the conspirator's family. The outcome of the visit would be quite a change in the brothers' morning plans.

The Bell copter roared along the New Jersey coastline as the pilot spoke out, "Our ETA is one minute. We're about to pass over the ground assault teams."

The Wolf turned to Hassan and spoke up assertively, "We're setting down on your group's Libyan freighter. Tell me where your brother's at, how many are with him, and who's got the cell phone detonator."

Hassan's expression appeared sincere as he responded, "I spoke to him just before you picked me up. He said we'd wait until noon in the galley. He's got the cell phone that will be used. There shouldn't be any unexpected resistance."

Captain Herbert Potter watched curiously as Helen began to stare intently into a small pocket mirror. He queried, gently, "What going on, Helen?"

The College professor replied, "I've always told my students, 'The mind remembers what the hand writes.' We're programmed to our paws. It's tied into my survival instincts. I have all of Molly Brown's marksmanship, but I'm not nearly her psychic equal. I've been practicing for weeks. The next voice you hear should be that of a hundred-and-fifty-year-old woman."

The Wolf and Herbert watched as Helen gripped her right wrist with her left hand with all her might. Helen blinked hard as she began breathing deeply. She turned to the Wolf's jet black stare as she spoke out, "We've got twenty-one minutes to get the code and disarm the bombs."

The lady from a less gentle, but more sophisticated, era reached out and viciously grabbed the back of the Egyptian's hair as she twisted his head sorely around to her intense jade stare, "Now, say the exact words you just spoke!"

Hassan repeated his words as the greatest trick shot of Hannibal, Missouri, exclaimed, "He's only half a liar. The bastard's brother is in the Galley, but the main corridor is lined with killers. You lead him in. I just saw the whole layout. I'll knock off every thug that gets in our way."

The Wolf's eyes spoke even more clearly than her words as she peered at the murderous traitor and hissed, "I thought you terrorists all wanted to die for Allah. It's pretty obvious that this ship is just past the blast radius. With the ship's hull, you expect to survive this. You get out of this chopper and walk across the deck like we're just one big happy family, or yours will be the first brains that I splatter."

The team walked casually across the ship's deck to the watertight door entering the ship's control centers. The Wolf hesitated and spoke quietly to Hassan, "When we step through this hatch, you call out your brother's name and tell him that we're coming down to the galley."

Molly Brown interjected, "You know a lot about the paranormal. I just proved to you that I'm quite proficient at telepathy. If you say the wrong thing, it'll be a race to see how fast you die. Say it right this time!"

The group stepped through the hatch and entered a long starboard corridor as Hassan called out in native Egyptian Arabic, "Jamal, I'm coming down to the galley. I have my team with me. Everything is all right!"

The group approached a set of stairs as Molly Brown spoke up, "Herbert, this leads to the bridge. I don't get the impression that there is a large crew. Get up there fast and take control before anything starts. Herbert nodded his head and darted up the steps.

Molly tapped the Wolf on the shoulder as Hassan continued to walk ahead. She motioned to a descending set of steps. She spoke up, quietly, "You follow Hassan. There's another set of steps ahead. I'll enter the lower galley-way from the opposite end."

Molly continued forward as the Wolf and Hassan descended. Peering down into the forward stairs, Molly overheard two sailors talking. The card-carrying 3rd-degree psychic concentrated on the voices as she considered their motivations. She felt a calming spirit as she considered that these two men were, in fact, void of darker influences.

Stepping into the galley-way, the 19th Century lady smiled broadly and curtsied as she stepped around the two Middle-Eastern men. Molly stepped into the ship's galley and saw that the Wolf had indeed managed to get the drop on Jamal.

The Wolf looked at Molly and called to her, "Close the two hatches to the room. Lower the bars. We'll a have a few seconds' warning if anyone tries to enter."

The Wolf stepped up to Jamal, with Hassan standing next to him. "Hand me the cell phone."

Molly's mind began to experience the same delay, in time itself, as she listened to the Wolf's words. It seemed to the green-eyed star of Burlesque and the New York City stage that Jamal Rahami knew something that gave him the upper hand.

Molly quickly walked over and tore open the Egyptian Islamic terrorist's coat. The phone fell to the floor as Molly picked it up and watched a counter ticking down on the 21st Century's dubiously evil device. She watched as the screen displayed numbers spinning downward from triple digits.

The woman who held a lifeboat crew at gunpoint and demanded that freezing men, women, and children be pulled from the water, stood wide-eyed before the face that would kill millions as she shouted out, "You've activated the triggers!"

The Egyptian terrorist stood silently as a wry smile filled his face. At that instant, both galley doors snapped open as the sounds of gunfire and shouting commenced.

Molly dropped to her knees as she simultaneously pulled her Colt revolver. The intruder entering from the starboard hatch fell in an instant as his face evaporated into a red mist.

Spinning back to the aft hatch, Molly saw that the Wolf had dispatched the second assailant. Helen's horror emerged in slow motion as Hassan leveled a pistol and shot Marguerite Cohen squarely in the chest. Helen's eyes grew wide as the screams from her mouth fell silently on the closed eyes of the fierce blonde warrior. The Wolf did not strike the deck before Molly had spun back to her feet and blown Hassan's head quite cleanly from his shoulders.

Molly's jade fire raged as she stepped up to Jamal Rahami and held the pistol fiercely under his chin, forcing his lower jaw forward. Before the eyes of the talented 3rd-degree (psy), the man's face began to morph into a hideous red creature. It seemed to the flamboyant lady of the 19th Century that she was, in fact, seeing not truly the physical face of the man, but his soul.

Molly took several steps back as she again shouted, "Disarm

the bombs!"

The voice emanating from the creature was heard as much a growl as speech, "You do not want to kill me, you cannot kill me, and death will be your only companion."

Molly blinked hard as she reached down and again picked up the ticking cell phone. She looked up at the grotesque vision and spoke out, "I know the 9 digit code. You cannot stop me from entering it. You cannot help but know the fear that I will enter it. I will enter it, and then you will die, and death will be your only companion!"

Molly held her gaze steady on the horrifying image as she relaxed her mind and focused on the demon's thoughts. As if in a total-mind state with Hell itself, the talented entertainer knew the magician's trick. Speak of something important and the audience's mind will follow. Demand that the listener not consider their own age or the address of their own home and it will be the only thought that fills their mind.

The Unsinkable Molly Brown stood her ground and entered the digits as easily as the memory of her own birthday. She punched in 5.7.0.9.5.1.2.2.1.

The cell phone's timer ceased and began to chime as it blinked the words, "CANCELED . . . CANCELED . . ."

Molly watched as the man-beast lurched forward. The rapid fire marksman from Hannibal, Missouri, casually releveled her Colt 45 magnum and squeezed off the round.

The beast's head exploded in a red haze as Molly peered downward at the pathetic being. She muttered calmly, "Oh, yes, I want you dead. I can kill you. And death will be your only companion."

Molly Brown turned to the collapsed form of her dear friend as the timeless soul's green eyes began to water. She whimpered softly as she knelt and lifted the beautiful woman into her arms. "Oh, dear (Y), please, dear Lord, tell me this fabulous woman wore her body armor today."

The Wolf's dark eyes opened slowly as she peered insistently back at her partner. "You didn't send the 'disabled' signal. Hurry, do it now. Don't think. Just Act!"

The copter sat down next to the Wolf's transport as Admiral Sasha Cohen and Commander Aaron LaSalle emerged. Aaron held Sasha close as they walked towards the three figures emerging onto the ship's deck.

The aging professor of physics held his child in his arms and spoke softly, "You see, my darling, as I told you, there walks the woman with the Halo above her head, and in her hand she holds the Devil's tail. The wretched red beast crawls before her on all fours. The shackles clatter between its two hands and two feet; their wicked claws are rendered harmless."

Sasha Cohen held Yuri close as they neared the approaching smiles of Helen Lovelace, the Wolf and Captain Herbert Potter.

Sasha nearly sung out the words, "Yes, Yuri, the shared dream we had when I was just 10 years old. Seventy years could not prevent the truth of it. You said we would see it together in the flesh. Look at the hatch on the water-tight door behind Molly. It shines brilliantly in the sun above her head. And in her hand is the terrorist's cell phone. The four nuclear bombs have been disarmed and captured."

Aaron spoke softly, "The Lord's love will never depart from his children."

Sasha Cohen added, thoughtfully, "As long as his children remain true to His Word."